The Esfah Sagas:
Cast of Fate
25th Anniversary Ed

By

Allen Varney

Revised by

Christopher D. Schmitz

Additional content by D.J. Heinrich, Lester Smith, Joseph Joiner, and Christopher D. Schmitz

A Dragon Dice Novel

PUBLISHED BY TREESHAKER BOOKS

THE ESFAH SAGAS

Rise and Fall of the Obsidian Grotto
Cast of Fate

The Relic Quests
Ashes of Ailushurai
Rise of the Champions (coming 2021)
Drakuwar (coming soon)

The Cyrean Songs
Chill Wind
Eye of the Storm
Secrets of the Shadowlands (coming 2021)

STAY UP TO DATE ON THE WORLD OF ESFAH!

Get a free copy of book 1 in the Esfah Sagas by visiting:

www.subscribepage.com/getfreedragondicenovels

Subscribers who sign up for this no-spam email list will get free books, exclusive content, and more! You'll get a digital copy of *Rise & Fall of the Obsidian Grotto* immediately… if you would like more details or want to follow the author, you can find his details at the end of this book.

BACKGROUND

Dragon Dice™ was originally created by Lester Smith and produced by TSR in 1995. It is an Origins Award winning strategy game where players create mythical armies using dice to represent each troop and is one of several collectible dice games that emerged in the 1990s. The game combines strategy and skill as well as a little luck.

After several years, TSR, now owned by Wizards of the Coast, had put Dragon Dice™ on hold to work on other projects. In October of 2000, SFR Inc. purchased the rights to Dragon Dice™.

Most of the races and monsters in original TSR Dragon Dice were created by Lester Smith and include some creatures unique to a fantasy setting and others that are familiar to the Dungeons & Dragons role-playing game. While the world of Esfah, where Dragon Dice™ takes place, has many similarities to that of Dungeons & Dragons, it is distinctly different in many respects. In some ways, there are greater unknowns and its history is both newer and older all at once.

Around the end of 1995 I was a teenager and avid board gamer who had a burger-slinging job (which gave me a disposable income) and a car (that took most of my disposable income.) In addition to many other games I played as part of a regular quartet of gamers, Dragon Dice™ was one that we all enjoyed.

I fondly remember how the four of us would-be delinquents often cut out of elective classes, study halls, and independent learning periods to meet up for gaming sessions. Dragon Dice™ came in a pocketable carrying bag which made it perfect for that.

We also had a mutual acquaintance. Lester Breitling was an older gentleman in town who owned a new and used bookstore that also carried a limited supply of gaming products. Though he did not stock Dragon Dice™, he did have a copy of *Cast of Fate*, the first Dragon Dice™ novel which included a special promo die. I snapped it up right away as the most avid reader of the foursome (which lent itself to me becoming the dedicated DM for our role-playing game sessions and solidified my path as a story-teller.) The included promotional die was our bright and shiny object for months. I may or may not have called it "my precious."

Cast of Fate by Allen Varney was not the only book set in the world of Esfah. The kind of Sci-fi and Fantasy I tend to write are the stories that I've always wanted to... and I've always wanted to have a voice in a shared universe. Creating a story within the Dragon Dice™ universe is something I long wanted to do, so I give a special thanks to SFR, who I've had the opportunity to re-launch this literary universe with as Dragon Dice enters its 25th year of existence. They are a company composed of true and like-minded fans who have kept alive a product that was one of the gems of the 1990s.

-- Chris

Dedications

In the original 1996 edition, Allen Varney thanked Aaron Allston, Beth Fischi, Kim Graham, Warren Spector and Don Webb. He also thanked Rob King.

Christopher D. Schmitz would like to also thank Leister Breitling for his part in this crazy journey. His old bookstore in Wadena, MN was also a place to discover many wonderful pieces of old and new sci-fi.

FOREWORD

In eons past, when time was young and creation malleable, the four powers of Nature -- earth, air, fire, and water -- the children of Nature, the Mother goddess, and each gods in their own right, brought forth two races of beings to care for their fledgling world, Esfah, which was created by the All-Father, Tarvanehl. One race, the selumari or coral elves, was created to husband the fluid forces of air and water. The other race, the vagha, a dwarvish race, embodied the stability of earth and the tempering power of fire. Together, these two peoples worked to nurture their infant world into something glorious and beautiful.

But Nature had a nemesis in Death, the spirit of entropy. In imitation of Nature, Death brought into being its own races: the morehl, or lava elves, who worshiped fire and destruction, and the trogs, a race of goblins, who sprang from earth and corruption. From the moment of their creation, the morehl and trogs sowed conflict, defiling the very world that gave them life and corrupting the other races who tended it. War sparked over land and possessions. Soon, hordes of dispossessed selumari, vagha, morehl, and trogs swept back and forth across the lands of Esfah, locked in endless battle.

In their struggles for supremacy over the fledgling world, the First Races pressed other magical beings into their service. The morehl were the first to do so, bringing up fire-breathing Hellhounds and web-casting Driders from the deepest caverns below Esfah. The trogs followed suit, leading Trolls, Harpies, and other monsters into battle. In response, the selumari called forth Coral Giants from the ocean and swarms of Sprites from the skies. The vagha enlisted Gargoyles, Androsphinxes, and other creatures of the crags.

Conflict raged across the face of Esfah and Death delighted in the carnage.

Back and forth across the world, darkness battled against light. Each side escalated the conflict, seeking victory, and the battles grew ever savage and desperate. New races arose, each pressed into the fray of the bloody struggle that seemed to have no end in sight.

Saddened by the bloodshed, Nature, the goddess-mother Ghaeial, dealt death to preserve life. Death, the bastard child of Ghaeial and Selurehl, the god known as Void. Death reveled in the chaos, terror, and pain that war brought.

A time of champions arose to safeguard the realm. Wars continued and an entire age passed. Pockets of tenuous peace grew from apathy—Death engineered a new trick to soften the resolve of Nature's troops, and seemed to have abandoned his playground for the comforts of the Abyss—but his attention has never truly waned.

Esfah has never known true peace. It is not in the planet's makeup: this is where the children of gods war on their behalf. Both old and new races struggle ever onward—creatures inspired to greater ends, forever in search of either an end to the bloodshed, or carnage renewed, as each is bent towards his or her own ends.

Esfah cannot know peace. The god known as Death will not allow it. Only a few know his true name—and to speak it aloud is to court Death himself.

For a short video overview of Esfah's origins, visit

https://youtu.be/JhF8RPFkF9I

SPECIAL ANNIVERSARY EDITION

Part of what makes this edition "special" is that it includes *all* the officially released TSR stories SFR has a record of from the 1990s*. It also includes one additional new story which is a prequel to *Chill Wind*, a fan- based project completed in 2011. The prequel, only partly written as fragments, was printed in part by SFR and is available only in this edition.

The original edition of Cast of Fate included a playable promo die which introduced the powerful eldarim race via a Dragonslayer die. If you purchased this book from either SFR, Inc. or TreeShaker Books you will have received a promo Dragon Slayer from them at purchase.
The contents of this book includes the following tales:

Cast of Fate

The Tale of Creation
The Beard and the Spear
The Soldier's Journey
(originally collected as Tome of the Tarvanehl)

Heart of Stone and Flame

Thunderfist and the Dragon

* Astute collectors might note that Army of the Dead by Edo Van Belkom is not in this list. It was originally teased in the back of the 1996 edition of Cast of Fate… however, that rare book's printing did not occur until the early 2000s.

CAST OF FATE

Year 18 of the First Age

Chypshik the sage moved blindly through the dark. He could sense the shift in the air. Things were changing in Esfah.

As an eldarim, he knew keenly how the gods paid such little attention to their lesser cousins, the eldarim. As a people, they called each other *Shara*, meaning "little gods."

As one of the sages, Chypshik had studied the birthing pangs of their young planet. Their race had crawled from the primordial muck and witnessed the warring gods, the coming of the dragons… and later, the creation of the first races: elves and dwarves.

Chypshik had been among those sages who helped establish a center for peace and learning in Daur-Bor-Nin, *the first city*. The sages' university had brought the two fledgling races together: different races from two sets of parents— different creator gods.

The eldarim sage noticed something else stirring in the swamps beyond the plains of the Crechelands—a ravenous breed of imp. The trogs, folk had called them. And then came new visitors to Daur-Bor-Nin… more elves. Chypshik had never seen an elf with skin any color but blue. The red-skinned people were quick to insert themselves into the culture—but something about them… these lava elves… did not sit rightly in his gut, and Chypshik had quested far from his home to learn more.

Chypshik had snuck into the volcanic mountain where he knew some of the red elves had come from. Drawing deeply on his connection to Esfah—to the magic of the realm—he obscured his presence as he slinked through the shadows. He'd heard plenty: the lava elves were not seeking alliances, *they were invaders readying an attack from within!*

Deep inside the lava tubes, Chypshik delved further still. He felt an ancient presence: an elemental spirit of great power slumbered. The sage knew how to deal with elementals. Only the eldarim interacted much with them in the centuries before the selumari and vagha arrived, and Chypshik was something of an expert on the rare, but willful spirits of magic that were elementally attuned to the gods. Elementals were a step closer to the quintet of gods than the shara, and every bit dangerous as dragons.

Chypshik set about his craft. He gently prodded the elemental with his mind… he had to first learn its name for this to work… *Mountain,* he learned, and then pulled back before the spirit was roused from slumber.

He dug his fingers into a tub of colored paste and began drawing a sigil upon the bedrock at the heart of the mountain. He paused when he felt something stirring.

"Shhh…" he cooed, trying to console the presence of the elemental. "Slumber here and grow," he said, completing the magic symbol which would bind the elemental to this location. It felt powerful, perhaps the most potent one he'd ever felt before.

Perhaps this elemental will come in handy, should the red elves treachery prove as great as I fear. Their attack will come soon and will be terrible.

Chypshik stood to leave. He turned around and found a lava elf regarding him curiously.

"What have we got here?" the elf asked. "An invader… one of the Old Ones."

Chypshik said nothing. He could already sense the elf's intentions as he pointed a short-barreled object at him. Some kind of mechanism clicked into the ready position.

The elf's black eyes burned even darker, despite there being such little light in the tunnel. "Not many eldarim around these parts," he said. "How does it feel to know that your race will never subdue Esfah… will never dominate her and rise to greatness?"

"Greatness comes not with domination," Chypshik said. "Rather, greatness is achieved in *cohabitation.* We must live together in symbiosis." He thought he recognized this elf now—

this one had been the one he'd earlier heard speak of instigating a war at Daur-Bor-Nin.

The red elf scrunched up his face as if he neither understood the word nor cared to try. Instead, he pulled the trigger. A flash of fire and blue smoke filled the tunnel. Chypshik fell dead with a hole punctured in his chest from the flintlock's ball shot.

…and the elemental slept.

Prologue

Year 520 of the First Age

"Hack a line in the bark of this tree, here, about three and a half cubits from the ground," said the dwarven warlord, reaching up to slap the ailanthus trunk with his mailed fist. "Then we march the whole city past it in single file. Anyone taller than the mark… cut off his head."

Calantha, demarch of Emmiria, frowned. She was a Coral Elf, a blue-skinned selumari. *If I were a dwarf,* she thought, *I also might judge enemies by height.* Looking away from the volcano slope where they stood and blinking against the light rain, she gazed down at the tree that Lord Burgard had struck. *Genocide in a scuff mark.* "So, you would spare the children," she said. "Generous."

Burgard missed the sarcasm. "It is bad strategy, I know. The red elves have not spared our children." His eyes hardened. "But some things we do not do."

The two warriors, and one other figure, stood on the battle-torn outer crater of the volcano Karakto. A dragon, slain in the fighting, had fallen to ground here, and it had leveled the forest on one side of the volcano. Its tail had torn a furrow nearby, crashing through the rim of the crater. A single ailanthus tree still stood, untouched amid the ruin. Its slender limbs rose gracefully, each branching exactly in two, then each half dividing in turn, until the twigs formed a fan that seemed to brush the storm clouds overhead.

Seeking shelter from the rain, the warriors had chosen the tree rather than the gigantic tail that loomed beside it. Even in this young world, called Esfah, the First Races knew that trees in a lightning storm mean danger. Beside Calantha, though, Lord Burgard had no fear. Lightning never struck a selumari enchanter, at least not by accident.

Calantha was taller than most coral elves, due partly to an old battle injury that had fused a length of her spine. Her collared moss green jacket, open at the waist, revealed a bronze breastplate. Apart from knee pieces over her riding trousers and moleskin boots, she wore no other armor. Beside Burgard, she looked practically naked.

The dwarf wore gray shoulder pieces, elbow pieces, and soon, new pieces carved from an earth drake's tooth and inlaid with silver would join his armor. He had removed his helmet, showing his scarred face and mane of red hair. The great axe slung across his back still bore stains of morehl blood, though the blood no longer smoked.

The third figure, visible only to Calantha, stood behind her like a shadow. She only saw an elven shape rippling in the air. At its heart curled a bright mist.

Burgard seemed concerned about the tone of Calantha's comment. "Is there a flaw in my plan?"

Calantha asked in return, "Are we to slaughter a whole city?"

"These morehl have slaughtered a dozen cities They are insane creatures of atrocity and corruption My own children died on their rapiers, and your husband—that is, I need not remind you…" He trailed off.

Calantha's sea-green eyes grew moist She looked down the slope, picking out the spot where her husband Devin, hero of the battle of Farnoch, had fought the morehl empress. Raised aloft by magic winds, he had struck the wyrm with his Dawn Blade, banishing the creature's spirit. In falling, it had crushed him, and the empress, and a hundred others.

A tear fell on the blue skin of her cheek, but she kept her voice steady. Calantha had been the one to summon the winds. "We have all suffered. Since we have known suffering, should we not refrain from bringing it on others?"

Burgard's anger overcame him. He addressed the diplomat directly. "If we do not end this menace now, these morehl will cause still more anguish to the selumari who elected you, and to my people at Gundakhor, and to all the stewards of Nature. Your Quietude philosophy is fine for the academy in Emmiria, but here we face real danger, real evil!"

"Evil? What word do you give to the murder of fifteen thousand?"

Burgard's fist fell into his palm as though crushing the argument. "Survival is my word! Survival against lunatics who would happily destroy themselves to destroy us. These lava elves are touched by…" he nearly spoke the name of the Death god aloud and then thought better. "They are touched by Death. From the womb to the grave, they are corrupt. To let these creatures of chaos live and bring more grief to our world— because of some arcane humbug philosophy—"

She cut him off. "Thank you, Lord Burgard You have made your point. As your commander, I shall take full account of your advice."

Burgard fell silent, frowning. He had never questioned Calantha's authority as supreme commander of the alliance between her own Emmirian forces and the kingdom of Gundakhor.

But she knew he had never liked it. Calantha strove to stay calm, using the Fourth Quietude Meditation: *All beings save myself are secretly wise. They pretend ignorance and difficulty so as to teach me. What lesson does this one offer?* Breathing deeply, she said, "I have examined all my beliefs. One very strong belief is that it is wrong to murder thousands of innocent people. If this belief is false, I dearly hope I shall not live to see the proof of it."

She turned sidelong to glance at the third figure. It said nothing, but seemed to gesture at the branches above them. Calantha looked up at the tree. Selumari elves called ailanthus the tree of destiny for its endlessly dividing paths upward. The enchanter knew that her own destiny moved toward such a fork now, and it wearied her.

Calantha sighed, "I have decided. Let us cross into the crater and address the people." With a flick of her wrist, she summoned a raincloud.

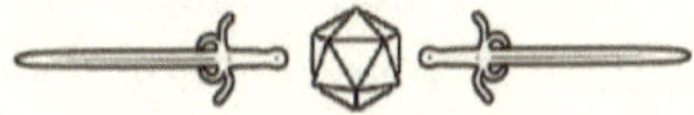

Fortunately, the elder dragon, Hwarrm, had died on the shoreward slope of Karakto, where the basalt was thickest. The dragon's fall had cracked the volcano's crater without opening a new lava vent. In his final thrashing, Hwarrm had turned head downward. His long, skull now lay in the breaking surf of the bay and much of him had been turned to stone where vagha spellcasters had encased or transmuted as much of the beast as possible for fear that it might have only feigned death.

No one had named this bay yet on coral elf maps, but the selumari would soon mark Hwarrm's Doom. A thousand paces up the slope, Hwarrm's tail stretched over the jagged lip of the crater.

In death, the tail had swept out a deep notch wide enough for a royal highway.

Through this gap, Calantha and the others walked, heading toward the morehl city. The stench of sulfur deepened as they entered mold-green slopes of twisted and sickly grasses. Around them, vents steamed like cauldrons. The mists occasionally parted, giving glimpses of the city below.

Half a dozen square buildings clustered at the low point of the huge crater. They looked like pebbles in a shallow bowl. In their midst rose a tall spire, from which the late empress had incited the hordes to conquest. She'd been a wretched conqueror and a loyal worshipper of the Death god, treating her own kind as cattle and her enemies as worse. The ground around the city bulged here and sagged there, riddled with tunnels.

Calantha could never look on the city without thinking of an infected sore. She'd known and met many of the red elves in her journeys apart from her native Emmiria, and over the course of several generations the late Empress had turned Karakto's culture into something fouler than any other morehl city she'd seen—twisted, silenced, depraved, and more devoted to destruction than any other Calantha had experienced.

Burgard paused, turned away, and then turned back. In a low voice, he said, "I say we should burn the place... and the people."

Calantha said nothing, only staring grimly forward. Ahead lay a line of huge boulders, chunks of the dragon's shattered tail. As the diplomat and the dwarf picked their way among the stones, they talked for distraction's sake. Both were experienced warriors, but Hwarrm's unmatched size still made them shiver. Keeping their eyes on the grass, they spoke of the morehl royalty. The third warrior said nothing.

"These people baffle me," Calantha said. "We may need a figurehead, a lava elf whom the rest would follow, and one we could control."

Lord Burgard squeezed through a stone gap. "The old empress was grooming her daughter for the throne. The dragon crushed both when he died. A second child, a boy of two or three, seems to have vanished."

"A missing heir. No doubt he will turn up someday. They always do. Meanwhile?"

"I suspect that a high-ranking warrior would be next in line to rule. Of course, we just watched all the warriors die in battle." Burgard shook water from his gauntlet. "I recommend against a noble—most of them are crazy. Perhaps we can use one as an advisor, but..."

Emerging from the boulders, Calantha made for a huge crowd of morehl that had clustered down the slope. Thousands of the lava elves stood silently in red-stained grass, among their fallen kin. Calantha's lieutenants had rousted Karakto's residents from their grottos and herded them onto yesterday's battlefield. The diplomat frowned.

Lord Burgard struggled to keep up. "I suggest that instead of a figurehead, we appoint an interpreter, someone who can explain their customs. We need a morehl we can talk to, someone less mad than the rest. I know of one, a minor noble named Fohlin."

"Very well," said Calantha absently. She had noticed a heavily guarded pile of morehl pistols. They'd used their signature flintlocks ever since the Dawn of War when the morehl revealed their treacherous nature and sacked Daur-Bor-Nin.

These weapons, though, were far more advanced than any the coral elves or dwarves used—even more nefarious than the cursed bullets engineered by the gremmlobahnd once kept in slavery beneath the Obsidian Grotto. Some strange gnomish tinkering made them every bit as deadly as the cursed bullets, but their magic allowed them to fire without reloading shot and powder.

Karakto had developed a warrior culture centered around these guns. Calantha hoped that the breaking of that class would change the people.

Guards from both victorious races surrounded the pile, and a few examined the flintlocks curiously. A strange light glinted off their silvery inlay wear they'd been modified with eldrymetallum, magically enhanced by the star metal.

"Put those down!" Calantha cried. "They are weapons of evil."

The guards hastily dropped the firearms and stood at attention.

"No need for worry," said Burgard. "Only the morehl warriors were able to fire them. In our hands, the pistols are just dead metal. Perhaps if we investigate them, we might—"

"No investigation. I order those weapons destroyed. And destroy the forges, or whatever they used to make them."

Burgard looked uncertain and seemed about to speak, but he only nodded.

They came to a crude wooden platform that the Emmirians and Gundakhorians had fashioned from a morehl gallows. Calantha climbed up and looked past the bodies scattered on the field, past the Emmirian guards with their drawn bows and cutlasses.

She watched the huddled morehl. Even in defeat, they had an uncanny beauty. They were slender and lithe, their skin as red as hot iron, their hair mostly blacker than their obsidian sacrifice-knives with a few of silver or white as spider silk and a rare and scattered few colors between. The morehl stood, poised like statues. Calantha saw nobles and merchants in purple silk, artisans in peaked hats, priests in black smocks, peasants wearing cotton shifts and holding naked babies, and slaves in any rags they had found.

Nobles no doubt took offense at mingling with the rabble, but in that field of fifteen thousand, Calantha heard not a sound except the rain. Every one of them stared at her in a hateful silence, knowing she held their lives.

Uneasily, she glanced around to find the wavering elf-shape. The sight of the hazy wisp curling at its heart reassured her.

She began, "I am Demarch Calantha Farandelin, leader of Emmiria. I extend both my hands to the morehl. The left hand I extend to the servants of Death, who brought this war upon my people. This hand is a closed fist that will try, convict, and execute them. But my right hand, the open hand of friendship, I give to those morehl who obeyed their leaders unwillingly, who sought no war, who wished no ill on the peaceful peoples who serve Nature. To you, who wish only to live your lives and raise your children in peace, this hand represents—"

Calantha stopped, puzzled. The crowd had begun to murmur. Hisses and angry mutters rose above the rain, like hornets stirring. She knew that a change of mood could spread among the morehl with eerie swiftness, for they had an innate empathy. A family argument in a marketplace could become a riot as strangers felt the anger. Now, she saw, this crowd could become a mob in an instant. But what had angered them?

She remembered her diplomatic training from the Emmirian University. *They use the open right hand as a gesture to slaves.*

In alarm, Calantha drew both hands sharply to her sides. The guards had already sensed the crowd's hostility. Their bows were drawn, their cutlasses out. Calantha foresaw disaster.

Then a high, thin cry, a young child's cry, cut the air. The guards looked around, for the cry did not come from the crowd.

Between the platform and the crowd, amid the soaked bodies, a morehl infant lay trapped under a corpse.

A selumari guard lowered his cutlass and moved toward the child. Calantha, knowing his training, understood he would rescue the child. Only belatedly did the horror strike, when she saw the morehl grow angrier. They thought the guard meant to—

Now the lava elves screamed and waved their fists. Paralyzed, Calantha found herself staring at one young morehl at the forefront, a young man with a high forehead and a pointed beard.

He struggled furiously, teeth clenched, as women on either side held him back. Then, as the demarch watched, the women shook their heads as though dizzy, and the man's fury grew in their own black eyes. Unarmed, the three launched toward a guard. In moments would come ten more, and fifty, and a thousand.

Fighting panic, Calantha projected magic into the air. Then she whispered: "Stand away."

STAND!—AND!—ND! The guard halted, as if frozen.

AWAY!—WAY!—AY! The crowd fell back, holding their ears.

The infant stopped crying and stared in awe at Calantha. Echoes fell into silence. No one moved. Leaping down from the trestle, she ran to the baby, with Lord Burgard clanking along behind.

Missing heirs always turn up, she thought, and then: *No, stop the line of succession and educate them to better ways*. But politics left her mind as she looked into the child's black eyes. A beautiful boy, she realized, *I've never seen such beauty. Surely he can serve good.*

She raised the boy high. In the rain, he began to cry again. Not knowing what effect she would have, and not caring in the least, Calantha called out confidently, "Hear me! I want only the best for your people and for mine. I want you to live! I want our races to live in peace. As a sign of that pact, I take this child. I shall adopt him and raise him as my own!"

For a long moment, the crowd made no sound. Calantha had time to wonder if she should call forth a water spell for protection. Then, suddenly, the mood changed. She heard laughter, a strange gulping sound. Then, smiling, the morehl walked forward.

The selumari guards, blue figures against the oncoming wall of red, raised their swords. Calantha, looking from her child to the crowd, sensed their mood. "Let them pass!"

The people of Karakto, who moments ago had wanted to destroy Calantha, now trampled the bodies of their kin and gathered around, silent but for an occasional laugh. A few reached out with black nailed fingers to touch Calantha. The rest watched her as they might watch some intriguing animal.

Holding the child close and murmuring in his ear, Calantha hardly knew whether to feel exhilarated or more frightened than before.

Lord Burgard tried to speak to her, but the crowd held him back and the rain drowned him out. She saw the dwarf's stern eyes and read his lips: "Corrupt from womb to grave." But Calantha smiled, or tried, and hugged her child.

She thought, *Lunacy!*

Part 1
Corruption

1

Mountain considered. In most times, the long years of Esfah passed Mountain in moments. The rains of summer and fall seemed to him only a splash, the winter's snow a dusting.

When Mountain watched the sky, he saw the racing sun as a thick rainbow of white light. It blinked. It crawled up the sky near zenith and back down with the seasons. The huge hurtling moon that crossed twice each day moved too fast for the elemental to watch, and as for the darting sparks that lived in his crater, the First Races—well!

Mountain had been aware of his binding to this place for many years. Time seemed to pass differently for him than for the little sparks.

Like wasps newly hatched, he'd watched the morehl set to building their hive city. From their first breaths, they planned war. After that, Mountain had fallen into sleepy thought. He watched the sun's path rise and fall in lazy arcs across the sky, one rhythm among countless others in the world.

Suddenly something jostled him. Mountain awoke into fast time. He felt an agonizing movement deep within him. Hwarrm, largest and cruelest of elder dragons had come— drawn by the chaos of the warring factions upon the volcanic slopes. Mountain watched in horror as Hwarrm laid waste to whole armies of the First Races. Mountain felt relief when the sparks, gathered on his outer slope, finally destroyed Hwarrm. Of course, he himself could do nothing to stop the carnage.

Now Mountain considered. His mind, a blend of light and earth, conceived new thoughts—slowly. He pondered one now, heedless that the sun path once more rose and fell in gentle arcs, that the seasons passed in moments.

At last, Mountain sighed. In the year of that sigh, a bulge rose and fell on his east flank, too slow for the First Races to notice. He had decided. He must rouse himself into fast time once more, to learn what he could of the sparks upon him.

Fitfully, he focused his perception. In time, his senses reached outward. There: he found a spark.

They threw Yort off the meat cart about noon. The goblin had snuck in the night before, just ahead of the reinforced Hagrond patrols which policed the lower sections of the Narcea Marsh from Lyander's Pass to the Nhur-Gale Forest on behalf of their capital, Gundakhor.

As soon as Yort crawled under the canvas and lay amid the carcasses, he fell asleep. He needed plenty of sleep, after three weeks of butchering dwarves at Hagrond Mount, and he was quietly snoring when the cart stopped. Someone spotted a black-clawed foot sticking out, and they threw the goblin off. He tried some banter but got only a cold look. The two drivers kept their yellow hands on their axes. They gave him a chew of tingleleaf, though, and with it, Yort had set off down the trail, looking for something—or someone—to eat.

After half the afternoon, he had found nothing and nobody.

The trail stretched away across green flats to the coast. The coast! He had come all the way from Bent Morass, so far inland that some goblins in his tribe refused to believe in oceans. The ocean itself bored him, but he had become hypnotically fascinated with seafood.

Yort had never eaten seafood, but he'd eaten people who had. He thought he tasted a savor in their flesh, heard a peculiar vigor in their screams. "Fish," as he'd heard it called, must be a delicacy, a source of great strength. With such strength, he could return to Bent Morass and—

"And then I'll dismember that treacherous Hulg," he said aloud as he walked. "The treacherous goblin who ruined my name, stole not just one *but both my wives*, and drove me out like a whipped dog from the tribe, which I joined even before he did, the Vaum-cursed sneak!"

Thinking of past offenses and future revenge, of anything except the present moment, Yort trudged along, bony yellow head down. He ignored the broad silkgrass meadows dotted with low clumps of cranesbills in pink and violet, snapdragons of radiant pink, speedwells, milk vetch, and tulips so vividly orange they seemed backlit by invisible flames. Beside the trail, green-winged orchids and yellow irises stood tall in rows, as though waiting for inspection. No parasites, no disease, few weeds… Wild flowers bloomed in all seasons with a vigor that elated travelers and hinted at a world of beautiful possibilities.

Yort paid no heed, eyes on his aching feet.

"Trout, salmon, clam, oyster, eel, shark, dolphin, goldfish, whale—" He had demanded from his baffled victims all they knew about fish. They had gasped the names before they died, and now he recited them in a marching chant—actually a marching grumble that matched the grumbling of his stomach.

Yort walked west in what goblins called the hunger-trance. He could have dug up a handful of dirt and found enough worms and grubs to satisfy any goblin. But Yort, like other worshipers in the disreputable Enlivening Hunt sect, had sworn not to eat "that which cannot flee"—except as a garnish.

A commotion off to his right jarred him awake. The trail had widened to a dirt road through fields of kasha, and a hullfruit orchard stood to his right. As though Vaumb, Leader of the Hunt, had heard Yort's stomach grumbling, a small human crashed through a stand of broomcorn and ran straight at him.

It had long brown hair woven in two braids (he thought of sausages) and tanned skin (cooked pork!) and it wore a clean shift of bright red (blood!) Recognizing it as a female child, he thought, Lamb, kid, piglet, veal! She ran while looking backward, as though pursued. Would she race right into his arms—could Vaumb be so generous?

Oh please, oh please, please.

But while still out of arm's reach, the young female looked ahead and saw him. Her almond eyes (almonds!) widened, and she stopped dead.

With boundless affection, Yort said, "Hello, small human."

She screamed, turned, and ran into the orchard. Yort took half a second to close his eyes in silent thanks, another to rub his clawed hands, and then a third to set off after her at an easy lope. In lieu of prayer, he recited a litany of recipes as he ran:

"Parboiled, blackened, chopped, pan-fried in meat gravy—"

Spreading boughs reached gracefully down from the hullfruit trees, their branches curling up at the tips like many-fingered hands held askance. As the goblin chased the girl across the dappled orchard grass, Yort imagined the trees saying, "No, no, that's quite all right—no, really, by all means continue chasing her, don't mind us—" Exhilarated by the hunt, he laughed and stomped his feet madly. The girl's ragged gasps delighted him. He hung back to draw out the moment.

Drunk with joy, and distracted by his own recital ("Seared with mushrooms, steamed with pepper, cubed and served in broth—") Yort failed to note that beyond the next row of trees, someone else was running and chanting recipes. The two chants converged on the girl from opposite sides of a huge hullfruit trunk.

"—coated with crumbs and baked—"

"—marinated and skewered—"

"—bathed with grease and—"

"—cut in strips, served in—"

The girl circled the trunk and dodged.

Yort collided hard with three other goblins. He fell onto the leader, a runt. Yort's forehead rammed into the knee cap of the one just behind. It buckled sideways and collided with the hulking brute in the rear. Both fell on Yort, who lay atop the runt.

The girl raced off into the trees. Stunned, Yort awoke to a cavernous chorus of stomach rumblings. He tried to lift his head, then said, very clearly, "Owww."

"*Eh ahh mee,*" came a voice from below.

"Hah?" Yort said groggily.

"*Eh ahh mee igh oww!*"

"Uh." Yort thrashed like a landed trout. "These two louts have pinned me."

"*I ohn air! Eh OFF!*"

"This is no great fun for me either, you know."

"*OFF! OFF or I gih you!*"

"Oh, indeed, you're on the bottom and you'll kill me. What'll you do, gnaw my vitals?"

The runt's screeching roused the other two, and they quickly heaved away. On his feet and rubbing his hurt spots, Yort faced the runt, who looked young but long of snout and fierce of eye. He wore a filthy leather jerkin.

The other two—one tall and hulking, one stout and stinking, both in leather armor—stood sulkily behind the little one. All three had wedges clipped from their left ears, just behind the points, and they carried stone axes and slings in their belts.

Troops. Yort hated troops.

"So, mutts," said the runt, brushing loam from his armor, call out the parts of this gurk you want to cut." As he pulled his axe, he eyed Yort with a ferocious grin.

Yort avoided sighing. "I don't suppose you soldiers want to join me in getting that human?" Suspecting the answer, he weighed six or seven routine escapes: kick-up-dirt, look-there, I'm-a-spy—

The tall one said: "I wants his giblets, Fenny!"

"Liver 'n' lights," said the fat one, licking his lips.

"I want his heart, and I want it fresh," said the runt. "And stop calling me Fenny." They moved forward, separating to circle Yort.

—my-gang's-coming, I'm-your-cousin—

Like a bubble of swamp gas, an idea suddenly surfaced in Yort's mind. "Recipes. You mutts serve Vaumb!"

They stopped. "You're already in trouble, gurk," said the runt, Fenny. "Choose your next words carefully."

Yort waved his fingers under his receding muzzle and made the Enlivening Hunt signal. "'Mine is the prey, mine the chase, mine the good eating thereafter!'" he said. "My name's Yort. Thirty-Third Circle initiate, Bent Morass Posse."

A moment of pregnant silence.

The tall one said, "I gots a brother-in-law and three litters of nephews and nieces in Bent Morass!" He waved the blood-stained fingers of his free hand. "Murget, that's my name, Murget. Praise Vaumb!"

"Praise Vaumb!" said Yort fervently.

The fat one looked surprised. "Praise Vaumb," he said, then smiled and tucked away his axe. "I'm Blodge."

Fenny, after a glance at the other two, peered at Yort. "Who's the trickster for the Posse in Bent Morass?"

"Harmaughan the Many-Blessed. Little greenish fellow with two pupils in his left eye, one yellow, one green. When he blesses you, the air smells like vinegar."

"Praise Vaumb!" the runt shouted. Grinning, he reached up to slap Yort on the shoulder. "You call me Fennevaunce. I lead this gang, the Wild Things."

"Gang?"

"Well, say 'independent patrol.' We were in King Kor-Kor-Bog's Third Regiment, fighting the vagha at Gundakhor, and it got too active. We heard of work with the morehl at Karakto, some kind of action against the blue elves, so we're heading that way. Know anything of it?"

"No. Is that on the coast?"

"I think so."

"Then I'll…" A spear struck the earth a few rods away. The goblins saw movement far across the orchard and heard many angry shouts.

"The small one's tribe," said Fennevaunce. "I think we'll get on toward Karakto. Coming with us, Yort? Good." They loped toward the road. "Bent Morass, aye? My regiment marched through there under King Kor-Kor-Bog a few years back—" As simply as that, Yort had joined the Wild Things.

Among goblins, things like this happened all the time.

2

Mountain's concentration blurred and lapsed. As he struggled to reawaken, years raced by. His fitful rousing brought him glimpses of the sparks living on his slope, images that cascaded like the last moments of a lingering dream.

In his studies, Orric kept falling asleep. Calantha had enlisted a tutor, an Emmirian scribe named Shantric, to instruct her adopted morehl son. But Shantric, thin as a bean pole, and no more engaging, made history, art, and geography into a long unbroken buzz.

Orric's days in the sunlit library of the demarch's mansion were a series of falls into slumber. He'd even tried snoozing in different postures to keep his interest up. Orric was small, with apple-red skin, black eyes, a tall, angular face, and long backswept hair that stuck out in spikes despite his nannies' best efforts. He wore a green linen tunic and simple black breeches, for Calantha believed a demarch's son should dress like any selumari boy.

Early each day, Orric's three selumari governesses sat him in a hardwood chair and left him at the aged Shantric's mercy. Shantric—a tall, emaciated coral elf with wrinkled sky-blue skin, many scars, and thinning white hair—always started with history.

"Almost two centuries ago, the Wanderers settled Emmiria, a reef-state on the Talvatic Coast. They were the fourth generation of selumari after their Making on Esfah— hence also the third after Death's Curse, and second after the Revolt and dispersion from Daur-Bor-Nin, the first city, also called the Dawn of War."

In these morning lessons, Orric found sleep hard, so he asked questions. "What year is this?"

Shantric treated questions as obstacles in the smooth course of his lecture. "This is year 520," he said with a touch of testiness.

Orric tried to imagine five hundred years. At age six, he could not grasp such a long time. What an old world!

Shantric continued, "By Year 512, in the seventh generation, Emmiria had grown into a thriving center of learning and music, of parks and pavilions both underwater and above. It was one of the illustrious cities called the Six Jewels. Then the morehl invaded.

"After two years of relentless struggle, we won the war but had lost our city. Emmiria lay in ruins, its academy submerged, its Pantheseum shrines sacked, a sixth of its populace dead, the rest homeless. Against our wishes, we perforce settled in the only shelters to hand: the tunnels of Karakto."

"Why live in the volcano? Why not rebuild the old city?"

A sigh, quickly stifled. "Many ask that question to this day. But your mother made the decision. The demarch's prestige had dimmed during the War, but with victory, her popularity swelled to new heights. If she had told us, 'Let us rebuild Emmiria,' the selumari would have pitched in with a will. Instead she said, 'Let us resolve the lasting threat by taming our enemies.' Not slaughtering our enemies, but taming them—so she put it.

"Many of us were skeptical, but perhaps you already know that your mother can be a powerful orator. She moved us. We are not obedient, not as a dwarf or human is obedient, but suggestible. We respond to wise guidance. Calantha hopes to guide us not to destruction or escape, but to a lasting peace. And so, we ten thousand survivors live among fifteen thousand of our enemies."

Listening to the drone, Orric slouched across the arm of his hardwood chair and let his eyes glaze over. By midmorning, when Shantric moved on to geography and cultures, his words fell like quiet, monotonous rain. "The four First Races each bring their own strengths to the endless fight for Esfah; of course, that omits the eldarim, of course, who predate our calendars, but they are an anomaly and were not created by the gods. We selumari have unrivalled skill in archery, and—I speak now of Emmiria in particular—our system of rule has made us resilient in defense and flexible in response to aggression."

Orric watched dust specks dance in the sunbeams and let his eyelids droop.

"The vagha, our dwarven allies in service to Nature, show uncommon toughness and expert tactics, as well as unshakable resolve. Even so, our adversaries, the races that serve Death, present a formidable menace. The trog race—wretched goblins—use nothing but stone axes and slings, but their dog-riders can cross the worst swamps as if on a paved road. Also, they breed in staggering numbers."

By now Orric could usually let Shantric's words lull him into groggy placidity.

"But worst of all, if you will pardon my bluntness, are the morehl. Nothing personal, of course, young sir. Their savagery in battle is infamous, their insane sense of risk appalling. Yet, even these traits do not frighten the servants of Nature so much as the morehl weapons... in particular the variety of them found only in Karakto."

And so to sleep until lunch. Shantric never woke the boy—unless Calantha looked in, and the demarch only rarely occupied her mansion between dawn and sunset.

Calantha's mornings gave her no rest. Sleeping every second night, meditating only briefly at dawn, she spent every morning supervising the rebuilding of the morehl city within the volcano and the construction of a selumari district on its shoreward slope. She labored endlessly to blend two enemy peoples without bloodshed.

Quietude philosophy called for awareness of the young world's beauty. But Calantha seldom had any chance to admire a sunrise over the shadowed crater, nor the pale downy blue of the midmorning moon. She lost track of time. In her memory, morning events jostled against one another like ships in a squall.

When had she formally canceled the morehl sacrificial rites? Soon after the victory, to be sure—but before or after she ordered the morehl temples rededicated? At her direction, the five basalt amphitheaters, spaced evenly around the crater's inner slope, began honoring five of the seven virtues of selumari society—integrity, justice, forgiveness, prudence, and mercy— in place of the five qualities that morehl society valued—honor, destruction, dominance, vengeance, and compliance.

Lacking two shrines, Calantha found no elegant way to honor the last selumari virtues—temperance and artistry. It seemed a minor point, for the morehl had no vices of indulgence and no conception of art. At least, none that compared to those of the selumari and could be comparable.

For all that she could recall now, six years later, the temples might have received their new directives the same morning that she freed the morehl slaves. Or a week afterward, or a season.

Today, in the summer of Year 520, she honored a group of former slaves, "free folk," who had learned to read and write. Now Calantha was in the sixth year of her nine-year term as demarch. Should she choose to stand again three years from now, the citizens would certainly award her another term. Her own people credited her with the victory over Karakto, and the morehl could not vote.

At the literacy ceremony, she stood beside a dozen morehl free folk on the high balcony atop Karakto's central windswept spire. Two years of decent living, after a lifetime of appalling cruelty, had made these former slaves firm of flesh and clean.

Even so, they looked at Calantha blandly, without emotion. Their coolness disconcerted her, until she stole a glance at the hazy figure beside her. The sight of her constant companion, visible only to her, always reassured her. The "spirit guide" was how she connected to the heart of Esfah. The Source. Some spell casters felt their connection as a kind of arcane mathematics, others crafted spells as an artisan works with clay. But for Calantha the connection was a sense of relationship with the spirits of the gods she served, and she managed that relationship through her training in the Quietudes... the shimmering apparition was her idealized form—the *goal self.* Those who practiced magic through the quietudes had a more philosophical approach to spellcraft as opposed to blunt arcana—magic use had to serve a greater purpose.

Below the balcony waited an audience of both selumari and morehl, who stood far apart from one another in segregated crowds: one sea of blue faces and green clothing, another of red and black. Aided by magic, Calantha's voice carried to every ear.

"We of Emmiria did not seek conquest. We sought, and still seek, a secure peace. Our way is not slavery but stewardship. The wounds of war do not heal quickly, and I will not speak of partnership. But if our races are ever to mean anything to one another beyond constant danger, we must win not only this city, but the loyalty of its citizens."

Grumbling came from the selumari. The morehl, of course, stared in silence.

"As these people beside me are reaching out to a better life, a life of new hope, let us all reach out. As these morehl have cast aside their shackles, let us cast aside our old grudges and dare to think of the new."

Silence.

"To the morehl, I say: Think of what calamities your service to Death has brought. What worse disasters must inevitably fall on your heads if you continue in Death's service?" She gestured to the free folk. "Then think of the opportunities that await you in service to Nature."

Sporadic applause from the selumari. From the morehl, nothing.

"To the selumari, I say: We are the stewards of Nature. Is this the way of hatred? The way of constant battle? Of revenge? The way of Nature is constant change, adaptation to the new. To all from Emmiria, I say that you are now of Karakto. Adapt."

A few selumari shouted angrily, but others quieted them. The sullen silence spread across the crowd. Reflecting afterward on the speech's failure, Calantha pondered her position. Would three more years even begin to bring trust between the races? She doubted it. Stupid people did not become demarchs, and ideals died quickly in office. Calantha knew the power and the persistence of hatred, but what could she do? Let Burgard march thousands of people past a line on a tree?

Calantha glanced at the dim elf outline beside her. With new resolve, if not confidence, she set about her duties: closing monster-infested tunnels deep beneath the city, tearing down morehl fortifications and transferring lumber to the selumari district, and closing the morehl government chambers.

Destroying these rooms would produce unrest, but leaving them intact symbolized revolt. Calantha declared them historic landmarks and turned them into a museum.

Such maneuvers had taken up the mornings of six years, and looked likely to take up six more.

By afternoon, the moon had rushed overhead and vanished for a while over Karakto's eastern rim. The sun climbed high, and in her light, the sky turned a deep sea-blue.

After lunch, Orric could never sleep. It didn't matter. When Shantric offered his afternoon lecture on Nature, Orric usually found something to argue about.

"The spirits of the elements created the selumari and vagha not long after they made Esfah. We serve as the stewards of Nature, in opposition to the races that serve Death. Now—"

"Who serves Death?"

Shantric sighed theatrically. "I told you, young sir. Several times. The morehl and the goblins."

"Do I serve Death?"

"N-No! No, ah, of course not!—Do you?"

Orric considered. "It sounds bad. What do people who serve Death do?"

"Why, evil things. They mean to kill everything that lives!"

"Even themselves? That makes no sense."

"Indeed. Thus we see the fundamental insanity of the servants of evil." Shantric returned to his scroll. "Now--"

"And if everyone served Nature and no one served Death, would no one die?"

Shantric opened his mouth, then closed it. He pointedly smoothed the scroll. "If I may resume my lesson, young sir—"

Orric looked up at the row of windows under the library roof.

He yawned.

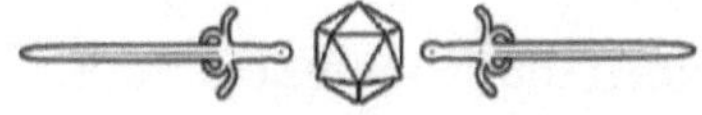

Calantha's afternoons, like her mornings, merged into a single long session in the new Court of Justice.

This looming block of granite, three stories high and charcoal-gray, had once been a hall for the priest class. Here, they propounded arcane doctrines and, three times each year, consecrated obsidian sacrificial knives in brass vessels filled with slave blood. By morehl custom, a clay molding around the building's base had displayed skeletons of battle victims, both morehl, *head up*, and their enemies, *head down*. Calantha had ordered the molding pulled apart, the remains decently buried, and the building rededicated. As they dutifully hauled the bones away, the elders had made not even a whispered protest.

Around the court, week by week, selumari landscapers planted a succession of trees and bushes, hoping for one to survive in the crater's sulphurous air.

Each afternoon in the echoing Supreme Hall, Calantha donned the white robe of judgment. She sat in a wooden chair of plain design on a dais three steps high. The dais was carved from a single stone that had fallen from the sky twenty years ago, not long after Karakto had formed. From this platform, the demarch delivered justice to the morehl.

Peasants withholding taxes from their noble masters—one male assaulting another over a female—an urchin stealing copper coins from a potter in the marketplace… Calantha found the cases tiring, but oddly heartening. These morehl endured the same frictions other races knew. Emmirians thought of their red-skinned counterparts as fiends, unified in a single evil purpose. The fact that a morehl urchin could take time from plotting the world's downfall to steal a copper coin—how reassuring!

From this endless afternoon, which spanned years, Calantha later recalled two incidents. In the first, she recognized a morehl man, charged with theft. She realized with dismay that this felon, Shaulf by name, was one of the freed slaves who stood beside her in the balcony ceremony.

"Freedman Shaulf," Calantha began in anger, "why in Nature's names did you steal—?" She looked to the bailiff.

The bailiff supplied, "A wheel from a mining cart, demarch."

Shaulf was a shark-eyed fellow with short hair spikes and a flat nose. He brushed one long finger on his black vest and spoke in the usual morehl stage whisper. "I don't recall why I stole the wheel. I have no use for a wheel, having no cart of my own."

Shaulf's distracted tone perplexed Calantha. "But you do have a profession, do you not? I instructed the tutors to find positions for all the trained free folk."

"Aye." Shaulf blinked slowly. "I teach others to read, as your people taught me. I have learned much." He paused. "I daresay I committed no crime against the cart owner, but rather performed a service. If the cart had functioned on its three remaining wheels, that would have proven its excellent workmanship. As it was, the rear axle broke at once. My act revealed its fault."

"Nonsense!" Calantha became aware of her own anger. While the demarch attended to her breath and calmed it, Count Fohlin plodded up to the dais. He was a misfit among the morehl, a massive, broad-shouldered man who moved with ponderous grace, like a ship leaving dock.

Watching the man bow to her, puppet-like, Calantha wondered if his physical strangeness determined his strange nature.

This morehl man seemed the most sane to the selumari—which meant the morehl viewed him as mad. Fohlin spoke in a cavernous baritone, so unlike the morehl whisper. "Perhaps the demarch will remind me whether a freed slave who steals may be restored to servitude and suffer the punishment due a slave."

A "reminder." Fohlin was making a suggestion to the demarch. Calantha could overrule him without appearing to contradict the noble—a grave social violation. Calantha spoke quietly to Fohlin. "The punishment for a slave?"

"Amputation of both hands, demarch."

Calantha addressed Fohlin courteously. "'Once free, always free' is the rule you are trying to recall. In such cases, the thief must make restitution for the damaged cart and labor for a week in service to the community, according to the dictates of the nobility, with counsel from the selumari court."

Count Fohlin affirmed this with a precise nod. The marshals led Shaulf away.

The other afternoon incident that Calantha later remembered took much less time. Not long after the occupation of Karakto, Lord Burgard and two selumari generals, Gleda and Osmaral, met with Calantha in a stuffy conference chamber outside the Supreme Hall.

Burgard, one of the war's greatest heroes, had stayed on in Karakto as military advisor and ambassador from Gundakhor. Gleda, a plain selumari woman of middle years, had led a charge against Hwarrm in the final battle on the volcano's slopes. She had scars and a limp to show for it. Osmaral's injuries, deeper and less visible, had been inflicted by subtle morehl torturers in an amphitheater before a chanting crowd.

Like Burgard, both Gleda and Osmaral hated the morehl and wished them all dead. But like Burgard, they deferred to the demarch.

"We face a problem with production," the dwarf began. "Morehl warriors once enforced the production of food and goods, but the warriors all died in the war. In their absence, free folk and peasants are much slower about growing food and mining metal. With child labor outlawed, we face the possibility of famine and shortage."

Calantha saw no great problem. "Offer rewards to those who produce more. Higher status, or more coin."

"A sensible idea," said Osmaral, a bony young selumari with long moss-green hair. "But these wretches don't respond to anything except compliance."

Gleda broke in, her voice slurring as she spoke through scarred lips.

"We've tried rewards, but conditions in the mines and mushroom farms are so unpleasant, the peasants and former slaves will not work unless forced to."

"Have the nobles issue the commands," Calantha said.

Osmaral replied with arrogant sarcasm, "The nobles are like drones in a hive. Peasants respond only to the warrior class, which is now dead. For that I, at least, am glad."

"Recruit new warriors."

"Apparently, the only way to become a warrior is to defeat one in combat," said Burgard. "Without old warriors, we can't create new ones."

Calantha thought for only a moment. "You have all defeated morehl warriors in combat. Install yourselves and the other officers in the positions, then give the orders."

The three generals looked at one another. "Us?" said Gleda.

"Try it. It is only temporary, after all. Now, if you will excuse me, the court docket is full today."

When she next met Lord Burgard, he said the morehl had accepted the victorious generals as warriors, and production had resumed. The entire meeting had taken ninety seconds.

Among the thousand problems she faced each day, Calantha thought this one trivial.

Both Orric and Calantha enjoyed the evenings most. Only then could they spend time together. For half a watch, Orric escaped his tutor and nannies, Calantha her legions of aides, supplicants, and adversaries. Mornings and afternoons merged in tedium, but mother and son remembered each evening distinctly.

Often she made tea. Selumari cropsingers cultivated sweet-root and ginger on the volcano's eastern slope, and the spice families of New Elrannin brought nutmeg from the south in merchant sky ships. Once Calantha somehow obtained actual Anvil Highlands tea, luxury of luxuries, and Orric listened in awe to her talk of the plantations where it had grown.

Holding his steaming mug in both hands, he asked, "How do you know so much about tea?"

Stirring her own mug, Calantha added a drop of honey from the mansion's hives. "I learned about it when I traveled up and down this entire coast, many years ago. Travel is part of the path, as is education. But most important is awareness, and tea is useful for that.”

“'The path' means the Crafts?”

“The Crafts are secondary. 'The path' means the journey through life, the search for understanding and the right way to live.” She sipped carefully, then held the liquid in her mouth a long time before swallowing. She looked to one side. Orric had seen her do that often, but never understood what she looked at.

“I'd like to do those Crafts,” he said dreamily. He sipped and swallowed. “Throw lightning bolts, walk on the wind, summon a dragon—”

“Hush! Wyrmcraft is no goal to aspire to! They are nothing but danger.” Seeing Orric's wide eyes, Calantha caught herself, breathed deeply, and quieted. She smiled. “At any rate, you come of different elements than I do. Your aptitude lies with Firecraft, and with—” She broke off, then resumed. “And you won't master any Craft, young man, as long as you cannot even drink tea.”

The boy looked puzzled. “I'm drinking it now.”

“You are not. You are drinking your fantasies of walking on the wind. Drinking dragons.” She shuddered. “Drinking anything except the tea. Listen, Orric: Until you can drink one sip of that tea, you can never drink the tea. Do you understand?”

“No.”

“Well, you will someday. Now finish up. I'll put you to bed, and then I must meditate. Tomorrow we go see the bats.”

“Bats?”

Orric almost fell into the bat cavern, an inconspicuous crack in a tall black outcrop on Karakto's eastern slope. He and several other children climbed out over abrasive volcanic rock to peer down into the narrow gap. Below, there was only blackness and a powerful smell of guano. High squeaks drew Orric closer, closer. The cleft did not look deep—

Then he slipped. He scrambled back up amid raucous squealing, and Calantha and the other parents called the children back.

On this early evening, as on every night during spring and summer, dozens of families gathered here. The selumari stretched out linen cloths and ate bread and honey. They were the very old and very young, with few of military age between.

The war had wiped out a generation of Emmiria. The morehl stood silently on the opposite side of the crack. All appeared of prime years. Orric saw but few children like himself among the morehl.

Calantha had brought not only Orric, but Shantric and some of the other servants as well. Orric asked Shantric, "How many bats are down there?"

"Over a million, I am told. That would be about four times the entire population of all the First Races on Esfah— even the goblins—when the gods were done with the Making. A million bats, just in that one cave."

Orric could not imagine a million of anything. "Are the bats Death monsters?"

Calantha laughed. "No, no. They are little, no larger than mice. They eat insects. Thousands and millions of insects, so mosquitoes don't pester us."

"Doesn't that make the bats Death monsters for the insects?"

His mother smiled thinly. "It's a bit more complicated than that. We'll talk about it another time."

With his employer present, Shantric seemed eager to display his knowledge. "Do you know, young sir, each baby bat inside that cave clings to a wall in the dark, helpless? The mother bat leaves to find food for it. Then, when she returns, the mother flies past all the thousands of baby bats straight to her own child. How does she do that?"

Orric thought of hanging alone in darkness, in a seething mass of children, waiting for Calantha to return. He tried not to shiver. "I don't know," he said. "Magic?"

His mother laughed. "Not quite," said Calantha.

"Look! The bats!"

Orric whirled, the children gasped, the selumari adults called out to one another, and even the morehl stood more alertly—as two starbirds flitted up from the cavern. Orric sighed.

Shantric spoke in his most learned voice. "It is early yet for the bats. Human foresters introduced starbirds while wandering through this area shortly after the war—"

Ignoring him, Orric wandered down the slope and looked out across the cultivated plains east of Karakto. He had never seen this view before, and the land's flatness interested him. In the fading sunlight, he saw green fields of leastleaf and kasha, salt marshes, and to his left, a gleaming inlet of the Narcea. In the distance, at the level of the lowest clouds, a red-sailed sky ship made its way north.

Here and there, megaliths of granite stood in grassy fields. Orric knew vaguely that Karakto had erupted from the plain less than three decades before. Were these rocks debris from that birth?

As shadows stretched across the landscape, he pictured it: the ground shaking, the first fracture, a smooth cone shouldering its way upward and throwing off colossal chunks of rock, molten rock pouring forth in a magnificent orange fountain!

Something fluttered past his ear, too fast to be seen. He heard flapping, high chatter, children's shouts. He turned. Silhouetted against a violet sky, a whirling cloud of specks raced past him.

Squeaking creatures flew straight at his eyes, veering away at the last second. Crying out, he reeled back and almost fell, but suddenly his mother stood beside him, and he clutched the hem of her jacket. "I am here," she said. "Be calm." She extended her hand, and across her fingertips ran an emerald glow. With a sweep of her arm, she conjured a sphere of green light around them both.

Such a light might fall on the ocean floor, and in Orric's mind the tiny bats darting crazily past became a school of furry fish. He laughed.

For a long time the cloud of bats stretched from the volcano, a twisting ribbon rising through the dark sky. From either side of the cavern, a few families slowly crept up to watch mother and son, selumari and morehl, standing together in the green sphere of light.

Suddenly a child broke from her parents and ran to stand beside Calantha. Then another and another. In moments every child of both races stood with her and Orric, laughing, pointing, staring in wonder.

Their route back to the selumari district took them around the outside rim, along a trail Calantha had recently ordered widened. The moon, Rhaudian, had not yet risen in his day's second orbit, but twenty-thousand stars glittered, and the Hand Nebula's orange-red glow gave light to see by. Steam from Karakto blurred only a patch of the brilliant sky.

Orric lagged far behind his mother and her servants, wanting the evening not to end. While Calantha talked with them about a forthcoming formal dinner, Orric noticed a twitch of movement at his feet. A bat, no larger than a field mouse, lay on the path. Though its black wings were huddled against its body, the creature looked unharmed. Orric could see it breathing. But when the boy gingerly touched it, the bat only trembled. Was it dying?

For the first time, Orric confronted the idea of death— or, as he considered, of Death. Some hostile force had thrown this sad animal on the path, simply to suffer, alone and without reason.

No thought occurred to Orric that his mother, or anyone, could help. He alone must decide: Walk on and leave the poor bat to die in agony, or—

Drawing a long breath and setting his jaw, Orric raised one foot. For a moment he trembled as the bat did, in sympathy.

Then his heel fell hard, crushing the bat's skull. Feeling dirty and helpless, he looked down at the dead thing. The smear of blood and brain across the rock drew his gaze. Its pink color, pulpy texture—he stared, caught up in a fascination he had never known. The veins, like threads, awaited his reweaving…

"There you are." Shantric sounded bored, but as he saw the bat, his mood changed instantly to revulsion. "Did you kill that bat? Yes you did! You bloodthirsty—" He grabbed Orric's arm. "Fire and Death! Death and fire, that's all you red rascals are!"

"Enough!" Calantha ran up and caught Orric in her arms.

Understanding all with a glance, she spoke coolly. "Shantric, go on ahead. I shall speak to you later."

The old elf's mood changed at once. "My apologies to the demarch. I did not think—"

"Later!"

As Shantric meekly departed, Orric asked, "What does 'fire and death' mean?"

"Never mind. Orric, why did you kill that bat?"

"It wasn't moving. I thought it was hurt."

He felt her relax. "Very well. We can talk about it at home. Now it is getting cold, and we must go."

As it happened, Shantric must have smoothed over his trouble with Calantha, for he remained Orric's tutor. But in thinking of that night, Orric recalled it as the moment he started to dislike Shantric.

By Orric's tenth birthday he was still small for his age, but graceful and highly intelligent. His thin nose and piercing black eyes had begun to show the unearthly morehl handsomeness. His ears grew more pointed by the year.

Shantric had never talked of "fire and death" after that night three years ago, and carefully avoided discussing the morehl. For his part, Orric still remembered, with a thrill that remained his secret shame, the blood of the dead bat at his feet.

In spring, Shantric began lecturing on the epics of Cormian, a mad selumari poet of the second generation. But the lessons brought difficulty.

"At the start of the second canto, Cormian uses the kiss of the moon spirit to represent the beginning of Starmor's insanity. The imagery of dim white light is echoed later in the poem each time Starmor kills one of the seven Landweaver monsters. Every time, Cormian describes the light as a different color, first violet, then deep blue, and so on down the rainbow to red. This shows the hero's descent into madness—What is it? Why are you crying?"

Orric clumsily wiped the teardrops from his scroll. "I don't understand!"

Shantric pursed his lips. Orric had made trouble from the start of the poem. "This is not difficult! What is the mystery?"

"It—It isn't real. There isn't a real Starmor—you said so yourself. This is just a name on parchment. How can a name go insane?"

"Once I might have wondered how a tutor could go insane. Have you not heard of stories?"

The boy was shaking. "I don't understand them either!" "It is simply a matter of imagination! You are not stupid. You must see that where the poet writes, 'He struck a hundred cuts upon the serpent's throat, And from the monster blood poured

red as wine,' that this describes not only a great battle, but also Starmor's victory over his own—"

Shantric broke off as the boy's eyes rolled back. Limbs thrashing, Orric fell from the chair.

From his ears gushed thin, smoking rivulets of blood, brighter red than wine.

In the healer's chamber Shantric was apologetic. "This is apparently a cultural defect of the morehl. These folk have no experience with the language of imagination. They understand only what they believe to be literal truth… Please believe me, had I suspected—"

"What of the blood?" Calantha asked.

"That is a normal sign of this sort of seizure, which morehl call 'the strange.' It is harmless, like a nosebleed. Only the young give way to such fits. In later years, they learn to control themselves. Again, I entreat the demarch to recall that I—"

Calantha fixed him with a green glare. "Master Shantric, if you apologize once more, I'll discharge you on the spot."

Shantric clapped his mouth shut, bowed, and retreated. Calantha looked away and saw the elf-outline beside her wavering like a heat mirage. She looked back, then called after him. "Master Shantric." As he returned, she thought of the Third Quietude Meditation: *One with deep spiritual wisdom acts in my place.* What would she say? "I spoke thoughtlessly. I recognize that you were not aware of Orric's condition. Please accept my apologies."

"Of course."

Calantha drew aside a woolen curtain and entered the sickroom, a small boxy chamber with clay walls. *Tch, tch*— white sunlight shone through an open skylight, healthy for selumari but not morehl. Stepping around the deep heal-water tub carved in the rock floor, Calantha loosed a cord that dropped a wicker screen over the skylight. Then she turned to the single cot of stretched shark leather, where Orric lay unconscious.

The healer, Desmi, rose from beside the cot. "He sleeps. I am sorry, but I cannot heal a morehl. The elements are different. I have smoothed his energy flow, that is all. Please understand."

"I know." Calantha looked down at the thin, mousy Desmi and tried not to think ill of her. For over three centuries, ever since Death's Curse of painful injury had struck the second generation, healing had been clumsy and crude. Any journeyman in Aircraft or Firecraft could restore elemental energy to the dying, but none could cure injuries. So had come the abundance of scars, limps, and lost limbs to the war-torn world.

Desmi looked back at Orric. "Has the demarch thought this might be part of the youngster's growth? His voice should break soon, and for all we know, this, too—"

"His voice will not break soon. Morehl sexually mature around fifteen or sixteen. Evidently they take no interest in the opposite sex until their mid-twenties, after the mind matures."

That, at least, should be a relief, she thought for the hundredth time.

"Mmm." Desmi looked at Orric with—envy? "Bred for fighting and little else, mmm?" She left the chamber. Calantha sat on a stool beside the cot.

Without opening his eyes, Orric said, "What does that mean, 'The elements are different'?"

Startled, Calantha realized that a moment she had long dreaded had suddenly arrived, and she was unprepared. She looked to the elf—shape but found no guidance. "The healer is accustomed to selumari. We are attuned to the elemental forces of air and water. Our life energies derive from them. The morehl…"

"Fire and Death. Death and fire." The boy opened his eyes. He seemed older, more reserved. Distant. "What does it mean to be attuned to Death?"

"It only means that Death created the morehl, and they can use a Craft that harnesses its force. Nothing more."

"Shantric says Death is evil, and so is anything that comes of Death."

"Orric, evil is a choice, a decision. Whether or not Death created the morehl, you are a thinking person, not a puppet. You choose your actions as anyone does."

"I saw visions." Orric sat up on the cot. Calantha noticed new exactness in his movements. "Something dark ate the words on the scroll, and then in my head. Bats ate bugs, and then the bats fell and worms ate them. Fish ate the worms, swimming elves ate the fish, and sharks ate the elves. I saw much more like that. You say Nature is the enemy of Death, but everything in Nature kills to live."

"People use the name 'Death' for the Corruptor who cursed the world, because they fear their own deaths and think the idea evil. But the Corruptor means far worse for the world than natural death. It is the force of decay and imbalance. Servants of Death seek the brutal exploitation and destruction of Nature. That is what is evil."

The boy considered that. Calantha thought she saw unusual depth in his gaze. He said, "I think the selumari and vagha cannot win against Death. As stewards of Nature, you preserve things as they are. You wait, while the morehl and the goblins act. Action seems to be necessary for evil. If they sat in their caves and swamps and thought bad thoughts, but never acted, why would they be evil? But if you take action yourselves and kill all the morehl and goblins, you would be serving Death as much as they do. You cannot win."

With suppressed fear, Calantha thought, ten years old. Does this happen to all of them? "Whether they would be evil if they sat harmlessly is moot. They do not. As for whether we can win, we won this city. We would only serve the Corruptor by adopting its methods, and I don't intend to let that happen. You are proof of that, Orric. Now I ask you: Which side do you serve?"

As she spoke the question, she regretted it. Realistically he would give no reply except the one he did: "I serve Nature, as you taught me." Yet his words left her no more certain than before. "May I have some water?"

For a moment he seemed a child once more. Almost relieved, Calantha fetched him a ceramic cup of water from the tub's pump. Orric took the cup, then cried out. A misfired shard of clay on the rim had cut his finger. "Dear me, let me get you—" Calantha began, when suddenly Orric dashed the cup to the floor, shattering it. He pounded the cot, tore at the leather with his fingers, leapt up and kicked it over, then kicked madly at the clay shards.

Five long seconds. Suddenly the boy seemed to awaken, panting, from a trance. Mother and son stood frozen in shock.

The next day, Lord Burgard called to Calantha outside the Supreme Hall. The dwarf was accompanied by a young morehl woman with flowing black hair, full lips, and small, even teeth.

She had a bronze shackle on her right wrist, a symbol of peasants, but wore a black dress of flawless cut. A small wyvern design was branded on her cheek. Dressed outside the dictates of class, she could only be a Crafter.

"A moment of the demarch's time, please," said Burgard. "My peasants have alerted me to an upcoming event—"

Calantha's eyes widened. *"Your peasants?"*

Burgard pursed his lips, as if trying to draw back the words. "Ah, well—that is a figure of speech. My position as a warrior bears certain duties. Among them, I must see to the welfare of over a hundred peasants, who sharecrop their late master's fungus gardens. Gathering the harvest, marketing it—what a chore!"

Calantha silently noted the dwarf's fine coat, pale orange with red buttons, and his waistcoat of ribbed white silk.

"But to continue: Jandith, here, tells me the morehl stage a cycle of dramas every nine years, and now a new cycle approaches. These plays seem to have ceremonial importance, and the elders have been preparing them for some time. They planned to stage the first play tomorrow night at the former honor shrine. But today, the shrine's deacon forbade the performance. I wonder if the demarch may see fit to let this important event go forward?"

Calantha's mind whirled with questions. How had she not heard of this? Were the priests, whose doctrines depended on blood sacrifice, so little supervised? Most of all, the mention of "dramas" struck her like a hammer, as she remembered Shantric's words: "These folk have no experience with the language of imagination. They understand only what they believe to be literal truth."

"Lord Burgard, what is the nature of these plays? Do they involve the sacrifice of victims, as the elders have done in the past?"

"No, not at all! As I understand it, they are productions by volunteers. These plays are odd hybrids of dramatic arts and sporting contests. Or so I'm told. I am eager to see one." He looked up at Jandith and smiled.

Disconcerted yet intrigued, Calantha too felt eagerness. If this was a staged dramatization in the selumari fashion, it would prove Shantric wrong. There would be hope for Orric to understand the selumari view—for him to be, after all, normal.

She granted Burgard's request and arranged to attend the performance with Orric.

The play began half a watch past sunset, but what with duties and meditation, Calantha and Orric arrived very late. The night sky of spring glittered with a colorful spray of stars. A gentle breeze off the ocean had dipped into the crater, carried away the stench of sulfur, and brought the tang of salt. With the air crisp but not chill, the evening seemed perfect, like so many in the young world.

As they labored up the northern slope, mother and son glimpsed the integrity shrine. In former times, it had been the shrine to honor, chief of the morehl virtues—the debased honor that called for proud, reckless valor and vengeance. The amphitheater occupied a gaping hole halfway up a basalt cliff, an open-ended lava tube that plunged straight back into the mountain. The hole poured firelight and declamations out into the night. When this was a morehl shrine, worshipers stood in the lava tube and faced the crater, so that they looked out from the hole to the city below, source of the morehl's birth and strength. Now the audience for tonight's play faced the same direction, but sat in rows of amphitheater seats built in the tube. The stage was the integrity altar, positioned right at the hole's lip.

Orric pointed. "What is that square in the middle of the hole?"

"That is the tower shield, the symbol of integrity that stands on the altar. Cadal the Moralist, from the first generation, used such a shield."

The trail passed under the cliff, doubled back to rise to the shrine's level, then turned into an unlighted tunnel. Morehl doctrine required the worshiper to enter the shrine from darkness. The stale air of the tunnel made Calantha gasp, though Orric seemed unaffected.

From past visits, the demarch knew she did not like the amphitheater. Only the front seats near the altar, reserved for the higher classes, had good ventilation. Rows farther back, the domain of peasants and slaves—or rather, free folk—were hot and airless.

A large, bulky form loomed near the tunnel entrance: Count Fohlin, the morehl go—between. He wore a black linen coat without fasteners and, beneath it, an orange vest that bulged across his rotund midriff. Calantha recognized a yellow sash at his waist, designating elevated status within the noble rank of count. Quite the rise for Fohlin, she thought, who began life as a poor baronet.

With solemn courtesy, Fohlin greeted Calantha, bowed ponderously, and then stood upright like the stern of a sinking ship. "And my greetings to you, young master," he said to Orric in his odd baritone voice.

"Hello." Orric had never liked Fohlin, for the man's somber manner disturbed him. "Now and then," Fohlin continued, "the groundless speculation arises that this is the lost heir to Karakto's throne. Does the demarch not find that amusing? Mm-hmmm, mm-hmm-hmmph!"

Calantha could not interpret this simpering chuckle. And what prompted the odd gleam in Fohlin's black eyes? Calantha encouraged rumors of Orric's supposed ancestry, for it lent her credibility among the morehl, but she preferred that Orric himself should not hear them. She changed the subject. "Are you not interested in the play, Count Fohlin?"

Fohlin sniffed. "Ah well, the simulation of the Firehill legend has passed. Now comes the action that pleases the rabble." He plodded alongside the demarch and her son as they headed down the tunnel.

"I had been led to believe that the morehl had no drama. I am glad this is incorrect."

"Errrmmm… Well, some might call it drama. The contestant and his adversaries don masks and play out their struggle in the persons of heroes from the myth of Tynalis."

The three entered the main lava tube, deep inside the mountain. They doubled back so that they now moved toward the crater's center, approaching the amphitheater from the rear.

Ridges of rock marked the cylindrical shaft. Calantha imagined it as the intestine of some giant rock-beast. Here it was only ten paces across, but it widened at the amphitheater entrance, just ahead. There she saw a mob of ragged free folk silhouetted in fiery light. Calantha almost choked on the acrid smell from cauldrons of burning oil, but neither morehl noticed the odor.

As they neared the entrance, Fohlin lowered his voice still more. "In each cycle, the priests stage three of the seven Firehill plays. The first always depicts the hero Tynalis emerging from the Firehill to battle mythical monsters such as the Fish-Bird and the Mammoth-Horse. The contestant's win or loss determines which of the two following plays is performed, and that play in turn has two possible outcomes, each leading to a different third play.

"If the contestant playing Tynalis wins all three plays, he becomes a warrior and receives the benefits of the class: peasants, wealth, prestige, and incontestable authority."

Calantha thought of Lord Burgard's fine coat. "So it is a sport."

"The demarch may so put it, although not in the manner of the selumari. For the morehl, this is sacred ritual, a playing out of their role in the world."

"Then why did you leave the performance?"

Fohlin spoke with grave humility. "Unlike the rest of my kind, I have no taste for blood."

Horrified screams came from the amphitheater.

"Orric, stay here!" Calantha said in dread as she ran into the amphitheater. Yet Orric ran close at her heels. She did not see the eagerness in his eyes.

Shouldering her way through the free folk, Calantha had only a brief impression of the high-roofed oval amphitheater: the semicircular rows of red faces, the steep flights of stairs descending to the stage, the void behind the stage, and the distant lights of the city beyond. Her gaze fixed on the tower shield, which had been draped with a black elder's robe embroidered with the morehl symbol of honor, two intersecting crosses.

She stumbled on the narrow stairs. Her legs buckled, and she very nearly fell. But Calantha, like other enchanters, could conjure protections from various minor spells and a gust of wind bore her up and she rode the eddies down the stair. Her eyes fixed on the distant stage.

There, beneath the shrouded shield, stood two morehl, dressed in black loincloths and wearing featureless masks. A masked morehl lay wounded at their feet. As Calantha watched, the two drove rapier blades into the victim, who thrashed in silence, then fell still. Smoky vapor curled from his wounds. Tynalis had lost his battle.

Just before Calantha reached the stage, two selumari leapt up from the front row: a round—faced woman with lined features and many scars, and a lank young man with long hair. Generals Gleda and Osmaral, each looking horrified and angry, pinned one of the masked morehl actors.

Landing lightly, Calantha whispered, "Stop." The word echoed through the amphitheater: STOP!—TOP!—OP!

Morehl and selumari alike covered their ears. Only then did Calantha realize that there was no commotion among the morehl in the audience—at least, not as the selumari or vagha interpret emotion. They had watched the death of Tynalis, and then the struggle between actors and generals, in sacred silence. They were worshipers at a temple. When some felt deeply moved, the emotion spread to the rest.

"It was—just a play," said a voice behind her. Lord Burgard of Gundakhor stood at the foot of the stage, his skin gone pale. The peasant woman Jandith stood behind him.

The dwarf continued shakily, "We were watching a story, a myth. And then…"

Calantha looked at the body's multiple punctures, the bloody orbits of the eyes. "And you did nothing?"

"The butchery came suddenly, after he fell." He licked his lips. "We did not think it real until then."

"It is true, demarch," said Gleda as she held the actor. Calantha noted that she and Osmaral both wore rich, perfectly tailored clothing and shining jewelry.

"Elders!" Calantha looked around for the morehl priests. "Where are the—"

She stopped as a gaunt morehl in a long-sleeved black smock emerged from behind the draped shield. He had thin, appealing features, but a blood-red scar like a burn reached up his neck and across the base of his scalp, as if something groped upward from his body. The man wore the bizarre ceremonial hat of an elder, a partial cone sliced at an angle. The shape and height of the hat indicated the priest's rank.

A moment after noting the cap's unusual height and steep angle, she recognized this high official, a former slave named Cennard. All priests in Karakto had been recruited from among slaves, for reasons she had never understood.

"Elder Cennard," said Calantha, "I outlawed sacrifices!"

Cennard's whisper was pure oil. "We adhere to the demarch's command with rigor. This was not a sacrifice." His hidden hands moved in their voluminous sleeves. What was he hiding? "The performer, the avatar of Tynalis, gave his life in the cause."

"What cause?"

The elder's sleeves separated, revealing a device that made Calantha and her generals reflexively step back. Cennard held a curved mallet of oak and iron, with a hollow barrel at one end and a trigger and hammer halfway along its length. Runic inlays of bone marked the polished wood handle.

The most feared weapon of the morehl: the flintlock.

Then came a second shock as Cennard said, "The ceremony we have just staged, drawing on the spirits of our people—acting in concert, feeling in unison—powers our sacred weapons."

And a third shock. He walked over and placed the flintlock pistol gently in the hands of Lord Burgard. Burgard and Calantha were speechless. Gleda's mouth hung open.

Osmaral, all trace of his usual arrogance gone, stared at the elder. "You charge the pistols through this ceremony? For years we have tried to learn the secret! Now you simply tell us?"

"You are the warriors."

Calantha asked, "Why would you produce a weapon for your enemies?"

Cennard favored her with a catlike smile. "Your folk and ours are no longer enemies. We have always served our warriors faithfully."

Hearing his smooth speech, Calantha suddenly understood why it bothered her that priests were promoted from the desperate ranks of the slaves. It guaranteed that elders were driven, that they would do anything at all to achieve their goals. Anything.

Burgard looked down uncertainly at the pistol. "We cannot fire these. They work only for the morehl."

"This rite has made you morehl. This weapon is attuned to you—to all of you, the warriors." -

"They are not—" Calantha started to reply, but Burgard suddenly raised the pistol and fired straight at the tower shield behind the stage.

A brilliant white flash erupted from the barrel, and the report deafened them all.

The symbol immortalized by Cadal—who alone of the first generation resisted Death's temptations and trickery, who held Daur-Bot-Nin's gate single-handedly against the Corruptor's first assault, before the arrival of Davian Whisperwynd and reinforcements from Maris-ta-Sehlim. Cadal's symbol, the shield, shattered and fell to the stage.

These flintlocks or Karakto proved more powerful than even a reinforced shield.

The echoes died. Burgard looked at the pistol in wonder. He murmured, "Light, powerful, long range, easy to use—" The elder smiled.

Calantha realized what was "happening. Gritting her teeth, she looked to the elf-shape, and it spoke silently to her. She heeded it and called out, "These plays are canceled!"

At last, the audience members broke their silence. In their low hiss she heard more than discontent. A single morehl's revolt could spread like disease to those around.

She stared them down. The hiss ceased. Without looking away, she said, "Gleda, Osmaral, come with me. Lord Burgard, will you please join us?"

Turning, Calantha stopped dead. Orric stood over the dead body and stared in fascination. He looked up at her. Only one word could describe his expression: ecstasy.

Tension ruled the conference chamber. Lord Burgard said, "The demarch must recognize that destroying a culture's sacred rites is as bad as killing its people!"

"I will not recognize that, not when the rites are evil." Calantha did recognize the inversion of the quarrel she had had with Burgard after the war ended, seven years ago. The irony brought her no amusement.

"Evil is a strong term," said Gleda reasonably. "The morehl sacrifices were evil, but Elder Cennard rightly observed that this was no sacrifice. It was a fair combat that ended when one side died. We have all fought such combats in the cause of good."

With equal control Calantha replied, "This is simply self-interest. You all desire those weapons so strongly that you have lost your reason."

Osmaral, most temperamental of them all, said, "To defend our city is not a loss of reason!"

"'Our' city is not under attack."

"It will be!" Belatedly Osmaral tried to control his temper.

"Esfah is filled with enemies. The battle against Death is endless."

"More accurately, the battle against the Corruptor." Calantha's tone was sharp. "This battle has shifted its ground, and none of you stands watch. You, Osmaral and Gleda: You must resign at once from the warrior class. Lord Burgard, I suggest you do the same."

Their faces fell. After a moment, Burgard said, "That may prove difficult. We still must persuade the peasants and free folk to continue their production."

"You have had three years to develop rewards for production. Have they had no success?"

"There are… difficulties," Gleda said vaguely. "I believe we do the most good by working for change within the system."

Calantha stared. "Seldom have I heard more dangerous words. The order stands. Tender your resignation from the class, or sever your relations, or whatever the practice is, by noon tomorrow. Lord Burgard, what is your decision?"

The dwarf thought a while. His eyes briefly wandered to one side. Calantha wondered if he, like her, consulted with a figure visible to him alone. But then she guessed Burgard merely sought his morehl peasant, Jandith. Calantha had forbidden her to enter the chamber.

Lord Burgard cleared his throat. "I believe in the importance of clear paths of communication. I shall remain as a liaison to the morehl, using the class position they respect. Of course, I will work with fixed purpose for the safety and defense of the servants of Nature."

Burgard rigidly obeyed the letter of the law, but not always its spirit. In the war, nothing had worked so well with him as outright authority.

Calantha spoke solemnly. "Lord Burgard of Gundakhor, my authority over you and your forces ceased when the alliance did, at war's end. You are not bound by my orders, but I still rule this city. My explicit commands to Gleda and Osmaral, and to all residents of Karakto, are that these ceremonies must not be staged, and that these flintlocks not be manufactured, made to function, brought into or out of the city, or otherwise allowed to exist here in any fashion whatever. Embassies from other kingdoms must heed these orders or risk expulsion. Do you understand?"

Instantly Burgard responded, "As the demarch commands." But he did not look her in the eye.

Osmaral looked sullen, and Gleda's face had gone as blank as a morehl's. Calantha suspected she had not seen the last of the flintlocks, but she could do nothing else for now. Dismissing the generals, she turned to the companion issue: the plays.

4

Happy gangs are all alike. Every unhappy gang is unhappy in its own way.

Over the years, everything had gone wrong in the Wild Things gang. The most recent disaster occurred just three days back. That was when the runt leader, Fennevaunce, had found out that his third wife was having a fling with Yort, and so announced that Yort could not go on living in the same gang with him. The rest of the gang—Murget, Blodge, a crazed war-dog rider named Giddy Duff (whose dog had died of bloatbelly), and Fenny's six wives—liked Yort better than their leader. None were eager to oust Yort.

This state of affairs continued for three days. It distressed Fennevaunce, Yort, and the third wife, particularly. The whole gang began to feel there was no sense living together under the same volcanic city. Any group of goblins who met while eating someone along a wayside road would have had more in common than the Wild Things.

On the third day, Fennevaunce began taunting Yort behind his back, and then in front of it. As the gang lay sprawled in their small cave, no one more than a leg's length from the others, the runt dispatched a message to Yort, four feet away.

"Tell that treacherous gurk Yort that his stinking armor is stinking up the cave, and he should clean it," Fennevaunce said sullenly to his third wife. She was an ordinarily spritely female named Fennevaunce's Wife Three (maiden name: Shroggard's Daughter Two). Then he took another long pull on his clay flask of gutchurn.

Yort sighed heavily at this memorandum. "I'll clean it right now," he said. After a few draughts of gutchurn, the runt got mean. When Yort left the cave and entered the hot, smothering tunnel, however, he glimpsed the leader rising to tiptoe after him, stone axe in hand…

Over the years, Fennevaunce had led the gang into many problems. By the time they reached the battle between the red and blue elves, the Vaumb-cursed blues had already won. Then, far short of the coast, selumari patrols caught the goblins sleeping off a heavy dinner of farmer. After a brief trial, the Wild Things wound up on a chain gang of goblin prisoners in the deepest grottos of Karakto, mining copper.

After eight weeks of insulting toil and a great deal of talking, Yort finally convinced two guards he could lead them to a buried cache of fire rubies. In a tunnel outside the mines, he pulled an oww-I've-gone-lame routine, and then bashed in their skulls with his manacles. He wanted to head for the coast and, finally, eat a fish, but he thought he would need allies to get out of the city. In any case, he had a poor sense of direction, and only the Wild Things knew how to get back to Bent Morass.

Besides, there were potential wives in the prison gang.

Breaking the Wild Things and a few wives out of captivity was Yort's worst idea ever, he later decided. Over the next three years he thought of a hundred ways he could have escaped Karakto alone and found his way home. Instead, he led a hand-to-snout existence as a fugitive beneath Karakto. They scrounged morehl garbage heaps and made short, desperate raids into the upper tunnels. Food was so short that all the wives had reabsorbed their litters each year, which made everyone sad and tense. Seventy or eighty imps gone! None of the 888 goblin gods would approve. The Wild Things were living in sin.

This series of calamities happened because Fennevaunce, at the moment Yort freed the gang, grew vindictive. Rather than escape clean, as Yort had arranged, the runt decided to set fire to the local mining foreman. Then—this part always set Yort's teeth on edge—on the rock wall over the body, he scrawled a message:

FENEVAUNSE VIKTORIOUS!

At least once a week thereafter, when the gang had to escape relentless selumari patrols by fleeing still deeper into the tunnels beneath Karakto, Yort reminded Fenny he had committed four spelling errors in two words. Dislike grew between the two. Once the runt had discovered Yort's affair with Wife Three, conflict was certain.

As Yort walked down a dark tunnel, stepping carefully over rough, pumice outcroppings, he knew this was the moment. Fennevaunce meant to bash his skull, the pathetic, drunken lout!

Yort's jowls twitched in annoyance. He had never killed another goblin, and had no wish to start now. Not that murder was bad form, but… though a gifted liar, Yort had never been good at tricking himself. He felt squeamish about killing Fenny. He hoped his family, 162 close-knit goblins in Bent Morass, never found out.

Yort came to the fetid pool of water that the Wild Things used for washing and, in desperate times, drink. He suspected the pool had formed out of the drippings from some privy overhead. As he knelt down in the darkness to wash his armor, Fennevaunce crept slowly up behind, stealthy as a mammoth.

Cut and run? No, now that the blue elves were hunting him, Yort needed the gang more than ever. He couldn't imagine a lie that would heal the breach with Fennevaunce. Resigned, Yort mulled half a dozen plans of attack while waiting for the runt to reach striking distance.

Closer… hurry up, gurk…

A point of orange light flashed in distant blackness. It darted at the two goblins like an arrow, then stopped just over Fennevaunce's head. Glowing like a candle, it cast a tight beam across Yort's skull. The runt lowered his axe.

From the light came a small, high voice. "Freeee meee!"

Yort found words first. "Gang! Wives! Come see this, quick!"

Fennevaunce said weakly, "Y-You see it too, Yort? What is it?"

"I don't know."

Nine pairs of clawed feet echoed loud in the tunnel, along with many curses as the Wild Things tripped in the darkness.

They reached Yort and Fenny just as the light spoke again: "Brinnng weaponnns…"

"Weapons? Who are you? What do you need them for?" Yort and several others spoke at once, but the light said nothing more. It began to glimmer.

Giddy Duff cried out, "Goin' out like a light, she is!"

Fennevaunce seemed irritated with the light. Like a dog, he snapped at the light, swallowing it. Darkness fell.

Murget's plaintive voice came, "Why did ya eat the light, Fenny? Does it taste good?"

Suddenly the glow returned, lighting Fennevaunce's skull like a paper lantern. The runt looked alarmed. His eyes widened. Abruptly, with a meaty *thoomp*, his head exploded. Thick blood and shattered bone sprayed across the other goblins. The point of orange remained over the beheaded, be-necked body.

"Ewww!" said Fennevaunce's Wife Three.

After a long moment the body collapsed like a sack of laundry. The light zipped away down the tunnel. Darkness and silence.

Murget remarked thoughtfully, "Eating that light was really stupid."

"Handy that we're right by the pool," said one of Fennevaunce's other wives. "I have to wash."

Some days later, Orric went looking for a bird and found a philosophy.

Not long after the selumari victory, Calantha had a demarch's mansion constructed on the southwest crater ridge. She called it Windhome. Placed between the selumari and morehl settlements, Windhome had two fronts, entrance rooms, and courtyards. The courtyard that faced the shore of Hwarrm's Doom Bay held a large pool of sea water surrounded with coral mosaics. Here, selumari servants refreshed themselves during the day, disliking long intervals away from the sea. Orric never went there.

Windhome's opposite atrium faced the crater. Its courtyard held an elegant rock garden of red boulders on a field of white stones, ornamented with cactus and succulents. Here, Orric spent each afternoon.

"Lemarin? Lem! Le-e-e-em!"

Orric had befriended an old pouchbeak that perched each afternoon onthe red tile roof. He loyally fed it fish from the pantry. But today, for the first time in several weeks, Lemarin the pouchbeak did not arrive. Holding a trout by the tail, between two fingers and at arm's length, Orric quickly grew impatient.

Against his mother's instructions, he stole out the crater-side entrance and searched north along the ridge. Cool wind blew in from the ocean. He wrinkled his nose at the salt smell and squinted in the white sunlight. To his left, the moon hung huge above the western horizon, the same sapphire blue as the sea below. In the crater to his right, Karakto's central spire towered above clouds of steam from the vents around it. A few gray, blocky buildings stood on bare rock around the tower, but the bulges of the inner slopes hid the tunnels of the true city.

Soon Orric came to a cluster of huge gray boulders in white sand, adorned by a few stubborn blades of beach grass. Alerted by a foul odor, the boy found the carcass of Lemarin. It was stripped of flesh and crawling with ants.

Not of analytical temper, Orric could make no sense of the feelings that rose in him. Shock, chagrin, anger... He had laughed to see this bird gulp down fish. Now he would never see his pet again. The loss struck him far more deeply than had the sight of the dead body on the amphitheater stage.

Along with the other emotions, though, there came fascination. The arc of the ribs, the intricate mechanisms of the joints! Insect trails like veins, a pearly sheen on the ligaments… In a moment, this gave way to a guilt that made him hunch as if under attack. He was not sad for Lemarin, and that fact itself saddened him. Torn by warring desires, he fell to his knees.

Then an outside force moved in his mind. Suddenly, without evident cause, Orric felt anticipation. Eagerness. He looked around, puzzled. Someone else was here.

A hollow voice behind him: "A friend of yours?"

Orric sprang to his feet. There, beside a boulder, stood Fohlin. Next to him was a familiar-looking morehl in black. Seeing the man's cone hat and scarred neck, Orric remembered: the priest from the Tynalis play, Elder Cennard.

"Forgive us," said Fohlin somberly. "We did not mean to startle you." His formal black coat and yellow sash should have looked out of place in this open sand, but Orric could not imagine Fohlin in any but the most proper clothing.

Orric grew suspicious. "Why are you here?"

"We mean no harm, I assure you." Elder Cennard took the same fawning tone he had used with Orric's mother. "We only wish to talk to you, young master."

Suspicion turned to alarm. "Did you kill my friend? Just to bring me out here?"

They stared intently at him, and at once he felt calm. *They are changing my feelings,* he thought, but he could not feel angry.

Cennard smiled tightly. "No, we did not kill the bird. In the priest class, our lesser Crafts can read the paths of chance. All the world is happenstance. I asked of my Craft, 'Where will the young master be this day?' and a whim seized me to take the air on the ridge. Hence—" With a flourish, he gestured to himself and Fohlin.

"Who killed Lemarin, then?"

"If that is the late Lemarin—" Fohlin nodded toward the bird, "—we do not know. Any wild creature is subject to the cruel accidents of Nature."

Orric asked Cennard, "How did you burn your neck?" His mother had said the morehl could not be burned.

The priest exchanged a brief look of surprise with Fohlin. "I fought in a slave company in the war. In one battle, a vagha moved among us with hands of flame. That is not the flame of a torch or even lava, but something worse. Only a few of us survived the carnage. But—" Cennard favored Orric with an ingratiating smile. "—I do not hold this deed against the wise rulers of our city, who have introduced many valuable reforms."

Though irrelevant to Lemarin or the morehl's sudden arrival, this straightforward answer lulled the boy's suspicions—somewhat. "Why did you want to talk with me?"

Fohlin countered. "Will you walk with us? We will show you a view you may find entertaining."

"How do I know you won't kidnap me, or kill me?"

"My, what a lot of questions. If we cared to do either, we could so already. We are well away from your mansion."

This was true. Calantha had never explicitly told him not to associate with other morehl, though he did not actually know any. With a long backward look at the body of his friend, Orric walked with the two older morehl north along the crater ridge, farther from his home.

The breeze slackened. Fohlin spoke in his odd baritone. "In Karakto, our custom is to speak of important matters when a child reaches ten years old," he said. "In your unusual situation, perhaps you have not yet had such a discussion."

"What kind of important matters?"

"Oh, many!" Cennard appeared enthused. "Insight into problems, awareness of the world, expression of purpose, embrace of self-assurance… All of them add up to the same issue: the enlightened exertion of your will."

"What does that mean?"

They turned onto a path along the outer ridge, on the southwestern flank of the volcano. Far below, like sea foam fixed in stone, a line of whitewashed selumari homes marked the boundary of slope and ocean. Each gleaming home stretched half into and half out of the surf.

Ignoring the view, Cennard said, "The ability to control your life and influence others depends first on the awareness of your own mind."

"My mother says that, too."

"Just so. Do tell us, then, young master, of your mind."

The request caught Orric off guard. He fell into thought as they walked, then resolved to talk freely. Somehow he found it easier to confide in these total strangers than in his own mother. "When I see something like Lemarin's body, I feel—I feel—interested." There, he had said it. "And then I feel bad about that."

Cennard's face showed infinite compassion. "Here we can offer relief at once! You need not feel guilt. The mystery of life bewitches all thinking beings. Death is part of that mystery."

"Mother says Death is opposed to the beauty of Nature."

Cennard adopted a tone of wounded protest. "Nature's servants deride corruption, but what of the corruption in Nature's own domain? Do they abhor the shingletail, which lays its egg in the nest of another bird so that its chick can push the mother's offspring out of the nest? Do they despise the silkworm's larva? The vagha harvest its cocoon for their clothes, but the worms can devour every leaf on a tree."

Fohlin said darkly, "Perhaps you know, young master, of the wasp that lays its egg inside living caterpillars. The wasp egg hatches and eats the host alive. How abhorrent! Yet should we then destroy all these wasps? No! That would lead to disaster—infestations of the mites and pests on which they prey, and starvation for the birds that feed on wasps."

Hwarrm's gray bulk loomed ahead. Years ago, Dwarven magic had transmuted much of the creatures' flesh to stone while it threatened to resist its death throes upon the slopes of Karakto.

The selumari had mined the area around the beast's wings and belly for the stone in every wall of the selumari district. The wings were gone, mined. The deep gouges in the quarter-mile-long body looked like bites made by some still larger monster. Orric imagined the dragon coming alive, rearing up as it had years ago on the war's last day.

The three morehl turned down slope alongside the body. Cennard kept up his hissing whisper. "Look at the creatures of Nature that some think 'evil.' What makes them so? The shark's remorseless hunt, is this evil? What of the spider, the snake, the flea, the maggot? Some find them repellent. But Nature created them, just like the 'noble' dog and mammoth and gryphon; what are the troll's crimes? He is ugly, and he eats humans and elves. Yet feed him on food of lower order—the meat of wild horses, or grain—and he withers. Is this evil, his refusal to starve?"

"Mother says Death created the trolls."

Cennard dismissed the point with a wave. "And though a troll is no worse than any of Nature's predators, servants of Nature exterminate all trolls on sight. Convenient, yes?"

After a time they reached Hwarrm's shattered foreleg, made of stone too hard to mine. Artisans had carved murals across the shoulder, scenes from their great-grandparents' stories of the founding of Emmiria.

Disturbed by the elder's words, Orric looked at the murals.

"The first elves didn't have to worry about war with the servants of Corruption, did they? They still had many problems."

Cennard agreed forcefully. "Truth, truth! Their problems made them stronger. Those who test a person's limits, his strengths and weaknesses, perform a vital service for that person and all his fellows."

They descended to the rocky beach. Angerwings and shearwaters flew overhead, circling in the warm spring wind and screeching. Hwarrm's diamond-hard skull lay upside-down but intact. Its flattened forehead rested in the surf. Its square upper jaw and fangs were encrusted with barnacles. The lower jaw pointed to the sky. The sea-cave of its mouth made a popular playground for selumari children.

Here Orric stopped, vaguely annoyed at the elder. "What do you want, really?"

"Ah." Cennard touched his fingertips together. "We come to our purpose. Perhaps you are unaware, young master, that your mother has kept influential morehl from talking with you, as we are talking now. It is because of your importance."

"What importance?"

"Earlier I mentioned the minor craft that located you. A similar rite has shown me that a high destiny awaits you. You, Orric! Its nature remains, shall I say, foggy. But this I know: To achieve it, you must exert a will guided by philosophy and honed by discipline. An awakened will."

Elder Cennard knelt beside the boy. "We of Karakto's first generation are blessed with the sure knowledge of our creator's interest, which gives us unending strength. Draw on this same strength as you grow! As one of our second generation, you lack our inborn knowledge, but we can teach it to you—if you wish to learn. As matters stand, open instruction is not possible. But we can meet in secret, with no one the wiser, like adventurers! Wouldn't that be thrilling?"

Orric decided he did not like Cennard, but the idea of a destiny excited the boy. To think that his anxieties and guilt might be guiding him to a high purpose!

Suddenly, it seemed, Fohlin noticed the dragon's head. "I have just recalled an intriguing folk tale popular among morehl children. They say that if you search in the dragon's mouth, you may find a sign that foretells your destiny. Do you suppose the young master could hope for such a sign, Cennard?"

The priest appeared astonished. "Why, I, too, recall that fanciful notion! Yes, many omens are possible. For instance, finding a gold coin is supposed to indicate future greatness.

Why not? Orric, would you care to look? In the event you find anything, I would gladly interpret the sign."

Orric scrambled up the rocks and into Hwarrm's mouth, mainly to escape Cennard. He searched among the huge stone teeth.

The priest's whisper carried even into the shadowed mouth. "Yes, the omen speaks clearly. The condition of the coin carries meaning, as well. In fact—Ah, you have found something? Come forth, let us see the coi—unnh." As he saw the treasure that Orric brought out, Cennard broke off.

The smiling boy held a bizarre sea shell, tan and white with a fat body and a long, thin spire. Along the spire grew opposed rows of long spikes, like the teeth of twin combs placed back to back.

"You—um—did not find a coin, then?" Cennard sounded disappointed.

Orric gazed at the shell's glistening spikes. "I know this kind of shell. It's a murex. When you build a new home, you put it over the doorway. It brings wisdom to the people inside. Or does the murex bring excitement, and the triton brings wisdom? I don't remember. I should ask Mother."

"In any case, a great sign in its own right, no doubt!" said Fohlin heartily.

Cennard recovered. "Yes, of course. Listen to me, young master." He ran a delicate fingertip along the boy's cheek. "Reflect well on what I have told you. This is the weapon of weapons, the strength that can carry you to greatness. Your spirit awakens in four stages. First comes the initial insight, then awareness of the world in which you act, expression of your purpose, and finally a sense of your unshakable destiny. I have now marked all four signposts on your path. I hope you follow it.

"Among the people that you spring from, that you have been kept from, there is a saying: With a pistol, the gunner kills a soldier—with a Craft, the warlock destroys an army—with an idea, the thinker uproots a world."

Without a nod or sign, Orric turned and climbed back up the trail. He cradled the murex protectively in one hand and used the other to steady himself against Hwarrm's side. He felt disdain for Cennard and muted fear of Fohlin. But in his mind, thoughts of purpose and destiny flew like the excited birds overhead.

On the beach, Cennard turned to Fohlin. "How did that shell get in there?"

Fohlin stared at him. "Perhaps all the world is happenstance. We shall hope he found us convincing nonetheless. Will you retrieve the coin, or shall I?"

When he returned to the mansion, Orric met Shantric. "Ah, you are well!" said the tutor. "Good." He looked around the rock garden. "I took it you would be playing with your pouchbeak friend."

Orric suddenly remembered, and his face fell. "Lemarin died."

Shantric appeared disappointed but not surprised. "Ah, me. I feared as much. Too bad."

The boy started as though an alarm had rung. "Why? What did you do?"

"In the first place, you must not take such an abrupt tone with me, young man."

"What happened? Tell me!"

"It—it was sheer accident. A few days back, I saw a whole fish on the waste pile behind the kitchen. The pouchbeak was outside, so I threw it the fish. Later the cook said she had 'laced that fish with banewort to kill the crows. Why do you stare? It was mere mischance! I regret your loss, but I accept no blame."

Orric saw a red glow engulf Shantric. *A hateful glow!* He pounded his fist in the old man's belly, tried to stab him with the murex spikes, and screamed. People ran at him—hands grabbed—he twisted and kicked—his arms became wings like Lemarin's—a black void filled his sight—a pattern of hungry sparks ate outward from behind his eyes—the ants ate Lemarin—Orric woke in his bedchamber, halfway into evening watch.

His head throbbed. He saw first the butterflies embroidered on his bed quilt, then the pile of simple wooden toys, the desk where he wrote and studied, and last, on the desk, his murex shell. Nothing had changed, but it all looked entirely different. The room was itself no longer. It had become a set of tools to bring about a destiny he still could not see.

The boy recalled Cennard's doctrine: "Those who test a person's limits, his strengths and weaknesses, perform a vital service for that person and all his fellows."

Orric resolved to perform just such a service for the murderer, Shantric.

5

A servant entered Calantha's drawing room in Windhome and announced Lord Burgard. Calantha had been expecting a different dwarf, a poet. Puzzled, she asked Burgard in and showed him to a wooden bench.

Burgard wore gold rings, an emerald necklace, and even richer clothing than before. His mood was odd, a blend of excitement, tension, and reticence. As usual, he shunned polite preliminaries. "I wish to discuss a matter that requires a certain—discretion."

"Of course." Calantha dismissed the servants. *If he asks to make those flintlocks,* she thought, *I shall expel him from the city.*

Burgard said, "I will not keep the demarch long. I have someone waiting outside." He paused, uncertain. He looked at portraits hanging on the whitewashed walls, at the couches around the low table, at anything but Calantha. "I suspect I have been enchanted. I would rather not say why."

Calantha failed to conceal her surprise. She wanted an explanation, but after a glance at the outline beside her, she did not ask for one. "Really. Well, I—I can see that this would cause you concern. If you like, I can use my Crafts to discover the truth."

He seemed relieved. "Yes, that would be most generous."

"—Now?"

"If the demarch pleases."

The drawing room had a large circular window facing the seaward courtyard and, opposite, a bay window facing the crater. Calantha rose from her chair and opened both windows, letting a moist breeze sweep through from the ocean. Catching its sound, she hummed a tone and focused the energies of Esfah, channeled it, and drew the magic to herself; a shadowy copy of an elf figure formed and she knew that Burgard could not see it.

Her skin suddenly felt damp. The air itself thickened. She walked to Burgard and placed a fingertip on his forehead. The phantom beside her did the same, and the moisture spread to envelop Burgard. It seemed to take on his coloring, yellow around his face, red amid his hair and beard, orange along the trim lines of his velvet clothing. Burgard became a blur. Calantha focused on her breath. The phantasmal figure merged with her. At once, she saw the room with greater clarity, and all the world echoed the song sounding in her mind. She felt transfigured and moved through her Quietudes as if they were a warm pool.

After examining Burgard closely, Calantha stopped humming. The trance dissolved, she blinked as though waking, and Burgard returned to normal. "You have no Craftwork upon you," she told him, trying to breathe evenly.

The dwarf seemed first relieved, then still more troubled. "I thought as much. Yes, my feelings are—Yes. Well, I, ah, must be going. My thanks to the demarch." He bowed and turned to go.

"Lord Burgard, do you wish to talk?"

Burgard faced her and said clearly, "No, thank you." Bowing again, he left.

Calantha stood at the bay window. She watched Burgard leave the mansion, walk out to the ridge, and join his morehl companion, the woman Jandith. As they walked down the path into the crater, Burgard's hand stole up and tenderly brushed the red hand of the lava elf.

Soon a servant showed the poet Hornbeam into the drawing room. Hornbeam was a much different dwarf from Burgard. The poet looked as though a couple of trolls had thrashed him soundly, scrubbed him with turpentine, and rolled him downhill in a barrel of nails.

Hornbeam had the vagha's red hair and golden skin, but the hair looked thin and dirty, and brown spots made his skin look like an overripe banana. Hornbeam's huge nose continued the banana comparison, and his teeth were crooked and yellow. His eyes were sunken, a nauseous pink, and deeply bloodshot. And his breath! Calantha moved to shake his hand, but decided instead to nod from a distance.

This vagha, supposedly the finest poet on the Talvatic Coast, stared blearily at Calantha without a word. He looked ill. Actually, he looked barely able to stand up.

"Er—hello, Steward Hornbeam," she said, using the title due a stranger from one of Nature's caretaker races.

"Are you well?"

"Madam, I am desperately hung over," he whispered. "With all my diseased heart I implore the demarch to speak more quietly."

"Oh." To the servant she whispered, "Please ask Cook to prepare one of Devin's refreshers." The servant nodded and left.

His footsteps made Hornbeam wince.

"Please have a seat." She supported him as far as the bench where he landed like a sack of beets. "I appreciate your keeping this appointment. At least, I think I appreciate it."

Hornbeam choked out words as if dictating from his deathbed. "One learns as a traveling bard not to let opportunities slip. Sad to say, one apparently never learns not to drink oneself into a stupor the night beforehand."

"Mmm. Please do me the courtesy of not dying here."

The dwarf opened one eye. "Already your requests tax me. Are the other details equally demanding?"

She hesitated. "You arrived in Karakto only recently. You may not know that the morehl here have a cycle of seven plays—I suppose you could call them mystery plays—"

"The Tynalis cycle. Every morehl city has them. Death planted the myth in their minds when it created them. Death is a better Corruptor than a playwright. What of the plays?"

"The first play led to a death. In some fashion, that death helped empower morehl flintlocks, which I have banned. I wish you to revise the existing plays to remove their violence and their link to the flintlocks, and to promote the cause of friendship between morehl and selumari."

Silence from Hornbeam. For a moment Calantha wondered if he had fallen asleep. "Steward Hornbeam? Are you..."

"The worst part of a hangover," he said dully, "the greatest torment, I believe, is when the throbbing in one's temples falls out of rhythm: first one temple throbs, then the other. In that moment after the first hammering blow but before the second, with one's senses sharpened by some evil agency, one feels the dreadful surety that the pain is not over. As inevitable as death, the companion blow will descend. Torture lies less in pain than in the apprehension of pain."

Breathing deeply, Calantha meditated on her frustration and so freed herself of it. She stood. "I am sorry to have taken you from your sickbed. Enjoy your stay in Karakto, if possible. Now I must—"

He interrupted, his voice still flat, his eyes closed. "Perhaps in the second play, Tynalis will learn from the Fish-Bird that both it and Tynalis himself have been tricked by the sinister—ohhh, what shall I call it—'Firesnake.' The Fish-Bird represents the selumari. The Firesnake will represent the evils of the old morehl ways. Morehl traditionally regard the snake as repulsive because it sheds its skin and grows more beautiful. I shall say that this Firesnake has lurked within the Firehill since the Making, charming all the mythic creatures in the plays. Morehl despise being used, for all that they delight in using others.

"Let's see, now. Tynalis must ride the Fish-Bird to reach the summit of the Firehill, the home of the Firesnake. The FishBird flies our hero to the battle, and together they fight the Firesnake. The snake uses a flintlock—no, hold on, no arms. The snake has a mad servant, portrayed as a slave—no, no, a priest!—owww, oh, how can a living being know such pain?—Yes, a priest. That will be a rich prank on those smug leeches. Where was I—ah. The priest fires the flintlock. But Tynalis has already fetched a secret weapon from the Mammoth-Horse, who of course represents the vagha. The weapon, the weapon—well, I shall come back to that—the unspecified weapon removes the saltpeter that powers the flintlock, rendering it useless. And so, the hero and his allies handily defeat the treacherous priest."

The flintlocks of all the morehl used the saltpeter, sulfur, and charcoal mixture to fire the weapons. Karakto's used a mystic alchemy, but it was a moot point and Hornbeam's ideas remained serviceable.

A servant entered and offered Hornbeam a tall clay mug on a brass tray. The dwarf opened one eye, took the mug, sniffed gingerly, and sipped. His eyes bulged. He snorted and blinked many times.

Something like vitality entered him. "A refreshment I developed for my late husband, Devin," said Calantha.

"I do not often drink, of course, but he did. I might have saved his life with that drink."

"Humm! Hmmm!" Hornbeam gazed at Calantha with admiration. "But the Firesnake sheds its skin and so escapes into the Firehill. Then, in the third play, we send Tynalis into the heart of the mountain, subjecting the poor wretch to endless tortures until he reaches the Firesnake in its lair. He battles the snake and he defeats the monster. All is well. The end. I will need a week to write both dramas. I do not provide masks. My fee is free lodging, food, and unlimited drink for two weeks in your coastal district, starting today, plus a pack full of food, and comfortable transport on the next coralship heading south. Oh, and the recipe for that drink."

Calantha stared. She cleared her throat. "What did you say about saltpeter powering the flintlocks? Is that true?"

For the first time, Hornbeam's ugly eyes showed a spark of life. *Apparently, not all spell casters also had knowledge of alchemy or chemistry.* "True of the flintlocks in other regions, at least. My fee includes what I know about flintlocks. Do we have a deal?"

She could not quite smile. "I shall instruct my staff."

Late that afternoon, Orric returned from his trip with Gleda into the morehl city. Ever since the pouchbeak died, the boy had wanted to look around Karakto, but his mother had had no time to show him around. Gleda, overbearing Orric's request, had told Calantha, "I am about to tour the mines and fungus gardens to check production levels. I would be happy to take your son along." Calantha agreed with thanks.

Now Orric sprawled happily across the bench, rubbing his feet.

"You two were gone so long I started to wonder," said Calantha brightly. "Did you walk the entire city?"

"I think so. My feet hurt. It was better in the afternoon, when we left the crater and rode horses. Now my thighs hurt too. Why won't horses enter the crater?"

"The odor upsets them." Calantha could not imagine what business would take Gleda outside the crater. "Where did you go?"

"Gleda took me all around the tunnels. I saw the mushroom gardens and talked to people everywhere. Then we went down to the ocean, and she met with some people in one of the rich homes. I don't know what she talked about with them, but when she left, they were all smiling. Laughing."

"Didn't—Didn't she come back with you?"

"Yes. She asked to use one of the rooms to change."

"Change?"

Gleda walked in, alone and wearing her formal military uniform: a green, tight-sleeved tunic and breeches, blue belt and boots, and a brilliantly polished cutlass hanging at the belt. Her green cap's band of blue silk carried the four shield symbols of general rank. As Calantha watched in astonishment, Gleda took the band from her cap and placed it in Calantha's hand.

Radiating confidence, Gleda said, "I hereby resign my commission and my service in the demarch's army. I tell the demarch as a courtesy that in the upcoming vote I intend to run for the position of demarch, myself."

As if a sword had swung at her from darkness, Calantha gasped. Instantly she controlled herself. She would not show weakness before (the thought rose without warning) an enemy. *No, no, keep perspective,* she thought. *Gleda had every right to resign her position, and any selumari citizen eighteen or older could stand for any position.* Yet Calantha's face flushed deep blue with anger. "And how, then, do you object to my policies?" She asked in a tight voice. "Flintlocks for everyone, I assume?"

"That is beneath the demarch." Still, Gleda appeared pleased at her reaction. "Many loyal Emmirians believe the city's defense is not properly provided for. Also, the experimental reforms in morehl society have produced disappointing results. We should investigate a return to proven ways."

Calantha noted Orric watching intently, but saw no reason to send him away. "'Experimental reforms'? Such as freeing the slaves?"

Gleda's smile tightened, but only briefly. "The free folk are helpless and discontent. They have little education and no opportunities. Many say they were happier in the roles society had assigned them. After all, they were created to fill those roles."

"No doubt the Corruptor appreciates your regard for its plans. And you? Will you be taking back the warrior role you so easily grew accustomed to?"

"I will take whatever role necessary to guarantee Emmirian authority in this city." Gleda's words flowed as smooth as the Narcea. In her assured manner, Calantha saw a genuine rival: an officer of real accomplishment, toughened in battle. Very likely, her contempt for the morehl was shared by more Emmirians than was Calantha's tolerance.

If Gleda had led Emmiria at war's end, when Burgard hacked a notch in the tree bark, she would have made the popular decision.

"I accept your resignation." Calantha casually tossed the blue band on her chair. "I shall face you in—what is it now?—forty days, more or less. What of Osmaral? Will he also visit soon?"

Gleda showed no expression. "I have not seen Osmaral recently and have no idea where he is." Her studied composure disturbed Calantha. Distracted, the demarch let her former general leave with barely a nod.

Orric watched his mother like a cat at a mouse hole. "What would happen if Gleda wins?"

Calantha did not answer until she had called a servant and sent a summons to Osmaral's home. "She would bring back slavery. I suspect her notion of justice is harsh."

"That sounds bad. But it is no worse than the morehl had before the war, is it?"

Calantha went to stare out the round window at the bright sea. "The question is whether she would stop with the morehl—or whether, ultimately, the morehl and the selumari are different."

Orric, the morehl boy, red of skin where hers was blue, looked at his mother and said, "I think we are very different."

But Calantha had fallen into worried thought. She wasn't listening. Orric went on. "I think Shantric would learn from a trip like mine, down into the city." He leaned back and stretched in contentment.

She paid no heed, coming around only when the servant returned to announce that Osmaral had vanished from his home. No one knew his whereabouts.

6

The original Tynalis cycle occurred nearly five centuries ago. Ever since then, Karakto's elders knew when to perform each play in the Tynalis cycle; it had become part of their cultural consciousness. The second play must occur on a night when the moon, as seen from atop Karakto's central tower, rose straight over a certain crag on the crater's rim. The timing was instinctual, perhaps based on the same impulse that made bats migrate south on a particular autumn day.

Calantha feared that the plays' action was as in-bred as their timing. She would find out tonight, at the staging of Hornbeam's revised play.

With the same instinct, the elders had chosen the play's location: a gigantic stone half-circle open to the sulfurous air. Here the morehl had once honored their virtue of vengeance.

Calantha had rededicated the shrine to the selumari virtue of forgiveness.

Around the amphitheater loomed seven bare pillars. Beside one, Calantha stood with Hornbeam, the poet, watching thousands of morehl and several hundred selumari who were seated below. The warm night air reeked of charcoal. The smell came not from lamps but from light-peasants, who stood with flaming red hands around the theater.

While waiting nervously for the play to begin, Hornbeam talked with Calantha about the pillars. For once, the dwarf was cold sober. "These stand for the seven aspects of Death. Let me see—Harrower, Destroyer, Calcifier, Putrifier, Liberator makes five—I can never recall all seven—oh, yes, the Aging One! And that large one directly facing the crater represents the Tester."

The Second Quietude Meditation had not calmed Calantha's heartbeat, so she tried conversation. "I've meant to have the pillars carved with murals from the life of Bialle. But we have only so many artisans."

85

Hornbeam snorted. "You will win no favor by carving murals for the morehl. Pictures bore them. The selumari never see them, except during some rare curiosity like this. Build coastal homes instead."

Once again Calantha was taken aback by the poet's familiar manner and casual tactlessness. Hornbeam had done a fine job on the plays, and his acid wit amused her, when he was sober.

But with the wit came brutal candor. So much for diversion, she thought. Calantha did not care to recall that in two weeks, she would face the election. She looked down at the rows of seats. A narrow aisle bisected the rows. On one side, the morehl in their thousands crowded in deadly silence, ranked by class: three rows of nobles, two of unhappy-looking elders, a dozen of merchants and artisans, and the rest peasants and free folk. Fohlin stood discreetly to one side. As for the warrior class—

Calantha looked to the opposite side of the aisle—empty save for a few hundred selumari curiosity-seekers and one candidate. Down in the front row sat Gleda and Lord Burgard, with Jandith close beside him. Surrounding them sat a dozen influential selumari merchants, artists, performers, and scholars, jovial and talkative. They supported Gleda's proposal to arm all selumari troops with flintlocks, and to increase morehl mining production to benefit selumari victims of the war. And who would not? Only those few selumari who had actually seen the nightmarish mines.

Calantha saw none of her own generals or advisors in the audience. They always kept a tactful distance from Gleda— but tonight had not gathered around Calantha either. She sighed. This play was critical. If it eased tensions between selumari and morehl, Calantha could claim some success for her policy of tolerance, raising hopes of peace between the races. But if the play failed—

Without warning, a morehl man in a black loincloth walked on stage. The young man carried a rapier with blunted edges and a covered point. He wore a red Tynalis mask, featureless as before, but now with wire mesh strung across the eye holes. Two more morehl, dressed the same way but wearing black masks, entered and began a rehearsed attack on Tynalis. They mimed a sequence of fencing moves, a recap of the end of the previous play. The pantomime ended as Tynalis dropped his sword and fell clumsily to the stage. The two attackers left the stage.

Among the morehl in the audience rose a low murmur of discontent.

Hornbeam quietly groaned. "The morehl may be masters of deception, but they cannot act."

"Who is the actor?" Calantha whispered.

"Just a peasant. The elders had already picked him for their second play. He wanted what all the contestants want, warrior status. But the priests forbade that after I wrote the new play. He settled for rescue from the mushroom farms."

Now a morehl boy wearing the blue mask of the Fish-Bird walked onto the stage. The scalp of a selumari had formerly adorned the mask. Hornbeam had replaced this with a crest of gull feathers dyed green. The morehl resumed their annoyed murmur… until they recognized the boy. Calantha had not wanted to put Orric in the cast, but Orric recently had become fascinated with the crater city. He tagged along into Karakto with anyone Calantha would approve—a governess collecting mushrooms, guards patrolling the free folk warrens, scholars teaching peasants to read. When Hornbeam suggested Orric as the Fish-Bird, the boy begged to take part.

The idea made sense. The Fish—Bird stood for the selumari, and in this play it brought Tynalis back to life. The morehl would never accept an actual selumari in the role, but Orric had a clear connection to the coral elves. He had always been popular in Karakto, because (despite Fohlin's objections) many thought him the lost heir to the throne.

Orric walked gracefully to the prone actor and recited:
This iron-hearted hero must not die,

For I have learned that we were cruelly duped
And made opponents through another's craft.
The Firesnake—the coiling, broiling serpent
At the darkest heart of yonder flaming hill,
The enemy of elves and dwarves and trogs—
Has put us at each other's throat.

The amphitheater's design carried even his morehl whisper to the free folk standing at the rear. The audience had fallen back into silence, though without the reverence of the first play. She looked at Hornbeam. "'The coiling, broiling serpent'?"

Agitated, the dwarf looked left and right. "I was forced to work under enormous pressure of time. You cannot expect a creator's best work on an unreasonably tight schedule."

Orric's hands traced circles over the actor.

At once I must call forth the sacred spark
That dwells within this man of bravest heart
And bring him back to this fore-destined world!

The boy waved his fingers, and Calantha watched with interest. This was Orric's first venture into the Crafts. Calantha had watched warily during rehearsals while her son was taught by a morehl adept. She did not want him to learn Deathcraft, and she did not trust the instructor: Lord Burgard's peasant, Jandith. The woman was somewhat adept in Craftwork. Odd, to Calantha's mind, that the Corruptor had scattered talented Crafters across all the morehl classes.

Even Orric's study of Firecraft struck Calantha as premature. Ten was a bit young among selumari, but apparently not among morehl. Before Calantha outlawed child labor in Karakto, she had seen slave children lighting their way through the mines with flaming forefingers. Now this same light glimmered fitfully at Orric's fingertips. A guttering flame—a burst of sparks—Orric's flame faltered. Ah well, Calantha thought. Orric was no prodigy, but few children were sensitive to Esfah's elements.

When the boy grew up and entered military service, he would learn the rudiments of Firecraft. On stage, Orric stamped his foot in frustration. He accidentally kicked Tynalis, who cried out and scrambled to his feet.

From the audience rose a buzzing, gulping sound. The morehl, who had coldly destroyed Emmiria and slaughtered thousands without remorse, were laughing. They had laughed that way when she adopted Orric on the battlefield, years ago.

But now only some were laughing: the peasants and free folk, and a few merchants. Down in the front rows, among the nobles and elders, expressions were stern. Across the aisle, Gleda and the selumari warily watched the crowd.

Morehl silence or morehl laughter—Calantha didn't know which disturbed her more.

The actors played on stolidly, allying and traveling to the Firehill. The drama was remarkably crude. Calantha could not decide whether Hornbeam lacked talent or was simply beaten by his material.

No more laughter rose from the audience until Tynalis and the Fish-Bird met the Firesnake's servant. This thin actor, who looked much like Elder Cennard, wore a mock elder hat and a featureless white mask, and he carried a flintlock. Before he said his speech or made a move, buzzing erupted from the peasants and free folk.

Puzzled, Calantha looked to Hornbeam. With pure joy the dwarf said, "White represents sloth and dishonor."

Nobles and merchants looked back, frowning. The real Cennard leapt up from his seat, raised his arms, and spoke to the peasants in evident anger. Calantha caught the word "impious," but otherwise laughter drowned out his whispers. By some trick of echoes, she distinctly heard a peasant respond, "Sit down, priest! Let's hear what Orric tells your brother!"

In the boundary rows between merchants and peasants, confused struggles broke out. Caught up in the anger from the rows below or the laughter above, class fought against class.

"This is the power of art," Hornbeam proudly told Calantha. "Show me the Crafter who can match a poet's magic!"

Selumari guards stood ready behind the pillar. Six warriors, lightly armored in shark leather, kept their cutlasses sheathed as they moved to break up the fights.

Many morehl did not notice. In back they stood laughing like children, entranced by this novel amusement. While the mock priest desperately played on, the merriment grew, and then something black flashed in the firelight: a shard of obsidian, one of the morehl knives. A laughing young peasant had thrown his blade at the actor.

The blade hit the false elder lightly in the shoulder, then fell to the stage. The actor twisted, and drops of smoking blood flew. A drop landed on the figure beside him: Orric. The boy stared as if transfixed.

Once one peasant had done it, they all had to do it.

"Guards! Stop them!" Calantha ran toward the stairs.

The guards could not break free from the struggling artisans and peasants. Countless hands lifted, each holding a knife, and let fly—

—*Too late,* thought Calantha, *I can't make it, oh, Orric*—

A flash of green, and suddenly Gleda was on the stage. She rushed past the adult morehl and tackled Orric. Both hit the stage and rolled a hand's breadth beyond the shower of knives.

At once, Gleda jumped to her feet and screamed, "Stop! Or I shall have you all killed!"

The drone ceased. In the stark quiet, the other two actors, each pierced by a dozen blades, fell to the floor and died.

Calantha reached the stage, rushed to Orric, knelt, and examined him for injuries.

Gleda spoke again: "I say this to the people of Emmiria: These morehl have not changed. Calantha has not remembered that. When I am demarch, I shall not forget!"

The selumari applauded and cheered. The morehl, their faces gone blank as slates, stared in silence.

Having found Orric unharmed, Calantha rose to her feet and said, "With all my heart, I thank Gleda for saving my child's life. Yet sincere gratitude cannot mute the voice of reason. When my opponent can swear she will—Orric! Orric!"

The boy ran offstage and up the stairs.

With one backward glance at Gleda's firm smile and the suspicious faces of the selumari, Calantha ran after her son. She was surrendering the demarchy.

The selumari endorsed Gleda's suspicions of the morehl—and the morehl could not vote.

On the lightless slope outside the shrine, Calantha almost stumbled over Orric. The boy sat facing the crater's center, where cracks in the earth glowed dim red. "I almost died just now," he said flatly.

She sat beside him. "No. I would have summoned the elements. The infusion of energy keeps you alive." If I could have summoned them, she added to herself.

Orric seemed not to hear. "I would have been like that bat. Dead." He was not crying, but she heard his fear, and she put her arms around him. "Those people would have killed me. They didn't even think about that. They were having fun. That was scarier than the sacrifices or the blood you always talk about. Just killing people by accident, for fun. Is that evil?"

"I suppose that is part of it—reckless action without regard for its price. I think of that as thoughtless ignorance, even madness, but not as corruption." She laughed. "We all do reckless things. I recklessly adopted you, and that turned out happily."

She hugged him. "Why did Gleda rescue me?"

"That is interesting, isn't it? I imagine she thinks of you as selumari. Or at least not lost to evil, as she treats other morehl. You must remember to thank her."

"You don't think of the morehl as lost, do you?"

"No rational person is beyond hope. Are you feeling all right now? I must go back and cope with these latest deaths, at least for the two remaining weeks I can expect to keep the demarchy. I'll get Shantric to take you home." Then Calantha realized she had not seen the old scholar all day.

"Do you know where Shantric has gone, Orric?"

He sounded troubled. "I wonder."

Shantric had never traveled this deeply into the morehl city. He hardly ever entered the crater. It was filled with foul air no horse would breathe, foul people no sane mind would tolerate, and foul dark tunnels twisting like snakes.

Dash that foolish child! For the hundredth time, Shantric thought longingly of a nice dinner in his cozy home, followed by an evening of study. A perfect day! Instead, here he was, scrabbling in the deeps of this hot anthill, searching for Orric.

A note he had received had taken Shantric completely off guard. He had returned to the library after lunch and found only a scrap of parchment written in the boy's unsightly hand:

I am running away because you neglect me and you killed Lemarin, my friend. Jandith in the coinery will take better care of me and teach me better than you. GOOD-BYE.

Well, of course one could not show such a note to one's employer. But the coinery, the tall building by the central tower—he knew that much. Coinery, Court of Justice, patrol stations, the late empress's palace: the imperial district. It stood near Windhome.

Shantric had set out at a brisk walk to fetch the young master before Calantha returned home. No preparation, no supplies. Daft! Monstrously senseless! Now it must be night up above, under the sky, the clean, beautiful sky. His mouth parched, his limbs shaking with hunger, Shantric made his way carefully down yet another foul, dark tunnel.

He stopped. Had he heard footsteps behind? No. His heartbeat slowed. Relieved, he breathed deeply, then choked and coughed. Death and fire, fire and Death—that was all this air held!

The morehl bladesman at the entrance to the coinery had regarded Shantric knowingly. "Jandith, the peasant, and a boy went to market half a watch back," the guard whispered.

"Check there with her friend, Halatri the firemonger." With his rapier, the guard had pointed to the stone stairs leading down into the nearest steam vent.

Well, it was only a few steps farther, after all. Shantric had sighed and gone down into the chasm by its curving stairs, wondering why the bladesman wore that insolent smile.

The market district, Shantric had come here once before to buy liquid fire—a coming-of-age gift for a niece up the coast in Aurora Bay. This time, as before, the market disturbed him.

Sunlight struck down through the steam only at midday. This afternoon, shadows and firelight flickered in the hot, humid air. Worst of all was the silence. Morehl crowded among the stalls, artisans plied their crafts, and merchants offered them, but it all occurred in dismal silence. A potter's stone wheel turned, a hammer shaped a sword, and occasionally transactions were whispered, but otherwise, the place seemed a domain of walking corpses.

Shantric had found Halatri. Thin and handsome like all the rest, he sat amid clay bowls of flame that burned in different colors and shapes. Their heat was stifling, their odor mysterious.

"What fuels these flames?" Shantric asked the firemonger. Staring fixedly, Halatri spoke in a deferential whisper. "Bad thoughts, oh master. Different flames burn away different bad thoughts."

"Thoughts? What blather. Where is Jandith, or rather, where is the boy with her?"

A smile came with a low whisper. "Ahh, the scholar."

"What? What was that you said?"

"Nothing. Merely a stray bad thought. See now!"

He thrust one hand into a purple flame…

Shantric gasped as the morehl's face contorted in agony. "Stop, stop!" the old tutor cried.

At once, the red elf grew calm and pulled his hand unharmed from the fire. Halatri whispered, "See now. No more bad thoughts here. Jandith has taken the boy to dine at her chamber in Highlight. They will not be back for some time. But it is not far, if you wish to find him."

Not far… The firemonger had said it so innocently. Now, lost in the depths of the volcano, Shantric felt certain he heard footsteps behind. Not those of morehl or selumari, either—not just two feet.

He had gone to Jandith's apartment in Highlight, the artisan district. Lord Burgard's favor must have raised her from the peasant tunnels. And yet, what a beastly pit! Narrow walkways, homes burrowed in living rock, low crude doorways blocked with animal pelts. Only dim sunlight filtered down from the crevasses overhead. How dreadful things must be farther below!

Shantric had to ask directions three times before he found Jandith's hovel. Each time, the informant favored him with a mocking smile. Was he so amusing to look on?

He assumed Jandith would be gone from here, too, and that he must simply return home. But no, the Crafter had been at home—-without Orric.

That woman. Shantric shivered now, in the hot tunnel, not only in fear but in recollection. Her long black hair was fine, not the usual oily spikes. Her robe of intense purple did justice to a sensuous figure. Her eyes, oh, her magnificent black eyes!

One look into those eyes, and he had forgotten his aching feet.

Even her whisper was alluring, not like other morehl. She spoke so quietly that Shantric had to lean in close, where he smelled the burning-leaf scent of her hair. "You are the boy's tutor? Ahh. He has been most unkind to you. He ran to me because he hoped I would teach him more of the Crafts. I have taught him a bit already, as part of the new play. But Orric is still too young.

"He was hungry, and so I sent him with a dear friend to pick mushrooms."

"Oh." Shantric tried to stop staring into her eyes. "When do you expect them to return?"

"I cannot say. But I have an idea!"

As though struck with a happy inspiration, she smiled, revealing sharp white teeth. "I'll take you there, and show you the sights of our city on the way. The deep tunnels always rouse my emotions—perhaps they will also rouse yours."

Well.

Shantric gritted his teeth to think of it now. The adept had led him quickly through Altars, the priest district, its high, torch-lit tunnels silent as a tomb. Then they had gone into the ill-smelling passages of the peasant district, where starveling free folk with burning hands served as lamps. Artisans carved symbols at intersections to indicate which noble family controlled what.

All the while, Jandith had walked close by him, talking in her alluring whisper. Her description of each sight contrasted with his, as when they came to the elders' devotional refectory.

The priests ate here communally at long stone tables. Ceiling glyphs showed lines and shapes. Jandith had whispered throatily, "The doctrines of our race are as meat and drink to the elders." But Shantric had only smelled the actual meat they ate, the flesh of wild horses, wild cattle, and rats. Nauseating!

She had sensed his reaction. As they walked deeper into the tunnels, into the foul depths of the Warrens, she said, "When outsiders tour a place, they never visit the city that its residents live in, but instead a city of dreams. The sights go directly into a dream world, with a wealth of detail that even we, who have lived here all our lives, cannot see. How I envy you."

No morehl in Karakto had ever visited another city except to destroy it. This woman may well never have left the crater.

Her observation came from the source of all her thoughts: Death.

Had Shantric felt repelled… or fascinated?

Finally, they reached the fungus gardens. These caverns echoed with scrapes of chisels, picks, and hooks, which grubby free folk used to harvest waist-high parasol mushrooms, shelf fungus, earthstars, smoothcaps, and countless other growths.

More than half these delicacies, savory to the morehl, would poison a selumari in one bite. Shantric had breathed shallowly for fear the air itself was noxious.

Where was that dim lavender light coming from? Did these things glow?

"Orric is truly a rascal," Jandith had said as they walked through that garden, then another. "He got so mad at you because of his pet. I must tell: He has been planning a small prank against you."

Shantric had thought the fungi here larger, the workers fewer. "A prank? Of what sort?"

"It hardly matters now. It has gone awry. He has no gift for seeing consequences, that boy. Do you?"

They had reached yet another cave filled with huge mushroom caps in rows. No one was around. Shantric, by then thirsty and footsore, had grown annoyed.

"I do not see Orric."

"He is hiding, the scamp. Look here, he is hiding behind that puffball."

She pointed to a tall growth with a round orange cap. It had white spots as large as his head. He peered left and right, past the stalk as she reached up to touch the cap.

A popping sound came with a strange powdery smell. Then, agony! Fire in his eyes! He had fallen to his knees, choking. In panic he'd expected a blow, a stab, even a gloating explanation or laughter! But only an appalling silence greeted his plight.

Now, a watch or more later—it would be deep night above, no doubt. Shantric was exhausted, aching, desperately thirsty, and lost in a tangle of dark tunnels. Something in the mushroom's powder was fogging his mind. Even in this danger, he began thinking, blearily, of the hero Starmor.

Canto Four. Starmor hunts the Land-weavers in the Cursed Palace. Fears to go in. Spirit of Earth comes to Starmor—or was it Fire? "Five doors you must needs pass, to break the shackles of your suffering. Doors with five fell guards, child—youth, man of strength, decay, and..."

He heard scuttling feet behind. Heart pounding, Shantric groped along the wall of the passage. He sought a crossing tunnel, a recess—anything! There, yes, he felt it! A gap in the rock, and in an instant, with many bloody scrapes, he squeezed through.

He sidled deeper, between rock walls that left barely enough room to breathe. Pausing to listen, he heard otherworldly steps passing, *clatta-tac clatta-tac*, where he had just stood. Then they stopped and returned. In fear and pain, Shantric worked his way deeper into the rock.

Suddenly he stumbled out into another cavern, this one dimly lit like the mushroom gardens. He shook his head to clear his thoughts, but the muzziness lingered. What was that strange, musky smell?

Looking down, he saw bones. *Why have they not buried these?* he thought dully.

Then fright struck. *A bone yard! Talismans of Deathcraft!* Morehl necromancers used the bones of the dead to summon their dark powers. These skeletons had once been embedded in masonry to line the buildings and tunnels of Karakto until Calantha had ordered the skeletons removed.

The morehl workers must have simply deposited the bones here, in this cemetery. Skeletons lay in heaps, as after a terrible battle, with chunks of clay still hanging from their bones.

Like a terrified boy, Shantric ran clear of the bones, his strides absurdly high. Long ago, his mother had told him tales of morehl skeletons that had come to life and walked out of the Obsidian Grotto in the northeast… after its fall hundreds of years ago many of its refugees had come to Karakto.

Gasping, Shantric found a passage that sloped upward. He wriggled into it. In darkness again, he fought a sense of doom.

Now what? Torchlight? He stole to the lip of the tunnel where it crossed a larger passageway. Looking around a rough-hewn corner, the old scholar saw thin, hunched figures walking toward him. The bandy-legged creatures had stooped shoulders and long dog-like snouts. A clutch of goblins. Shantric almost fainted.

In the light from their torches, they looked haggard and filthy, nothing like soldiers. At the fore marched a short, misshapen figure—a dwarf? No. With still greater horror, Shantric saw that this lurching creature was a dead goblin. Its head, and also much of its chest, was entirely gone. A brainstem and small chunk of grey matter flopped uselessly where it attached to the busted spinal column like a useless, insectoid antennae.

Two living goblins followed close behind, one tall, one stout, both with low brows wrinkled in frustration.

"Wake up, Murget," said the fat one. "You're not keeping your side in rhythm. Look at Fenny, he walks like a hunch back."

"This is hard!" said the big one petulantly. Prodding it with sticks, the goblins steered the animated body of one of their peers as if it were a hoop they pushed with a stick: a terribly slow and stubborn hoop. They poked it as it ambled aimlessly; sickly black and pulsing lesions spiderwebbed across its already mottled skin. Whatever the fiend had gotten into at the time of its death, it had brought the goblin back in a state of unlife.

"Urrh, another crossing." The fat one yelled ahead. "Yort! Which way?"

The goblins were marching their dead companion to the cemetery. *Down this tunnel!* Shantric crept back. A voice came from the other direction. "Nothing up this way, so—why, hello!"

Shantric turned and looked right into the warty face of a goblin with small fangs and a cunning demeanor. "A good evening to you, venerable sir," said the creature in a silky voice. "What brings you to this humble passage?"

"I—ah—" Shantric looked left and right. The other goblins had come abreast of the tunnel.

"Indeed? Well said! I must apologize for our headless companion. He ate something that disagreed with him, or disagreed with being eaten. Luckily, he landed upon ths black goo and it's helping us get his body to where it belongs."

The goblins laughed.

Shantric took a deep breath and charged straight through the clutch, then ran up the far passage. Amazingly, they let him go.

Behind him, the smooth talker called, "You caught us at an awkward moment. Perhaps we shall return the favor!" The goblins laughed again.

Ahead, Shantric thought he detected a faint breeze. He stumbled on with new hope. The tunnel narrowed. Once again he scraped through a tight opening. He felt a brushing against his cheek like the itch of stubble, and spider webs clung to his shoulders. If spiders lived here, could not other creatures of Nature live close by?

Shantric went on, the passage sloping ever upward. Oh, Nature, if he actually survived this ordeal, he would leave the demarch and work heartily to support General Gleda. That woman, and her worthy friend Osmaral—they knew the truth of the morehl!

Like all members of the First Races, Shantric had seen his share of battle. In his youth he had defended Nature with a strong bow of heartwood and whalebone. At Gundakhor, in a flying coralship he had shot many morehl. He smiled grimly. The goblins were foul enough, but there was a madness to the morehl, an evil that threatened to engulf the whole world. If Gleda won the demarchy, there would be fewer of the vermin. Many fewer.

Now Shantric distinctly felt a breeze, coming from a wide crack in the tunnel wall. He smelled an acrid odor: the bat cavern! He could climb out onto the volcano's slope! "The sky," he whispered, and crawled into the crack.

For once he passed through easily. He got few scrapes, and the cool fresh air, however bad its smell, invigorated him. When he found room to stand, though, Shantric saw no opening. Of course, it would be dark outside—and a cave of a million bats must be fairly large.

He moved forward in darkness and silence. Wait, there ahead, a glimmer of torchlight—in this cavern? *People!*

He tried to call out, but his parched throat betrayed him. In a moment, he gave thanks for this betrayal. A huge, dark shape eclipsed the light. Shantric glimpsed a long insect-like body and an arching tail. He heard a sound whose familiarity stopped his breath: *clatta—tac, clatta-tac.* The sound of many thin legs.

A scorpion. One of the monstrous morehl steeds. Shantric had seen them in battle, seizing enemies in their claws and impaling them with a bitterly sharp sting. He had thought all of Karakto's killed in the war.

Shantric froze. The thing passed by, and its footfalls receded into the distance. How large was this cave? He seemed to be in a side passage or crevice off a main chamber. The floor was coarsely textured, but flat as a board—a cooled lava pool?

None of the people working under torchlight seemed alarmed by the dark creature's passing. They kept shoveling white, powdery heaps of bat droppings into pails, emptying the pails into carts, and wheeling the carts away. Mining the droppings? Shantric had never heard of such a thing.

The workers were elves. They wore nothing, and white powder coated them from head to toe, so he could not tell their race. If they had scorpions, they were morehl.

Shantric had never heard of this mine, so it was probably secret. He had blundered into still greater danger. Danger or no, he desperately needed water. He thought of peeling off his sweat—soaked clothing, rolling in the droppings, and passing as a worker. But to an elderly scholar of the works of Cormian, this scheme sounded as bizarre and impossible as turning into a bat and flying out of the cave. Instead, he stole out from his hiding place and crept along the cavern wall.

Smooth floor, sheer wall—Shantric could almost pretend he walked in his own home. He could cry for that sweet idea, if only he could find a drop of water! A pool, a cistern—did the workers need no water? The bats? The scorpion?

He barked his shins on a high carved step. In the light of the distant torches Shantric saw that this was an arching doorway into a small grotto, less than a dozen paces across. On the walls he perceived strange carvings, impossible to identify in the darkness. In the center of the circular grotto lay a heap of—bones? Branches?

A cart rolled toward him. Shantric crept through the arch into the grotto, where he hid behind the bulge of an unrecognizable carving. Directly after him came a powder-white worker bearing a pail of droppings and a torch. Moving listlessly as if tired, the elf male approached. In the torch's light, the space was revealed:

A monstrous black face, staring with alert eyes straight at Shantric. Involuntarily the old scholar yelped. In his dry throat the cry came out a cough, clearly audible. The worker only glanced at Shantric, then poured the pail's contents into the face's gaping mouth.

Shantric realized, to his embarrassment, that this was only a carving, one of many tall faces in the grotto's circular wall. But how lifelike were those obsidian eyes!

The worker returned to his cart to fetch another pail of droppings, then poured these into another carving's mouth. The elf obviously saw Shantric but showed no interest whatever. From the curve of his nose and the point of his ears, Shantric guessed the man was selumari. Hopes rising, Shantric whispered, "I need water."

The worker stopped and stood before Shantric. He inhaled, then said hollowly, "There is no water." The voice carried through the cavern, but no one bothered to look.

Shantric still whispered, for he could manage no more. "Is there a way out of here to the surface?"

The worker distinctly drew another breath. "There is a way out of here to the surface." He lifted his arm like a puppet and pointed. He inhaled again. "The scorpion enters and leaves by a passage at the other end." Pause. Inhale. "A young elf enters and leaves. He gives orders. I do not know him."

Listening, Shantric gradually realized that this man, who stood talking to him within arm's reach, was dead. He spoke as if merely reacting to stimuli. He, too, had splotches of pulsing black threading through his skin.

On his eyeballs, a thin coating of white grit shot through with black weaving—a swelling at his joints—his fingernails torn and split—this was one of the bloodless, a corpse animated by something far fouler than even the morehl—it was a new evil and often in league with the practitioners of Deathcraft. The scholar had heard of this pollutant—necralluvium!

Shantric's heart pounded as he cringed against the carved face, but the bloodless seemed no threat. "Wh-What do you mean to do with me?"

Inhale. "I do not mean to do anything with you."

"What do you do here?"

Inhale. "I mine saltpeter and place it in the mouths." Pause. Breath. "I place wood, bone, and metal in the mouths."

"Yes, but why?"

Inhale. "The elders speak. The mouths close. They open later." Pause. Breath. "The elders remove the flintlocks."

Comprehending, Shantric looked down at the items piled on the floor. The wood branches would become pistol handles. He knew that deadly flintlocks had come from Karakto—all of Esfah knew that... *but how? Is there some sort of Gremmlobahnd forge nearby? But why would the undead be tending it?* The gnomes made the deadliest weapons, inlaid with mystic metals: the eldrymetallum and other star metals and he'd heard tales of the mortality faces—perhaps...

The bones, runic inlays. Scraps of sword-metal, barrels. At the morehl plays, the flintlocks gained their power and links to their users—but the morehl actually made them here in this grotto, using these unliving servants. The scholar suddenly knew the nature of his fright. He was not afraid of the bloodless proper—for it could do no more to him than any living soldier—but of the fact of death, the common fate of everyone. He would one day die and be no more than this pale, decaying thing. And as a bloodless serving the morehl, or simply as food for worms, his body would serve some purpose he could not control.

Groaning, breathing hard, Shantric stumbled away from the dead man and out of the grotto. Straight into the selumari general, Osmaral.

"Oh, oh, sir!" Shantric found his voice. "Oh, I am so very glad to see you! You know me, Shantric. We met at Windhome. I'm tutor to the demarch's boy, the young master—"

Shantric stopped and stared at the man's long black smock and black leggings. A morehl elder's costume. Osmaral looked down on him benevolently. "I remember you, Shantric. Would you like to help us here?"

Shantric looked past Osmaral to see many morehl bloodless standing obediently in formation. "Whuh—well, I— Y-Yes, of course, how can I—help?"

"First, I must introduce you to a friend of mine." Osmaral gestured, while removing a tube of inky, black fluid. It crawled towards the cork stopper as if the sludge had a life of its own. From the darkness came a familiar sound. Clatta-tac. Clatta—

Shantric bolted. Despite endless walking and dire thirst, he found the strength to run for the cavern wall. The crevice, he felt the crevice! He could escape!

Frantically he thrust himself into the narrow gap. He pushed and struggled, and in a moment he came to—

A blank stone wall. He had taken the wrong path.

Torchlight flickered behind. He meant to turn, when something black dropped swiftly down before his face. He felt a sudden pressure in his chest, and then searing pain like a hot brand. Writhing, he saw that the scorpion's sting had torn a long gash straight down his chest. For a brief moment before he fell unconscious, he looked with wonder on the miracle of his beating heart.

7

When Shantric did not appear at Windhome next moming, Calantha canceled her morning appointments. From a warded closet, she drew forth a discolored coral urn dating from Esfah's third generation. Filling it with sea water and a drop of perfume, she cleared her mind. Then she focused her thoughts.

After a pause, a voice spoke coolly in her mind reassuring her that she was connected to the heart of Esfah. This was how Calantha communed with her mystic energies and how her faith bisected that arcana veil and connected to her power: to her, it was as if her magic had form and personality.

She sent the thought, communing with the essence of the gods she served. *The matter of finding my servant, Shantric, a problem that vexes me greatly, must certainly present no challenge to the gods!*

Calantha felt the answers come as it speaking with someone who politely dodged direct questions. *Do you like my new dress? –it certainly brings out the sparkle in yours so I can tell that* you *love it.*

Something awful must have happened to Shantric. Disturbed, Calantha politely stopped scrying. She summoned her lieutenants.

After yesterday's lunch, a chambermaid had seen Shantric enter the crater. Recalling this now, Calantha gave way to a moment of selfish dread. If the morehl have killed him, she thought, I can never hope to win.

Reluctantly, she ordered a search of the city, especially—and this she kept confidential—the lower morehl tunnels. "This could take days," she told Orric. "But do not worry. He may return at any moment."

"I hope so." The boy looked frightened, and she held him close. His fear gave her perspective.

I worry about politics while my son endures the loss of his mentor, she thought. *I can always rely on Orric to remind me of what is really important.*

The search lasted days and found nothing. With guilty relief, Calantha canceled the inquiry. A mysterious disappearance affected her chances less than would a murder.

Though Gleda's victory looked likely, Calantha retained a shred of hope.

Then, the day before the election, a selumari jailer uncovered a clue—from a gang of goblins.

Fennevaunce was dead, to begin with. There was no doubt about that. The register of his burial was not signed by any morehl elder, vagha undertaker, or selumari dirge-singer, but by Yort. He wrote FENNEVAUNCE on the cemetery wall over the runt's body—and underneath, TO WHOSE CRIMES HIS FOLLOWERS WERE UNWITTING ACCOMPLICES. That was good enough for the Wild Things. Young Fennevaunce was as dead as a hangnail.

After they buried him, the Wild Things took a moment to marry off his wives to the surviving gang members. Yort got Fennevaunce's Wife Three, who took the name Yort's Wife ("One" being understood until he married again).

Then they needed a new leader. They started to look at Yort, but he wanted none of that, so he said, "Blodge, lead us!" The gang accepted this. Blodge was a pleasant fellow, not quite as stupid as Murget and not given, as was Giddy Duff, to berserk rages.

"All right, I'm leader," said Blodge. "Yort, I order you: Tell us what to do."

So Yort said they should run for Bent Morass and, if the blue elves caught them, plead that Fennevaunce had misled them into villainy.

The gang ran, the elves caught them, they pled, and now they were back on a prison work detail. Yort pointed out that the court had reduced their sentence from eighteen to six years, but the Wild Things did not find this heartening.

Yort seethed with self-loathing. I might have abandoned the gang as soon as Fenny blew up, he thought, but no! I was too busy thinking I've a wife now—these gurks can still help me—things will go better with the runt gone. Yammer, yammer.

What held me back? He wondered with each swing of his stone pick against the mine wall. *Why did I stay?*

Pure craving for security! Brainless attachment! What a dullard. All these years, and he still hadn't eaten a fish.

Some guards remembered Yort. Word got around about his last hitch on the work detail. Now nobody listened to his smooth talk. They laid on the lash, too. Worse than the exhaustion and pain was the indignity.

Yet salvation came quickly, from—of all trogs— Blodge.

Overhearing a couple of blues talking about some old missing elf, he said, "We saw him!" The blues thought Blodge too foolish to invent a story, which was true. After he told his tale to some patrol captains, a squad of troopers led the Wild Things to the tunnel where they had disposed of Fennevaunce. It had taken fire to burn away the black stuff that had made the body get up—but it had ended him all the same.

No sign of the old elf. But they headed in the direction he had run. In a cave passage along the way, Yort spied a stone wall, freshly mortared.

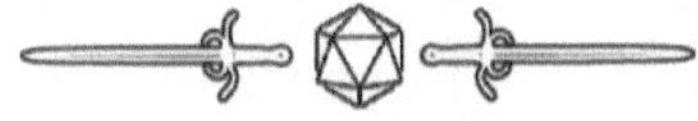

Here in this high tunnel, Calantha felt the taint of Deathcraft. The stale, scalding air clung heavily to her as she supervised the goblin work team. On her command, they had begun wielding their crude picks and hammers against the freshly mortared stone wall. Behind the goblins, a selumari patrol and a squad of bowmen waited tensely, weapons ready. Not knowing what to expect, they had prepared for the worst. So had Calantha. For the first time since the war, she wore armor and carried her cutlass and shield.

What lay beyond the wall? If she faced some monster or morehl necromancer, then this place, deep within the volcano, could give full play to the elemental forces of Fire and Earth.

The goblins had almost broken through the stone wall. "My lady!" one worker called suddenly. Lowering his pick, the creature spoke in an unusually smooth voice, "We have alerted you to a possible danger, when we need not have. Might you show your—oww!" A lash and a correction from the patrol captain. "Pardon me! Might the demarch show her appreciation? If this clue proves valuable, might she consider a full, free, and unconditional pardon for our trivial infractions?"

Calantha rolled her eyes. "Keep working."

"Thank you—Ouch! Argh! I mean, we thank the demarch for considering the matter."

"Look!" Another goblin, short and stout, brushed away rubble and pulled a white object from the growing hole. "It's a skull. What do you make of it, Yort?"

Calantha glimpsed a line of red runes written across the skull. Drawing back, she shouted, "Talisman! Get away!"

The guards and bowmen fell back, and the goblins scattered—all but the one holding the skull. He looked around in confusion, then belatedly thought to drop it. Before it left his claw tips, the Deathcraft focus struck.

The goblin trembled, then shook head to toe. Thin ribbons of skin peeled away from his warty neck. With a pop, the muscles of his right arm tore loose, and he screamed a wobbly shriek.

"Blodge!" The biggest goblin had stopped, far back in the passage, and was looking on in horror. Then one of the others—Calantha thought it was the smooth talker—ran back and grabbed the big one by the arm. "As the demarch commands!" he shouted, and then they were gone in the darkness.

"After—" Calantha began, but suddenly the skull talisman finished its work, unleashing whatever dark warding spell had been pent up in the object. The goblin Blodge's howls filled the cavern as the arm-bone tore from his shoulder, each leg ripped at hip, knee, and ankle, and his spine twisted and snapped like a green branch.

Blodge's scream cut off sharply as his body and head wrenched apart. For an instant, the hand holding the skull hovered in the air, but then it fell to the stone floor, limp. The skull rolled free and dissolved into powder.

Bowmen and guards stared wide-eyed. The last of the wall crumbled. In the passageway beyond, Calantha saw a slim, standing figure: Shantric. Dead… or worse.

The old scholar still wore his usual leaf-green tunic and breeches, but they hung loose and tattered. Through the rents in the cloth Calantha saw gaping wounds, and a green scab covered one side of his head. Shantric's bloodshot eyes looked back and forth, blinking in utter confusion as spalts of black riddled his pale, blue skin. But his arms, commanded by some unseen agent, steadily held a loaded crossbow.

"Walking dead!" a guard whispered. Gasping, the bowmen nocked arrows and drew.

"Archers, hold," Calantha said steadily. "Shantric, can you hear me? Drop your weapon."

The dead elf kept looking around. He opened his mouth, and his jaw sagged, broken. In a parched voice he said, "I— Where am I? Where is—is young master—?" Though he did not look at her, his arms lifted the crossbow and aimed straight at Calantha.

"Fire," she said. The bowmen let fly. Shantric fell with coral tipped arrows in his forehead, throat, and both eye sockets.

From the wounds spouted wisps of green—powdered blood.

Calantha's teeth were clasped so tightly that her jaw hurt. *The poor, innocent man,* she thought. *Orric will be crushed. I shall make someone pay for this.*

Despite the damage his body had taken, Shantric's form still tried to rise and Calantha frowned. "Burn it," she said. The thing was no longer Shantric.

Distracted by thoughts of revenge, she did not notice her Goal Self waver—her connection to the magics of Esfah were uniquely tied to her philosophy, and her commitment had begun to waver. "Guards forward by threes. Archers, two ranks behind. Fire at will. Be ready for flintlocks."

Cutlasses high, the six guards formed two ranks. They stepped gingerly over Shantric's body and moved forward into a rough stone passage.

One rank would advance a few paces, then watch as the other moved past, and so on alternately. Just behind, six archers pulled arrows from the corpse and entered the passage, three abreast.

Calantha, close at their heels, cast green light ahead from her fingertips.

As soon as she smelled the place, she knew where they were. Squeaking and flapping high in the darkness confirmed it. She murmured, "Watch overhead, but do not let the bats distract you."

Blackness and echoes swarmed ahead, ideal for an ambush. Calantha halted the troops and conjured a globe of flickering green light. She sent it forward, upward, panicking millions of bats but lighting the entire cavern.

Shantric had seen this cavern and died in it. But Calantha's light, falling where no light had struck since the mountain's birth, showed far more than the scholar had seen. The main force of that eruption, decades before, had fractured the volcano's whole eastern side. An immense gash in the char-black rock stretched jaggedly up and still farther up, measureless to left and right, rising to small sunlit rents near the mount's summit—such as the cave opening Orric had almost fallen into.

Caves of this early time had no stalactites or flowstone decorations. But these sheer stark sweeps of rock and these bats in their flapping millions, made Calantha and her troops pause or stumble in their steps.

Here at its bottom, the vast cavern narrowed to a smooth floor, a flat stretch of cooled lava just thirty paces long and fifteen wide. In a shadowed grotto at the far end stood stone faces, monoliths carved from, and still embedded in, the living rock.

Calantha knew of these monoliths. The morehl called them "mortality faces," but she'd thought them myths born of superstition and corrupted tales of trading with gnomes bent and twisted by the spider queen of the Obsidian Grotto.

Calantha whispered, "All these years…" The selumari had occupied this city, traced its tunnels. They thought they knew it all. And all this time—Knew it? She could just as soon know the minds of the morehl!

In the dark grotto, Calantha saw movement. Yes, many figures stood behind the mortality faces—excellent cover. The grotto looked small, but for all she knew, it might hold two dozen men. And anyone could hide in those crevices in the wall to her left. Anyone, or anything.

She nodded to the guard leader. He shouted, "In the name of Calantha Farandelin, demarch of Emmiria and Karakto, I order you to come forth unarmed!"

A flare of white within the grotto, and suddenly the rock wall beside Calantha erupted in a spray of molten lava. A pinpoint speck of dust, fired from a morehl flintlock, had struck and conjured lethal forces of fire and death. Ducking behind her shield of shark leather, Calantha searched for her connection to The Source. Only magic provided enough protection to halt the bullets from these weapons.

She heard the rock sizzling, felt its heat on her arm. "Send off a warning volley," she said. "Call!" Just as the soldiers in her forces would launch arrows or swing swords upon her command, so now they lent her their minds.

They had learned, in crude fashion, to marshall the Nature magic that flowed strongly in the young world. Kneeling behind their shields and concentrating, the troops added their minds to her own, amplifying her summons.

Calantha sensed interference, some maligning emanations from the grotto. At the thought, the mortality faces began to chant.

The gaping stone mouths drew shut, then shaped strange, booming words—if words they were—that sent the bats into still greater panic. The words beat like weapons against Calantha's ears, and drummed against her limbs until she shuddered. Her troops leaned on their shields like old men. She had no will to try magic again, but could only shout a command: "Fan right! The soldiers staggered out, tramping through thick, muddy layers of droppings, to form a line across the cavern floor. She drew her cutlass and waved them forward, then followed, holding her ears. Bowmen tried a few dispirited shots at the grotto, but their shaking hands sent arrows far wide of the target.

Calantha still could not see a clear target within. Abruptly the faces ceased chanting, and she gasped as though relieved of a weight. From the grotto came a searing glare. Flintlocks—easily a dozen!—fired in unison. As the invisibly small grains struck home, six brilliant orange flames erupted behind six bowmen's eyes. They fell hard, their life energies burning away within their skulls.

Calantha fought panic. Without enough magic to command, she foresaw only disaster. She cast a despairing glance at her Goal Self, and saw that the phantom elf shape point upward.

Looking, she saw the maddened bats fluttering wildly out of the cavern, their wings beating, the air turbulent high in the cave—

She could work with that.

The air turned cool and clear and strong around Calantha. She thought of summoning a windstorm, and yet these wounded men had not long to live.

More flintlocks flared in the grotto. Calantha shouted, "Down!"

As one, the unhurt troops dropped to the cavern floor, burying themselves in the filth. Winds rushed across the dying selumari, whose bodies partook of air and water, the elemental forces restored their energies. They would bear the scars of today's wounds all their lives, perhaps, but now they revived, ready to fight.

With a twitch of her cutlass blade, Calantha signaled the troops to crawl forward. Leaving muddy furrows, they crept toward the grotto. Within a few steps of the entryway, Calantha glimpsed the powdery figures within. Even in the sea-green light, she knew them at once for bloodless, and her blood ran cold.

A parting gust blew a thick cloud of powder into the grotto. A single cough issued from within.

One soldier actually breathes in there, Calantha thought, *but not for long.*

Her simple maneuver gave the selumari time to gain their feet. Now, covered with droppings, they looked no different from the morehl within.

Her cry echoed to the ceiling: "Charge!"

The guards struck first, while the archers dropped bows and drew blades. The unliving morehl threw their flintlocks at the invaders and clumsily drew rapiers. Four stood abreast at the entrance, and many more waited behind. A taller figure loomed behind. Could it be—?

A bitter smell of venom, and a whispered alert from her Goal Self. She whipped around, right into a charging scorpion. It was twice her size, gleaming black, with two thin, jagged pincers and a terrible tail. On spidery legs, the creature raced toward Calantha. Its curved stinger lanced toward her neck.

By reflex—for she had faced the morehl scorpion-knights in earlier battles—-Calantha jerked aside. She stumbled, and then rolled to the only point of safety—beneath the creature's body.

Her cutlass and shield went flying. For an instant, she glimpsed her own frightened reflection in the monster's belly plate.

Before the scorpion could move away, Calantha clutched wildly at one of its segmented legs. Thrashing and circling, the creature dragged her like a doll through the gray muck. Its stinger swung down within a hand's breadth of her eyes, but she held on. Fear strengthened her. *If I die here,* she knew, *I join the bloodless!*

Calantha realized the animal had no rider, but still had attacked. Some Death-influence from the grotto must be guiding it. Urgently she tried to sense and nullify it, but again the creature began throwing her back and forth, and she lost concentration.

Calantha saw her phantom companion standing aloof nearby. Frustrated and terrified, Calantha faced the Crafter's greatest challenge—mindfulness in battle—this was the particular problem for followers of the Quietudes.

Her grip was weakening. She could smell vinegary poison on the stinger, so close to her. The demarch of Emmiria and Karakto struggled to regain purpose.

The dead scholar, she thought. My boy's sadness. Still the shimmering outline did not move. *The thousands—they have nothing but endless, bleak, sickening struggles like this one, with no prospect for peace*, she thought, *unless I am strong!*

She called to her Goal Self and it slipped down and merged with her. The scent of venom grew sharp, the surroundings vivid. There, her cutlass! As the scorpion dragged her by, Calantha snatched the blade from the floor. She knew with perfect certainty she could now cut off the scorpion's stinger, dismember its legs, and drive the blade deep between belly and back. But killing the beast would not serve her purpose.

She sensed a flickering in the air, like a heat mirage: Death magic.

With her heightened awareness, Calantha extended her Goal Self's arm and, as if snapping a thread, canceled the influence of whatever magic user had commanded it. Calantha felt the creature shake, and she loosed her grip on its leg. It scuttled away across the cavern, once more a simple creature of Nature.

Catching her breath, Calantha rose to her feet. Heaped in the entryway to the grotto lay her fallen bowmen and guards, gray as their victims, the twice-dead morehl—and a few selumari, she now saw.

What graveyard had offered up those bodies? It did not matter now. All were dead again. Splashes of green blood mingled with sprays of powdered red where heads had been severed: the most effective way to kill the undead.

Why this calamity? Because her generals wanted to increase production in the mines. Without a thought, she had made them warriors.

Warriors. In the shadows behind the bodies, she saw one. "General Osmaral. Drop your weapons and surrender."

The young selumari man walked to the barricade of bodies. He wore a breastplate and helm over the black smock of a priest, and he carried a flintlock and cutlass. "You made that request once," he said with utter calm. "I have no different answer now than before." He raised the flintlock and fired.

Calantha dodged, but the particle struck her arm, where it burned like a brand. She screamed. The forces of fire and death rushed in from the wound, seeking her mind. Her bowmen had almost died this way, as dark fire destroyed the elemental pathways that gave them life. But Calantha was an enchanter of air and water. Mastering her pain, she channeled her energies to quench the burning.

With firm strides she walked toward the grotto. Filthy from helmet to boots, she still embodied her Goal Self, an unseen presence that struck fear into her enemies.

Osmaral backed away, deeper into the grotto. He threw the pistol at her, missing, and readied his cutlass. He kept his voice steady. "Keep back. I have done a great deal to protect Emmiria, and I will not stop now."

Coldly, Calantha walked over the piled bodies as if up a staircase. In the close confines of the grotto, she backed him against one of the mortality faces.

"I shall not ask what you did here, Osmaral, nor why. The court will hear that. But hear me now: It is over. Drop the sword."

"You are the enemy of Emmiria!"

"Says a user of Deathcraft. Now drop…"

Osmaral regained his composure. "That is a temporary measure. I do what is necessary for my cause. You could never understand."

"I shall not debate the—" Calantha began, when Osmaral suddenly launched himself at her, sword high. She dared not block, for he had weight and reach. She twisted aside as the blade fell past her shoulder. On her cheek, she could feel the breeze from the stroke.

In that breeze she sensed victory. Even as she threw herself back from Osmaral's next stroke, she flung down a vial of air and summoned the elemental power. It rose in her like a wind. In a breath, the air grew warm and humid. A distant rumble echoed down from the upper reaches of the cave. Osmaral stopped, suddenly wary.

He looked at her, saw the sparking at her fingertips and eyes, and sprinted for the entryway.

Too late. Calantha marshaled her new force, the merest spark of thundercloud. Her arm lifted of its own accord, and along its length ran a tendril of force. Jagged white fire burned the air. It struck Osmaral at the neck, blazed down his spine, and made a blinding arc to the ground. Paralyzed, he trembled.

In a moment Calantha noted, with faint heart, the sizzle and smell of burning flesh. Then he collapsed, one more body on the heap.

Calantha's other self slipped away from her, and she felt weary. Looking at the dead general, she began to weep.

"You idiot," she said to him, or perhaps to herself. "You poor idiot."

The cavern stood silent. Even the scorpion had gone. She hoped it would find its way to the surface, where it belonged. And she hoped the bats would return.

What a loss, she thought. *I must salvage something from this.*

The faces. She must have them destroyed, but she might invite selumari scholars to study them first. She noticed that the gaping mouths seemed filled with ash and debris, like fireplaces. Gnomish sigils adorned their heads like an inscribed crown.

But among all the faces, one had its mouth closed. She gazed at it, and suddenly, it dropped open.

Startled, she leapt back, but nothing more happened. Cautiously she stepped forward. In the mouth lay a flintlock pistol, its hilt polished, its barrel shining. Had this face just created it?

From within the mouth, a light flashed out. Calantha stumbled back. A small orange glow danced briefly before the enchanter's astonished eyes.

"Morrre! More weaponnns!" said the light.

She found her voice. "I am Calantha, demarch of the city. What—who are you?"

At once the light flickered and dashed away. It rose high in the cavern and rushed straight out to the sky.

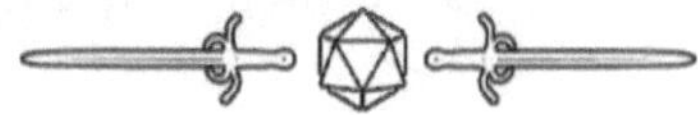

Election night. The blue—white moon shone full as the selumari descended from their whitewashed homes into the calm sea. Each thinly dressed elf walked out to chest level, concentrated, ducked under the waves, and drew a bracing breath of cold salt water. Invisibly thin gill slits opened along their rib ages, showing dark green membranes. Webs of water, tough as leather, formed between fingers and toes, and the pupil of each eye enlarged.

To a selumari, it all came as easily as a breath of air.

Some ten thousand coral elves swam by twos and threes out from Hwarrm's Doom Bay to a long, foamy shoal not far offshore. The coral giant was called Ogan the Reef. Now grown large beyond calculation, Ogan could hardly move. At war's end, years ago, he had barely managed to uproot and move from Emmiria down the coast to Karakto. But he loved the Emmirians as his children. Now he sent forth impulses that drove away sharks and monsters, so that his coral elves might gather in peace.

Just under the ocean surface, the Emmirians converged on a familiar bone-white hollow. The sandy basin was ringed by corals, seaweeds, anemones, starfish, urchins, and shells. To the elves' dark-adapted eyes, moonlight made the infinite colors as vivid as fireworks. The selumari stayed close within the basin, which Ogan kept clean of life. Though Ogan had wiped out more than one armada over the centuries, the delicate corals that made up the giant's skin could break or die at a touch.

At ordinary gatherings, elves fell to discussing Ogan's age. But this night, every selumari in the city had heard about yesterday's events in the bat cavern. As they gathered to select the next demarch, they talked of nothing else.

Some few old veterans had vocally supported Calantha ever since she (as they put it) won the war. They passed among the citizens, listening, then retired to a sheltered part of the reef where Calantha discreetly waited. The Emmirians were sharply split, said the veterans.

Everyone, it seemed, felt that Calantha had blundered by trying to make peace with the morehl. But some thought that Shantric's death and Osmaral's corruption showed continuing danger. The selumari now must either destroy the morehl or retreat to a safer locale.

Others said that whether or not General Osmaral had turned to evil, he still had a sound idea in harnessing the power of the flintlocks. The morehl could serve the good by continuing to produce the weapons for Emmiria.

Some in each faction supported Gleda. The veterans had not found anyone, however, who supported Calantha.

"I shall enact long—delayed justice! Acclaim me demarch, and the death of that poor Emmirian scholar can become a turning point. Where, once before, we coddled these servants of Death, now we shall turn them, however unwilling, to serve Nature! Where the morehl once planned the murders of innocent Emmirians, now we shall plan how they will serve our goals!"

General Gleda spoke to the gathering from an elevated coral platform that Ogan had graciously extruded at one end of the basin. At the opposite end, Calantha stood on an identical platform and watched as Gleda's final words brought her one last ovation. Here underwater, the selumari indicated approval by holding up their hands and releasing air bubbles from their fingertips. The volume of bubbles floating upward indicated the degree of approval.

The people liked Gleda a great deal. The Emmirians stood at the center of the basin between the two speakers. After each spoke twice (argument and rebuttal), the citizens would move toward one or the other platform.

Whoever attracted more people would become demarch of Emmiria and Karakto. Calantha had already spoken about her success in rooting out corruption, and her promise to keep doing so. She had emphasized Osmaral's treachery, his likely connection to Gleda, and the dangers of the flintlocks, but she had said little about lasting peace with the morehl. Even so, the citizens had not favored her. Now, as Calantha began her rebuttal, many were already moving toward Gleda's side of the basin.

Calantha had one more choice. She had hoped to avoid it, but—she glanced at her ghostly companion and repeated a Quietude proverb in her mind: *Unconsidered acts bring uncertain outcomes.*

She disdained that one. She knew the consequences if Gleda won: oppression, war, genocide. Anything but these! Bitterly she recalled her thought in the cave: *What a loss. I must salvage something from this.* She drew a deep breath, then spoke.

"My opponent speaks of making the morehl serve our goals. In that cavern yesterday, just before he died a traitor's death, I learned of Osmaral's goals—or rather, General Gleda's goals. She and Osmaral intended to establish a warrior class among the selumari as well as the morehl. She would give only a few loyal followers the ability to use the flintlocks. They would eventually take full power to pass and enforce laws for both societies!"

A deathly silence. People in the basin stared with peculiar intensity at Calantha. Seeing Gleda's expression—not shock, not outrage, but a tight frown—Calantha understood, with deep sadness, that her lie had hit home.

She talked a bit more, reinforcing the horror of the idea, then casting herself as a tried and proven servant. But she closed quickly, so that Gleda might have less time to prepare an effective response.

By now Gleda had assumed the carefully bland expression Calantha had seen before. "I—I deny these outlandish accusations," said Gleda flatly. "Can the demarch produce a single witness to support her claims, her completely false and—and outlandish claims? The demarch is desperate indeed to indulge in such slander, when—when the real issue is not some imagined conspiracy, but the need to impose our will upon the morehl!"

With mixed satisfaction and sympathy, Calantha saw that Gleda's small ability to deceive had reached its limit. As the general struggled on, the selumari noted her change of manner. Here and there, a few bubbles rose from the audience, then no more. Gleda ended dispiritedly, and the moment of decision came. Almost as one, the people moved to Calantha's platform. The genial Ogan marked her victory by surrounding her with a swirling column of bubbles. But the people's mood seemed grim.

Not so grim as Gleda's. Before she left the basin, Gleda paused to look hatefully on her former commander. Her scars made that glare remarkably ugly. Then she swam away into dark waters.

In victory, Calantha projected graceful confidence. But back at Windhome she reflected on the trouble she faced. She had united the Emmirians by deception, playing on the two notions they all held: distrust of the morehl, and flat hatred of morehl customs. Now cooperation between the races appeared even more remote. Now she must lead a divided city.

She sensed reproach from her Goal Self, but by sheer resolve, Calantha subdued the shape. She had developed this idealized personality during her apprenticeship. Its manifestation had marked not only her skill in air and water, but also the self-awareness required for Craftwork.

Now Calantha thought the outline appeared thinner than before, more drawn. Yet she observed with grim satisfaction that it did not waver. Her Goal Self would always remain clear, so long as she pursued high and selfless ends. She had found a way to extend her mission by nine years. No one would dare deny that she embarked on this road with the best of intentions.

8

One day after the election, Calantha stood in the Supreme Hall of the Court of Justice. The granite walls of this high and gloomy chamber, stained with decades of grime from fetid volcanic air, today smelled of lye and ashes. On this, the first afternoon of her new term, Calantha had ordered the walls scrubbed clean.

She noticed that, as Karakto's sulfurous air made the selumari choke, so the soapy smell bothered the morehl. Watching Elder Cennard rub his bloodshot eyes and snuffle like a boar, Calantha felt guilty delight—then dismay as Orric's eyes, too, grew red. She rarely brought her son to court, but at this session, custom required that prominent Emmirians and ambassadors congratulate the demarch on her victory. Given the city's continuing tensions, she wanted every positive influence she could find. Orric, the sole citizen in Karakto who was popular with both selumari and morehl, could help. She also hoped this visit might cheer up the boy, who had been sad ever since Shantric died.

The officials filed past her chair, offering good wishes with varying sincerity. "The kingdom of Gundakhor sends its best respects and hopes for continued peaceful relations," said Karakto's only ambassador, Lord Burgard. Gundakhor's best respects seemed muted, at least as he delivered them. Before the election, he had never openly endorsed Gleda, but his sympathies had been clear.

Just behind Burgard stood Jandith. The Crafter, somehow unaffected by the lye odor, addressed Calantha but smiled thinly at Orric. "What lesson has he learned from Shantric's death?" she asked in a whisper.

Calantha began, "I would prefer not to—" but then she noticed Orric's expression, not grief but rage. His sharp, even teeth were showing, and his eyes had almost rolled back in his head. His words sounded strangled. "She—she—"

122

"What, Orric?" Calantha looked to Burgard, who seemed as baffled as she.

Elder Cennard, standing nearby, spoke in equal anger. "This Crafter has acted without propriety or guidance. Headstrong!"

Beside him, the unflappable Fohlin spoke with irritation, and his booming voice carried to every ear. "A low-born disgrace to her class and her race! She is a Crafter. They never know their place."

Orric's fury had spread by contagion to the other morehl.

Even Jandith seemed to succumb.

"Fah! Your efforts grow weak, your goals over-subtle, as you shore up your own petty positions!"

She pushed Lord Burgard aside and seized Orric by the arm. He struggled futilely in her grip. The bailiff rushed forward, but with a sharp gesture Calantha stopped him. She did not think Orric in danger.

Meanwhile, she listened closely. The crowd in the chamber had fallen dead silent.

"This boy frightens you!" Jandith said. "You do-nothing nobles and elders cannot manipulate him, and so you ignore him and hope he disappears. Meanwhile, the lower classes wait and hope for a new leader, the rightful heir, to lead them—"

Elder Cennard glared at Count Fohlin, who shouted. "He is not the heir! He is a battlefield foundling!"

Jandith arched her eyebrows. "How can you know? His mind is strong." The other two morehl paused, then shook their heads as if awakening. They looked at Orric, and their expressions went carefully blank. Jandith smiled. Had she sprung a trap? Calantha wondered whether the adept had actually succumbed to Orric's anger, or merely pretended.

Calantha knew from long experience to follow her original course. "I have heard enough for now." She gently pulled Orric back to her side. "Bailiff, arrest her."

The bailiff moved forward—then fell on his back. Before Jandith stood Lord Burgard, fists up. His golden eyes flashed. "The one who touches Jandith will get an axe in his gullet!" To Calantha, he hissed coldly, "I extend to my peasant, Jandith, the protection of Gundakhor, which may not be breached without grave consequence."

Calantha's scowl matched his own. "Lord Burgard, that woman is a citizen of my city. Rights of embassy do not extend to an ambassador's servants."

"No. But they do protect his spouse. Jandith and I are soon to be—be m-married."

This news astonished everyone, possibly even Burgard himself. Jandith's eyes were unreadable. Did that smile mean she had sprung another trap?

Calantha decided not to press the issue. "Lord Burgard, I trust Jandith will cooperate in an inquiry into Shantric's death. It appears she has something to tell."

"We all have something to tell," said Burgard. "We shall be available to the demarch or her servants at my home, or possibly at my estates in the city, as my schedule dictates." Amid deafening silence, he bowed and departed with Jandith.

Exasperated, Calantha thought, May Nature hear me, this is my last term.

Orric looked up at Calantha. "What is a gullet?"

The demarch had hoped Burgard's outburst would distract attention from her proclamation later that afternoon. The hope was unfounded.

"The recent discovery of General Osmaral's treachery has justly alarmed our city," she said to an audience of selumari citizens and the morehl upper classes. "Clearly, corruption is widespread.

"To recapture our lost security, I am instituting foot patrols throughout the city. Squads of Emmirian troops, known as diligence patrols, will move regularly through the tunnels and the coastal district." Now Calantha's heart beat faster, and she tried not to sound apprehensive. "That they may guard effectively against subversion, the diligence patrols will have limited authority to enter dwellings and interrogate suspicious persons."

The morehl stared in silence, of course, but among the selumari she heard whispers and saw exchanges of nervous looks. A scholar, whom Calantha recognized as one of Gleda's supporters, raised his hand. "Of course the demarch means that these 'diligence' patrols will confine their activities to the morehl."

"The patrols will fight corruption wherever it is found. As we have seen, there is corruption within our own ranks."

Silence fell. Then the scholar, exchanging a look with several others, pointedly turned away from the demarch and walked out the rear door of the chamber. Others who had supported Gleda followed, and then more who had not. The remaining Emmirians simply stared, their blue faces as dead as the red ones on the other side of the chamber.

Calantha ended the session, then met Orric in the hallway a short while later. He had eavesdropped on the selumari as they left the chamber. "What did you hear, Orric?"

"They did not say much. I heard someone say something to a group, and then they all looked around, saw me, and left."

"What did they say?"

"'Something must be done.'"

After sending Orric home with the bailiff, Calantha met in private conference with Count Fohlin and Elder Cennard. "I want to hear what you know of Shantric's death, and of that Crafter. And perhaps, Elder Cennard, you can explain what she meant by your 'over-subtle goals.'"

He did not know. But of Shantric, Jandith, and Orric, Fohlin and Cennard had a great deal to say.

Late that night, Orric sat on a stone bench in the rock garden at Windhome, staring up at the moon. At half phase and waning, it showed through a dusting of white clouds. Orric wondered if anyone lived up there.

Calantha arrived home, looking tired. She carried a folded black cloth under one arm. Sitting, she hugged him. "I've brought a gift."

He looked without curiosity as she shook out the cloth. It was a black wool cloak with a red silk lining, much too long for him. "This is for me?"

"It belonged to me, and before me to my teacher, Riddan. He was a powerful Crafter and the father of Devin, my late husband—a warrior of great renown. I know he received this cloak from his own teacher, but he never told me more. Now I give the cloak to you."

Her reverent tone interested him. "What is it? A uniform for Crafter apprentices?"

"No. It teaches discipline of the mind. Today, after you left, I talked with Count Fohlin and with Elder Cennard. Both told me your mind is showing unusual power and will need training."

"They volunteered to train me, didn't they?"

They exchanged a knowing smile. "I think this will serve you better. Here, try it on."

"It's too big."

"Try it on."

Orric stood, and Calantha placed the cloak across his small shoulders. Thinking of its history, he felt honored to wear it. The cloak fit across the shoulders, but was too long. It fell in bunches around his ankles. He thought his mother was taking a long time to adjust the fit and pat the cloak into place, until he realized she was standing beyond arm's reach. Suddenly he felt uneasy.

"Gather it in your arms and walk," she said. Baffled, he walked around. The rock garden looked very pretty tonight. Under blue moonlight the stone field became a frozen sea, and red boulders loomed up like the frontier of an arctic continent. The cloak seemed lighter with each step. On an impulse, he let it drop—and it fit perfectly, reaching no lower than his knees.

Amazed, he looked to his mother.

"You have nothing to fear," she said. "Do you remember how I taught you to meditate? Try it."

Years ago Orric had learned how to follow his breath, but it bored him and he never practiced. Now he closed his eyes, cleared his mind, and attended to the slow passage of air into and from his lungs.

Soon an image rose of a beautiful sunlit garden. He noticed the thought, set it aside, and returned to his breath. At once, there returned a vivid vision of bright blooms and green grass. Each time he cleared his mind, the scene manifested more strongly. For a moment he thought—

Beside him Calantha said quietly, "I suggest that you pause for now."

Startled, he opened his eyes. "I saw a garden. It seemed that I could go there."

"You can. But do not go too far too quickly. That is one of many lessons the cloak can teach." She looked at him intently.

"Orric, why did you send Shantric down into the crater?"

He felt surprise, but not anxiety. In the days since Shantric's death, Orric had expected she would find him out, but he did not dread it as he once would have. Since his seizures, the idea of confronting others no longer frightened him.

"I only wanted Shantric to walk around a lot and get sore feet. He killed my friend, Lemarin." His gaze fell. "Though I think that was an accident."

"Indeed. And now Shantric has died for your prank. Do you understand how it went wrong?"

"That Deathcrafter, Jandith—"

"No, Orric. She played her part, but your action went wrong because you had no clear view of the result. Had you foreseen the danger, I know you never would have carried out your trick. Had you thought clearly, you would never have stooped to even a harmless prank."

His face burned with shame.

"What now?"

She sighed. "Had matters gone as you planned, with Shantric returning footsore and angry, you would merit punishment only for your cruel joke. But this is a serious offense, Orric. Still—"

She stared to one side for so long a time that he stared after her, wondering what she saw. At last she said, "Punishment for its own sake is the morehl way, the goblin way, not our own. In that single respect my duty here is easier.

"The selumari punish to teach, to prevent a crime's recurrence. As demarch, were I hearing this case from strangers, I would consign the child to his parents' closer attention, that they should raise him better. I can hardly excuse myself from my own laws.

"Therefore, you must accompany me through each day as I attend my duties. Bring along whatever scrolls suit your current studies, and do your work while I do mine.

"And you will wear that cloak. But do not tell anyone of its purpose."

Orric's heart sank. Court and administrative duties bored him. Worse, though, was his mother's disappointment in him. Later that night, as he lay awake in bed, guilt struck him like a seizure. He struggled against his feelings, and fell to wondering how much Shantric's death was really his fault.

Sending the old scholar into the crater was a mistake. Enlisting Jandith's aid was a terrible mistake. Possibly even the prank, as his mother said, was wrong. But his underlying idea—

those who test a person's limits perform a vital service—was that wrong?

He looked curiously at the cloak by his bed. In the darkness the red lining glowed faintly, as though lit from within. Resting the cloak on his shoulders, he meditated, and soon the garden vision returned. As he concentrated, its aspect grew clearer: rows of dazzling flowers, a vast and brilliant sky, somewhere the trickle of a brook…

A warm wind blew in his face. In panic he opened his eyes on the dark, familiar room.

Thrashing and gasping like an animal in a trap, he threw aside the cloak. He stared at it with bulging eyes, and he could not fall asleep for a long time.

9

Calantha expected, and heard, cries of outrage when she sponsored the third Tynalis play. No one had seen Gleda since the election, but her supporters vocally condemned the demarch's irresponsible invitation to further disasters." The morehl elders had never liked the revised plays, and Elder Cennard protested by withholding the correct place and time for the performance But Calantha believed this play, if it succeeded, would overcome the two previous disasters. She selected a likely time, the next full moon, and place, the justice shrine—once the morehl Temple of Dominance. The new diligence patrols, squads of three selumari troopers and three guards, carried out their first task: announcing the new plays to all and sundry throughout the morehl city. Before the play began, the patrols took on their second assignment—searching the audience for weapons.

The patrols had much searching to do. Many thousands of morehl attended this third play. Aside from a few curious merchants and artisans, all came from the peasant and free folk classes, a point that fascinated Calantha. Save for Count Fohlin, who appeared at the demarch's order, not a single noble or elder attended. Lord Burgard showed up with Jandith, but no Emmirians.

Calantha had chosen an informal outfit—a sea green jacket and trousers with broad bands of blue. She first thought to observe from beside the stage, as she had at the second play. But Hornbeam, the Vagha poet, proved unpleasant company.

Drunk again, he grumbled about working conditions. "Had to remove the Fish-Bird because you didn't want your boy up on stage again… Had to bring in the story from the second play that didn't get performed, fold it into this play… All on a week's notice?" A burp and a belch. "What do you think this is, quilt-making? Patching and replacing as you go, all on a horrendous schedule… You know what you end up with?

Cordwood! Fabric goods! Churning out lines to run some troll-brained obstacle course—that is no way to write."

So she sat in the front row, Orric beside her in his new cloak. She knew the boy had not used it yet as anything but a garment. There was no hurry.

For all the poet's whining, the play went well. At least, the crowd seemed undemanding. As before, they lost all sense of the sacred as soon as the mock elder went on stage. Hornbearn had added a mock noble and merchant, as well. The lower classes loved it all.

Seeing them laugh and jeer, seeing even Orric laughing, Calantha thought that the morehl could enjoy stories, at least on some level. Did they comprehend that the play was not real? She would ask Orric after the play ended.

A diligence patroller crept up and whispered in her ear. Orric looked at Calantha curiously as she gasped.

Calantha cast green light ahead on the crooked trail. "How much farther?" she asked the selumari bowman.

"Only a bit, demarch. The child fell from that crag, there." The soldier pointed up at the crater wall, but Calantha could not tell what crag he meant. With the moon barely visible through a blue lace of cloud, the crater here lay in deep shadow.

Calantha looked back at the justice shrine, a wide stage atop a mighty spur of granite. She and the bowman were going farther away than she liked, for she had left Orric alone. But she expected to heal this injured child and return before the play ended. The breeze blew fresh tonight, and Calantha foresaw no trouble summoning magic to heal the poor girl.

Calantha made idle conversation with the bowman. "I don't think I know you."

"Fillhial is my name, demarch."

Climbing the slope almost to the volcano's rim, they passed a steam vent. "What in Nature's name took you to this part of the crater?"

"A friend and I were hunting. We have no idea why the girl is here."

"Hunting? In this miserable terrain? Hunting what?"

"Here we are. The child is just ahead."

They approached a narrow crevice in the rock wall. Just down slope from this gap, many jagged boulders thrust up from the ground like teeth. Fillhial pointed into the crevice and said, "In there."

Calantha looked in—Gleda's arrow hit Calantha just under her right collarbone and drove straight through her shoulder. Screaming, Calantha twisted in agony. Fillhial's arrow missed her neck by a finger's breadth. Calantha started to fall, but summoned winds to form an invisible air cushion beneath her and bear her up. The enchanter, racked with pain, had only one thought: *Out! Away!*

Gleda cried, "Catch her!"

The winds carried Calantha from the crevice and into the maze of boulders, depositing her gently on a patch of rankweed.

Calantha yelped as she bumped the arrow, but then realized she had alerted Gleda and the bowman to her new position. *Were there others?*

"A friend and I were hunting…"

Calantha staggered down slope and tried to gather her wits. Her light had gone out, and in the blackness she almost collided with a boulder. Veering to one side, she heard footsteps and froze. Someone up the slope—Fillhial?—ran past without seeing her. Gleda was still up there, and possibly others, all still in arrow range. She tried to concentrate.

A strange calm rose within her, and a warmth in her chest and face. She felt sleepy. *No—no, drug on arrow*, she thought, *stay up, stay up.*

She gripped the arrow, braced herself, and pulled. Pain overcame sleepiness, but she could not stifle a moan as the coral arrowhead tore loose.

Footsteps came around the boulder. She gripped the arrow and stabbed with it at eye level. The attack hit only air, as a small figure darted in and hugged her.

"Mother!" Orric whispered.

"Orric. G-Get out, go—" She could not think why he had followed her. She could hardly think at all. If this was morehl poison, she was dead.

"They'll find you here. Come with me." The boy clutched her sleeve and pulled her back the way she had come. *Stones, more stones—all alike. How did he find his way? Morehl know this place,* she thought distantly. *They listen to the mountain.*

Silly idea. Where was she? Why were they running? She drifted off...

"Mother, wake up. They're coming."

Hot. Steam in her face. Moonlight. Orric's face in the steam like some being of fire. Fire and—

He spoke flatly but quickly. "Do something."

She coughed. They were lying on black, ashy rock. As the moon emerged from gray clouds, she saw they were lying on a ledge inside the lip of the steam vent she had passed. The vent's floor, if it had one, was lost in darkness. *Like a mouth,* she thought drowsily. *Mouth of the mountain.*

Hello, Steward Mountain.

What was Orric doing? She gazed with bleary eyes as the boy's hands began to glimmer. *Yes. At the last play,* she thought.*No, different now.*

His hands seemed gloved in oily black smoke. One of his fingertips had gone dead black, like a cold brand. And like a brand he laid it on his mother's neck.

Burning pain! Calantha screamed again. Her mind cleared, and she realized his finger had felt, not hot, but deathly cold.

"Deathcraft," she said dully.

Gleda's voice rose from the darkness: "Over here!"

"Mother, please. Do something quickly."

She felt terribly hot. Another few moments in this vent would roast her alive. At least Orric was in no danger. When he grew to full strength, he could walk across molten lava unharmed… at least for short times.

The steam—steam was water. She amplified the power of the cloud and steam from the vent billowed forth tenfold, in surging clouds that blanketed the slope like a winter morning's fog that obscured all view.

Startlingly calm, Orric whispered, "Good. We should move now." He rose and stood over her.

"N-Not yet." She struggled to stay alert. Dispelling poison was not beyond magic's ability, but it was delicate work.

She still held the arrow and opened her palm. With her other hand she drew a dagger and cut her palm. Her wounds leaked with a green tint.

From the wound at Calantha's right shoulder, a thin trail of tainted blood spurted into the steamy air. It crossed her body in a high arc and fell, cleansed, into her slashed left palm where it re-entered the body. Orric watched in wonder.

The enchanter felt her mind clearing. In fact, the after-effect brought exhilaration.

Suddenly, at the vent's edge, two dark shapes loomed in the fog. Together they shot at the only moving figure they saw—not Calantha, but Orric. One arrow went wide in the fog, but the other drove into Orric's throat.

Calantha screamed. "Orric!"

Gleda's angry voice: "Oh, gods, we shot the boy!"

He did not cry out when wounded. Calantha's son fell motionless across her body.

Holding him. feeling his hot blood burn her hands, Calantha glared at the silhouettes in the fog. Her mind was now absolutely clear—and cold.

Icy hatred swelled in her chest. She would gladly summon a drake, a wyrm, even the prime elementals themselves! But as it was…

Calantha climbed to her feet, inhaled deeply, then blew out a strong puff of air. By sheer will, she marshaled an array of dust devils at the curling edges of the gust. In the vent, a wind grew, blowing clouds of vapor over the two archers.

The air cleared in an instant, but winds had already raised to a gale. Calantha stood motionless, easily visible on black rock in blue moonlight. The assassins could not hope to send an arrow through that wind.

Fillhial turned and ran.

Calantha said, "*No.*" Her voice carried straight to his ear. Sending the wind under his feet, she lifted him bodily and transported him, struggling, over the steam vent. Then she dashed him headfirst, with tornado force, straight down into the vent—a cauldron of roiling, super-heated moisture that would boil him alive in the same way many humans cooked their shellfish..

Gleda never moved. She shouted, "I acted for the good of my city and my race!"

Calantha coldly replied, "And so do I." She strained. The winds gathered under Gleda, lifting her a finger's breadth. Calantha looked down at Orric, lying motionless at her feet, and she clenched her fists. With an imperious gesture, she hurled Gleda high in the air. When she was no more than a black dot, invisibly small against the clouds, Gleda vanished over the crater's rim.

Then Calantha stilled the wind.

She stood in utter silence, listening harder than she had in her life. There! Orric still breathed, shallowly. Calantha tried to summon more magic, but could not instill that which was required for healing.

Still, she might—

Another figure, carrying a make-shift club, rushed at her out of the fog.

It was Lord Burgard.

She could not contain a despairing moan. "Oh, no. No. Not you, too." Exhausted, her arms full, her magic was spent. She had no chance against the warlord.

He looked at her, at Orric. He lowered the club. "I heard screams. What happened?"

The rush of relief made Calantha dizzy. She explained quickly, and found solace in his shocked reaction. "Lord Burgard, can you heal my son? Quickly!"

Without a word, Burgard closed his eyes. His brow furrowed, and across his golden skin ran a shimmering orange flame. He held out one hand. Fire flickered at his fingertips. If Burgard could summon his connection to the fire god, Firiel, and restore a spark of life to Orric…

But the flame died on his hands. The warlord opened his eyes and sighed. "I am no Crafter. But Jandith—"

"There is no time." Seeing the cloak still wrapped around her son, Calantha thought, I can save him. But who shall rule in my absence? The woman felt sudden fear, even despair. She no longer trusted her usual aides and lieutenants. She had not one single trustworthy ally anywhere in Karakto, save for the boy dying in her arms.

She saw no choice. She fixed her gaze on the vagha warlord of Gundakhor.

"Lord Burgard. In the war, you stood by my husband and by me. We knew your steadfast honor and loyalty to friends. Now I must leave this city in crisis, to save my son's life. I may be gone a day or more. In memory of our old alliance, I ask you to govern in my name while I am gone."

The dwarf looked surprised, then resolute. "I shall!"

"You might reverse my decisions, overturn decrees, subvert the populace, while I am helpless to stop you. I entreat you, on your honor, to govern as I would."

He looked at her silently for a long time. At last he said, "I give you my word."

With no further thought, Calantha pulled the cloak from Orric's body and whirled it one-handed onto her shoulders, where it billowed and sank gently to cover her wholly. She pulled it close around herself and Orric, and in a moment the cloak fluttered to the ground, empty.

Orric woke up underwater. He looked up at a rippling blue sky and felt whole, at peace. Thoughts rose in his mind with perfect clarity.

He remembered following his mother outside the shrine, in hopes of glimpsing the wounded child. He remembered a feeling of infinite cold space, frightening yet thrilling, as he— he, Orric!—focused the powers of oblivion to revive his mother.

Finally, he remembered the sharp jolt at his throat. The thought came with detachment, without hatred of Gleda or that bowman. As if overlooking a map on which they walked, he saw how they had gone astray. He had been no better, lost as they were in a maze of unrest and frustration.

Orric wondered at these thoughts. He had never reflected in this way. In that moment, he realized he was breathing water, and then began to choke. Flailing, he broke the surface and coughed wildly. He was standing naked in the shallows of some pond or pool, with grass all around.

"Ah, you're awake. How do you feel?" Calantha lay on the grassy shore near him. She wore her outfit from the shrine. Her boots lay beside her, and her bare feet just touched the water.

Orric sputtered and spat. "Where is this? How was I breathing water down there?"

"I don't know the name of this place. This is the healing pool. I don't have a real name for it either. All the features of this land are unnamed."

The brightness of the sunlight, the warm summery breeze… "This is what I saw when I wore the cloak!"

"Yes. The cloak transported us here. I brought you to the pool. How do you feel?"

"Fine." Surprised at his own answer, he touched his neck. He felt no wound or scar. Now he saw that her jacket had a hole in the shoulder, but the skin under it was intact. But where he had touched her throat, she had a puckering white scar. Orric looked around. The sky, a fathomless blue, showed not one cloud. Beyond the pool, the grass fell away on all sides. The hilltop was engulfed in crystalline air, above plains that rolled like folds in velvet. Trees, numberless trees, dappled the plain. Each grew free and unobstructed by its neighbors. At the skyline, tremendous flat-topped mesas rose, red as fox fur. They had fluted sides and many ridges and spires. In all the panorama, no leaf trembled at any breath of wind. The stillness—the stillness was immense.

"What is this place?" he whispered.

Her tone matched the solemn calm of the landscape. "I dearly wish I knew. We may still be on Esfah. The sun is similar, but I have never seen the moon here. Still, he rides low in the sky, and the world is said to be huge."

"No, but—how is it the cloak brings us here? Is it magic?"

"There is no such thing as magic. Come, let us walk. Your clothing is over there." She pulled on her boots. He found his clothes on the shore—including the cloak, which in this place was red with a black lining.

Dressed, he stared down into the pool. Its pure waters extended down into sapphire depths. "How deep is it?"

"As deep as it need be," Calantha said confidently as she led him down. The pool surmounted a round hill clad in short lemon grass. From the pool, down a sloping course bedded in smooth pebbles, flowed a creek that chuckled as it ran. They walked down beside this brook, beneath an arching promenade of branches. They reached a wide bower, where the stream ended in a shallow basin of earth.

Here grew a terraced garden of many bright flowers, their names and types unknown to the boy. He wandered wide-eyed on unpaved paths amid fascinating colors and shapes. Plants on the upper terrace grew from rich black earth; in the middle terrace, from a bed of thatch; and at the lowest level, from an expanse of thousands of small stones.

Orric knelt to examine the stones. They were identically smooth and flat, no longer than his finger. On each stone he saw a crude drawing: circles, spirals, animal shapes, fish, a strange hunchback playing the pipes, suns and stars—no two stones bore the same glyph. "Who drew all these pictures?"

Calantha shook her head. "No one, that I know of. I have never seen another person in all this land, save for my teacher who bequeathed the cloak to me."

"Then who keeps this garden?"

"I did, for a time, and my teachers before me. Now you will."

He looked up at her, puzzled. "I don't know how."

"You needn't. As you are attuned to the elements, so these plants are attuned to the cloak's owner. As you grow, so they grow. That is how the cloak teaches discipline. "I had not planned to give it to you, actually, until the morehl convinced me it was needed. The cloak is for Crafters, particularly for those devoted to Quietude. As a gardener makes Nature's garden grow, a Crafter makes straight his trembling and unsteady thought, which—" She broke off. "Ah, we have company."

Over the trees floated a pair of strange creatures, long white eel-shapes with flattened heads. Like ghosts, they settled downward in silence, guided by short featherless wings. Their rippling scales were radiant like clouds in the sun. From each creature's round face peered two black disk-like eyes of enormous size and depth, separated by a vertical ridge. The circular mouth was no bigger than a fingertip.

"Before you ask," Calantha said, "no, I don't know what these are called. I call them windsnakes. They are harmless."

The two windsnakes blinked curiously at Orric. He shied back, they shied away as well, and Calantha laughed. Hesitantly, Orric observed the creatures. Their fluid motion reminded him of the long chain-kites he had seen at selumari festivals. "Are they intelligent?"

"Not that I have found. You will see many strange creatures here. Some are dangerous, but in my experience one can avoid or befriend them all, if one is wise."

The windsnakes floated away. With wonder and sadness Orric watched them go. "I want to come back here all the time!"

Calantha ran her fingers through his hair. "You will find that is not easy. You cannot always reach this place—I do not quite know why. The reason has much to do with mental discipline."

She looked to one side. "You will learn to hear an inner voice, a guide that embodies your wisdom and awareness."

"And the guide brings me here?"

"In a sense. Sometimes it guides you, sometimes you guide it. It is hard to explain. But I will tell you how to start: You must promise me, Orric, you will not use Deathcraft."

Orric frowned. "Jandith said it is part of my heritage."

"Indeed, and you must overcome that heritage to avoid disaster. She has started you on the Craft of the Corruptor, but I tell you with absolute certainty that nothing good comes of it." Just then, she reminded him of Gleda. "I offer you instead the way of Quietude," she continued. "The way to freedom from suffering, by the elimination of selfish desire. The way to joy, through compassion for all people and the creatures of Nature. It is a fine and enlightened path, but you cannot walk that path with Deathcraft."

Orric said stubbornly, "Any Craft can be used for good. If I had not wakened you with it, Gleda would have killed us."

"Your touch wakened me because it aged me! A month, a year, I have no way to know, but this scar on my throat will never heal. Firecraft would have done as well, at much less cost. Deathcraft can never be used to serve Nature. Promise me."

Orric suddenly recalled Cennard's comment about trolls—that feeding on people was their nature, and if prevented, they starved. Was that true? He was attuned to fire and Death—would this promise deny his own morehl nature? Would he somehow starve?

Or, perhaps, he should deny that nature. Nothing in the morehl city seemed so beautiful as this realm his mother had given him. "I promise."

She smiled and hugged him, and that felt wonderful. But misgivings haunted Orric. He felt unsure whether he was morehl or selumari—or something other, without a name.

His mother's beliefs had set her against the whole city. However beautiful this garden, her beliefs in the selumari virtues of integrity, forgiveness, justice, mercy, and the rest might be wrong. On an impulse, he decided to test them. If she passed the test, he would follow her way.

What test? If she could convert an enemy, that would foretell her ultimate success in Karakto. He asked, "What will you do about Gleda?"

He felt her tense. "I am not sure," she said, too smoothly.

"Perhaps now that she has failed, she will flee the city."

Even at ten years old, Orric could tell when his mother was lying. "What happened? Did you kill them?"

"Of course n—I—We can discuss this later. Now I must—"

"Did you kill them?"

She seemed to sag. "Yes. I had no choice. They meant to kill us both."

She looked to one side. "Well, perhaps I did have a choice. I don't think they meant to hurt you. But after they did, I was so angry—I'm sorry. I know Gleda had been good to you before."

Shocked, he said nothing. "I'm very sorry," she repeated.

"Given the chance to do it again, I don't know if I would, or should, choose differently. It was… This is like a war, Orric, in its way, and in war we sometimes follow different rules.

"Now I must return to the city. I left Burgard in charge, may Nature help me. Will you lend me your cloak?"

Silently he handed it to her.

She whirled it in the air, and when it settled on her shoulders, it matched her height perfectly. "If all has gone well, the other aspect of this cloak is still lying on the volcano slope where we departed. I shall carry it to your room. When you are ready to leave here, put on this cloak, meditate, and you will see your room. Then you simply decide to be there. Do you understand?"

He nodded.

"Do not be too long here," she said. "I love you." She closed her eyes, and in a moment she grew transparent as the air. Then, like a dream image, she blurred and vanished. The cloak dropped to the garden path. He picked it up and donned it absently, his mind lost in confusion.

For the actual killings, Orric cared nothing. The two assassins had meant to murder his mother, so if they died in the attempt, well and good. But Calantha's evasion, her merciless execution, these troubled him greatly. If his own mother could turn morehl—so he thought of her act—why should he not?

Disturbed, he walked among the clear paths of the garden. Its tranquil air made him feel part of the place, like a figure in a mural. What were these bushes that grew in a wall around the bower? Blackberries, and in fruit! Carefully avoiding the thorny branches, he plucked ripe berries and ate them by the handful, while his thoughts sped on a hundred tracks.

She had made a single error. That did not prove her way wrong.

He thought of Cennard's strange talk about the awakened will: insight, expression of purpose—he could not remember the rest. On the instant, between chewing a blackberry and swallowing it, Orric conceived a plan and resolved to carry it out. He would keep testing his mother, observing, offering choices—whatever it took, as long as it took, to prove the worth of her beliefs. If she bore up through the tests, he could follow her with a high heart, living as a selumari. Otherwise…

Orric reached for another cluster of berries. Suddenly a branch of the bush sprang out, whipping across his hand. A thorn drew blood. The boy yelped and jumped back. Watching the branch swing lazily back and forth, he decided it had simply jostled free of a cluster of branches. For a moment the bush had seemed almost—scolding.

PART 2
OBERVANCE

10

Distracted by a minor earthquake elsewhere on Esfah, Mountain lost concentration. He took a personal interest in earthquakes. They often came from some marauding earth-dragon… or another elemental spirit bound to earth, such as himself.

Mountain's unyielding dislike of dragons stemmed from his sole encounter with one, the great wyrm Hwarrm. Now there was a foul creature. Its remains still littered his seaward slope after all these years—how many? Mmm… The living sparks within him had summoned Hwarrm at the final battle of their war, many years ago—how many years, now?

Mountain suddenly noticed how the sun raced overhead, how the sparks moved invisibly fast. Why, he had drowsed! He grumbled in fiery temper, and in his deepest tunnels, fumes rose strongly for most of a year. But in the impassive fashion of earth spirits, he simply gathered his concentration again.

The red sparks within Mountain, and the blue ones colonizing his western slope, fascinated him. Their little lives were boundary events, and Mountain understood a great deal about boundaries. The sparks lived between his profound, predictable world, and the smaller world of animals, gnats, and elementals—just as predictable in its own way. Like shoreline tidal pools teeming with weird life, the sparks produced infinite complexities.

Focus—focus—Mountain first sensed the organized diligence patrols moving through his tunnels and on his slopes, in greater and greater numbers. Then he felt, like tiny pinpricks, the flintlock attunement rituals—an unnatural kind of magic instigated by creatures not of Esfah: the gremmlobahnd… different sparks altogether.

But hadn't the leader, that queen or demarch, banned those ceremonies? Their existence troubled Mountain. He associated these flintlocks with the appearances of that strange orange light that talked, bouncing around from time to time, ever in hiding, but always encouraging their creation. *Hmmm... its magic felt connected to both the gremmlobahnd and that of Esfah?* Mountain sensed something of that light's nature, but nothing certain—and his guesses were so ominous that he wished no confirmation.

That leader, the demarch… ah, there. But what had happened? Mountain hardly recognized her.

In spring of Year 532 Calantha, in her eighteenth year as demarch, ordered a new cycle of the morehl mystery plays.

The order provoked no controversy, of course. She had ordered the plays half a dozen times in the nine years since her triumph over Gleda. Though the elders had originally staged the plays on a nine-year cycle, Calantha found more frequent stagings desirable.

Without them, she could never have obtained enough flintlocks. Though they could have switched to the traditional firearm used by the morehl elsewhere in Esfah, it was a point of pride that the local law enforcement carry the dreaded Karakto flitlock with its improved range, accuracy, and arcane ability to fire with rapidity far improved over its powder and shot kin.

The premiere of the first play in the new cycle drew thousands of morehl peasants and free folk, and thousands more selumari of low status, to the integrity shrine. Diligence patrols, armed with flintlocks, seated all attendees as they arrived, mixing the races efficiently. The front row held a long line of selumari—newly trained diligence guards awaiting weapons.

Calantha, in a private box built into the wall of the shrine, looked down with satisfaction at the large audience. Now near the end of her second term, the demarch had grown thin, almost bony. Her green hair had started to whiten, very early for the selumari, and this lent her distinctive authority.

Calantha wore a loose black jacket with enormous cuffs, green ruffed vest, moon-blue hose, and short-toed green slippers. The coat bore an embroidered design of circles and lines in the morehl "blind stitch"—so called for its exquisite fineness, which inevitably destroyed the weaver's vision. Calantha had outlawed the stitch long ago, but she had rescued this coat from the shuttered imperial palace rather than let such a fine piece gather dust.

To the demarch's left stood a detachment of two diligence bodyguards—one selumari, one morehl. To her right stood two more morehl guards, and behind her, a squad of six selumari men and women. All carried pistols in sharkskin holsters strapped across their chests, as well as selumari cutlasses.

Calantha knew all ten guards. They had become attuned to their flintlocks during the most recent plays, a year before. Of the two dozen enforcers scouting the audience, though, she knew few by name. There were so many diligencers now.

Sedition is everywhere, the demarch thought as she opened a gold locket at her neck. Gleda showed me that. Thoughts of enemies at hand always made her nervous. Thank Nature she had sana.

The locket held ointment, a thin pink paste scented with lilac. With one finger, she daubed a touch of the sana paste behind her ear. She never took a dosage of sana without silently thanking both Gleda and Orric. If Gleda had not shot her with that arrow, all those years ago, Calantha would never have known the tremendous calm it inspired. And Orric, dear Orric— had he not encouraged her to investigate that potion, she would never have found its source, a small sea-slug on Ogan the Reef. *Marvelous sana! Ahh*—already it began to soothe.

"Suffrage! Suffrage! Suffrage!"

An uproar began at the rear of the amphitheater. Many morehl Balloters chanted in hoarse whispers, with a few selumari shouting in unison. The rest of the audience fell tensely silent.

Calantha's calm shattered. She pointed at the protesters. The diligence patrols were already charging up the stairs. They drew hardwood truncheons and set upon the chanting morehl. The quick ones fled, but most fell. Guards dragged away the unconscious morehl and roughly escorted the selumari sympathizers from the shrine. After some time, people in the amphitheater again began to talk in low voices.

Balloters. Troublemakers, Calantha thought bitterly. *Sedition is everywhere.*

Orric had infiltrated the protesters' organization, and he had told her of the secret genocidal purpose behind their "representation" claims.

If not for me, they would all die at one another's hands! She thought, and welcomed the return of the familiar sana calm. A guard received a message and whispered to Calantha, "An informant, demarch."

Calantha rose from her seat and, with her diligence escort, went down the stone stairs carved in the amphitheater wall. As she passed up the aisle, selumari and morehl again fell silent, row by row.

Carvings from the legend of Cadal now ornamented the walls of the narrow lava tube that was the amphitheater's entry hall. Calantha looked around in the dim torchlight. "Flig?"

"Here I am!" said a piping voice by her ear.

On Cadal's granite nose perched Flig, a white-winged sprite from the Supremely Masterful Flyers swarm. The choker at her throat designated elder status. It held a single bead of tredaine, the pearly stone that sprites wove from the first breaths of newborns. Flig's advanced age was not obvious in her young elf-girl face, but her size betrayed it. Over the centuries she had grown as tall as the length of Calantha's arm, and sluggish by the standards of sprites. Nowadays, Flig would probably be hard put to outrace a falcon.

But among the sprites, age never brought manners. "If I'd been a bug, I could have bitten y—the demarch," Flig said.

Calantha avoided sighing. At their first meeting, years ago, she had corrected Flig regarding correct address of a demarch. Forever after, the sprite conspicuously corrected herself just in time, a practice far more annoying than straightforward rudeness. The demarch waved the diligence patrol out of earshot, then whispered, "What have you to tell me?"

With a flutter of her butterfly wings, the sprite danced up within a hand's breadth of Calantha's left ear. Then she cleared her throat, flexed her frail white arms, adjusted her sword and moonsilver scabbard, brushed at her autumn-red tunic and trousers of butter yellow, and said, "How much are y—is the demarch paying?"

"You know the rules. Talk first." Calantha practiced patience when dealing with sprites. She had recruited them a few years earlier, when Orric warned her that Gleda's erstwhile supporters meant to instigate a morehl riot. Thanks to her early warning and Nature's blessing, the riot never happened.

But vigilance must be eternal, she thought. Flig's voice dropped to a dramatic whisper. "The Burgardans are planning to raid Winter Spear's ice cavern and steal the pistols."

The demarch stared dumbly. Lord Burgard's covert clique of selumari had grown wealthy by exploiting the morehl peasants and free folk. The dwarf and his followers evaded the formal title of "warrior," but controlled large morehl estates, as the warrior class once did. For years, the Burgardans had been a political threat to Calantha, sheltered from the law by the Gundakhorian ambassador's diplomatic immunity.

But they had never planned open insurrection, so far as Calantha knew—and she had investigated very thoroughly. This planned raid, if true, marked a worsening of the long conflict.

"When?" she asked Flig.

"I couldn't find out. Tomorrow, next week, a year? It is all just wing—flapping for now. They are dull to eavesdrop on, don't y—doesn't the demarch think so?"

Calantha opened an eelskin pouch at her belt and brought forth a vial of honey from the Windhome apiary. "Keep listening. As you leam more, report on the instant."

The sprite appeared to ponder her instructions. "I'll move quickly, so long as the honey flows." She flirted away down the entry tunnel, into the open air, and vanished straight up.

My enemies are all alike, Calantha told herself, thinking about the treason. *Only I protect peace and freedom.*

She looked sidelong at her Goal Self. Years ago she had stopped wondering at the outline's thin, drawn shape, and at the dullness of the mist curling at its center. These signs, she had decided, marked the path toward detached wisdom. As the sana calm returned, she felt wonderfully detached.

The play told the adventures of two young vagha, played by morehl free folk who wore plain orange masks topped with mammoth fur. Morehl plays had never before represented dwarves as such, and so the actors began by announcing their race and heritage.

The morehl audience—Calantha found this curious—the audience, instantly broke into laughter. Over the years they had gradually understood acting as a concept, but apparently the idea of morehl portraying dwarves amused them. Most of the morehl were peasants, free folk, and a scattering of merchants and artisans. For years, the higher classes had stayed away from these performances.

On stage, the two dwarves—one talkative and one silent—received a summons from the Mammoth-Horse to travel across the land and help Tynalis fight the newly resurgent Firesnake. He gave them quarterstaves, which they promptly tripped over.

After much loud boasting from the one and vulgar, comic noises from the other, they set out. On the journey, goblins (actors in yellow masks framed with swamp grass) attacked the dwarves. Here the narrative broke off as the actor-contestants took formal positions for battle.

A new figure stood up behind the tower shield, and a murmur of approval rose in the crowd. This morehl, the drama-captain, wore a mottled mask of red, blue, orange, and yellow. He judged all combats and, after each, provided an explanation of how the winners resumed the story. On his right forearm he wore the symbol of his position, a small shield studded with four kinds of stones. When he waved the shield, the combat began.

The contestants fought strongly. Meanwhile, in the audience, a clamor rose as the spectators began to wager. These low class morehl and poor selumari, who had fewer coins than any others in Karakto, seemed most eager to bet them. With distaste, Calantha watched frenzied hands pass coins back and forth.

"Orange! Orange! Yellow!" As each contestant landed a blow, the bettors chanted the color of his mask.

As always when she saw this, the demarch felt soiled, tainted. What a beastly display, and she herself officially encouraged it! She kept reminding herself it was all for a good cause. Her diligence guards needed weapons. For linking guards to their flintlocks, this sporting frenzy had proven just as effective as the old sacred silence. Whatever magic was in the linking had less to do with ceremony than ever thought. How fortunate! Orric had suggested the link—dear Orric—and experiment confirmed it. That had certainly put the elders in their place!

The problem was that audience hysteria often spread to the combatants. On stage, the actor playing the mute dwarf launched himself toward a goblin, his quarterstaff drawn far back to the side for a mighty two-handed stroke. When it landed, the blow slammed the opponent into the other mock goblin, knocking them both down. Then, as the contagion took over his mind, the attacker dropped his staff, seized his own teammate by the throat with one hand, and pounded him in the face with his other fist. Calantha hid her eyes.

The thought took her by surprise: *My fault! My fault!*

In such a crisis, the drama-captain had to keep his thoughts clear. He launched himself over the shield, landed beside the maddened actor, caught the actor's fist in mid-swing, and threw him to the stage. The captain, raising his shield, declared victory for the dwarf side.

The audience responded, "Orange! Orange!"

As attendants carried the wounded offstage, Calantha kept reciting reasons to herself. Morehl customs should be honored insofar as they are not evil. These dramas help keep the peace.

At least I changed the weapons to staves instead of rapiers—those actors will live because of that.

As she thought all this, she avoided looking at her Goal Self. The demarch felt trapped between her Quietude philosophy, which advised compassion for all beings, and the city's refusal to adopt compassion themselves. Was she the only one who cared to build peace between the races?

The narrative resumed, but Calantha's thoughts drifted elsewhere. Another election loomed. She had long since decided to retire after this term, but it distressed her that one of Burgard's puppets would certainly take over. Unlike Gleda, the Burgardans would proclaim no genocidal policies. The lower classes were too lucrative to destroy. But the Burgardans showed no interest whatever in lasting peace. Oppress, exploit, yes—but teach, reform, treat as equals? Never.

Heavy footsteps sounded on the stairs up to the box. The diligence guards tensed, but it was only the author of tonight's play: Hornbeam the dwarf. Nine years ago he had come to Karakto for a visit of two weeks, and he had never left. Usually nine years changed nothing of a vagha's look, but they had made Hornbeam fatter and, if possible, uglier. Drink had swollen and darkened his nose, so that now it resembled a red-veined banana. He now wore clothing of velvet and silk, and on his finger a ruby ring gleamed. These plays had made life easy for Hornbeam.

He looked down at the stage. "What are your thoughts so far?"

Calantha whispered back, "It's all very—novel."

"Yes, and about time. I have taken to inventing new characters and narratives independent of the old cycle. I've grown heartily sick of the elders' resistance when I try to establish consistency. Those beetle-brains!"

Calantha suppressed a yawn. "Fortunately, it seems the audience does not care either way." Indeed, the morehl peasants and free folk laughed and stamped their feet as the mock vagha stumbled around. "But why did you portray your own people as fools?"

Hornbeam shrugged. "Am I, through an accident of birth, an ambassador for all vagha? Spare me. I give the audience what it desires. I want only to tell a good story."

As the drama went on, Calantha thought the story dull-witted, not surprisingly, given the poet's lack of ambition. When the drama-captain signalled the play's end, though, she dutifully rose with the rest of the audience and threw coins at the stage, keeping a motherly eye on the play's guide, the drama-captain.

To recruit better actors after Calantha banned promotion to the warrior class, Hornbeam had instituted the practice of coin throwing. Audience members tried to hit the actors squarely. In turn, the actors presented themselves as tempting targets, hoping to draw maximum fire and maximum profit.

The dwarf poet himself went down and joined the actors, dodging coins and then scrabbling for them. Calantha shuddered. Hornbeam had many clashing traits: contempt for elders, bridled creativity, pride in his craft, willingness to pander, and shameless greed.

The drama-captain, ignoring the coins, walked easily up the aisle beneath Calantha's booth and removed his mask to reveal himself as Orric. Hopping onto a stone bench, he vaulted up over the railing and into the compartment, landing gracefully beside her. None of the guards moved. The captain removed his mask, revealing a long, well-favored face with a prominent forehead and chin, arching eyebrows, thin nose, and wide mouth. "What did you think?" he asked in a whisper.

She smiled. "Of you, or of the play? You kept control very skillfully, as always. It was a pleasure to watch you. As for the story, well—"

"You flinch? Why? Hornbeam has given us an amazing new weapon. Simply stage the play in the swamplands. When the goblins fall asleep, we attack."

Noting his dry tone, she saw with satisfaction that the crowd's exuberance had not infected Orric. He always kept his thoughts clear during a performance, and in recent years he had made progress off stage as well. She nodded to the audience.

"They have not fallen asleep, thank the elements."

"I have the flintlocks ready behind the shield."

Calantha sent a squad of guards to fetch them. Even as she gave the order, a wonderful idea struck her. How had she never considered it? She said, "I have your cape. Walk home with me, I'd like to talk to you." She handed him the black cloak from the empty chair beside her.

He took the cloak, but she wondered why his smile looked strained. He must be tired, she thought.

Escorted by two squads of diligence guards——five troops in front, five behind, and two on each flank—Calantha and Orric walked home in the beautiful night. Tonight, a gentle breeze had cleared the crater's air. The Daybringer comets were back this spring, on their cycle of twenty-three years, and they formed a chain of brilliant white orbs across the sky. They seemed closer than the clouds, than the birds. Their long tails stretched each to each, firework-bright, a luminous line that held four dozen pearls and a hundred shimmering stars.

Calantha looked at the Daybringers and thought of their last visit, when she was younger. She recalled little from Year 599 beyond work and tension: study with Riddan, backbreaking work in the city's undersea gardens, endless marching drills, and even in her spare moments, Quietude arguments with fellow students at the academy. And always the fear, fear of invasion from the south. From here.

"Beautiful," Orric whispered. Seeing her son's delight, Calantha suddenly remembered rejoicing at the comets, long ago, and feeling the same joy when she woke each morning. Despite all the stress, she had been eager to meet the Emmirian day. For that instant, he made her feel young.

"People are saying it's an omen," he continued. "Chaos and disaster."

She sighed. "Omens provoke fear without giving guidance. Yes, of course there will be chaos and disaster. There always is, somewhere on Esfah. We have evaded it so far, but what do we learn from this so-called omen? 'Watch with alertness'? Many thanks."

Descending the trail, they came to wide gravel roads bathed in the yellow light of tall Firecraft lamps. Along each road stood the new black buildings of the aboveground districts, which the morehl had built to cater to increasing selumari traffic and commerce within the crater. They passed by the jails and the empty stalls of Aboveground Market. Calantha turned wide of Blackshutter, where slow-moving morehl women leaned against buildings of many windows, all shut.

Orric, now a strapping young nineteen-year-old of mature agility and intellect, took no more notice of the women than he had at age ten. "What did you wish to talk about?"

"I had a marvelous idea for—Look!"

Calantha pointed down a crossroad. That way lay the old imperial district and, nearest to them, its massive Court of Justice. There five young selumari were furtively painting the building wall. From here, Calantha could not tell what they painted, but she could guess. "Guards. Call!"

The diligencers knelt and concentrated. Calantha reached out with her mind, and summoned the air. At ground level, a hot blast of wind lifted Calantha and her party off their feet. Upright, with hardly a hair out of place, they blew like dry leaves down the road toward the courthouse.

The young vandals saw them and ran, but the guards broke formation and glided smoothly to intercept them.

As the diligencers expertly wrestled their prey into armlocks, Calantha looked askance at the wall. Under yellow lamplight, the paint looked black, but from its odor she guessed it was purple fabric dye. A large clay pot held enough to cover the building. She had also guessed the picture: a stylized mammoth head, symbol of the Burgardans.

The vandals were boys and girls in their teens. They wore purple velvet in fashionable imitation of the morehl nobility, and on their fingers Calantha saw rings of emerald and pearl. She did not recognize these unruly offspring, but she would certainly know their Burgardan parents all too well.

Some of the vandals stood silently in the guards' grasp, peering at Calantha as though at some bug. Others shouted defiance. "Oppressor!—Let the people choose!—The jails will overflow before you get us all!"

"They sound like Balloters," Calantha said, bemused, "though Balloters are poor morehl who think they have too little, and Burgardans are rich selumari who think the morehl have too much. Well, these sprats seem harmless. I can set them to cleaning the courthouse, but beyond that—"

Orric examined her with an odd intensity that she had asked him about many times. He always told her he hoped to learn leadership skills. Now he whispered, "Is it true, what one of the guards told me? That the Burgardans train their own children as spies?"

With a chill, Calantha recalled Flig's report. She felt the sana calm fading. "What guard told you that?"

"I am sure I don't remember." He still looked at her intently. "How does one handle such potential dangers?"

Looking at the youngsters with new suspicion, Calantha pondered. "I don't care to confront the wealthy class in court."

But if I do not set an example, she thought, protests will only get worse.

She thought a moment, then called, "Guards! Look sharp there. If you're not careful, those vandals might accidentally fall into their own dye can. It would be terrible if they accidentally swallowed any. I understand it can ruin the voice." Then she pointedly turned her back on the guards.

She heard the youths scream and, one by one, choke. She did not look, but she saw Orric watching with obvious discomfort. Strange.

The fights in the plays always enthralled Orric, but here he winced. Did only bloody injury fascinate him?

The guards shooed away the screaming protesters. Calantha heard them go and dearly hoped she would see one or two bright purple faces in the days to come. "Don't concern yourself with these troublemakers," she told Orric. "If they cause mischief now, the guards can certainly catch them." She meant to comfort him, but he still appeared subdued—even, somehow, disappointed. Well, better disappointment than one of those terrible rages. Opening her locket, she rubbed another touch of paste behind her ear.

As they walked on toward Windhome, she asked Orric, "Has the cloak helped you any more? I must say, its small benefit so far has surprised me."

He seemed to grow tense, but in her warm calm she could not be sure. "I improve, I improve," he said dismissively. "But you never told me, before we were interrupted, about your wonderful new idea."

"Ah! Oh, yes. When I leave office, these Burgardans will sweep in and ruin everything. But I have the perfect way around that: a new and perfect candidate. You."

He stopped in his tracks. "Me? Stand for demarch?"

"You are the ideal choice. Any citizen eighteen or older is eligible. You have the right ideas, as I of all people should know."

"Morehl cannot hold office."

"Not true! They simply cannot vote. No morehl in the past could hope to win over the selumari. But you are popular. Everyone looks at you as one of their own."

"Everyone but me," he whispered.

"What?"

"I said, 'Everyone likes me.' But I—I lack experience."

"You have followed me in my work, and often guided me, every day for nine years. You know more than anyone about this city and all its people. True, I wish you had studied your lessons instead of practicing all that combat training with the veterans. But then again, everyone on Esfah respects a trained fighter. We should not stand here parleying in the dark. We can talk further at Windhome."

"I—" he said foolishly. "I shall think it over. I'd prefer to walk on my own for a time." Without another word, he left Calantha staring in astonishment and walked rapidly away into the night.

11

He wandered a maze of his own making.

Years ago Orric had suggested that his mother order new aboveground housing for peasants and free folk on the pretext that she could avoid surprises like the mortality faces in the bat cavern. She had agreed! She ordered dozens of new buildings, recruited huge labor gangs of free folk to build them, and taxed the morehl nobles to pay the gangs. Now these miserable, blocky buildings housed not only morehl, but also displaced selumari.

Wealthy Burgardans had taken the whole shoreline for their spacious estates, so the poor had nowhere to live but in the crater, where they choked on brimstone-laden air.

His mother's reaction? "It promotes greater contact between the races," she had said absently, while daubing yet another touch of that hateful ointment behind one ear.

Now Orric passed among the buildings, heedless of the night sky's beauty. He wandered as one trapped, though he knew the roads like his own cloak—better, really. Where was the way out? Not from the city, but from this monstrous mess he had created and now must rule.

A fury grew in him. He walked faster in what seemed a pounding red rain, though the sky was clear. He felt himself falling once again into that unbalanced state the morehl called "the strange"—and he welcomed it. As he passed the women in Blackshutters, their faces surged forward through the rain. He thought them ugly and wicked, wantons of a vile race to which he was a stranger.

His strange mind influenced the other morehl. When he passed, they staggered as though dizzy. When they tried to hail him, they trailed off, frowning in puzzlement. Orric was the best-known young man in the city, but they could not remember his name. They only knew him as what he might be: *a possible heir to the throne.*

He counted five people. He could seize the arm of the nearest one, throw her against the two behind, jump over them, kick the fourth in one knee and drop her, lock his hands together and break the last one's jaw…

Fighting the impulse, Orric raced on into the night. The gravel road felt uneven beneath his feet.

He reached a road without lamps, paved with ash that glowed gray in Daybringer light, and his wolf howl echoed across the crater. He stamped, fell, and pounded the ground until his hands bled. Citizens looked down nervously from narrow windows, then turned away. Then—a rustling hiss, the touch of a thorny branch on his neck—At once Orric came to himself. He stood stunned, panting and listening, poised to tear off his cloak.

Long moments passed. Orric relaxed. The cloak had indeed disciplined his mind, though not in the way his mother had hoped. She imagined that he sat in the beautiful garden and meditated on Quietude. In fact, he had not entered the cloak's realm in years. Sometimes, though, when he succumbed to rage, that realm made itself known to him… Stubbornly, as a test of will, he still wore the cloak.

As he walked, Orric thought bitterly about his mother's Quietude, the path to peace through transcendence of selfish desire. A weak reed, and he had broken it! He had tested her by tempting her—with improved security, better defenses, political revenge, and eventually personal comfort. At every temptation, she had fallen farther. If she had ever once said, "No, I must hold to my principles…" He had hoped she would, oh, how he had wanted that! But no.

He had succeeded too well. What weak point had he used? Her wish to save ten thousand people from slaughter. Playing off it, he had turned Karakto into a city of corruption, and now he was to govern it.

Not for the first time, Orric wondered if, all those years before, his mother should have chosen genocide. He had strayed back to the lamplit part of town. The still air carried sounds of hissing argument. On an impulse, he moved toward them. Turning the comer of a huge gray building, he saw a crowd of morehl, and beyond them a woman walking away.

Her swirling robe, her smooth gait—*was that Lady Jandith?*

The people were peasants, dressed haphazardly in ragged robes or loincloths, their wrist braces indicating the noble family they served. The half-dozen commoners spoke in loud stage whispers, the morehl equivalent of shouts.

"If the nobles don't want suffrage, that tells me I do want it—no, they would never let us vote—You watch, the warriors will make our choices for us—I tell you now, I don't intend to swim out into the ocean for whatever it is—"

Balloters. When they saw Orric, the peasants broke off and greeted him.

Some looked guilty, for his mother was fighting against the morehl suffrage movement, which had arisen mysteriously in the last few weeks.

Still, the peasants did not fear Orric. As the only morehl in the city without a class, he moved easily everywhere. He nodded to them politely. "A late night for argument. What prompts this?" Silence. "Did you like tonight's play?"

"Oh, yes—A good job, especially when you broke up that fight—Nord, here, won three coppers from me, and he's been gloating about it all evening!"

As always, when he heard such casual banter among the peasants and free folk, Orric thought how the selumari viewed all morehl as implacable, single-minded lunatics. The Corruptor had created them more skillfully than that. Death had given the lava elves creativity and ambition, that they might scheme against their equally creative enemies.

But morehl free will could turn on the Corruptor like a knife in the hand. In less than two decades, the lower classes had formed independent ideas. The peasants and free folk, especially those who lived in huge common houses with selumari, discussed the merits of different nobles, of the old war against Emmiria, and even of living their own lives, in some way they did not yet know. As the wealthy Burgardans had taken on the roles of morehl warriors, so the peasants and free folk had begun to resemble the selumari.

When they seemed at ease, Orric casually asked, "Was that the Lady Jandith I saw here, a moment ago?"

All the peasants fell silent, save one emaciated man who answered thoughtlessly, "Whatever her name, the demarch won't care for her words!" Then, as if only just recognizing Orric, he too went quiet.

Orric nodded again and walked on, hoping to catch the woman. If that was Jandith preaching Balloter talk—Jandith, who danced Lord Burgard like a puppet on strings—then the Burgardans were behind the Balloter unrest!

He could not imagine why the richest faction in Karakto would want the poorest morehl to vote, but if he found out why, he could…

Orric stopped in his tracks. What would he do? Maneuver his mother into another pointless temptation? Or attack the Burgardans and Balloters alike, weakening them, making his own detestable election more certain? Madness!

Where he stood, two roads met. The crossing road led toward the center of town, the old imperial district. He saw the central rock spire, with its ranks of balconies, silhouetted against the pearly sky. And there—wait!

An orange light raced toward him, high above the lamps. It glittered in the night's half-light. Orric had never seen this light, but at once he knew what it was. For years, ever since his mother had happened on it in the bat cavern, people of all classes had fleetingly glimpsed that light. From all reports, it appeared more regularly after a flintlock ceremony, such as the mystery plays. In recent years the light had supposedly grown bigger.

He called, "Ho there!"

His loud whisper carried, and instantly the light darted straight down to ankle level and flew toward him, a hand's breadth above the gravel. At Orric's feet it flew straight up along his cloak and stopped just in front of his face. It said in a high voice, "Helllp!"

Orric stared in wonder. He saw a hazy globe of light the size of his fist. Through its outline, as if through a sky ship porthole, he saw what seemed a realm of orange light. Within that domain writhed a sinuous shape he could not identify. "Wh-What do you wish?"

"Freeee meee from this prisonnnl Helllp the goblinnns!"

"Goblins? Who? Where?"

"Ice caaavem! Followww!"

It raced into the darkness. Without a thought Orric ran after it.

At the base of Karakto, a thousand paces north of Hwarrm's skull (or rather from the spot where the skull rested before a storm swept it into the bay) there lived an ice elemental called Winter Spear. This name was self-evident to any passerby, including the Wild Things, for over the spirit's cavernous lair there stood a pillar of transparent ice, seven times a trog's height and straight as an arrow.

The spirit had shown up a few years back. If it had another name, Yort did not know it. He assumed the demarch, or one of those weedy blue Crafters, had discovered the elemental's name and detained it—why, he had no idea. Or perhaps Winter Spear had wandered here at random and never left. Yort knew all about that!

Nine years ago, the Wild Things had escaped the work gang that broke down the wall to the bat cavern, and had finally gotten free of the volcano. Now, years later, the gang still lived almost in its shadow, in the marshlands just north of the city. In thatch huts near Winter Spear's pillar, Yort, Murget, Giddy Duff, and their six wives lived a sleepy and sloppy existence—

eating, sleeping, and raising imps. Doing nothing. Every spring, as each wife dropped her litter, Yort went a little crazier.

What bothered him wasn't just the strain of herding one hundred sixty-five imps, most still teething and even the nine-year-olds saying nothing more intelligent than "Worm, worm!" In his day, nine was considered the perfect age to join the army and have considered spawning one's first litter. The lack of culture certainly had an effect on the growing brood.

What bothered him was also not the nuisance of counting heads each evening, only to find one gone and send the rest out into the swamp to find the body. Nor was it the agony of eating fish all the time.

No, Yort knew exactly what was driving him "stone brained." With Blodge and Fennevaunce dead, he'd never get home to Bent Morass. He didn't remember the way; Murget couldn't find his own claws at the end of his arm; and Giddy Duff and the wives had never heard of the place. Yort supposed he could just strike out on his own and wander until he found his way, but…

He had a guilty secret. He couldn't leave because he had fallen in love with his wife.

What a talker! Yort's Wife could spin tales all evening about her childhood in the Marshlight Stranglers, or her time as a mugger in Queen Lugger-Bhar's fifth regiment. Every day she and Yort chattered together like birds. She made his heart sing. She made everything… He could not think of the right word. He hadn't told her or anyone, of course, but the gang must have noticed him mooning around her like an elf. Loving a wife! It was perverse, but there it was.

Yort's Wife wouldn't leave the gang. If he went alone, he would miss her deeply. So, stuck with the Wild Things, Yort endured their current leader, Giddy Duff. Even at his best, the crazed war-dog rider wore a constant look of puzzled alarm. On nights when he drank more than a flask of gutchurn, though, the tall, thin goblin grew morose about his late mount: "Big Growler. A trog's bes' friend, he was." Then the whole gang had to run for the swamp, because Duff would soon start kicking and pounding anything that moved, and he always destroyed the huts. Yort's Wife would remark testily, "He does more damage in that dog's memory than he ever did riding it."

It amazed Yort when Duff actually got worse. On the first night that the Daybringers returned, he ate something—fish or beetles or a caterpillar-without thanking Shalbarrg the Sky-Renewer. The god didn't like that. Over the next week, Duff's skin flaked and split, and all over his body there grew pale yellow lumps that were springy to the touch.

Duff's biggest lump grew on his neck just under his right snout. It tilted his head to the left, making him look even more unsettled. Duff picked at it constantly. "Help me. Cut this thing!" he pleaded. But no one would come near it, and he seemed afraid to cut it himself. His drunken rages grew even more violent.

One night out in the swamp, while the gang waited for Duff to wreck the last hut, a whisper came from the darkness: "For goblins with fighting spirit and a tolerance for cold, I have a lucrative offer."

A morehl, here in the marshlands!

Duff's Wife Two and Three proposed eating the fool on the spot, but Yort and his wife wanted to hear the offer. When they did, even Duff's wives were glad they'd listened. Yort felt ecstatic. Never mind the coins this stranger would pay—after years, his tedious life would see some excitement!

"But will Duff lead us?" Yort's Wife asked, looking to the fallen huts where the war-dog rider had collapsed in tears.

"Of course," said Yort. "I'll tell him he can get a new dog out of it."

When the orange light led him over the crater rim and down to Winter Spear, Orric understood what was happening.

Years ago, the ice elemental manifested unexpectedly. It either found or carved a perfectly spherical lair in the mountainside. Its arrival prompted one of Calantha's few decisions that Orric had not influenced. She had enlisted three minor Crafters, evokers, to soothe and anchor the spirit—they had lost touch with the sages who knew the old magic and how to bind an elemental spirit, thus requiring the presence of at least one crafter at all times. Winter Spear had remained there ever since, and she had taken full advantage of the good fortune.

Orric had to admit, the ice elemental provided formidable defense. No fire-hearted morehl could fight well within the ice spirit's domain. Therefore, at the cavern's bottom, amid a kind of living glacier, Calantha had erected a small building with thick stone walls and bronze doors, a priceless treasure for any would-be conqueror: the armory.

Now Orric realized why the light spoke of goblins. Selumari already controlled the pistols, and vagha and morehl could hardly stand the cold. However, a small gang of trogs infested the Narcea delta. Attuned to earth and death, they could freeze solid and thaw without injury.

The light hovered above the icy passage leading down into the mountain. While Orric caught his breath, it repeated, "Helllp the goblinnns!"

"Help them steal the flintlocks?" he asked, panting. "Why?"

"Helllp themmm!"

"You move quickly, friend light, but your conversation is lacking. Why me?"

"You—Craaafter! "

"You are mistaken," said Orric sourly. "You will not find many in the city who are less skilled in magic." Then Orric thought of his cloak. "Did you sense this garment? My mother, the demarch, gave it to me."

At once the orange light whisked straight up into the darkness. It vanished over the lip of the crater. Alone, Orric stared upward. The light presents no threat to the city, he thought, unless it bores someone to death. Looking down the icy passage leading to the armory, Orric shivered. He had brought no weapon, and his cloak granted little help against the cold.

After a moment, he entered the cave of Winter Spear and made his way down a winding tunnel encrusted with icicles. In time, he heard footsteps below, and he stealthily ran toward them.

Yort could not find his way around. He could see well enough, for a blue-white light shone in the ice. The problem was that the cave was filled with ice from top to bottom, with only narrow channels through it. The path twisted and turned like the frozen bowels of a monster.

The Wild Things, never much for stealth, had moved fast—too fast. They had descended, wound, climbed, and descended again, each loop bringing them closer to the armory at the sphere's bottom.

On the way, Yort had gotten separated from the gang. He'd charged in with the rest—Giddy Duff, Murget, Yort's Wife, and four more wives. Yort had been excited and ready for the first battle of his life. As the gang stampeded down, though, the noise got to him—the strange, hollow echoes.

When Murget scraped his wooden shield against an outcropping of ice, the sound echoed up and down the tunnel, visiting them again and again. At last it fell silent. But when they came to a cross passage, they heard the same scrape again, from another direction!

This troubled Yort. He wondered if this frontal assault was wise, even with the talisman the morehl had given him. Axes, shields, Crafter talismans—he had no training with these. He wished the gang could just walk in casually and pull a your-boot's-stained or your-captain-wants-you routine.

At each turn, Yort fell a few steps farther behind. Then he lost the others completely. The passage branched four ways, and echoes came from all directions. This place was gigantic! He had expected a battlefield, but half a dozen armies could fight two or three independent battles here, and he'd be lucky to stumble on one.

With a sinking heart Yort ran down one passage, found no one, and tried to retrace his steps. Almost instantly, he got lost. Slipping, cursing, he charged back and forth, always trying to angle downward. At least he heard no fighting—yet.

Suddenly he thought to try the talisman. Taking the sight stone from its snakeskin pouch, Yort polished it with the hem of his brown tunic. In the swamp, the gem had sparkled emerald and gold in the moonlight. Here in the cavern, it gleamed red.

As the morehl had taught him, he held the stone's flat face to one eye.

He seemed to hover in emptiness, near the bottom of a broad globe streaked with ruby and topaz. He perceived twisting rock layers, fractures in leaf-vein patterns, and blinding orange rivers of lava. He traced their paths down, down, into crystal depths. Above and below loomed the volcano itself, whole, too large to comprehend.

Dazed, Yort did not immediately notice spirit-glimmers at the base of the sphere. Rapid movement drew his gaze to a cube of stone—a building, the armory!—with four torches burning at the corners of its fortified roof.

On that roof stood seven blue elves. Three wore bronze armor and carried cutlasses and twin flintlocks. If the morehl employer was right, those were sharpshooters. Three more, with cutlasses, wore armor and feathered headdresses. Through the sight stone, these elves glowed ice-blue, as did the torches. The last trooper seemed to be the captain, with cutlass, pistol, and shield.

So few? Of course—in this defended position they probably expected they could hold off an army.

Not far below him and off to one side, Yort saw the attacking "army." Murget was foremost, wearing his leather jerkin and carrying a shield and stone axe. The five wives, armed and armored the same way, all were trained muggers blooded in many a battle. Yort pointed the sight stone here and there, but he didn't see—

"Yort!" Duff whispered in his ear.

Yort cried out. The stone clattered on the tunnel's icy floor. "Bargatt's Eye! You made me drop it, you lout!"

"Where's—?" Duff broke off and fixed Yort with a baleful glare. His head at an angle, he peered down over his swollen lump. "Here now, you don't talk t' me that way. I'm the leader."

"All right, all right," said Yort, retrieving the stone. It looked unharmed. "You're lost, too?"

"I'm not lost. I'm leader!"

"Well, the others are about to attack, so we have to bring the spirit fast. I hope we can do it alone."

"We can." Duff looked around the icy tunnel, as if staring through it. "Tricksters taught us in base camp about those gurks. Here underground is real easy, 'specially with that thing." He closed his eyes tight.

Wonderful, Yort thought. He raised the sight stone and tried to concentrate. Yort, who had never served in a fighting unit, could no more summon an earth spirit than call down a Daybringer. But the sight stone could help Duff enact some actual magic. Or so Yort hoped.

Duff opened his eyes. "It's here!"

Yort did not see the earth elemental manifest, transitioning from its spirit form to one that was physical, tangible, and in possession of the power of that element. But Yort felt it happening. His own body suddenly seemed odd, misshapen. Slow, alien thoughts formed in his mind: *Pretty. Your zingbauble glistens nice.*

Yort breathed deeply. Thoughts of earth magic filled his mind, flowing from the sightstone and feeding him arcane knowledge beyond his ken.

Orric had visited Winter Spear's cavern twice before with his mother, and he remembered the straight paths to the armory.

Apparently the orange light didn't realize it could have led him a shorter way. Though few knew it, this cavern actually connected with the volcano tunnels.

Orric heard sounds of battle, and he ran faster. Here and there in the icy passage he saw clawed footprints. Both elated and chilled, he knew he was about to enter battle. For the first time in his life, he might have to kill someone. The possibility of his own death never occurred to him.

The cave's bitter cold had Orric shivering as he reached bottom. Here, Winter Spear had arranged a great hollow, its turquoise-white walls contoured like the chamber of a seashell, its roof heavy with icicles. In the room's exact center, separated from the walls by an expansive floor of icy black stone, stood the armory.

When Orric saw it, he stopped short.

The armory was a tall, cubical, stone stronghold with castle-style battlements—usually. Now, the building was a shapeless heap of black mud.

Torches, somehow still burning, stuck out at four places.

Earth magic! Orric thought. *Some earth spell has destroyed the armory.*

At the foot of the building, seven mud-covered selumari troops were floundering in waist-deep mire. Orric could see the tracks on the mudheap where the hapless soldiers had slid off the roof. With axes held high, half a dozen yellow goblins were running across the mud, effortlessly firming it beneath their clawed feet. One huge thug was leading, with five smaller monsters behind him. Before the troops could draw their flintlocks, the goblins were upon them.

Orric sprinted for the battle, fifty paces distant. As he covered the first ten paces, the goblins struck. Each trog shouted a wordless war cry and swung its axe at one helpless soldier. In the mud, the sharpshooters and their captain tried to roll out of the way of the attackers. Meanwhile, the three evokers gestured desperately, trying to protect their struggling fellows. It worked—at great price.

A roar like a rapids… As Orric ran ten more paces, a sheet of ice erupted from the mud between goblins and sharpshooters.

Its jagged edge rushed straight up, and the clear and glistening barrier held firm against the goblin axes. The creatures pounded on it as though angered by their reflections, then tried to dodge around the wall. It extended to stop them. Winter Spear, like all spirits, moved at speeds that made statues of the living races. Yet like all elementals, Winter Spear was a capricious and fickle spirit, and its attention wandered. The Crafters who incited the spirit could not stretch its wall to cover themselves. Three goblins rushed in.

No, Orric thought as he pushed himself faster. No, if they die, then the spirit will become unfettered by any mortal will—

Three blows fell. Three skulls split like eggshells. As the bodies sagged onto the reddened mud, the goblins howled in triumph.

At that moment, a tremor ran through the cavern, and the roar grew louder. Vapor rose in swirls from every surface. Calamity followed faster than thought, making statues of the living races.

Lost in the ice passages, Yort felt the tremor, and his expression mimicked Duff's. "What's happening?"

"Crafters are dead, must be," said Duff, as if anyone could see the link. Though he always looked startled, Duff could occasionally greet crisis with startling calm.

"Why? Does that do something to the water spirit?"

"Sometimes, sometimes not." The entire passage shook, and both goblins fell to the passage floor. Duff said, "I'm thinkin' this is 'sometimes.'"

They ran down the passage. Behind them, a freezing mist surged down as though shot from a pistol.

At a dead run Orric threw himself to the ground. He slid and spun on the ice, moving fast, yet clouds of mist jetted past him as if he lay still. Wind deafened him, needle-sharp ice crystals cut his face, and he pulled his cloak around him. For one moment he thought, I could escape into the cloak. At once he put the idea aside. Rather than face that realm, better to freeze to death in this one.

Orric realized then that Winter Spear was leaving. Whether the evokers' deaths had freed it from servitude or only alarmed it, its manifestation was evaporating from the physical world.

No one could predict the nature of its exit. The spirit might depart in a shower of harmless mist, or with fist-sized hailstones—or it might plunge the cavern into deep winter.

Feeling the temperature drop, Orric climbed to his feet. He would have to move to keep warm. And he still meant to fight, however appalling his disadvantage. He could see nothing in the thick mist, hear nothing in the wind. Could the goblins?

He felt so calm, he might have been contemplating one of Shantric's exercises, or watching one of the old morehl mystery plays, the sacred dramas of violence.

He recalled the other time he faced such danger, with Calantha against the assassins. He had found the steam vent. He needed his sense of the volcano, of looming masses of rock above and below, lava coursing through channels like veins… *I am the descendant of this land*, he thought. *Speak to me.*

Orric started forward with a sure, silent step. The ice was dissolving under his feet, leaving hard granite—the goblins' Earthcraft had waned. Still blind in the thick mist, he knelt and extended one hand. His fingers closed around a bronze hilt.

From the body of a fallen evoker, Orric lifted a twin-edged blade, smeared with mud but fearsomely sharp.

The wind ceased abruptly. From the fog came sounds like a cleaver cutting meat, then two guttural yells. At once, as if Winter Spear had waited for that signal to finally desert the cavern, the air cleared.

The enchanted torches had kept burning through the storm. In their light, Orric saw that he stood directly behind one of the goblins who had killed an evoker. It had short pointed ears and muddy black hair falling over stooped shoulders: a female.

Sensing him, she whirled.

Orric swung wildly and struck her forehead with the flat of the blade. She dropped hard.

A wordless cry came to his left. Without looking, he leapt forward. The stone blade missed him by a hand's breadth.

Already the goblin was readying another swing. Orric danced back lightly.

One quick glance told him two more goblin bodies lay nearby, the corpse of the selumari captain atop them.

Can't reach the pistols, he thought. Sharpshooters, where are the sharpshooters? Three goblins are still up, two females and the huge thug.

Axes, shields, glares of pure hatred. Raising his cutlass in a steady hand, Orric adjusted his cloak around his shoulders. He felt warm again, and more: serene, like a worshiper at the shrine of honesty. As the three goblins closed, he eyed them with solemn focus.

Yort woke up, felt a hundred pains, and looked around. That blast of air had blown him into the mouth of a dark stone tunnel. He felt around for the sight stone, but he had lost it. And his axe. And his shield.

Looking blearily out at the torchlit cavern, he saw Giddy Duff running toward the destroyed armory, across a floor of solid rock. The earth spirit must have gone, and the ground gotten firm again.

"I didn't know spirits could do that," Yort said aloud.

A familiar whisper issued from the darkness behind him. "That is obvious. Your gang has bungled this task in several ways."

Surprised, Yort tried to get up, but he had hurt his ankle, and his ribs, and both arms. "Why are you here?" he groused to the morehl. "We arranged to meet at the river." He glanced toward the speaker and saw two red elves.

Both morehl ignored the question. "Somehow you idiots have drawn the demarch's son here," said Yort's employer. "If he dies, matters will go badly for everyone."

"The demarch's…?"

With dread, Yort looked out on the combat. One morehl man was holding his own against Murget and two wives, but he didn't see any blue elves. Then Yort remembered something he heard on the work gang, years before—that the demarch had adopted a red son. And there was Duff, howling and charging right at him!

Yort started to shout, "Hold off, hold!" but his blood ran cold. Tall stacks of wooden crates, the crates of weapons, stood forth from the heaped mud of the former armory. He saw the sharpshooters clambering up those crates, gaining the high ground.

My wife, he thought.

Orric slipped in a pool of blood. He barely brought up his blade in time to block the huge goblin's blow. Through constant movement, he kept the thug between him and at least one of the others, but even so, he was hard pressed.

If I slip again, he thought with a curious calm, they have me.

His foot slipped. He stumbled. The two nearest goblins raised their axes—

"Mine! I'm leader an' he's mine!"

The nasal voice caught them all by surprise. The goblins froze, giving Orric an instant to right himself. From somewhere across the cavern ran a tall goblin with a fierce expression. The other trogs stepped aside to let this one have at him. Raising an axe, the goblin leader shouted a war cry—"Bring Growl—!"

From the mudheap came a series of sharp reports. A volley of flintlock particles struck the cave floor near the goblins, carving pits of flame. One particle sliced through the lump on the leader's neck, then struck the floor with the rest. From the wound poured a thick yellow gas. The goblin choked on the gas, fell, and died. Orric, at the edge of the cloud, accidentally breathed a whiff of the gas, and he doubled over, coughing.

The other goblins had shied back from the pistol fire. When they saw this gas, they turned and ran.

The sharpshooters fired at the fleeing goblins but missed. One called down to Orric, "Are you all right, sir?"

Orric pointed. "Af-After them!"

The guards leapt down from the stacked crates and raced to catch the goblins, who were escaping through a tunnel. Coughing and wheezing, Orric looked around, saw no danger, and dropped his cutlass.

Goblins. Why would they want flintlocks? They could not fire them any more than the selumari could before the rituals that attuned the pistols to them. Were they working for that talking light? But why would it—?

"Aaaahhh!" Orric hissed at a sharp pain in his back. Twisting, he saw the female goblin he had felled with the flat of his blade. She held a short dagger, its obsidian blade as black as the claws of her yellow right hand.

The goblin looked amazed that Orric was still standing. The cloak, Orric thought, but he had no time to plan his action.

When she tried to stab him again, he moved with pure instinct. With his own right hand, he grabbed the goblin's wrist. Then he pulled her hand toward him, crosswise up and over his left shoulder. Pivoting, Orric drove his elbow hard into her snout.

The goblin stumbled hack, blood streaming from her nostrils. She dropped the dagger, and Orric caught it in the air.

Stepping forward, the morehl flipped the blade and held it to the goblin's throat. "Hold still," he said. He had never seen a goblin before and did not know if she could understand him, but felt something wild and violent rising in him. He watched himself as a spectator, not knowing what he would do.

In one swift motion he carved a crude stroke on her sloping forehead, then returned the blade to her neck. When the goblin finished screeching, Orric whispered, "I leave you that scar to remind you that I. Orric, held your life in my hand. If you ever attack me again, I shall kill you. Do you understand? Do you believe me?"

The goblin grunted. "You wait, red one. I'll raise you high and strip your skin, I'll—"

Orric's brow furrowed in disbelief. As if a puppeteer had jerked a string on his wrist, he flicked the dagger upward and deep into the goblin's yellow eye. He stepped back to avoid drenching his cloak. With—not pleasure, but solemn interest, almost reverence—Orric watched his victim jerk back and forth in agony.

"Aaah! Aaah! You gurk, you blinded me!" Hunching over, the goblin rushed Orric.

He sidestepped and tripped her. He knelt with one knee in the small of her back, the other across her right arm, the dagger again at her throat. She thrashed futilely, then moaned.

"That was your second lesson, which I had thought basic: when an enemy holds a blade at your neck, you agree with him. What is your name?"

"Y-Yort's Wi—" She trailed off, groaning in pain.

"Well, Yortswy, you will have no chance to master the second lesson, given your breach of the first." Orric drove the dagger into her neck, then pulled at a slant. The goblin jerked and tried to cry out. She choked, and blood poured over the ground as from an open bowl. She went on thrashing for quite a long time.

Rising, Orric felt overheated, excited, unclean, transcendent, hateful. He had killed the goblin in perfect calm, yet now he breathed hard, and his heart pounded. He could make no sense of his feelings. He fastened onto the only certainty he could find: his victim was dead, he himself alive.

Alive! He had never felt it more, but he had never desired it less.

Orric heard a shout. "Let go! You! Red elf, over here!" Then the voice—a goblin's voice—suddenly cut off.

Orric picked up a cutlass, willed his hand to stop shaking, and ran, or stumbled, toward the sounds. His back ached abominably.

The voice again: "Mmmph! Let me go! See, here he is, coming over! Think, do you want him to tell the demarch you were here? Let me go, help me kill him!"

Orric came to the mouth of a tunnel. There, a single goblin, an unarmored male with many bruises and cuts, struggled in the grip of two morehl, one gaunt and the other large and heavyset: Elder Cennard and Count Fohlin.

Orric had no presence of mind even to feel surprise. "A good evening to you, Orric." Cennard and the count toiled to restrain the goblin, but the elder spoke as if chatting idly in the shrine of mercy. "We have happened upon an item that has sworn undying vengeance against you. Fohlin and I are unhappily unarmed. Will you do us the courtesy of killing this creature?"

The goblin shouted, "You killed my wife! Killed her! Mmmr-rmph!"

Fohlin's heavy hand clamped the trog's snout shut. "Pay the thing no mind, Orric," he said, trying to smile. "Even by the villainous standards of its race, this one is a born liar." And then he chuckled, as if some force held his own mouth shut.

Elustered, Orric said, "I—I didn't know goblins married."

"Hah! These filthy creatures?" Fohlin almost laughed again, but the goblin thrashed and distracted him. "Only a primitive parody of the selumari custom."

Elder Cennard said, "A spirited animal. Would you be so kind, Orric?"

"Quiet, the both of you!" Orric tried to gather his thoughts. He said to the goblin, "Your wife tried to kill me. I acted only to—" He meant to say "to defend myself." But when he recalled what had possessed him, his throat tightened, and he could not speak the words.

He raised his sword point to the goblin's throat. Something within him said, *Pull his head back, impale him from throat to heart!* Fighting the impulse, he said, "I do not wish to kill you as well. But if you attack me, I will. Note, you are unarmed, and there are three of us. Will you throw away your life so cheaply, when your wife died in fair battle?"

Orric stepped back and lowered his blade. The goblin quieted, though his glare still spoke volumes. Cennard and Fohlin reluctantly turned him loose.

With dignity, the goblin straightened his tunic and made to head toward the battle site.

Orric raised his sword. "No. Leave her. Go back up this tunnel, take the left branch, and you will end up outside the crater."

The goblin spoke one distinct word: "Later." He turned, went into the tunnel, and vanished in the darkness.

Cennard began, "That may have been a mistake—"

Orric ignored him. "Now, gentlemen, three points. First, you are in territory forbidden to morehl. Second, you are unarmed and I hold a sword. Third, and most important by far, I am in a foul mood. Let's dispense with lies and evasion."

Count Fohlin cleared his throat and nodded assent.

Elder Cennard said, "We are fundamentally of like mind."

Orric loathed that notion. He had avoided both men as much as possible since the day Lemarin died, long ago. Nine years had not changed a hair on either one. "Why were you trying to steal the pistols? You gave them to us to begin with!"

Exchanging a glance with Fohlin, Cennard said, "We gave them to the selumari, young Orric, in hopes they would destroy themselves. They have gone some way to that end, and in the long term, I still believe destruction the likely outcome. Yet we had not foreseen the danger that the selumari present— their corrupting influence."

Orric almost laughed. "Corrupting?"

"The ridiculous moaning of the lower classes," said Count Fohlin with passion. "The upstarts, the climbers, malcontents who do not know their place—"

Cennard interrupted. "This is no place for full discussion. The guards will return soon, and we may reasonably suppose that the ice spirit's explosive departure will soon draw more. Orric, for the moment please accept this. The pistols will help us—you, me, all the morehl—free this city from oppresson."

"Then why do you not create them for yourselves?"

Cennard made a fretful gesture. "I do not speak of mere armament. The explanation is complicated. We did not succeed in theft, so I shall try a direct approach. We hope to persuade you that our cause is worthy, and that your own interest lies with ours. Shall we meet to discuss our proposal, say, tomorrow night?"

Orric found the elder's nerve incredible. Fohlin's expression was blank—had Cennard surprised him, too? Both stared at Orric, waiting for his decision. A backhand swing, a thrust: He could kill them in an eye-blink. The blood pouring across the cavern floor, the goblin struggling under him…

Orric heard echoing footsteps from another tunnel, the sounds of the guards returning. He drew a deep breath. "Very well. Tomorrow night, half a watch past sunset. Under the ailanthus on the seaward slope."

The two others—he thought of them as "those morehl"—nodded and turned to walk quickly up the passage.

Orric thought of something else. "Wait. At our meeting, will you tell me of that mysterious light?"

Turning, Cennard and Fohlin traded bewildered looks. "What light?"

"Never mind." Orric waved them off, watched them vanish in the tunnel, and went down to the armory, or what was left of it. He rehearsed his lie: "I looked around, but found no one else…"

Orric staggered up the trail to Windhome, growing more determined as he walked. He looked up at the Daybringers and remembered his mother's talk of omens. This evening had brought him an omen, complex in form—the light, the killing, the meeting—but clear in its import.

He, personally, had to set matters right in Karakto.

That light. The more he thought of it, the more he became convinced it meant only danger. The light was no part of Cennard and Fohlin's would-be rebellion, so why had it sought help for the goblins? Because it wanted the pistols? Its past appearances were tied to the flintlock rituals…

The answer came to him in a flash. The light wanted the flintlocks gone, so that the selumari would create more of them. Somehow this strengthened the light.He reached the mansion. Standing on the crest of the ridge, swept by a gritty gale, Orric looked out on Hwarrm's Doom.

The tide, shouldering its way into the bay, turned the choppy waters pearl-white. He saw, far offshore, a speck of black—fisherfolk, seeking the elusive nightbreeding surf-tracker. Keening song-lures drifted ashore on the wind.

Orric thought of how those two had casually asked him to kill the goblin. He, having just killed, saw nothing routine in murder. Earlier he had wondered if his mother had been wrong to oppose genocide. What an awful thought!

But that thought, however terrible, would not leave. Now he had a clearer idea why Emmirians hated the morehl, who destroyed whole cities with such routine cruelty as Cennard and Fohlin had shown tonight. If he had simply beheaded those two, and all the rest like them, wouldn't the city be better for it?

Revulsion struck him like waves hitting the shore. Would the city improve for having one more cold-blooded murderer in its midst—as its demarch? Was he to become worse than his mother, not only seeing danger everywhere but killing out of suspicion? Angry, he bolted into the mansion, stopping in the rock garden.

He did not trust the light, nor Cennard, nor Fohlin, nor—really—himself. But he saw well enough how to solve the immediate problem—meet with Fohlin and Cennard, learn the nature of their plot, identify other conspirators, and then smash the scheme. If the nobles and elders were worried about "corruption," there might be hope for the city yet.

And he would correct the damage he had done to his mother, as well. He had manipulated her toward temptation, and now he must guide her back to righteousness.

As for whether he should stand for demarch—well, one crisis at a time.

"Congratulations!"

Calantha entered the rock garden, wearing her green brocaded evening robes. She smelled strongly of lavender, the odor of sana, and she walked with care, as if on a wire. "I sensed Winter Spear's departure from the cavern, and I contacted him to learn what happened. He kindly told me your battle against the goblins, although he stayed only long enough to tell the first part. I am proud of you."

Proud of a murderer. "Thank you." He considered telling her of the conspiracy, but he decided to wait until she emerged from her haze. "Unfortunately, most of the goblins got away. One stabbed me with a dagger, but the cloak stopped the blow. Does it grant some special protection?"

"No, but it is good silk." Her eyes lost focus. "I once saw an ordinary silk cape stop an arrow. Or rather, the arrow tore through flesh, bone, and clothing, and penetrated to the heart of the poor man who wore the cape, but the silk was intact, wrapped around the shaft within his wound. I don't doubt that your cape took a dagger thrust without tearing, though it would not protect you."

"Very true." Orric felt at the wound and winced. "I think I've broken a rib."

Bending to examine it, she barely avoided toppling over. "Yes, it looks bad. I suggest the healing pool."

"I—yes, of course. Yes. Let me just"—I'll go from my room. Good night." He retreated quickly to his small, bare room, closed and barred the door, and considered the cloak.

Well, why not? He had made a new resolve, taken a new path. Surely the cloak would no longer…

Orric, who had calmly faced a goblin gang, fingered the red silk lining and shivered. He steadied himself, sat, and meditated. In moments he felt the brush of thorny branches against his skin and he opened his eyes.

A bird's shriek ripped the humid air. From rank undergrowth sprang a black, catlike shape, all teeth and claws. He lunged aside, into a razor-leaved bush laden with nauseous green blossoms. Choking pollen burst forth, and the cat-thing fled. Orric fell through the bush and rolled down, down, through briars and thistles, a buzz of brown insect wings across his face, splashed onto a shoal of gray mud, rolled toward a glistening black hump rising in the water, a puckering mouth bigger than his thigh.

With eyes shut tight he scrambled back, trying to think, think, think—calm, think of the room, the room. He fell gasping onto his sleeping pad and hugged his pillow.

Omens, he thought.

12

Fohlin had always yearned for acceptance. The other morehl had always looked at him strangely. Since childhood he had learned his name, the duties of his family's noble position, the workings of his estate, and the names of all his peasants and slaves. He had been educated in the best schools, but he had not known, and still did not know, why Death had created him different—the differences were subtle, yet he felt them keenly. He knew only that he hated it.

The slaves in the Karakto's fungus gardens needed supervision, and the mushrooms provided his income. Fohlin rotted in those gardens while other nobles chatted at fashionable gatherings. It was unjust! Why was this mere fungus field his lot in life? More importantly, and most unjustly, why was he created so different from others, hulking, with a loud voice that annoyed everyone? Acceptance by people of distinction and taste—surely that was not too much to ask!

It proved too much, until the last days of the war. News of the final battle against Emmiria swept through the lava caverns swiftly. Misshapen and lacking aptitude for war, Fohlin had stayed within Karakto as the battle raged on its slopes.

On the estate he sheltered wounded morehl of the better classes. In this way he met and cared for some members of the imperial family. Fohlin also met Elder Cennard, and they talked at length.

He did not see the elder again until just before war's end, at a ceremony held in his honor. The affair had been informal. Elder Cennard had simply spoken a few words of congratulation, mentioned Fohlin's "services to the city," presented him a red ribbon on a plate of brass, and named him a count.

This informal promotion was not really legal. True promotion came from the imperial family or, in their absence, from a member of the warrior class. But the warriors and royals

184

were away fighting Emmiria, except the infant heir, who remained under Fohlin's care. Elder Cennard had thus taken the initiative (or committed the treason) of promoting Fohlin. But he showed discretion in avoiding full ceremony.

All the while, Fohlin feared someone would say—he could not imagine what. Anything. And as abruptly as Fohlin and Cennard had risen, so would they crash, like twin meteors.

No one said anything. Most of the attendees had not even witnessed the knighthood, so busy were they casting bone dice or pursuing the serving women. Ah, those beautiful ladies with their burning fingers! Dressed in tight black wraps, the harashin used their fingernails to skewer flaming puffers and charred cavetails, then fed them to reclining guests.

On such a wonderful night, Fohlin hardly remembered the war. With Gundakhor's aid, Emmiria was turning the tide.

Rumor said that even now, Nature's armies were marching south toward Karakto. But the nobles kept their dignity.

It is vital to preserve the values we fight for, Fohlin thought as he nibbled a cavetail from fiery fingers. For the first time in his life, he felt like an aristocrat. Cennard happened to pass, and Fohlin waved him over, as one friend might call to another. The priest hesitated, then stepped over.

"I am having a wonderful time, Cennard!" said Fohlin loudly.

"How good," Cennard whispered. "I hope I do not spoil your gaiety by requiring you to address me as 'Your Sanctity,' and insisting that you never gesture to me as you would to a peasant."

Fohlin fumbled and dropped his cavetail. "Ah, oh, certainly—" he began.

"I am pleased to have promoted you," Cennard continued in a flat tone. "Certainly it will help you in your planned service to our high cause." Though otherwise he did not move, the elder's eyes darted left and right. "But for our common convenience, I think it best that we have no contact with one another from now on, save for ceremonial purposes. Is this clear?"

Fohlin gulped. "Perfectly."

At war's end, during the desperate retreat, Fohlin joined the mobs fleeing through Karakto's tunnels. In the rumbling depths of Karakto, he and a lower-class rabble crouched in the pitch darkness of a cramped lava tube, knives ready.

When selumari bowmen and vagha crossbowmen attacked, though, knives proved useless against the missiles. In the squad of attackers Fohlin saw, not death, but worse—ruin, abandonment, poverty. "Attack, you idiots!" he screeched. "Charge them!"

His fear spread to them. They shied back from the attackers. He could not control his panic. All was lost!

Something hit him at the base of his skull, and he dropped, stunned. He heard some low-born man call, "Charge!"

A dozen desperate peasants charged down the tunnel, straight into the oncoming arrows. Fohlin hung back with a few others, but caution did not save him. Hearing the whistle of an arrow, he dropped to the tunnel floor—too late. When a sharp pain blossomed in his shoulder, he thought he would die. He had been created to die pointlessly, in some war he did not understand, and he had never escaped that garden. He had been wronged, wronged!

The last defenders fled past him down the tunnel. Breathing hard, he heard vagha and selumari just beyond the tunnel bend, talking in ghastly, alien voices—the one like gravel, the other honeyed.

Two figures walked around the bend: a red-bearded dwarf in fine armor, who held a spiked axe ready, and a blue archer. They stalked cautiously down the tunnel, stepping around the bodies, then stopped when they saw Fohlin.

"Here's a big one," said the dwarf. "Built like a human. Look at the fancy garb! Cut his throat."

"Sir, the demarch's orders—"

"Hah! How will she know?"

"Lord Burgard, you cannot imagine how much she knows."

Fear drove Fohlin to desperation. In his loudest voice, the odd voice unique in all the city, he said, "I am of the nobility. Spare me!"

The dwarf started. "That's no red voice. You, red, who are you?"

Fohlin tried to shut out the pain. Did they kill nobles on sight? He was wearing his velvet jacket and fine linen trousers. Well, he would not stoop to pretending anything less than his true status. "I am Count Fohlin. I can be ransomed!" He tried to believe that Elder Cennard, or someone in Karakto, would care to ransom him.

"Why is your voice deep like that?"

His shoulder throbbing, Fohlin could think only, *What an inane question.* "I fear I was created with this voice. I am yours to kill, but it is in your interest to spare me."

The dwarf looked disdainful. "We won't kill you—Nature only knows why. Give me your name again."

"Foh—" he said, and fainted.

That fateful encounter led to a summons by the Emmirian demarch the next day. "I wish you to serve as my liaison to your kind," she said.

"My kind," Fohlin repeated. "The nobles?"

Briefly, she looked puzzled. "The morehl race. You would explain morehl laws and customs when necessary, describe typical punishments, translate unfamiliar gestures, and generally perform duties that increase our understanding of your culture."

It sounded like menial labor, artisan work. Fohlin cleared his throat and thought of how to phrase his refusal. She was still talking. "The duty is unpaid. However, so far as I am able, I shall restore your property and standing within society—"

"I accept," said Fohlin instantly. Thereafter, life improved wonderfully. The selumari took a liking to mushrooms, which greatly helped his finances. As his fortune and influence grew, Fohlin received more honors. Most important, Elder Cennard grew more powerful. Half a dozen years after their early, furtive relationship, near the end of Calantha's first term as demarch, Cennard finally renewed his acquaintance with Fohlin.

The elder received visitors in a cavern that dwarfed Fohlin's largest. Blind-stitched cushions and wide carpets covered the floor.

Benches and shelves, carved from the cavern walls, bore the skulls of many beasts. A lava font bubbled at the back of the cavern, casting a lurid glow over the room.

Cennard entered in company with a girl-child who had strange yellow eyes.

She stopped at the entrance and fell prostrate, ready to relay messages.

"Count Fohlin, so good to see you again," the gaunt priest whispered. "Please, take a seat." He gestured to the cushions beside the bubbling lava font, where the heat was pleasantly intense.

"Thank you, Your Sanctity." Fohlin waited for the elder to lead, then followed at a respectful distance behind him.

Elder Cennard seated himself on the finest cushion, his legs stretched out. Fohlin sat cross-legged on a pillow of lesser quality. Cennard seemed subtly pleased.

The elder lightly brushed the needlework on a purple cushion lying next to him, then eyed Fohlin with a sidelong glance.

"When you return to Calantha's court, do not make known to her my art objects, will you, my dear fellow?"

"I think we have both proven ourselves able to keep a confidence, Your Sanctity."

Cennard smiled. "You need not bother with such titles in private—though I must ask you to maintain the courtesy in the presence of others."

Fohlin nodded gravely. "Of course." He extended his legs. "I hear your work in the selumari court goes well. Calantha, in particular, finds it much easier to understand the morehl these days, thanks to your efforts. Many nobles have you to thank for protecting their interests! But I have not invited you here to recite morehl law or describe the proper way to drown a burglar.

"In a week, we hold a promotion ceremony for some of the young barons. The elders have studied the rites and determined that it should occur at Krikanua Crevasse."

"That is only a few paces from my caverns!"

Cennard smiled. "Precisely. I intend to stay at your estate for the ceremony and for a week afterward. Some of the better folk will join me. Can you prepare your household by then?"

Fohlin's heart raced. What a great honor! *But preparation for such an event would take weeks, even seasons to make everything perfect.* He heard himself saying, "Of course. Everything will be perfect."

Then followed a nightmare—and unspeakable joy. Fohlin hired ten new servants. From a trapper, he bought two magnificent gracethroat rock pythons (Cennard's favorite meal), new cushions, bone dice tables, an obsidian lava font, and a drum beaters' dais. He sent his slaves to all corners of Karakto to invite the appropriate guests—the higher nobles, a few rich counts, a Deathcrafter and Firecrafter for color, and some wealthy merchants with whom Cennard liked to argue.

When the guests arrived, his estate was perfect. Cennard's private rooms were clean, the fungus gardens were lush, the servants had rehearsed, and Fohlin was utterly exhausted.

Cennard loved the bone dice tables and the gracethroats. Fohlin's guests loved the haranshi serving girls and the water duels, in which morehl free folk in tanks of cold sea water fought to the death. The loser, along with the bloodied water, went to the scorpions in the caverns below. The illegality of the duel lent it a delightful savor.

For this feast, Fohlin spent an entire season's income. But he made a spectacular success. So many uninvited guests arrived at the door that a few days into the gathering, Fohlin hired two guards just to turn them away.

Not long after, Fohlin received a message from Cennard informing him that he would be arriving for another stay in a week. This time, Fohlin dipped into his inheritance to finance the proceedings, justifying the expense as an investment in his future. The preparations were just as harrowing and exciting, the results just as pleasurable for the guests.

Cennard gave Fohlin only five days' notice for the third and fourth gatherings, but somehow Fohlin managed to present a perfect household. These feasts had grown immensely popular.

Noble vied with noble for a treasured invitation, haranshi of sensational beauty inquired about employment, trappers sent their catches unasked to Fohlin's growing kitchens, and Crafters auditioned ornate sparklers, whirligigs, and lava-swirls. Aristocrats who had avoided the first gathering sent free folk to inquire about the next feast. The famed orator Krikil, also known as the Gadfly; Lady Akhien, the loveliest eligible aristocrat in Karakto; and many more attended his gatherings. Fohlin's household became the measure of status among nobility and famed commoners alike, and Fohlin himself an envied figure among them.

What joy! What a feeling of arrival!

During these gatherings, Cennard acted as raucous as a merchant. How different from the lesser priests, who behaved so stiffly, conscious of their lowly origin. Fohlin found him refreshing, and Cennard in turn found Fohlin's oddity intriguing. At times, they consorted almost as equals. Nonetheless, Fohlin took care around Cennard, for with the deaths of the imperial family and all the warriors, the elder had become Karakto's chief power—aside from the occupying forces.

During the fifth or sixth gathering, which Fohlin somehow put together on a day's notice, Elder Cennard, Krikil, Duke Sahrol, and other high nobles reclined around the lava fountain, sipping spicemead. Fohlin sat cross-legged among them, hanging on every word.

Krikil the orator said, "But in an occupied city, we must maintain, or re-establish, our dead traditions." Holding a parasol mushroom between a slender finger and thumb, he waved it like a wand. "Otherwise, the enemy has truly won!"

Lady Akhien, lounging across two large cushions, raised an eyebrow. "What do we gain by bringing back the warriors and imperials? The Burgardan elves are as troublesome as the warriors, but without the tiresome warmongering. We should kill them all, of course—but not replace them with those just as bad."

The discussion implicitly concerned the merits of Cennard's leadership, now that the elders had become rulers by default. Even so, Cennard sat without speaking, above it all. He could afford to. He had no real enemies among the nobility.

Duke Sahrol swallowed a honey-dusted cricket. "The issue of restoring imperials is moot. There are none to restore."

Krikil pounced. "What of Orric?"

Cennard's expression did not change, but Fohlin noted that his jaw tightened. "He is not the heir!" Count Fohlin said, far too loudly for polite company. "He is some orphan, a mere whelp!"

Krikil rolled his eyes. "No one knows what became of the empress's youngest son. Who can say?"

"Anyone who has exchanged ten words with him!" Seeing the others wince, Fohlin consciously lowered his voice. "Whatever the rabble believe, Orric is not of imperial calibre. You would not want him as ruler. The ruler's responsibility is the same as the nobles—to represent the state, to stand above and guide the lower classes, to symbolize our society's goals."

"And what might those be, Count Fohlin?" The others looked on like a pack of hellhounds at the kill. Fohlin cleared his throat. He had not thought of society's goals, having achieved his own with these feasts. "Umm—prosperity, happiness, enjoyment, such as I hope you are experiencing here at my little gathering."

"Indeed, Fohlin," Cennard broke in. "Your feasts always please. But as a noble, you surely aim for something higher than the stomach. No more sitting around, I say! Less personal greed and more service to our creator! We need no warriors nor rulers to lead us. We should work to overthrow the selumari, who have desecrated our altars and razed our shrines. We must rediscover our martial roots, we must—"

Stopping short, Cennard looked around at the nobles, who were staring in astonishment. He had never before talked openly of revolt. His excitement had infected the minds of the others, but they had controlled it. The nobility considered powerful emotion bad form. The silence stretched.

"So," Fohlin said heartily, "who will join me in watching two desperate men fight on a field of broken glass?" The nobles showed interest, and in moments all was right again. Cennard favored Fohlin with a smile of gratitude.

By the tenth or twelfth gathering, Fohlin was running out of money. His debts were enormous, and more than once he had dipped deeply into his inheritance. He had tried to borrow from the selumari, claiming that these gatherings were necessary for his function at court, but the demarch rejected this reasoning.

He wanted to ask Cennard for help, but was too embarrassed. After all, Cennard had never commanded him to hold the gatherings.

The elder seemed utterly impractical, always talking about rebellion but never offering a plan and certainly never talking about money. Cennard lived in luxury, yet he probably understood no more about money than a scorpion did about poison. So Fohlin believed.

At the most recent feast, not long before the raid on Winter Spear's cavern, Fohlin discovered a far different side of Cennard.

"I maintain that she's useful as long as she stems the tide of selumari resentment." Cennard's face was dark with spicemead and passion. "She will not change things—she serves only to let us regroup. We are supposed to live in harmony with the servants of Nature—hah! She does not grant us even the most basic rights!"

It was more of his usual aimless grousing. Fohlin listened without interest. While Cennard spoke, though, the missive girl rose from the floor just outside the entrance. A talented mindspeaker, she could talk to Cennard in words that sounded like nonsense to anyone else.

As the girl quietly stammered her private message to Cennard, Fohlin glanced across the dining area at Dharsi, a minor noble who also had noticed the girl. His head was cocked, as if he listened beyond the babble.

Fohlin, too, listened to the drone. Somehow, its words became clear: Daybringers align with Death and fire one cycle earlier, say the skyreaders. Prepare the apocalypse soon. Fohlin's eyes widened. He glanced over at dark-robed Cennard, who sat casually on his cushions. Fohlin thought the message a trick of the spicemead—until he noticed Dharsi's astonishment, and his furrowed brow.

The girl had misplaced her sending. It sometimes happened, especially when similar minds were close by. Fohlin wondered how closely Cennard's mind actually resembled his own. Judging from Cennard's deepening frown, he had caught the missive girl's error. Fohlin suddenly felt a stab of fear.

Cennard did nothing unusual, but he seemed distracted all night. The following day, Karakto buzzed with the news of Dharsi's death. In a mysterious accident, he had plummeted headlong into an uncharted crevasse.

Fohlin wondered if Cennard might silence him as well. His thoughts bounced back and forth. "He would never try to kill me, and we both know the reason. But, for that very reason, he could treat my death as a double convenience!"

Finally Fohlin decided he would not know a moment's peace until he confronted Cennard. He didn't at all like that message about "apocalypse." Fohlin decided to try—carefully—for an amicable break with the priest.

In Cennard's chambers, Fohlin bowed deeply as the elder entered. "Fohlin, what a pleasant surprise! Have a seat." Cennard drifted over toward Fohlin and the fountain, dark robes billowing behind him like the black sails of an ill-omened ship. The missive girl followed at a distance. Fohlin noted fresh scars on the child's face and body.

"Thank you." For once, Fohlin sat without waiting for Cennard to sit first. He drew a deep breath. "I wish to take leave of your service. In parting, I assure you that, as always, you may trust in my absolute discretion."

Cennard looked at Fohlin in surprise, as at an insolent child. He smiled and shook his head. "Is this because of that message you overheard the other night? My fond count! You cannot comprehend. Let me show you."

Fohlin could not refuse the invitation. He followed Cennard to the back of the chamber, where Cennard stopped before a giant leopard pelt hanging on the wall. He murmured, "Honor, vengeance, compliance, destruction," and touched the four corners of the pelt. A shadow, barely visible, seemed to slide off the fur and into a corner. Cennard lifted the pelt, revealing a small hole in the wall, and motioned for Fohlin to climb in.

As he did, Fohlin felt a shiver, the aura of Deathcraft. The room beyond was small and cluttered. Tables carved directly from the rock walls held inky vials of sludge. Scrolls lay scattered about. Lining the walls were empty, bloodstained cages, some animal-sized, a few Fohlin's size. He knew the place at once: a Crafter's chamber!

Fohlin concealed his astonishment. He always felt uneasy around Deathcraft, although in theory he was attuned to it like all morehl. He had never shown talent in any Craft.

At the table holding the black vials, at least one of which contained necralluvium—the foul substance used to animate the undead—Cennard held one up to the dim torchlight. "I have been conducting certain researches, and I have found a solution to the selumari problem. You have consistently proven your integrity and honor. I can trust you, Fohlin, with the secret by which we shall regain our rightful power." Cennard shook the vial, then returned it to its holder.

He picked up a scroll, on which red and black designs constantly broke up and fused. The script was distinct: gnomish. The gremmlobahnd were the reclusive designers of powerful and arcane artifacts created from metals found in stones that fell to Esfah from the skies. Seldom did their writings or research fall into the hands of arcanists who could both decipher their mad writings and ply the elements to gnomish tinkering.

The scrolls in Cennard's hands described the creation of a talisman: the Ring of Stars. These rings were known to amplify the power of mages as they drew power from the heart of Esfah; this one was different, however… something both corrupted and amplified to be far more powerful based on the runic scripts drawn in the margins. "With this ring, we will oust the selumari from Karakto and reestablish our rule. Then you will sit at my left, partaking in the glory." Cennard paused to draw a breath, and then shot a piercing look at Fohlin. "Can I rely on you?"

Fohlin wondered about the danger of creating a talisman, and of subverting Calantha's increasingly harsh rule. He weighed these against the vision of personal prestige.

Really, it was not as if he had a choice. He nodded gravely, renewing the allegiance he had nearly dissolved a moment earlier. "Yes, you may rely on me."

13

Over the years since Calantha and Burgard had argued the merits of slaughter, the ailanthus had doubled in height. Other trees now grew on the volcano's grassy western slope, though no plant could live in the rocky crevices of Hwarrrn's body. But the tree of destiny, oldest and hardiest of the war's survivors, overshadowed them all. Looking up its graceful, grooved trunk to the branches that waved high overhead, Emmirians remarked, "Here is a holdover from the First Years. Meriopa herself blessed this one!"

The morehl viewed trees differently, Early on the night after the armory raid, Count Fohlin greeted Orric beneath the tree. "Foul-smelling thing," he said, pointing up at the ailanthus without looking, as if he spoke to a poorly dressed peasant. "What the servants of Nature see in a tree I cannot understand. If they saw such a growth, no larger than my thumbnail and rooted in a carcass, they would call it a foul fungus."

Orric looked around. He moved carefully, for his back still ached. A light rain had fallen earlier in the day, and clouds coated the night sky. One coralship floated south across the heavens. The dragon's body, now a high, bare ridge that merged smoothly into the grass, was deserted. On a dock at the edge of the shoreline district below, a dozen fisherfolk readied their nets for night fishing, but Orric saw no one else. "Where is Cennard?"

Fohlin looked around nervously. "I must confess. I tricked Elder Cennard into omitting this appointment. I told him you had sent word to delay the meeting—that your mother had enlisted you to help move the pistols to a safer location."

This "lie" unsettled Orric, for he had in fact come here from the temporary armory's secret location. Did Fohlin know the secret, or was it coincidence? If he knew, was he hinting at his knowledge so that Orric would—?

Blind me! Orric though with disgust. *Suspicion of the morehl can lure even me into pointless second-guessing. If they suspect one another the same way, where do they find time to destroy cities?*

He asked bluntly, "Do you know where the pistols are now, Count Fohlin?"

Fohlin gave the predictable answer. "If I knew such a thing, would I reveal that to you?" But he did not chuckle. The count's deep voice was strained, and his hands twitched oddly.

Orric watched with interest. A morehl, fidgeting!

After a moment, Fohlin spoke again. "I know you are expecting a plea to join our cause. Elder Cennard, if he were here, would argue that your mother's demarchy has brought misfortune to morehl and selumari alike." Fohlin anxiously fingered his red topcoat.

"And what is your opinion?" asked Orric.

"My opinion is of no consequence. In truth, I believe the attempt to recruit you is doomed, and have told Elder Cennard as much." Fohlin hesitated again. "Rather than waste both our evenings, instead I report grave news. This goes against Cennard's wishes, so I ask you to keep your source secret."

"I make no promise. Say what you will."

"Well… Let me burn the matter down to its essence. Elder Cennard spoke with that goblin last night, after we left you. He learned that the trog gang plans violent revenge against you and our whole city."

"Oh, the sleepless nights ahead," said Orric, bored.

Fohlin frowned. "The threat is not trivial! The trogs have obtained potent talismans, as you yourself saw last night. Tomorrow night, between sunset and midnight, the goblins plan to use these items. They will summon enough power to turn the whole coast to mud, washing all the selumari homes into the sea or burying them in mudslides. They mean the catastrophe to occur just ahead of the festival."

Karaktos annual Cropsinger Festival would take place three days hence. It was staged each year on the south bank of the Narcea, near the goblin marshes, but Orric could see no reason the trogs would find the date significant for revenge. "That overwhelming horde of four trogs plans this, does it? Potent talismans indeed."

"In the cavern last night, they intended stealth, and so they sent a small party. We know they have been breeding out there in the marshes for a decade. There must be hundreds by now. And yes, I am told the talismans are quite powerful."

"Did Cennard, perchance, provide them?"

Fohlin rolled his eyes. "Issues of blame, though relevant, are not pressing. Your tone discourages me, but I still recommend that when goblins appear on shore tomorrow night, your diligence patrols should be ready to arrest or kill them."

Waiting outside the crater for most of the evening, Orric thought. What does Cennard plan inside it? He wondered why Fohlin, who had an entire day to invent some diversion, offered only this transparent lie. Almost, Orric began analyzing again, but he stopped himself. It was pointless!

Fohlin obviously meant to betray the selumari, but he would never, ever betray anyone in the morehl upper classes. He would keep up the lie forever. "I'll bring the matter to my mother's attention," Orric said. "As to how she will respond, who can say? Let us turn to another critical matter, Count Fohlin: recruiting me to your cause. I am not so unwilling as you believe. I wish to hear more."

Fohlin's expression was as bland as his own, and Orric imagined that the thoughts behind Fohlin's black eyes also resembled his—disdain for a transparent lie. "I shall bring the matter to Elder Cennard's attention," Fohlin said gravely. "As to how he will respond—"

"Very well," Orric said with poorly concealed irritation.

Walking away from the ailanthus in opposite directions, both men nursed regrets about the meeting.

Fohlin, making for the crater rim and the elder assembly hall beyond, knew he had been over-subtle.

Hmmm. Did that foul peasant woman, Jandith, say "over subtle" all those years ago in the courtroom? What grotesque irony!

Fohlin had hoped the youth would hear the silly goblin story and reason, "Fohlin could create something more convincing. Hence this must be true." He then would have told his mother to remove the troops to shore, leaving Cennard free to carry out tomorrow night's ambitious Craftwork. Orric had, however, not troubled to analyze even this deeply, instead rejecting the lie at face value. What a guileless, unreflecting boy! His upbringing had stunted him. To think that the vulgar classes imagined this dolt to be the lost heir to the throne!

What I could tell tell them about that, he thought. *More proof that low breeding always shows.*

As for Orric, nothing in the meeting had matched his hopes. Now, having aroused Fohlin's suspicion, Orric would learn no more about this conspiracy. He must simply report Cennard and Fohlin's treachery, so far as he knew it, to Calantha. She would have to investigate officially—with tensions already high in the city.

His mother would still be supervising at the temporary armory, so he walked the muddy trail down slope to the shoreline district. A road paved with flagstones, the only such road in the city, ran parallel with the coast. High red walls of pumice brick, topped by iron spikes, rose on either side. Behind these walls Orric glimpsed torch-lit tiled roofs and the spray of fountains. He could almost smell money.

Two diligence troops patrolled far up the road, near the sprawl of seedy fisherfolk huts by the docks. Orric saw two more down the other way, and three guards approached him, torches up and swords drawn. Security was always tight in the shoreline district, for the Burgardans valued privacy. But tonight, the patrols had reason to watch with special care.

"Is all well?" Orric asked the guards.

They relaxed when they recognized him. "Good evening, sir. All's well."

"Where is my mother?"

"The demarch has gone with Lord Burgard, sir, to see something Gundakhor has sent for the Cropsinger Festival."

Orric was surprised. He had not heard of a gift from Gundakhor. As he walked on, past high blank walls with arrow slits, past banded oak gates studded with spikes, Orric thought he must be the only morehl who could move ten steps on the shoreline road without taking an arrow in the neck. No, he knew of one other—A gate opened to his left. He saw within it a velvet cape, a glint of gold at ear and wrist, flowing black hair, and skin of pomegranate red.

"Hello, Orric," Jandith whispered.

Orric raised an eyebrow. That gate led to the estate of the Sehlisirals, longtime Burgardans and opponents of Calantha's policies. Matron Meliath Sehlisiral, who had supported Gleda in the last election, once boasted of slaying dozens of morehl in the war. She now talked much of teaching the red barbarians virtue through hard labor in her copper mine, worked by a legion of morehl peasants.

Now emerging from that estate was Lady Jandith, whom Orric had glimpsed last night agitating peasants. Orric wondered what old Meliath might say about that.

"A good evening to you," he said. On impulse, he added, "Your Balloter talk went well last night up in the city. I happened on one group just after you left, and they spoke highly of you."

She stopped in mid-step. "I am sorry I missed you," she said evenly. "Let's visit a little, now." She took his arm, and they moved south. "How cold the breeze has been of late—" she began.

Orric interrupted with another blind guess. "How ever did Lord Burgard embrace the cause of morehl suffrage?" He did not know if the dwarf really was aware of Jandith's activities, but Jandith could convince Burgard of anything.

She looked appraisingly at the walled estates, as if they were her private collection. "Burgard always promotes the cause of freedom and self-determination."

"Even for the peasants who tend his own garden estates? For the free folk who work his mines?"

"For them most of all, of course."

"And were they to choose my mother, or her designated successor?"

"Whoever they might choose—" Jandith gave him the same appraising look, "—would naturally win the demarchy, for the peasants and free folk outnumber all others in Karakto. Of course," she added carefully, "the morehl are unacquainted with the democratic process, and would look for guidance to those they trust."

Ah, Orric thought. Now he saw Jandith's plan. If the morehl could vote, the Burgardans who controlled the obedient lower classes would dictate their choice. Burgard's puppet—or Jandith's puppet, or Jandith herself—would sweep into the demarchy. Burgardans and Balloters: two sides of the same coin!

Orric did not need to guess Burgard's first request for the new demarch. For a decade the ambassador had tended a fiery ambition to attune the morehl flintlocks to Gundakhor's marksmen.

Why Jandith wished to further Burgard's ambition, Orric could not guess.

Since the raid on Winter Spear's cavern, Calantha had allowed Lord Burgard closer to the pistols than ever before. As the temporary armory, she had chosen, of necessity, the best defended building in the city. Prosperhome: Burgard's own house and the Gundakhor embassy. Along with Jandith and his staff, Burgard had consented to move to another home nearby until Calantha could build the new armory.

Orric and Jandith arrived there now, at the base of a rock spur that jutted from the southwestern edge of the mountain.

Steam vents along its steep faces sent up white plumes of vapor. The spur reached almost to the bay, where it rose to a low peak that overlooked the coastal flatland to either side. On that peak stood Prosperhome, a round keep of stone topped with an ever-burning brazier. Since this afternoon, the keep had held Karakto's whole stock of unassigned weapons, including two hundred flintlocks awaiting attunement ceremonies.

The paved length of the shoreline road ended here, before a gate of iron set in a wall of brick. The road went on as a wide dirt trail, turning right toward the bay before vanishing south around the spur.

Two selumari guards, diligence troopers with pistols, stood sentry at the gate. "I must retrieve a few items from my chamber," Jandith told the sentries. Two more guards descended from the keep to escort her.

In parting, Jandith said to Orric, in front of the four Emmirian guards, "Your mother does not trust Lord Burgard or his friends near these weapons. Why does one steward of Nature suspect another?"

Her remark was a prank, at least—perhaps even a test. "It is not a question of suspicion," Orric said, his tone pure politeness. "The demarch knows that the pistols are the key to Karaktos security. Obviously only those subject to city authority and supervision may have them."

As Orric spoke, he felt a faint trembling underfoot. He glanced around, as did the guards, but they saw nothing.

Jandith asked, "By the bye, have you seen the festival show piece?"

Trembling came again. With rising suspicion, Orric said, "No."

"I think you'll be surprised." Smiling slyly, Jandith went in.

As the gate closed, the ground shook again, and from the south came a sound of trumpets. Shocked, Orric and the sentries all identified the sound at the same time. The sentries started to run for the end of the spur.

"Stay at your posts! Sound the alert."

While a sentry sounded his horn, Orric ran down the dirt road toward the bay. His wound made him wince, and he hoped he would not have to fight. He rounded the Prosperhome spur and saw his mother standing with Lord Burgard, who carried a torch. They were looking up. Orric's gaze followed theirs, and he threw himself against the rock wall.

A snaking trunk, cloud-white tusks carved with dwarven heraldic symbols and capped with iron spheres, a knurled brow cresting in a casque of bronze—Orric's heart raced at the sight of the mammoth. Ears that looked soft as swaddling quilts swayed gently as the shaggy bull walked along the road. It placed its steps with stately deliberation and a kind of grace.

On the beast's neck rode a yellow-clad dwarf, almost hidden behind his huge shield. And behind that mammoth marched another, and another. A line of bobbing torches stretched into the distance. Orric could see no end of mammoths. With faltering steps, he joined his mother and Burgard.

Calantha watched the procession with unfocused eyes. The scent of lavender pervaded the air, even more strongly than the odor of mammoth. She spoke with forced politeness, but Orric heard the anger behind it. "Look, Orric! Lord Burgard has kindly favored this year's Cropsinger Festival with a surprise—an entire company of mammoth riders from Gundakhor. What a… surprise. Wouldn't you agree?"

Orric could not find his voice. A full company of Gundakhor's elite cavalry was not a festival showpiece but an invasion force. And the mammoths seldom traveled alone. If Burgard had a few companies of footmen and crossbowmen hiding outside the city, he could seize the shoreline district, and probably all Karakto, almost on a whim.

With a tight voice, Calantha asked Burgard, "Your troops have been traveling a long time, I think?"

"Many days." Burgard rose up on his boot-toes and back down, but he kept his voice free of smugness. "What good fortune that they arrived in this crisis, when the armory requires protection."

"Indeed. Enemies lurk everywhere on Esfah—often unseen, close at hand!" The dwarf ignored Calantha's angry tone. She continued, "Tell me, Lord Burgard, where do you intend to put these mammoths?"

"Why, near the fair," the dwarf replied with perfect innocence. "They are here for the fair, of course." The fair's site lay hardly a hundred paces from the north end of the shoreline road. The Prosperhome armory lay at the south end, a straight march of six hundred paces.

Orric drew his mother aside. "They can seize the pistols on a moment's notice, for any of a hundred trumped-up reasons. Why do you not forbid them entry?"

"And give them their trumped-up reason? We have a treaty of free passage with Gundakhor. Oh Nature, I have such a headache." With shaking fingers she fumbled open her locket. "Then we must move the weapons!"

"What was that?" Burgard moved closer. "My apologies, but I could not help overheating what sounded like a suggestion that the demarch should move the weapons. This, I suggest—speaking as an ambassador—would be a grave mistake. The pistols are safe in Prosperhome, my embassy, which technically is Gundakhor's soil."

Calantha snapped. Her face going dark blue with rage, she shouted, "And I suppose you are willing to fight for it?"

"Mother!" Orric pulled her away, around the rock spur. She did not resist, but her limbs trembled. "Don't worry, nothing to worry about," she said, dabbing ointment behind her ear. "I only need to relax. To relax. I shall be fine."

Orric could walk the sulfurous tunnels of Karakto with ease, but this reeking fragrance made him cough. She almost started a war, he thought. *Nature help me, but it would be my fault. She is my fault.*

Calantha breathed deeply, and her eyes lost focus again. She spoke with clarity and firmness, too low for the passing riders to hear. "Quickly, Orric. I need some excuse to station our troop near his."

Orric took the first idea that came to mind. "I just spoke with Fohlin. He told me a foolish tale about the goblins in the marsh. He says they plan to destroy the shoreline tomorrow night."

Calantha laughed harshly. "The goblins! What will they do, bury us in children?"

"Fohlin suggested that we move the patrols to shore. He has some reason for wanting them out of the crater." Orric felt strange telling Calantha the plain truth. Had he ever done this before? He saw with regret that this truth affected her no differently from his lies. She wore a bleak frown, and she fingered her locket fretfully. "Enemies within and without. Why in Nature's names were you talking to Fohlin?"

"That, I must discuss with you. But for now, if you seek an excuse…"

Calantha looked to one side. "I have never trusted Count Fohlin, nor the nobles he worships. Yet whatever mischief they plan, I can't imagine it matches—" She trailed off. The mammoths still marched past in an unending line. She took his hand. "I shall have to warn Burgard of the troop movements, may Nature help me, or he will interpret them as an attack. I want you with me as I tell him."

Dutifully, Orric listened to his mother delivering the news of troop movements, and heard Burgard's cold assent.

Whatever Fohlin and Cennard have planned, he thought, the crater will be utterly vulnerable.

In the Gundakhor camp, near the mouth of the Narcea, Burgard and Jandith talked with the cavalry commanders into the night. As they left the camp, very late, the dwarf lord and his morehl lady took the long way. Burgard strolled with approving eye past lines of sleeping mammoths. Both walked in comfort, for Jandith had set a minor flame spell to draw mosquitoes and burn them as they approached.

When they passed near a stand of swamp grass, a silky voice said, "My lord and lady, a moment of your time."

From the grass stepped a goblin.

"Guards!" Burgard's shout summoned the two nearest sentries, who seized and held the unresisting goblin.

"This is not necessary," the trog said. "I assure you, I mean no harm. I have information of unusual interest pertaining to the demarch's son, the red elf."

"Let him go," Jandith whispered.

Burgard called, "Let him go. Talk, goblin."

Yort talked. He knew talking.

14

The following night, Fohlin climbed—or as he thought of it, descended—to Blackshutter with Cennard. He saw the Daybringer comets overhead, magnificent diamond sprays woven into trailing ribbons of white silk. A favorable omen! Theirs was the strange silence of a morehl victory pageant. The comets lit the sky with a shimmering opal-gray twilight, like fire made into ice.

Fohlin was drawn to the cold, galactic grace of these vagabond stars, and everything else seemed strangely distant, suspended in time. The comets floated over the city like feathers held aloft by the wind. An unusual peace settled over him as he pondered the trails of shimmering stardust.

With detachment, he realized that before the night was out, he might be a hunted fugitive.

The distant cry of a selumari brought Fohlin's attention back to the ramshackle district looming ahead. The dirt path leading to the center of Blackshutter was muddy with spring rains. A few torches burned low. Males peered from alleys.

Fohlin had accompanied Elder Cennard to Karakto's crater this clear spring evening to help in his mysterious work. Fohlin knew only that there was to be Deathcraft and a certain amount of danger.

In a taut voice he murmured, "Forgive me for asking, but are you sure this is a good idea? We are not protected."

Cennard simply motioned him forward. Near a cavetail packing building that smelled of sulfur, two morehl women approached them. They wore black wraps in ragged imitation of haranshi serving women, and their faces were painted with coal stripes meant to be seductive.

A thin one with curled hair and glinting bracelets strutted up to Cennard and draped her arms over his shoulders. "Want to make a fire tonight, Your Sanctity?" The other put her braceleted arms around Fohlin's large waist.

207

Fohlin rolled his eyes. "These women are disgusting. May we leave?"

Passersby glanced up in curiosity. A shutter two stories above them squeaked open.

Cennard brushed away the women. "We have business here yet." He addressed the passersby in a dramatic stage whisper, loud for morehl. "Hear me, people: The aboveground districts have corrupted our ways!"

A few morehl shook their heads and moved on. Others, perhaps fifteen of them, stayed to listen.

"These women!" Cennard indicated the striped women. "Once their discipline found support in the shrine of compliance. Now, thanks to the corrupt selumari, they are out on the streets, engaging in business, using their arts for profit. What a sad fall!"

One Woman shot a poisonous look at Cennard. "If I had your Wealth, I could say the same, you skinny frog." To the crowd she cried: "Listen to his words, then think of the luxury of his caves!"

Cennard ignored her. "Honorable morehl must believe, as I do, that we should return to our roots, join in one mind to overcome the tyranny!" A few of the onlookers nodded, but many wandered off.

"I tell you, we shall do just that! I am Elder Cennard, come among you to throw off the shackles of Emmirian corruption. Join with me now, and I promise deliverance from the selumari!" He paused. There was no response. "Show your support it you believe it time to throw off the blue yoke!" Scattered hisses sounded, the morehl equivalent of selumari applause.

Cennard appraised the crowd. "Are you skeptical? I give you a sign by which you will know that the morehl will once again rule themselves—and someday, all of Esfah!"

Sudden lightning crackled across the sky, tracing the chain of comets. The crowd gasped. Light flashed in the northern sky where the last of the Daybringer comets floated, and a line of white fire darted down toward Blackshutter.

A burning white pellet struck a second-story shutter and burned a finger-sized hole through it. A tendril of smoke rose from the spot.

Morehl looked at morehl. Then the crowd burst into gulping laughter. A striped woman spread her arms and called, "Beware, blue ones! Slink away like sullen dogs, or we shall lob pebbles at you!" A few morehl threw pebbles at Cennard and Fohlin.

Cennard flushed bright red, the color of the scar on his neck. "Mark my words, this is just the beginning! Count Fohlin, please retrieve the stone from behind that shutter."

Startled, Fohlin nodded solemnly, though he considered abandoning Cennard where he stood. *We must maintain appearances,* he thought.

Fohlin plodded into the squalid building and up high, narrow stairs.

On a shadowed landing he found a piece of shining quartz—jagged, white, and fiery hot. He picked it up and examined it with only slight interest.

Fohlin went back outside, where Cennard stood imperiously, pebbles bouncing off his chest. Gravely, Fohlin held the stone aloft. The crowd did not care. Handfuls of smaller pebbles whistled toward him and Cennard.

Fohlin lowered his hand and whispered in Cennard's ear. "I suggest a strategic retreat."

Cennard spoke loudly to the crowd. "We will go then, but sadly, with regret that these folk do not desire freedom. They will learn tonight their mistake!"

As they left, a few morehl followed them, some, at least, to jeer.

Cennard stood atop a market stall near the center of the square. Eyes stared at him from Aboveground Market's corners and tent flaps, from empty wooden stalls and unshuttered windows. Some merchants standing in the square wore dark silks, earrings that glinted in torchlight, and ornately filigreed bracelets. Others—those who did little business with selumari—wore plain cloth, and jewelry studded with volcanic glass. And then there were the Blackshutter groundlings, in hemp cloth and black snakeskin.

A few selumari merchants, dressed in fine silks and linens of white and green, clustered at the outskirts of the crowd. They exchanged dark, angry looks among themselves.

As Cennard spoke, the wind blowing down into the crater caused his black robe to flutter like a dark banner. "These selumari have made us slaves to commerce, when we should be conquering the world!"

Resentful murmurs rose from the merchants—but a few hisses of agreement answered from the Blackshutter folk, who disliked the high prices of Aboveground Market.

Cennard raised his arms. The sleeves of his robe slid down to reveal forearms scarred with war wounds. "Join with me now—I give you a sign that the world will be ours!" More folk hissed.

Some murmured.

The elder's eyes rolled back into his head, and he swayed where he stood. Again, lightning crackled across the sky, and again came a flash.

From high overhead, a red fireball plunged toward the market. Fohlin's heart raced as he heard the rumbling roar of the flames, louder, ever louder…

Some elves stood in tense silence. Others broke and ran screaming. The meteorite gathered size and speed as it fell.

When it hit a large selumari tent, Pohlin felt the ground shake, and heard a hiss like lava quenched in cold water. The tent burst into flame.

The morehl began a chant to confine the fire. Judging from the smiles and in the crowd, the meteorite had destroyed selumari competition.

Cennard had already instructed Fohlin in his own task. He slipped through the crowd into the burning tent. Inside, tongues of flame raced up wooden poles, and metal boxes near the impact had already started to melt to slag in the unnaturally intense heat. Fohlin's gaze paused on a blackened body on a pallet at the center of the tent. The clothes had burned away, but patches of blue skin told that the selumari owner had burned with his tent. The smell was annoying, Fohlin bent over a pit near the burning pallet and thrust his arm into a pile of smoldering rocks—the meteorite. When he pulled forth his smoking hand, it held a glowing red gem that tingled in his grip. His coat sleeve was smoking, but Fohlin was so impressed he hardly noticed.

As he was about to leave, Fohlin noticed a shelf of curious items untouched by the flame. Skulls, vials of liquid, a tiny copper sphere—talismans, some of which had great value and significant power. On an impulse, Fohlin pocketed the copper sphere.

The night entered second watch. The full moon raced up the sky, casting brilliant blue light.

As he paced along the marbled steps of the Hall of Justice, Cennard's long shadow fell across a crowd of morehl. All of them had followed him from the market, for this district was deserted. The diligence patrols apparently had not yet heard of the—Fohlin surprised himself with the word—uprising.

Almost instinctively, the crowd had separated by class. Elders in black robes, from nearby Blackhand Cloister, stood in the front ranks. Only merchants and artisans dared to stand near them. The lower classes, their numbers grown enormously, hung back. Behind them stretched the paved expanse of the former imperial plaza, which the demarch had named Alliance Square. Across the square rose the tall central spire, silhouetted against a blue-black sky.

Cennard was finishing his speech. "Here—" he pointed to the Hall of Justice looming above him "—the selumari demarch enforces the laws that destroy our ways! This is not justice. It is tyranny of the worst kind! Let us have done with subservience to foreign ways. Let us serve our creator and find our freedom!"

A wave of enthusiasm swept across the crowd. Appreciative hissing erupted from all classes. Again, Cennard's eyes rolled back as he called down fire from the heavens.

Moments later, a brilliant explosion bleached the night sky. A tremendous boulder ripped itself from one comet and hurtled toward the imperial district. Green fire licked it as smaller boulders broke off and sped down to other districts.

Fohlin's heart raced as the mottled green meteorite, bigger than a vagha mammoth, plunged toward them, casting weird shadows across the square. Then, it struck! The front of Trade Hall collapsed with an explosive shudder that Fohlin felt a thousand paces away. A green blaze grew from what remained of the interior.

Rocks and burning wood fell as the building's frame collapsed.

We are doomed, Fohlin thought in horror. Cennard will destroy us all. Then he started, surprised at his own thought.

Cennard would drive out the selumari, which served the interests of the cultured classes.

Cennard spoke as if in delirium. "The fire, the green!" Fohlin plodded through the hissing crowd and, suppressing his unease, entered the building. He dodged chunks of wood and collapsing mortar as he picked his way toward the meteorite. The unnatural heat, intense even for a morehl, irritated his scars, but he managed to root through the glowing rubble and find the gemstone hidden beneath heavy rock and timbers.

Like the meteorite, the gem was mottled green, but it felt icy cold, painful to his hot hand; many fragments of other, mysterious metal flecked throughout it. He had no time to wonder at it, for the building threatened to bury him at any moment. As he walked back, Fohlin dropped the chill gem in a pocket.

Fohlin climbed the steps to Cennard and bowed. "Your Sanctity," said Fohlin with quiet reverence, "you said you would tell me what this Ring of Stars will do."

Cennard took the gemstone. He glanced down at the count, smiled, and then held the stone aloft. To the crowd, he cried, "Now I say to the morehl, let us take the selumari! We have the power, we have the will! Follow me!"

As Cennard descended the steps and headed west into the residential district, a mob of morehl milled behind him, hissing like a thousand cave snakes.

Fohlin trailed behind, angry at being snubbed.

Cennard stood on the steps of one of the blocky residences that the demarch called worker dwellings.

Worker warehouses, Fohlin thought bitterly. But then, they can't appreciate better.

In the yellow lamplight, he glimpsed a few frightened selumari peeking out at the mob from narrow windows.

Cennard spoke. "Here, our blue captors have insulted the traditions our creator gave us! Our workers have been torn from their assigned homes and put in these monstrous blocks, where they must mingle daily with the scum of the selumari race. And so, our established values decay.

"But I say to you, we must return to the old ways! As we did in better times, we must now once more honor the roles and stations that our creator assigned to us. Respect class compliance, my friends! if we do not, we shall remain dishonored in selumari shackles. But if we work our assigned tasks, respecting those who guide us, we will work efficiently and combine our various strengths to snap Emmirian bonds!"

Fohlin heard some appreciative hissing from the elders and merchants, but those of lower class stood in angry silence. Then one worker, pale red—almost pink—contorted his weathered face in a snarl. "Coming into our homes, talking class compliance! It's easy for you, with the nice life of a priest, to duck punishment from the blues. But we're in it. If we don't obey them, we're on the work gangs!"

Another, an emaciated woman with skin so red she was almost black, waved a knife. "Who wants to go back down in those black tunnels where we couldn't even breathe? Go away!"

Others nodded, and someone shoved an elder onto the road. A purple-robed merchant pulled a gleaming knife from beneath his robes and slashed at the attacker. Soon knives and swords showed everywhere in the crowd.

Fohlin felt anger sweep across the mob. Frightened, he slipped around the corner. He ran with heavy steps down an unlighted crossroad. As he went, the morehl's whispered cries and sword clashes grew fainter.

A few hundred paces away, on an unlit road, Fohlin stopped. Just then, a bright orange light zipped around the bend, veered straight toward him, and stopped abruptly a hand-span from his nose. "Freeee mee!" it whined, bobbing up and down.

Fohlin had seen too many wonders already tonight, so he tried to move on. But the light, a small sphere, zipped around Fohlin's head and floated before his nose again. Fohlin grew exasperated. "I don't know what you are, and I am preoccupied. Please leave me alone."

The glowing sphere zipped around Fohlin's head three times before he could manage to blink. "Freeee mee or I shall killll you!"

With fresh interest, Fohlin examined the sphere. Inside, through a haze, he glimpsed a curling, wormlike creature. It was black and seemed to develop tiny scales even as he watched.

"Who are you?" he asked. "What must I do to free you?"

"Mooore pistollls!" The light swirling within the sphere turned briefly purple. That tiny figure—a worm? No. It reminded Fohlin of something he had seen. Recently… with Orric… That was it!

Hwarrm's huge, sinuous body on Karakto's slope. Here was the same head, scales, talons, jaws—all in miniature. How remarkable, almost like—

Suddenly Fohlin understood. A shock of terror froze his heart, and he broke into a run. He did not know where he fled.

He knew only that he must get away—away from Hwarrm, greatest dragon in their region of this world.

Thunder cracked, the ground shook, and a jagged spear of lightning lanced the earth. The midnight sky flashed blindingly as something huge exploded within the Daybringer arc. Fohlin shielded his eyes and kept running.

A roar filled the sky as a huge meteor, the size of the Hall of Justice, fell toward the houses on Karakto's slope. As it slammed down, the earth shook again. Fohlin lost his footing and fell. He scraped his cheek against the gravel. Struggling to rise, he saw purple flames consuming an entire row of residences. Wind from the fire howled down the narrow roads. He heard the loud cries of trapped selumari children, and the panicked Calls of Emmirian horns outside the crater.

Fohlin looked around. The light had vanished. He lurched into a run—this time to find Cennard, who would know about the Crafts, and possibly about Hwarrm. Cennard had told him that the last place he intended to go was the integrity shrine, once the honor shrine before the selumari renamed it. Fohlin's legs pumped as he pushed himself up the crater slope.

The first of the diligence patrols crested the rim, entering the crater's western notch while Fohlin climbed toward the shrine. There on Karakto's heights, fires raged across the city. Figures clashed amid the destruction, their swords and knives glinting in the light. Dozens, then hundreds of diligencers swarmed into the area, some breaking up fights and some striking down morehl with swords and clubs. Then smoke rose to eclipse the view.

Fohlin looked away. *He will destroy us all,* he thought. *No, no—he knows what he is doing. He has training, refinement…*

In time, the count puffed up the last few steps of his climb to the amphitheater. On the oval stage stood Cennard, silhouetted against the Daybringer comets, the full moon, and the black smoke from below. Noble morehl had gathered in the front rows, but the shrine was otherwise empty. The aristocrats sat in utter silence, staring up into the sky.

Cennard wore an expression of severity and fanaticism. His eyes were wide, his face flushed, and his final, whispered word carried perfectly through the amphitheater: "… and it was here that we once staged our sacred plays. Now they stage raucous betting contests!"

As he left the stage and walked over to the nobles, they rose from their seats, nodded to him, and after a brief exchange, climbed the stairs and silently left the amphitheater, their faces blank.

Alone with Cennard, Fohlin descended the stairs.

Before he could speak, Cennard whispered, "On your life, you will not to reveal this to anyone else, Count Fohlin. I intend to use the Ring of Stars to summon a drake, who will destroy the accursed selumari."

Fohlin stared in shock. He had never seen a living dragon, but he had seen the ruin Hwarrm had left behind. In the final battle, he had laid waste to Karakto. The earth-wyrm had destroyed whole districts with whirlwinds from his beating wings. Thousands of selumari and morehl had died, crushed by a flick of his tail or turned to statues by his petrifying breath. A selumari army had killed Hwarrm—supposedly—using a talisman. But Hwarrm still existed, and here was Cennard talking of dragons. Dreadful! Fohlin said carefully, "Which dragon?"

Cennard raised his eyebrows. "I have no notion. They are eternal and most live now in a distant realm after being slain here in Esfah. I work the Wyrmcraft, and it calls whichever one is—"

"Only the empress knew Wyrmcraft," Fohlin replied. He rememberd her as a paranoid ruler who limited knowledge to serve her own position and assuage her own fears. "How did you learn?"

"I happened upon a useful informant, and then expanded upon what it—what that informant told me, using research in the elder archives."

No doubt Cennard's informant began its conversation with *Freeee meee*; he doubted the old Imperium would have deposited such powerful information where notoriously power-mad priests could access it. "But can you control a drake?"

"I need not. I have deduced a way to destroy it, once it has destroyed the invaders. A fascinating field, Wyrmcraft. Hardly so bad as its reputation would imply. It turns out that the mortality faces and our flintlock rituals have been making more than just these magnificent weapons."

Fohlin nodded along. Any person with a finger could use a normal flintlock, but Karakto's mystic forges made slug throwers that penetrated armor better than any magic arrow, and could hit with the force of the cursed bullets that originally flowed from the Obsidian Grotto four centuries ago—only these amazing weapons did not require bullets crafted with starmetal cores—they only require a weapon to be attuned to a user and to magic. *Any* bullet became a *cursed* bullet from these guns.

Cennard continued. "The flintlocks draw magic from a power source—the users who are attuned to Firiel, our fire goddess. But they also draw it from the forges themselves, which is why the selumari have been able to use them: the forges were given to us an eon ago by the gremmlobahnd and act as a sort of battery, and all that power is stored up for us to use… but the power diminishes over time—strongest closest to their creation, the power wanes as it is used up.

Fohlin did not know much about batteries, though he had seen a clockwork item or two brought out during a festival or at a bazaar. That Karakto's flintlocks operated like those items once a circuit was complete made some sense to him, but he still did not follow the logic connecting dragons to firearms.

"The more flintlocks we make, the more magic we can tap into. More flintlocks means it is easier for me to summon the drake!"

Fohlin suddenly understood. "You wanted to steal the selumari flintlocks so they would create more!" He struggled to contain his fear. To think, he had been party to this madness! "But why do you destroy this shrine? This is where flintlocks are made."

Cennard shrugged. "This shrine, that shrine—no great matter. And I want to use this one to make a specific point. Let us leave, so that I may continue my work."

If I am to mention Hwarrm, Fohlin thought, *it must be now.* He pictured the huge body on the seaward slope. That monster, returning—this madman, conjuring him…

Fohlin said nothing. He followed Cennard up the stairs and down the trail into the crater.

A smoky wind dipped across the rock, ruffling stunted brush and whistling past narrow outcrops. Last watch was beginning, the moon had disappeared, and the comets shone brilliantly above the western rim. About two thousand paces from the amphitheater, Fohlin and Cennard met with the nobles who had left earlier. They stood silently by an outcrop of huge granite boulders.

Cennard told them, "Take cover behind these rocks, friends, and lend me your faith in our new beginning!" Fohlin and the others took shelter, as Cennard stepped out onto the trail and faced the amphitheater. He raised his arms to the sky and chanted, swaying slightly every few syllables.

Fohlin braced himself against the granite, ready for the impact. Nothing happened.

After a few moments, the nobles crept out from behind the rock, again neither surprised nor disappointed. They walked toward the city fires below, untroubled by smoke. Fohlin turned to Cennard, whose expression remained ecstatic, crazed. The elder stood immobile, scarred arms lifted to the sky.

He's failed, Fohlin thought joyously. *He's failed, and the nobles have abandoned him, thank the Destroyer.*

A deep rumble shook the crater. Fohlin suddenly felt very cold. From the comets came an explosion like a bursting sun, and light whitened every crevice on the eastern rim. High above them, a meteor tumbled gracefully away from the largest Daybringer.

Fohlin stood transfixed. *It is over,* he thought. *We are dead now.*

An oblong ball of molten yellow flame dropped toward the city. It gathered speed, heralded by a deafening roar. Even at a distance, the ball looked larger than a building. Rapidly it multiplied to gargantuan size. Hurricane winds rose as it rushed toward the crater. Flames dropped like arrows and set brush afire.

Fohlin threw himself to the ground, protecting his eyes as sand lashed him. He heard the clatter of a rock slide. His heart raced.

Cennard still stood like a madman, arms uplifted, wind whipping his robes, fire raining down on all sides.

The meteor hit with a deafening clap, a scorching light, and dust enough to bury his estate. After long, terrible moments, the light waned and a roar grew. Fohlin looked up. The immense amphitheater and shrine began to crumble. An avalanche of pulverized rock, enough to destroy an army, tumbled down the basalt cliff. It left behind a gaping hole along the northern ridge, through which Fohlin could glimpse the placid Narcea River.

The integrity shrine was gone.

As if in response, the mountain rumbled one last time and fell still.

The wind carried dust and caustic gases, deadly to any but a morehl. It raced toward Fohlin and Cennard, flattening the brush across the crater and dislodging rocks. Fohlin crawled across the trail to find cover behind the granite boulders.

When the explosive wind had passed, Cennard stood untouched. Rocks were scattered around the elder, but a circular patch at his feet was entirely clear. Without a glance at Fohlin, he said calmly, "Go. Retrieve the stone."

Fohlin gulped. He wanted to refuse, and for a dizzy moment he thought to rush the priest and beat his brains out with a rock. But—but—He recovered his wits and went toward the mountain of smoking rubble.

Cennard smiled, his black eyes glinting strangely in the gem's light. He took the tiny diamond and held it with exquisite care between thumb and forefinger. "We are victorious, my friend."

"Victorious," Fohlin repeated.

"Now we must go to ground while I craft the ring. You have set up a refuge? Food, water? Told no one?"

Fohlin nodded.

"Good. Let us meet at our rendezvous at first watch, three days hence. Move with caution, but know that our goals are within reach. Remember, Fohlin, we live in perfect trust of one another. Now we share two secrets."

By separate paths, the two stole away, shadows passing unnoticed in the tumultuous night.

15

My plans go wrong. The spirits of Nature oppose me. Everyone opposes me. But I'll not break. These little minds cannot break me. Look at them: every variety of vandal, thief, rebel, and lunatic!

From her high seat over the silent crowd in the Hall of Justice, Calantha inspected the long line of criminals. She pictured them as insects—whole families of bugs, beetles, centipedes, worms, grubs.

And she? She stood over them in judgment like a tall, hungry bird.

Orric feared the worst. From the back of the court, among a large crowd of spectators, he watched his mother sag in her seat, glare at each looter in turn, and dip repeatedly into her locket for sana paste. Outwardly, she looked fit in her white gown of judgment. Only Orric knew she had not slept for three days.

Two nights back, when Burgard's mammoth riders had arrived, she had spent the night planning defenses against invasion. Then last night, as she was heading to bed exhausted, calamity struck the crater. Through the night and all morning, Calantha led efforts to quench fires, quarter the homeless, bury hundreds of victims in mass graves, assess damage—and apprehend looters. Many weeks of rebuilding lay ahead, but Calantha had put judgment ahead of such tasks.

Orric wanted to believe that she simply needed more workers on the labor gangs. Secretly he knew she sought to release her anger—anger at herself, for moving the diligence patrols out of the crater. They had stood idle, in sight of the Gundakhor mammoth riders, on the pretext of stopping a goblin attack that never came. Meanwhile, in the crater, the supposedly less dangerous elders and nobles somehow managed to destroy most of the city. Of course Calantha would be angry. Orric himself was furious!

But they could not bring the culprits to justice. Fohlin, Cennard, the lesser priests, and many nobles—all had vanished into the deep tunnels, or somewhere. Frustrated, Calantha was more than ready to sentence mere looters.

Morehl and selumari thronged the chamber in equal numbers. Sensing the crowd's range of moods, Orric saw quickly that the two races here were not red and blue, but rich and poor.

One selumari worker, who had stolen coins from bodies, received a week on the work gangs, rebuilding collapsed dwellings. The poor selumari and lower-class morehl whose homes had been destroyed nodded in approval. But Orric overheard the man's Burgardan master grumble, "And how am I to make up his lost work in my gardens?"

Next the demarch judged a young morehl noble who, infected by last night's frenzy, had assaulted a diligence patroller. "What have you to say for yourself, Count Dakiloth?" Calantha asked the youth.

He stared fiercely and spoke in a bitter whisper. "I would not have succumbed to the general fury had these workers been disciplined properly. Their minds run free like wild hounds. Nothing you do can match the indignity I have already suffered."

"For Count Dakiloth," Calantha said blandly, "three weeks digging privies for the workers, followed by half a year in the mines."

As the bailiff noted the harsh punishment, a cheer rose at the back: shouts from poor selumari, delighted hisses from low-class morehl. But among the Burgardans, Orric heard disbelieving whispers. One lavishly dressed selumari stepped forth from the crowd. "I implore the demarch to reconsider!" the old woman said.

Calantha's tone seemed to say, I expected as much. "Lady Sehlisiral, you have a comment for the court?"

"Is this punishment not extreme? The young man comes of a noble morehl family. To thrust him into a far different setting, where training and stature count for nothing, does him terrible hurt. And when the workers see a noble reduced to such straits, it produces in them worry for their own lots. The danger, then—"

Calantha leaned forward in her seat. "Lady Sehlisiral."

"Yes?"

"Refrain from further outbursts, or I shall find you in contempt and set you to digging privies beside Count Dakiloth."

Laughter came from half the audience, shocked silence from the other half. Lady Sehlisiral, her eyes bulging, turned and bustled out of court. Other Burgardans and morehl nobles followed, all with somber backward looks at Calantha.

Orric only then noticed Lady Jandith standing near him along the rear wall. She was staring at the peasants and free folk, her eyes lit with alarm, even horror.

He sidled up to her and indicated the laughing lower-class morehl. "Someone recently told me," he whispered to her, "the morehl are unacquainted with the democratic process. If granted suffrage, would they look for guidance to those they trust?"

Jandith assumed an expression of wounded resentment. "The old morehl warrior class managed the lower classes with unspeakable cruelty. We treat them far better. If they only reflected on the change, they would see how much they owe us."

Orric glanced at the remaining Burgardans, who carefully looked away from the taunting peasants. The rich had no interest whatever in the poor, he realized, except to milk them of all possible effort. To them, the poor were a separate species. Orric supposed it was an improvement. "In any case," he told Jandith, "it seems you founded your Balloter movement on a mistaken assumption. The wealthy class has less influence on the lower classes than you thought."

Cut of pure mischief he hoped to ruffle her composure. She gave him a sly smile. "There are endless paths to influence," she whispered. "To change the subject entirely, Lord Burgard and I wish to meet with you. At sunset, come to the tall yellow tent in the festival encampment. Do not bring your mother."

"How conspiratorial," Orric began. He meant to ask details, but a tense silence from the court audience distracted him.

When he looked back, Jandith had left by the back door. Now before the demarch stood a morehl man, a shark-eyed fellow with very short hair spikes and a flat nose. The bailiff intoned, "Shaulf, a freedman, apprehended by diligence patrol eighty-seven at midnight last night, in the act of looting broken pottery from a merchant's tent in Aboveground Market."

Frowning, Calantha peered at the morehl. She said to the bailiff, "This one looks familiar. Prior offenses?"

"The disaster has left our records in disarray, demarch."

Calantha said in exasperation, "Freedman Shaulf, why would you steal broken pottery?"

Shaulf's tone was distracted. "No other kind was available."

The demarch shouted, "But why did you want it?"

"I don't remember. It seemed the thing to do."

"The thing to do! Of course! When the city falls into chaos, with death and destruction on all sides, what response could suit us better than ransacking the debris and stealing garbage? Tell me, Freedman Shaulf, do you still think that 'the thing to do?' "

Shaulf looked back and forth aimlessly. "Right and wrong depend on the situation. Since I am no longer in that situation, the question is nonsense."

Calantha leapt to her feet. "Do you understand that I am passing sentence on you?" She staggered, then grasped the arm of her chair. "If you feel no remorse, are you so dense that you cannot make even a show of it?"

Shaulf spoke mildly. "Since receiving an education, I've considered this. I believe deception is unproductive and remorse pointless."

"Pointless!" Calantha stumbled down one step toward Shaulf. As she did so, her squad of diligence bodyguards emerged from behind the dais and moved with her, three on each side.

"At the back of the room, Orric began to shoulder his way forward through the crowd.

The demarch repeated, "Pointless! When you prowl among heaps of bodies, even bodies of children, thinking only of the coins you can rummage from corpses, you are no more than an animal. Some scavenging brute. Shall I punish you as I would punish a remorseless animal, Shaulf?"

Haltingly she walked down the wide steps, with the guards keeping pace.

"Can punishment influence your educated decision, Shaulf? What if I had your hands cut off, as the old empress would have? Would you find remorse productive then?"

She reached Shaulf just as Orric pushed past the front of the crowd. Vaulting the low wooden railing, he ran past the bailiff, who made no move.

Calantha was shouting again. "Shall I have your arms and legs severed, Shaulf? And your eyes and tongue burned out, and your eardrums, so that you live a long life in darkness and quiet? Would that give fair cause for remorse?"

Dead silence had fallen. Shaulf was staring blankly—the "morehl stare" that Emmirians found infuriating. Looking back at the audience, Orric noticed the same stare on almost every face, morehl and selumari alike—the safest expression when life hung in the balance. Or was it?

Calantha screamed, "Do you not care? Does your life mean so little? Does no one else here value life?"

Orric knew just how to distract his mother. He would bring up the conspiracy between Fohlin and Cennard to steal the flintlocks. In the continual crises of the last two days, he had not wanted to worry her still more, but now—He whispered, "Mother, I have urgent news."

She looked not at him but through him. "Leave me alone! Guards, remove him!"

The bodyguards hesitated, looking uncertainly from Calantha to Orric. The captain said, "Demarch, this is... Does the demarch wish us to remove her son?"

"Mother, please. It concerns the flintlocks."

Calantha shoved him away, and almost fell. "Must I give my orders twice? Take him out of here!"

In her wild eyes, Orric saw no one he knew, only a stranger. He felt a shock of insight: He had brought Calantha down, but he could not bring her back up. Having pushed a boulder down a slope, he could not persuade it back uphill.

The diligence guards gingerly took his arms. Angered, he pulled free, but retreated a few steps to one side.

Calantha said coldly, "Captain. I want this prisoner to kneel."

The guard-captain, a tall, scarred veteran in breastplate, helm, and pale green tunic, expertly wrestled Shaulf onto his knees.

"Captain, shoot this prisoner." She was looking straight down at Shaulf, perhaps hoping for some—any—reaction. If so, the morehl disappointed her.

Again the captain hesitated. Then he said forcefully, "As the demarch commands! Shall the scribes enter in the court record the demarch's formal sentence of execution?"

Orric understood the captain's delicate ploy. The law required a death sentence to be carried out at dawn, by the bay.

That would give Calantha most of a day to change her mind.

But the officer's question was dangerously close to insolence. Calantha glared at him. Then, with a snarl, she seized the flintlock hanging at the captain's belt and pointed it at Shaulf's throat. She pulled the trigger.

The pistol did not fire. It was not attuned to Calantha, nor was any flintlock in Karakto. Orric drew a long breath.

Enraged, Calantha gripped the pistol by its iron barrel and swung the hardwood handle at Shaulf's left temple. The morehl fell and lay still. Steam rose from the wound.

"Will that teach you?" Calantha shouted over him. "Do you feel sorry now?"

"Demarch," the captain said quietly. "He is dead."

She stared at the body. The morehl stared back, unseeing. Backing away with faltering steps, Calantha dropped the pistol. In the silence, the clatter of its fall was deafening.

She looked around as if waking in a strange place. "Where—?" She looked around with increasing desperation.

"Where is it? Wh-What happened to it?"

Orric stepped forward. "Mother. We should go home."

"Orric!" She started as if only now recognizing him. For long moments, she looked around blindly. Then she fell into his arms and began to cry. "It's gone, it's gone!"

He had no idea what she meant. So much was gone now, gone beyond recovery.

As the spring sun fell into the western sea, Orric and a squad of diligencers walked from Windhome down toward the bay. They turned right and climbed the slope over Hwarrm's body, then descended the steep trail to the Cropsinger Festival grounds.

Orric usually talked casually with the guards. This evening, he walked apart, preoccupied. He had not told Calantha about Cennard and Fohlin, for fear of provoking more brutality. His mother was an utter loss, and it was his own fault. He had broken her, disproved her Quietude philosophy, and corrupted her compassion and faith into callous suspicion.

What was he to believe? What path should he follow? This path, at any rate, led around the northwest curve of the volcano to a clear view of the flatland to the north, the festival site. Of course, the disaster last night had ruined hopes for tomorrow's festival, but without the fair, the Gundakhor cavalry would have no plausible excuse to remain so close to the pistols.

Orric turned at a bend in the trail. There in the sunset, lit by rays of gold, stretched a long line of festival tents. vagha and humans bustled among them like bees in a hive. They carted goods and food of all kinds. Well-dressed selumari onlookers surrounded the mammoths and their riders.

Orric stared, perplexed. "Captain!"

"Yes, sir?" said the diligence guard behind him.

"Did the demarch remember to formally cancel the festival?"

The guards conferred. "No one remembers her doing so, sir. She has been quite busy."

Orric stamped on the dirt trail. "I see! So in the absence of a proclamation, people decide to attend the fair. Never mind that the crater still stinks with unburied bodies!"

The captain looked down on the crowds. "The humans and the vagha are from outlying areas, sir. The selumari look to be from the shoreline district. No damage there."

Orric cursed. To them, the poor were a separate species, he thought.

In the spacious yellow tent that smelled of mammoth, Orric met with Lord Burgard and Jandith. Burgard wore the yellow uniform of Gundakhor's army, with his own symbol— three seven-pointed stars of moonsilver. Jandith wore violet robes and a cloak trimmed with black fur.

Four of Orric's diligence bodyguards waited outside the open entrance, ready to sound an alert to two more stationed in relay positions up the slope. Orric, who thought of the Gundakhor camp as enemy territory, had brought the guards as a precaution. Now he felt foolish. Here, amid crowds of shouting merchants, the vagha likely did not mean to kidnap or kill him.

But they did threaten him. "I shall not waste your time," Lord Burgard said, after Orric sat on a leopard hide and declined to give up his cloak. "We have reports of your doings, young Orric. You are keeping interesting company."

Orric knew then the purpose of this meeting: blackmail. He did not bother to ask what Burgard knew, nor how the dwarf—or more likely, Jandith—had learned his secrets. "You seem to find me—interesting. Why?"

"We know you are likely to stand for the demarchy at the next election, and you may win." Burgard moved and spoke with authority, never glancing at Jandith. She sat to one side, where she looked into her wine cup as if seeking oracles.

She must have coached him well, Orric thought. "But think, Lord Burgard," he said blandly, "if the Balloter cause succeeds and the morehl gain suffrage, can you not simply command your peasants to support someone else?"

Burgard's smile held. "Should you become demarch, it is obviously in both our interests to maintain Karakto's long alliance with Gundakhor. To this end—"

"—I should promise, here and now, to provide you with all the flintlocks your armies can carry. Otherwise you'll reveal your 'interesting reports,' thereby ruining my hopes for happiness."

The ambassador assumed a mournful look. "Now, would I do such a thing? We are all friends here, Orric. I must say, you have much to learn about diplomacy."

Orric kept his composure, but he thought of his mother's account of Burgard heatedly calling for the murder of every adult in Karakto. Odd that the former warlord had become so soft-spoken, so protective of the morehl who had made him rich, and yet had also become less honorable, less likable.

Orric said, "Some aspects of diplomacy I have never mastered."

"I look forward to helping you learn, so far as I am able." Burgard looked down into his mug of fermented bendhorn milk.

"Perhaps Elder Cennard and Count Fohlin will prove equally helpful. I understand you got along well with them at Winter Spear's cavern." He fell silent.

Now I am supposed to ponder the awful consequences if they told what they know, thought Orric. He saw no awful consequences. He had intended no harm to Karakto—unlike the ambassador and his wife.

How to get rid of Burgard and Jandith? They held diplomatic immunity and commanded a formidable army.

Orric thought of trapping the two in some clear breach of the rules of embassy, such as theft.

"Lord Burgard," he said, "perhaps you knew that the goblins who raided the armory two nights back used earth magic to destroy the building?"

Burgard glanced at Jandith. Staring down into her cup, she shook her head slightly. "Why, no," said Burgard. "How remarkable."

"After we defeated them, I found the talisman they used to attract the spirits." This was untrue. Orric did not know if the goblins had used a talisman, but it sounded likely. "I kept the talisman and hid it in my bedchamber at Windhome. I tried to use it, but the thing flared in my hands and made my joints go stiff." He flexed his fingers rigidly. "Children of Fire and Death, it seems, should not meddle with spirits of earth. I'll not touch the thing again," he vowed. He glanced at Jandith, then looked levelly at Burgard. "You, though, are vagha. I suspect you could wield it to great effect."

At a furtive nod from Jandith, the dwarf said, "Perhaps." His eyes were gleaming.

Orric continued. "As I say, I won't touch it. Nor would I trust it to any courier. But—I could arrange a diversion that would let you enter and take the talisman without risk… if you promise your discretion in certain matters."

Orric thought it a fair lie, but after a glance at Jandith, Burgard only smiled. "A kind offer, but I would feel uncomfortable entering the demarch's home without permission. If we were discovered, she might misconstrue our presence. Even so, I freely guarantee my discretion in all matters, when it is in the interests of both our homelands."

Failed again, thought Orric. "I shall happily cooperate with you in kind, both in my own person and in the event I become demarch. I believe we understand each other, Lord Burgard?"

"I believe so," said the vagha amiably, though his eyes looked hard as rubies.

As Orric left the tent with his bodyguards, he looked on the many merchants and farmers readying their wares, bards staking out their spaces, and vagha crafters shaping cookery pits. He wanted to shout, "Who will buy the bodies of the poor, a thousand paces away?"

No one here cared that disaster had blighted the crater. What folly! Bitterness rose in him, and he thought about the pressures that had driven his mother to desperation.

Orric passed a Crafter who, with a wave of his hands, had just hollowed a fire pit from the earth. The man brought down his fist, and the pit erupted into bright yellow flame. In the light, Orric saw a glittering pair of wings overhead, darting toward the crater.

A sprite, he thought without interest.

When he arrived at Windhome, dismissed the bodyguards, and went to his chamber, Orric found Calantha waiting. She had ransacked the room. She stood panting amid a jumble of furniture, bedding, and clothes. The broken shards of his murex shell lay at her feet.

"Where is the talisman?"

Amazed, Orric realized the sprite had been one of his mother's spies. "I invented it. I meant to trick Burgard and Jandith into looking for it, so we could accuse them of thievery."

"Hah! You'd like me to believe that!" She looked alert and steady on her feet. He smelled no lavender, but the look in her eyes frightened him. *She murdered a man today,* he thought.

She shouted, "I suppose you created that plan with your good friends Cennard and Fohlin!"

Her tone made him angry, but he bit back a retort. "I planned to tell you about that—"

"Oh, indeed!"

"Would you allow me to finish? You had a great deal to worry about already." He told her the entire truth, adding nothing. As he talked, the story sounded ever more unlikely, less believable than his many lies. Calantha's glare did not falter. "I meant to learn more about their plans," he finished. "I—I thought letting them go for a day could do little harm."

She stared, mouth open. Orric imagined her sorting through a dozen sarcastic replies. "Please don't say it," he said. "I made a terrible mistake. But you have no reason to suspect me. Why would I wish to harm the city? Why ally with a priest?"

"I cannot imagine. Perhaps for the same reason, whatever it is, that you have lied to me for years."

He opened his mouth to answer, but could not even breathe.

Watching his every moment, she said, "I have thought a great deal about this, since this afternoon, when I ki—" Her voice caught. "When I killed that man. I asked myself how all this happened, why I changed. And always I returned to you."

"I did not lie!" he said, lying. Through long practice, he spoke with conviction. "I have alerted you to the dangers all around you." He saw her expression soften, and he continued with confidence: "If I had not warned you, you would have fallen to them a hundred times over—"

Then, very suddenly, he thought, *Why am I lying? With nine years of lies I've tested her, and she has failed—why continue? To shore up her weakening love for me?*

That idea repelled him. His love for her was still strong. To corrupt that was to corrupt his very soul.

Orric had faced a goblin gang without fear. Without fear he now told his mother, "Very well. You are right. I have lied these many years. I made you what you are, and now I am profoundly sorry for it. But though I have worked to harm the city, now I am working to heal it. It all began when—"

Her glare returned, more vicious than before. "I am placing YOU under house arrest," she said flatly. "You will not leave this room until I have made a full investigation. And give me your cloak." She reached for it.

Reflexively he jerked back. Anger burned in him. "I am not your enemy! Cennard is plotting to expel or destroy the selumari, and Burgard wants the whole city. I can—"

"Guards!"

"Will you listen to what I say?"

"Why?" she shouted back. "Guards!"

Pounding footsteps echoed in the courtyard. Orric looked around like a trapped animal, then rushed out the door just ahead of his mother's desperate grab for the cloak. A dozen guards ran at him from all directions.

"In there!" he called to them. "I'm going for help!" He ran past them and out the entrance facing the crater. Down the dark trail he ran, with the guards in belated pursuit. In a patch of jagged rocks, he ducked down a volcanic shaft, eluding them. Then he headed at full speed down into the tunnels of Karakto.

He had lost any allies among the selumari, the vagha, the nobles, and the elders. Furious at the course of recent events, he gave way to the red haze of "the strange." In a deserted black tunnel, he cast aside his cloak, then beat the walls, tore at his hair, and shrieked. For a time, he lay unconscious.

When at last he woke, he saw with perfect clarity the path he must take.

16

Mountain pondered. He knew already that the sparks living within him were of two races, blue and red. The blue ones partook of the essence of air and water. These sparks were alien to Mountain, but he accepted them as stewards of Nature. The red sparks shared his essence of fire, but carried the taint of Death, the despised Corruptor. They had brought down sky fire two nights ago, the meteors that struck and wounded him.

He still felt the pain.

But there were other divisions. The blue race had "poor" sparks that lived in his crater, and "Burgardans" that lived on shore at his base. The red had upper classes that lived deep within him, and lower classes, the "Balloters" that occupied the crater with the poor blue ones. The Burgardan sparks had somehow gained control of all the poor sparks.

Slowly he sorted them out. The Burgardans wished to keep matters as they were and make more weapons. The upper red classes wished to destroy the blue sparks and, perhaps, everything. The poor sparks of both colors simply tried to survive.

Interesting, this "poor" and "rich." Mountain did not quite grasp the idea of money, though he knew the Corruptor had instilled the idea in its red servants. Wealth conferred some invisible power, like—what was that term the sparks used?— "magic."

The river Narcea flowed into the ocean at a wide, muddy mouth not far north of the volcano. There, twin-tailed stiltwings waded amid hummocks of grass, rushes, and spleenworts. Frogs in rainbow colors perched on rocks and sang a peeping chorus.

Between this marsh and the volcano ran a narrow strip of grassy flatland. Here stood a hundred open-air tents of canvas or hide, which flapped in the light afternoon breeze. The festival tents offered crafts created over the winter by cropsingers, farmers whose homesteads dotted the countryside. Merchants and artisans sold their goods, travelers displayed oddities they had collected in their wanderings, and bards performed. All catered to the only visitors at this year's festival, the Burgardans of the shoreline district.

Before this audience, the bard Hornbeam stood on a ramshackle wooden platform, squinted in the sunlight, and spoke in a slurred voice. "The great Lord Burgard, whose proud name and heroic—ah—identity are familiar to all of you fine people who have joined us here in this beautiful field on this marvelous day for this inspiring occasion, a host of the sort of folk that make this world great and—well, interesting—Pardon me." He downed a deep swallow from his mug. "May I congratulate you on the excellent barley beer that you brew here?"

The crowd cheered.

"As I was saying, Lord Burgard invited me to tell you a bit about the impressive mounts of the elite cavalry of Gundakhor. Though the mammoth's legendary prowess in combat is, of course, legendary, these hairy creatures have another and more lovable side seldom appreciated by those who—who seldom appreciate them. I tell you, my good friends, I have seen fully grown mammoths, as large as these sturdy creatures standing by us now, rise up on their hind legs and beg for a chunk of rock candy—"

As the crowd laughed, Lord Burgard, who stood beside the platform with Jandith, turned away in disgust. Under his breath he said, "This drunken dunce is making my cavalry look foolish!"

"It may serve a purpose," Jandith whispered. "Reduce the people's fears, then strike."

Pretending casual curiosity, the warlord glanced around for listening ears before continuing. "But we meant the riders to raise fears! Raise a threat of invasion to panic the citizens and bring our candidate to victory."

"Calantha may cancel the election. The nobles and elders—may they drown in their own blood—have done too much damage in the crater. Meanwhile, the pistols lie in our own home, guarded by a token force of sharpshooters. We shall not see a better opportunity."

He sighed. "We shall not be a worse ally."

She stared at him. "Do you doubt decisions you have long since made? There is no clearer sign of weakness."

He met her stare. "Except dangling like a puppet."

Abruptly, the Crafter's manner changed. In a wounded tone she said, "I am not your enemy, my love. Do you desire the weapons, or don't you?"

He sighed again. "Yes."

She seemed to examine him. "How good to hear. Well, let us talk more later. Now I feel like walking alone."

In the middle of his journey through the swamp, Yort came to himself within a dark wood where the straight way was lost. It was a stand of scrub poplars, their tangled branches already in full leaf. As Yort stopped, stonecrows squawked and flew away across the evening sky. He looked listlessly for the trail, then decided he was lost. With a sigh, he sat, accidentally crushing a toad.

Yort could not see the merit of vengeance, a prime virtue of his tribe at Bent Morass. He had made trouble for that red elf who killed Yort's Wife. Was he supposed to feel better? He didn't. He wanted her back, and he suffered agonies of loneliness.

Of course, he could not admit this stupidity to the other Wild Things—Murget and his three wives—though Yort knew they sensed his guilty secret. Murget himself was a mild leader, mainly because he was thick as a bendhorn ox. A couple of his wives, though, would hunt a gurk across Esfah if he so much as stepped on their toes. By Vaumb, Yort himself had held a grudge for years against Hulg, who stole his old wives in Bent Morass.

Now he could hardly remember what Hulg looked like, let alone the wives.

Yort no longer felt a passion for vengeance, or for anything else. He'd thought a lot over the years—another guilty secret—and decided that these tribal habits just kept getting him into trouble. Falling in with a gang of not-too—bright goblins—trouble. Hiring on with anyone who had coins to pay—trouble. Falling in love, big trouble. Even living years in the marsh, raising imps and doing nothing, seemed like trouble of a kind.

He needed to get back on the road. Wandering, not knowing or caring where he would go, eating whomever he met—that was the life!

"Yort! Where are you? This way, Yort!"

Murget. Wearily Yort rose and plodded toward the voice, absently firming the marshy ground with each footstep.When he found Murget and the wives, they were cavorting in a lily pond, trampling the blooms for sheer joy. "We got work, Yort!" said the elated Murget. "A red elf lady just gave us a job where you do your talking thing. She told me what you gotta say, okay? Coins and excitement, Yort!"

"Wonderful."

"—hate those guards. Cursed blues—"

Just past sunset—though the sun meant nothing down in these steaming tunnels—Balloters and others of lower class met amid the magma pools at the city's lowest reach.

"—not like the morehl guards're any better, the traitors—"

Red firelight played across domes of charred rock, and brimstone fumes rose from molten lava. The air shimmered with heat that would roast anyone but a morehl.

"—was bad under the empress and the warriors, but at least you knew what you were working for—"

The lower classes met in these chambers because the diligence guards, who were mainly selumari, didn't patrol here. Nobles and elders would never stoop to visiting.

"She'd kill us like she killed poor Shaulf!"

Peasants and free folk gathered here around flat stone outcroppings, much as nobles far overhead lounged around tables at Fohlin's feasts. They complained and argued, and the Balloters, a growing minority, whispered of revolt.

"What does that mean, 'Take over the demarchy'? Massacre them all and take back the city, I say!"

"All the blues, or all the rich classes? Can't say which is worse."

"Burn that! Death created us to kill blues and dwarves, not each other."

"Hah, Death wants us to kill everything everywhere! Why spare the nobles?"

"Well, Death put me down in the warrens with those mushrooms. Now I'm living up with the blues and cleaning the Court of Justice. Death hasn't made a protest that I've heard. It's turned us loose to do what we want."

The riot two nights before had not united the lower classes, it had only raised the pitch of their arguments. Whether the Corruptor created them without qualities of leadership, or whether they simply lacked chances to develop these qualities, no mortal could say. Whatever the reason, the peasants and free folk had no leaders. Their squabbling had gone on for years and could easily have lasted years more without result. But on this night, a slender figure climbed without ceremony atop one flat rock at the chamber's center and began to speak.

By a trick of the dome's shape, his whisper carried to every listener.

"Good greetings to you all," Orric said. The morehl nodded casually. "I bring exciting news. It has been a hard time for Karakto's workers, these last few days. Many of you have lost your homes. Most know someone sentenced to a work gang. All are doing work you hate, for a wage you can't live on, while the upper classes live well on your labor."

"Right!—Orric's got it!" Hisses of agreement answered.

Someone called, "But what will the demarch do about it? Shoot us!"

"I am not here to tell what the demarch is doing," Orric said, "but what I myself shall do for you."

"What, stage a new play?" The peasants gulped with laughter. Like so many others, they suspected that there was no magic in the play itself. The dramas merely took on the ritual form and performed what rite a priest would have otherwise done in its stead.

"I'll lead you into a new era in our city's history. For years, I've held my secret close, waiting. But in this time of crisis, I can wait no longer. You are good people, undeserving of the fate the wealthy folk of the shoreline district are preparing for you."

"What fate, Orric?—What secret?—Are you standing for demarch?"

"I am at last assuming my rightful position. I come to you as the only surviving heir to the late empress of Karakto, your new emperor!"

In the super-heated air, there was silence.

"I have long known of my true parentage. In my childhood, a servant of the empress, last survivor of the imperial household—a peasant woman, no different from yourselves—appeared to me in the night. She told me of my heritage, then vanished." Orric had had all day to invent the story. After much thought he had aimed for simplicity. In his mother's service he had learned that people can believe any lie, if it is large and simple.

"For a long time, I have worked in secret for the good of the city. But I have seen the rich take, and take, and take-stealing food from your mouths! Now they plan an even greater offense against you, using the weapons you have made for them. Now I must reveal my true self. I show you the way to power over those who have had power over you!"

He talked on. One by one, then in groups, as if by some silent magic, they knelt.

"So, after I talked with you three nights back, my lord, I spied on the demarch's son. I learned much of interest to the forces of Gundakhor." Inside the vagha tent, Yort and Murget stood before the dwarf warlord. Four vagha sentries stood guard. Yort struggled to sound interested. He had another batch of lies to tell, and these were not even his!

Yort's main interest lay in whether Murget would botch everything. The big thug looked uneasy, possibly because the vagha guards had taken his weapons. Yort had tried to persuade him not to come along, but Murget, saying "I'm leader!" After eight times, he insisted. He hoped to see their red elf employer again. Murget thought she looked "tasty."

She was not here, and that suited Yort. With a liar's gift for spotting liars, he could tell she was trouble.

Burgard asked, "What did you find about Orric?"

"Last night, he met with a selumari scout patrol, just in from the southlands. They said an army of Gundakhor is camped half a day's march south of here, two companies of footman and two of crossbows, preparing to invade Karakto."

The dwarf kept a diplomatic composure. "How did Orric take this unproven allegation?"

"He said to them, 'Tell this to no one. I shall report to the demarch myself.' But I followed him, and he never went to his mother."

Burgard's expression did not change, but Yort noticed that his fist clenched tight. Long ago, Yort had seen this gesture at Mount Hagrond—it meant triumph.

Murget picked this moment to speak up. "I saw him too! He came down here to the festival and drank a lot of ale!"

Yort avoided screaming, but he could not stifle a sigh.

Burgard scowled. "It is widely known that Orric does not drink."

"What my colleague has mistaken for ale was actually leastleaf herbal, sold in the third tent down from this one, on the left, a concoction said to relieve anxiety, even for morehl. Delicious. Murget, would you go and get the warlord a cup?"

Murget crossed his arms. "I don't get tea. I'm leader."

Yort shrugged and smiled at Burgard, as if to say, 'we must tolerate these trogs' churlish ways. "Well, to continue. The demarch's son—after a brief trip to the tea tent—met with some lower-class morehl who had an unclean and wayward look. I crept up behind the tent where they met, and I heard every word."

"I did too!" Murget thrust out his jaw, as though willing to fight anyone who denied it. "I was there, because—"

"Because he is leader." Yort tried to smile. "My leader will certainly vouch for what I tell you now." Good thing, too, for a sillier story I have never told. Curse that red woman for the poor job she shoved on me! "It seems the demarch intends to destroy the flintlocks in your embassy."

Burgard sat up in surprise. "Destroy them? Why?"

Yort aimed for a tone of sinister conviction. "To keep you from getting them."

"Anybody could guess that!" Murget added.

"Death take me," said Burgard hollowly. "I cannot believe she has descended to such madness. But then again—"

Seeing the ambassador seize on this idiotic lie, Yort thought the demarch must have changed greatly since the Wild Things saw her, many years back. Dwarves invading, fireballs falling from the sky, rulers destroying their own armories,

Yort's Wife dead for the sake of a few pistols… The whole world was going mad.

"I cannot believe it," Burgard repeated. "What more did they say? When was this supposed to happen?"

Yort started to embroider on the lie, but before he could open his snout, Murget said, "It's tonight! Isn't it, Yort? That's right, they're doing it tonight, and they'll burn down the house too."

Yort suddenly felt tired and depressed. Bowing to Burgard, he headed for the tent door. "My apologies for wasting your time, my lord."

Murget stared after him. "Wait, Yort! Where are you going?"

"I resign."

"You can't resign, I tell you when you can resign!"

Yort walked out of the tent. Behind him, Murget called, "Yort! I'm the leader, and I'm telling you to come back and make up more things!"

"Sentries! Get this dim-witted trog out of here. Chase them both off the grounds."

"Yort, I'll kill you! Here, you, give me my axe!"

"Look out, sir!—Get him!—Ungh!—Get the axe, get the aahnnnh!—Watch out, he's—Yaaaaah!—Got him!"

Walking into the swamp, Yort felt a deadening weight rise from his hunched shoulders. He stared up at the Daybringers in the night sky. How free they looked!

"Get after the other one, you dolts!—Yes, sir—I saw him go this way—There he is!"

Breathing deeply of the cool air, Yort hopped across a stand of sedge grass into a boggy pool. The earth firmed to support him, and he jogged lightly across the marsh. Behind him, vagha splashed into the water, stumbled, and sank in knee-deep. Only their curses followed him into the darkness.

With Murget dead, Yort was the last male left in the gang. When he returned to the huts, just west of here, he would be leader, with three wives and two hundred children. Yort considered this for the space of two heartbeats, then ran straight east. If he could not find Bent Morass, he would find something, somewhere—he hoped. He splashed across the marshes, made a silent vow never again to eat another fish, and disappeared into a thatch of grass.

So ended the Wild Things.

By coincidence, the story Yort told to Burgard, a story invented from thin air by Jandith, happened to be true in one respect. Though Calantha did not mean to destroy the flintlocks, Orric did.

In the caverns beneath Karakto, a hiss rose from the lowest tunnels. It was the sound of morehl voices, many and united. The chant mounted just ahead of the marching mob that made it: some four hundred lower-class men and women, and more gathering every moment. Born decades ago from a shoal of lava, they only now marched with a fire in their hearts.

The fuel of that fire had been gathered and stacked during thirty years of oppression, of resignation to the servile existence the Corruptor had decreed for them. They had worked away their lives without hope or imagination. Yet the fuel of their resentment was being stockpiled. Though they themselves did not know it—the fuel waited only for a spark. Now he had arrived. He marched in their vanguard.

The chant moved through the seaward tunnels, toward the shore: "Orric! Orric!"

Orric was leading them to an obscure side tunnel that a diligence patrol had discovered years ago. Not a natural passage, it led from the crater through the volcano's western shield. Calantha had examined its rough-hewn walls and guessed that, in all likelihood, the late empress had ordered the tunnel dug before the war, and then probably killed all the workers who excavated it.

The empress's passage connected with a natural steam vent beyond the shield. The vent climbed steeply from unknown depths to open in a rock spur near shore. When told of the tunnel's destination, Calantha had smiled and said, "Well, we must inform Lord Burgard of this—someday." Years passed, but she never did tell Burgard that only a thin rock wall separated the vent from the lowest subcellar of his embassy, Prosperhome.

When Calantha moved the flintlocks three nights past, she ordered the tunnel blocked at the earliest opportunity. Orric had checked the tunnel and found that the guards had set up only a thin barricade, easily destroyed by rudimentary Firecraft.

The meteor strikes had drawn away every spare soldier, and now Prosperhome held a token force of sharpshooters—the survivors of Winter's Spear cavern.

The way lay clear for destruction of the flintlocks.

To Orric, the plan showed brilliance. In a stroke, he was alienating the Balloters from the Burgardans who hoped to control their votes, and was also removing the main reason that Gundakhor would invade Karakto. The same stroke damaged the power of Elder Cennard and the other priests by resurrecting the imperial line. The destruction of the weapons did not leave the city more vulnerable, for no enemy threatened—save Emmiria's onetime ally, Gundakhor.

Of course, the vandalism would make further trouble for his mother, but she would be out of office soon anyway, and not a moment too soon.

When the mob passed any tunnel, the chant grew louder as new morehl joined. Even merchants and artisans fell in with them.

"Orric! Orric!"

Orric had no more ambition to rule as emperor than as demarch. But he could take power temporarily, then appoint some new "heir" more qualified and interested in ruling. With these people behind him, he saw at last a chance to remedy the ills he had brought to Karakto. He could reshape the world, assert his will.

The chant lifted his spirits ever higher. "Orric! Orric!" He raised a fist, spurring them on. Spurring on his people!

In the scorched rock tunnels of Karakto, the fire began to burn.

17

Mountain found it hard to track the sparks as they swarmed about his base and, soon thereafter, within his crater. Red and blue intermingled and flowed through the city, a river of people.

Not long ago they had been individuals—a washerwoman scolding her son for laziness, a merchant weighing opportunities, elders debating points of doctrine. The mob had swallowed them all. No individuals remained for they had no choices. Did the washerwoman feel caught up in the mania? Did the merchant get swept unwillingly along in fear and anguish? No matter. They were gnats in a swarm. They could only move with the crowd or be trampled, attack or witness attacks, plunder or destroy.

Consciously or not, each had decided to join the mob—and after that, no decisions mattered.

They crowded at the end of the steam vent, where a wall of stones blocked their path. As Orric examined the wall, his followers ceased chanting. He sensed them slipping out of mob mind and into individual thoughts again. It was a welcome turn for Orric, who had battled to stay free of the hypnotic fury.

"We can break through, Your Majesty," said one worker, his eyes clearing as his own thoughts returned. "But it will take hours. They will hear us and prepare."

"It will take mere moments," Orric assured him. "Stand back."

He knew his mother's thinking. This wall would be sturdy, yes, but she would have installed some means by which she could bypass it, should she need to get into Prosperhome swiftly.

He found it on the topmost row of stones: a carved sigil of the vagha. To his touch, it pulsed with their Earthcraft. "I'll wager Hornbeam did this in one of his sober moments," he said to himself. Then, to the others, he commanded, "When it opens, spread out in all directions. When you find selumari guards, you have found the armory. Remember: Spare the guards! And speak my name, so that all will know to join you."

Their voices rose in agreement. He placed his hand on the sigil again, and spoke the word he guessed would enact the spell: "Calantha."

The stone wall sagged, becoming almost liquid. A hole shaped like the Earthcraft sigil appeared and widened, like a firebrand burning through a parchment. It gave off no heat. Beyond lay a round-topped corridor like an empty catacombs, cut and stone-faced in the manner of the dwarves.

"Now," said Orric, "we—"

The voices of the morehl rose in a united roar and they spilled through into the corridor, pushing Orric with them. He found himself flat against the corridor wall, pressed by the passage of bodies. Again he felt the tug of their single purpose. He had to concentrate, lest he become part of it.

He heard the call ahead: "Orric, Orric!" He ran toward the vanguard, shoving past men and women massed ahead of him.

Cracking bursts sounded—flintlocks! "Spare the guards!" he called again, but his whisper was lost in the chant.

The corridor ahead angled sharply right, and morehl there were retreating. Orric saw a woman struck from behind by a particle. Her back exploded into fire, the elemental flame that could burn even the morehl. She fell shrieking, her garment and hair in flames, and the air filled with a terrible smell.

"Sharpshooters, Your Majesty," said a morehl man at the corner as Orric reached it. "They're firing from behind a table, up ahead."

"How many?"

"Four or six. Eight, maybe. We can win!"

Orric peeked quickly around the corner. The guards had turned up what looked like a large dining table and barricaded themselves behind it. He glimpsed four flintlock barrels across the top, and then he ducked back.

"Hail, sharpshooters!" he cried. "I am Orric, rightful occupant of the imperial throne of Karakto, and I have come for the flintlocks."

One guard laughed. "Step forward, traitor, and take them."

"You are vastly outnumbered. If you leave now, I guarantee you safe passage out of this place. I do not want to see you die."

"I cannot say the same of you, 'Emperor.' If you come forward now, I guarantee you safe passage to the Death you serve."

"If you do not leave," Orric began, but his followers were jeering loudly. Their open-mouthed hisses sounded like the howls of an angry cat. "Rush and crush," someone said, and in an instant they were chanting it, the old battle slogan of the lower classes. All, every one of them, surged forward.

Orric held fast to the wall. Helplessly, uselessly, he cried for his subjects to fall back, but not even he could hear his words.

The chant and the crack of pistol fire deafened him. He lost his grip and was swept along into the hallway, into range of the selumari sharpshooters.

Insanely, his followers rushed into the hail of fire, slowing as their front ranks died and the next ranks crossed the treacherous dying ground. The man beside Orric screamed in ecstasy against the selumari, until fire and smoke blossomed behind his eyes.

The morehl advanced into the face of death. Moment by moment, they gained ground, oblivious to the horrible cost.

They were almost upon the barricade. Orric saw the guards exchange long looks. Then—fog. A wall of white vapor flowed like a mighty river from the guards' position, filling the air. Orric could not see more than a pace away.

The flintlocks ceased. Loudest of all now were the cries of the morehl wounded. The mob behind shoved Orric farther forward.

He felt a stir of wind, then a sheathed cutlass rushed out of the fog and slapped him hard in the face. His head rocked back, and he heard a metallic clatter passing down the hallway.

"They're gone!" he called. A buffet of air had borne the guards over their heads to safety. Orric had seen Calantha use magic this way in the past.

The morehl cheered. Orric stumbled as they pushed him forward across the smoking bodies of the dead. Suddenly he and the rest had passed the barricade.

The fog cleared. Before them stood a heavy oak door with a decorative brass lock.

"Break that down," he said, unnecessarily. The morehl were already battering at it in rage.

"They've sent up a message plume," said the cavalry captain.

Burgard spun to face the crater. No puffs of smoke floated over it—but then the shoreline district drew his attention.

There, twin bands of fog curled into the comet-lit night sky.

"Green and yellow," Burgard said. "'Under attack.' Fog-stripes, so it's a selumari signal. Who would attack a diligence patrol in the shoreline district?"

The cavalry captain trotted toward the line and whistled for his mammoth, which knelt before him. He clambered up to its neck and whistled again. Awkwardly, the beast stood up on its hind legs. The captain gazed south. "Sir, it's from Prosperhome!"

"Fire and earth, those trogs were right." Burgard ran for his own mammoth as fast as his legs would carry him. "Form up!"

He stepped onto Khazbul's extended leg, found the stirrup in the neck harness, and swung himself up. "We killed the stupid trog for nothing," he mused.

His captain smiled. "Any reason to kill trogs is a good one, sir."

"True. Faster, men. The enemy waits!"

Orric walked among the crates of flintlocks. Some were new weapons, not yet attuned to owners. Others were burned out, empty of the forces that had once fueled them, stored in the event that the city's Craftworkers might someday find a way to restore their power. He began to issue orders, but the morehl were already greedily seizing and hauling the crates.

But not many morehl. "Where are the rest? Those who went down the other corridors?"

They stopped and looked down in silence. The reaction annoyed him.

"What is it? Why are you all stopping?"

One woman said meekly, "When Your Majesty asks a question, we must stop and answer, or if we don't know, say nothing."

Orric sighed and left the chamber. The peasants got out of his way.

Burgard didn't wait for full dress formation. As soon as the slowest rider mounted, he drew his axe, pointed toward the distant plumes of color, and cried, "Charge!" He kicked his own mount into the lead, heading straight for the target, his home.

"Warlord!" His captain, behind and left, shouted for his attention. "The festival tents!" They lay dead ahead, a sprawl of brightly colored tents and merchant stalls.

Burgard shouted back, "No time for niceties. This fairground must fare for itself!"

The merchants and fair-goers heard the trumpeting and felt the rumble in the earth. There arose a cloud of dust like nothing the watchers had ever seen. The mammoths ran, trunks raised, ears flapping, treelike limbs moving with speed that belied their bulk. On they came, heedless.

A maker of wood pipes, a human bearing her infant son, stared in disbelief, waiting for some signal that the charge would turn aside. When the beasts were fifty paces away, she seized her money pouch and ran shrieking.

A dozen goblin imps, hidden at the marsh edge, watched in wide-eyed wonder as the beasts approached. When the mammoths hit the line of tents, the imps cooed in delight.

"Go, go!" Orric said, impatient.

The two morehl hurried their crate of pistols down the tunnel by which they'd arrived. Orric sighed. When he'd found them, they had been looting upstairs, and were defensive about it. "Todris and Elemar led us here, your Majesty," one said. The mob mentality. Those in front ran, and those in back followed.

Orric felt a rumbling in the earth.

The mammoths reached full speed along the shoreline road, charging heedless of travelers. One wealthy selumari and his retinue drew back against an estate wall. "Protect me!" the rich man shouted. His servants hastily tried to boost him atop the wall, but his panicked kicks pushed the servants back into the road, where they died beneath the feet of the mounts. They dragged their master with them.

Burgard frowned in distaste. He didn't care for unnecessary deaths, especially among these well-bred people, his friends.

Ahead, the road ended at the base of Prosperhorne's hill. Clearly silhouetted against the night sky were the colorful fog-plumes sent up by the selumari guards. They rose above the tall estate walls, the walls of the keep, and the rocky ridge.

A selumari diligence patrol was fleeing toward Prosperhome. At the cavalry's approach, the guards ducked down a side alley.

Burgard shook his head in confusion. His gates were intact.

No enemy had penetrated the walls. Selumari inside were signaling for help. If Calantha meant to destroy her own pistols, this made no sense.

Now he heard the crack of flintlocks within the keep. At the gate, he saw two selumari guards firing at the keep. They turned, saw the onrushing mammoths, and raised their flintlocks uncertainly. But they held their fire.

Now entirely confused, Burgard took a chance. He shouted, "We are here to help! Open the gates!"

Incredibly, the guards bent to the lock, but the gates could not swing open in time.

Grimly, Burgard raised his axe and pointed straight ahead. It was a signal: "break through." In the instant before the impact, Burgard ducked as low as he could and gripped his riding harness.

Khazbul hit the metal gates dead center. The bar holding them fast bent but held. Then two captains, one on each side, hit the gate. It flew from its hinges, spinning. Trumpeting their triumph, the mammoths charged onto Prosperhome's lawn.

Morehl warriors were everywhere. They ran across the building's roof, concealed themselves behind shrubs and trees, or danced merrily on the lawn. Selumari warriors, holding the colonnade before the front entrance, fired on the morehl.

Smoke poured out of windows on the lower stories. Burgard's cavalry, trained to perfection, spread out across the lawn, forming twin wedges and charging the morehl. As Burgard rode Khazbul to the main doors. He watched the red elves scatter.

Most ran toward the rocky ridge leading to the volcano's crater. They scampered easily up its steep slope. Out of reach of the mammoth's trunks, they jeered at the cavalry.

Burgard addressed the six selumari guards at the keep entrance. "Good work, soldiers. I assume you've kept them from the armory."

The ranking guard gave him a contemptuous look. "Thick as a dwarf… That's where they struck first!"

"We'll descend and retake it, then—"

The guard trained his pistol on the warlord. "We'll wait for selumari relief forces, thank you, and then retake it ourselves."

Burgard glared, then wheeled and formed up with the other riders.

He spoke in a low voice to his captains. "You lot, barricade the gates. Don't let in any diligence patrols.

Captain Tatan, take two riders and seize the keep entrance. The rest, with me—we'll hit the invaders from below."

The selumari guards at the front entrance saw the cavalry form into several units. Burgard led the largest group in a chant of Earthcraft. The smallest, three riders, faced the keep entrance—and charged.

"Target the leader!" The selumari opened fire on the lead mammoth. Craters formed on its skull and legs, then burst into flame. The deadly particles burrowed into the creature's flesh, and it trumpeted its agony. The mammoth burst into a tremendous ball of flame. Dying, it stumbled and fell. Its rider pitched forward onto the lawn.

The two flanking beasts crashed onto the columned porch. One grabbed a guard in its trunk and smashed him against a stone column, and then slammed another with its curving tusk. The other mammoth trampled a guard. The three surviving sharpshooters retreated into the foyer—into air fouled by smoke.

Mountain felt a stirring in the little knob on his west flank, where the sparks had built a nest. He felt his very substance stir as tiny earth spirits moved it gently aside—Only a Path. He lost interest.

Protected by a fluid bubble that floated through living stone, Burgard and his mount descended into Prosperhome Hill.

Down a little, forward, and up, and he would emerge into his own cellar. Though he could not see, he was sure of the direction, and equally sure his troops were following. Khazbul sat calmly.

Then, too soon, the bubble halted and solidified. Khazbul shifted uneasily.

Burgard frowned. Somehow he had reached an open space. He'd have to break free from the shell and attempt this earth magic anew. At his signal, Khazbul rode forward, shattering the stone shell.

Darkness, a sulphurous smell, and—eyes! Fiery, canine eyes all around! Burgard heard new shells arrive and shatter as riders broke free, then cries of alarm as the troops saw what surrounded them.

"Call again!" he shouted. He did so himself, summoning the elemental magic that would carry him through stone. The shell started to form—

With deep growls, the fire-eyed things sprang forward from all directions. The shell formed around them all.

Two landed on his mount's flanks. Burgard smelled the odor of roasting meat and heard terrifying growls. Then

Khazbul shrieked as the hellhounds tore at its flesh, ripping away fur and muscle in their stone-toothed jaws.

Burgard almost sobbed. It had been a mystery, the disappearance of the late empress's hellhound guards. Now he knew: they occupied deep places in the earth, doubtless slipping up to the occupied tunnels to make their meals. He smelled his mount's free-flowing blood and knew the hounds had found food.

The keep entrance was too low for the mammoths. They charged in anyway, smashing the wall. Three guards fired, hitting mounts and riders alike. After the second volley, both beasts collapsed, crushing the flaming bodies of their riders. An eerie silence fell.

"Stopped them," said the lieutenant. "Back to the doors."

Outside, jeering lower-class morehl were running up the spine of the ridge toward the safety of the volcano. The vagha seemed content to let them flee.

Then the surface of the lawn boiled.

Five stone eggs erupted onto the surface and immediately shattered. Each contained a mammoth, its rider— and a hellhound. Or three.

Under the bright night sky, the hounds looked rust-red, and their eyes burned. Most were tearing chunks of flesh from the mammoths' flanks. One rode precariously atop a mammoth, killing its rider even as the beast reared and shrieked.

Sensing fresh blood, the hounds spread in all directions.

Flames leapt from their throats, spraying the mammoths at the ridge. The air carried shrieks of wounded animals and the odor of burning flesh.

Two hounds raced toward the main doors and the selumari.

The guards raised their weapons, fired—Missed—The lieutenant felt the hard floor of the foyer crack against his back, felt rending and tearing pain like nothing he had ever endured before. He tried to scream but failed.

Orric and a madly grinning morehl miner moved slowly down the tunnel, burdened by a large crate full of well—packed flintlocks.

"You were right, Your Majesty," the miner said, his voice a moan of admiration. "We have the weapons. By dawn you will be Emperor."

Orric gritted his teeth.

The miner's whisper grew harsh. "We will spread out into the crater. Nothing with skin of blue or gold will survive. We will dance on their bones!"

"Just hurry."

They were the last ones out of the armory, well behind the rest. Orric had told all the crate-bearers to wait for him at the exit. But, crazed as they were…

Burgard's shell stopped. With the next rearing of the mammoth, Burgard smashed through the top of the shell and almost cracked his head against the ceiling above. He looked around at the familiar high-roofed cellar. Khazbul's forelegs came down upon the two hellhounds, and there was silence.

Finally something goes right, Burgard thought. As the sulphurous smell dissipated, Khazbul calmed down. Burgard dismounted, landed in the bloody pool of hellhound bones, and headed up the stairs.

It took him only a moment to confirm his fears. The armory was empty, stripped. He found the passageway used by the thieves. When he opened the door to the main floor, thick smoke poured out, choking him. He heard distant baying and snarling. Where were the other riders? Had they all missed? All died in the depths?

He thought of his brave troops, and the speeches he'd have to make to their husbands and wives. But he had no time for grief. Leaving Khazbul, he entered the tunnel.

When Orric and the miner emerged from the tunnel, only one person awaited them, a morehl peasant woman. Orric blinked at her. "Where are the others?"

"Gone about your work, Your Majesty! They are attuning the weapons to themselves, spreading out into the streets, and sending death in all directions! And wherever they go, they let the doomed know who leads us. Our war cry is 'Orric is Emperor!' "

Orric set down his end of the box and sagged against the stone wall. In the distance he heard flintlock shots. "I did not order this!"

"We knew what you wanted. Orric! Orric for Emperor!" She danced off.

Orric stared after her, despairing.

In a side tunnel of Altars, Count Fohlin peered cautiously from his hideout, a small rock chamber once used to store implements of torture. There—he heard it again. Flintlock fire, echoing from the surface through air vents. And over the weapon fire he heard the cries: "Orric is Emperor! Orric the heir! Die, in Orric's name!"

Fohlin moaned and hurried toward the surface. He thought, *This madness must end, or I am done for! I must find Orric.*

Reaching in his pocket, he fingered the metallic sphere he had taken from the burning market tent. He touched it often these days, contemplating…

Flig hovered in the air before Calantha. "That is their cry. They kill for Orric. They die for Orric. Now even the poor selumari are joining the mob."

Calantha did not move. Flig would have thought her dead, had tears not flowed down her cheeks. Finally the demarch asked, "How do they stand against the diligence patrols?"

"More and more of them have flintlocks. Those without pistols throw knives or rocks."

Calantha turned to her guards. "We have no time for delicacy. Marshall the diligence patrols. Send couriers to the shoreline district to bring in those stationed there. Your orders are to shoot and kill rebellious morehl. Order selumari rebels to throw down their weapons. If they refuse, engage them hand to hand and arrest them."

The grim-faced guard saluted and left. In a hollow voice Calantha said, "That was my son."

Flig was surprised. "That guard?"

"Orric. Orric was my son." Weeping, the demarch fingered open her locket. Lavender smothered the room.

Night's last watch. With the Day-bringers gone beyond the rim, dawn bleached the eastern sky.

Orric wandered through the city, the destruction all around mirroring the devastation within. His army, the instrument of his will, was tearing through the crater. He watched the morehl peasants and free folk angrily assault merchants, priests, even buildings. Orric thought of a trapped animal gnawing off its own leg, never realizing its other three legs were also trapped, and it was caged, as well.

This has come of teaching them stories, he thought, of teaching me stories.

He had acted out an inner story, a happy vision of ousting the city's conquerors, but when his vision became real, it changed unpredictably. How could one's "awakened will" shape the world to a dream? Impossible! The dream would collide with other dreams and follow a path beyond reckoning.

He entered Alliance Square near the destroyed Trade Hall. Other buildings here looked hardly better. The morehl had raised fire inside. The selumari had countered with wind and water. By the time both sides were done, only charred shells remained.

From behind, a deep voice called, "Orric!"

He had heard the chant all night, and he did not turn around. It surprised him, then, when Count Fohlin ran up and grabbed him by the arm. The big morehl looked pale and agitated.

Furious, Orric wrenched his arm Free. "Fohlin! Many people have looked for you these three days. You and Cennard have been busy." Orric looked at the ruins of the Trade Hall, then at the rest of the square. "But then, I have been equally busy." He laughed without humor.

"Young man, I beg you to put to rest, once and for all, this foolish rumor that you are the imperial heir."

"How do you know I am not?"

"Please! I cannot explain just now, but believe me. You are not! I suggest you gather the mob, address them from the spire, and admit your error."

Orric gazed across the square to the looming central spire. He sighed. "I believe you are right."

The amber dawn, breaking over the east rim, showed Orric standing on the highest balcony of the spire. Below, thousands of lower-class morehl and poor selumari waited, drawn by criers that Fohlin hired. Their mood was jubilant, and the few who had not shot their flintlocks to exhaustion now fired straight up in the air, for the sheer joy of noise-making.

East of the square, badly reduced diligence patrols were regrouping under Calantha's direction.

In hiding at separate locations at the squares edge, two figures waited to hear Orric's words: Fohlin, in turmoil of fear and apprehension, and Lord Burgard, weighed down with an armload of blood-spattered flintlocks.

A few minor selumari Crafters, held in armlocks by morehl, invoked the winds so that the mob might hear its leader, and the selumari might hear the usurper.

In a tone of solemn calm, Orric began, "I have been asked to admit my error. Seeing the chaos I've inspired, I find that easy. To right a wrong, I created a mob. No wrong can be righted by a mob."

The jubilation subsided at once. Silence fell.

"You workers of Karakto, bystanders in the war between Nature and Death, have only sought freedom from tyranny. But the elders and nobles used you. Elder Cennard and Count Fohlin used you to rain fire on your city."

Aghast, Fohlin fled to his sanctuary in Altars. *This stripling has brought my death!* he thought. *Defenses, I must have defenses.*

"Some among you, seeking freedom, looked for a voice in the selumari elections. But the Burgardans used you. Lord Burgard used you in hopes of ousting the demarch for his own ends. Now that this has failed, he plans to lead the armies of our onetime ally, Gundakhor, in an invasion of the city."

Lord Burgard, furious, withdrew to the tunnel leading to Prosperhome. *First retrieve Khazbul, he thought, then head south to the army. I can still salvage the flintlock process, and strike before first watch tomorrow night.*

"With no other hope, you have at last sought freedom in a return to the old imperial ways. But I used you. I used you worst of all. I acted without wise purpose, as I have all my life. You see the result. With all my heart, I regret it."

Calantha, crying, turned away. A sharpshooter said, "Demarch, I believe I can find a clear shot." Calantha stared in shock, then shouted, "Get back to your position!" As she looked again at Orric on the balcony, she called to her guard captain. In a toneless voice, she said, "When the crowd clears, arrest the usurper." *This has killed me,* she thought. *I am dead. Now I must serve Death.*

"With confusion in my thoughts and goals, I have brought only confusion to this city. Had I simply stayed at home—had all these 'leaders' gone away—you all would be better off. From this colossal disaster I have learned that much. And one thing more: you will never find freedom in a leader. Now that you have no decent leaders left, I ask you to seek a clear path that you may walk alone."

More than his words, Orric's tremendous sorrow communicated itself to the morehl. It spread from mind to mind. As the young man fell silent, they dispersed in somber silence. The riot was over.

Now: judgment.

18

The next morning at first watch, Cennard met with Fohlin in the deep tunnels. In the glow of a lava pool, the two talked without sitting, without spicemead, without ceremony or friendship.

"The young heir is making a stir," said the elder. His chill tone contrasted with the heat of the chamber.

"Utter nonsense." Fohlin spoke as if to an unruly child. "He is no more the heir than I am. I have tried to stamp out such rumors."

"With obvious failure. Perhaps some—evidence—might appear?"

"There is no evidence. It has been twenty years."

"No burial site?"

"Only a lava pit, like that one there."

Cennard eyed Fohlin with impersonal hostility. "You are speaking from experience? Not from reports?"

"I—I, no, I did it with my own hands."

"You appear unsettled, Count Fohlin."

"I did it with my own hands!"

"Very well. But bodies may live again."

Fohlin thought back to the vial of necralluvium in Cennnard's secret chamber. His face showed disgust. "Orric may be one of the bloodless, do you mean? Nonsense. True, I did not display the head and hands on a platter, but be practical. Dead means dead."

Elder Cennard gave him a long, measuring state, then a sudden smile. "Very well," Cennard repeated, "I believe you."

"Your faith fills me with confidence."

"Come now, Fohlin. You cannot blame me for wishing to verify the competence of my most trusted assistant."

"I gladly embrace that honor. May I ask how the work goes?"

Elder Cennard showed satisfaction verging on bliss. "I have completed the ring. It waits in my chamber now, ready for the summoning a day or two hence. It took heroic effort, Fohlin, which I must tell you about at length. Which reminds me: To heal the breach that has troubled us, I offer you a gift. Have you heard the tragic news about the Dakiloths?"

"No. I have been hiding. I have not even returned to my own estate."

"Just as well. The diligence louts are watching for you. Sadly, the entire Dakiloth family was torn apart by their peasants in the uprising." Cennard spoke as if discussing his tastes in spicemead. "Claims on their property are conflicting and, especially during this unrest, confused. I shall vacate all claims and assign the property to you."

Fohlin's eyes widened, then narrowed. He assumed a broad smile. "That is certainly generous. I accept your kind gift in the spirit it was offered."

"Splendid! Now, your new holdings make promotion a necessity, don't you think? The current unease makes a formal ceremony difficult. With your approval, I'll make the award at my chambers. I have disposed of the enemies who watched it. I warn you, the ceremony will be unassuming, and in these circumstances, I cannot promise all the best people will attend. But I shall arrange the details. Tonight at first watch, shall we say?"

Fohlin nodded gravely. With a smile the two men parted.

By coincidence, shortly after the meeting, Cennard and Fohlin each murmured the same remark: "Dead means dead."

At first afternoon's watch, the demarch held court. In her white robe, she looked like a corpse, perfumed with lavender and wrapped for the grave.

Calantha deferred all cases but one. For it, she had directed the court to pronounce a speedy verdict, and now Orric waited on her sentence. She glared at him as she had at Shaulf, moments before she swung the pistol.

"I am sorry our friendly Count Fohlin is not with us today, and so I do not know the traditional morehl punishment for treason. But under Emmirian law, leaders of a rebellion are burned alive at sunrise." She stared with unfocused eyes, as if disbelieving her own words. "Has the prisoner anything to say?"

Orric stood calmly before her, shackled at wrists and ankles.

He wore black clothing—but not his cloak, which rested on the dais under Calantha's chair. Behind him, both races and all social classes packed the court like arrows in a quiver. Orric said, as much for their ears as hers, "I recall the demarch who sat on that dais years ago, passing sentence with a clear mind and refined sense of justice. For what I have taken from you, I am sorry. For what you have become, I am to blame."

She snorted. "You're most kind!"

"I hoped your way would prove fit for me. Now I have shown that Quietude does not work for me, nor for you. No one is more disappointed than I. The morehl philosophy has failed me too. I see no other way to live, no worthy goal."

"That is no lasting problem." She spoke sardonically, but her eyes focused on him, and he saw they were moist.

"But the people who followed me do not deserve blame. For many years I convinced you to think they plotted against you. I wronged them as well as you. True, they have given in to anger, as I did. It is our nature. But they only struggle to survive, a task that grows harder with each passing season. As I once urged you to suspect them, now I urge you to free them."

"You're—" She choked. "You are playing me like an instrument, as you always did! You are corrupt from womb to grave, like all the rest. This abject sorrow, this contrived pathos, are meant to make me spare you."

He could not restrain his anger. "Spare me for what? I cannot live here as ruler or subject. What can life offer me, Mother, that I should be spared?"

Equally angry, she shouted, "You are nineteen years old! Your entire life is ahead!"

He stood silently, face blank. In the back, a few morehl broke into chuckles. Calantha glared at them and shouted, "Remove those people!"

The bailiff removed them. Her anger tempered, Calantha looked at Orric wistfully. For a painful moment, Orric remembered her in the courtyard of Windhome nine years ago, when she decided how to punish him for his fatal prank against Shantric.

"Well," she said tensely, and then, "if you have no more to say, I must pass—" At last her control broke, and she sagged, hiding her eyes and weeping quietly.

After long moments she wiped her eyes and reached to open her locket. "I must pass sentence," she said. "Orric, for your crimes of sedition, treason, riot, theft, and other grave and dangerous offenses, I sentence you to—"

Her finger hovered over the sana paste in the locket. She stared at him, despairing. His face mirrored hers. She snapped the locket shut. The words rushed out. "I sentence you to exile for life from the city of Karakto and a vicinity of two days' walk from the crater. At dawn watch tomorrow you will be escorted by diligence patrol in a direction of your choice for a march of two days, then set free to make your way as you will, but never to return here on pain of death."

Orric let out a breath he had not known he was holding. He felt tension dissolve in the room. Calantha would not meet his gaze.

"May I take my cloak?"

A long pause followed. "Very well."

His steps shortened by chains, he wobbled over to take the cloak from her. Her hand brushed his. They looked into one another's eyes, and for a frozen moment, they were mother and son once more.

"Gundakhor! lnvading!"

A stir came in the courtroom. Through a high window flew Flig and a swarm of other sprites, their wings a rainbow of shimmering colors. They swooped down to Calantha.

"Dack and Lossil just scouted the camp."

"A watch's march south of here on a high hill."

"Two companies of footmen, two of crossbowmen, some with flintlocks. At least three Crafters."

"Burgard is leading the army, and Jandith is leading Burgard. They mean to move on the city at dusk, so they can 'restore order.'"

An angry clamor came from the audience. Burgard could not have moved troops from Gundakhor so quickly after the revolt.

They had been waiting nearby all this time, probably since the mammoths arrived.

A cold fury filled Orric, along with a keen sense of guilt. He, Orric, had weakened the city so greatly that Gundakhor could take it with ease. With shackled hands, he waved aside the sprite swarm. "Mother, let me fight with you against them. I have much to settle with Burgard and Jandith."

The audience erupted in cheers. Orric turned, surprised. How had he regained their loyalty? Then he realized that, in the minds of the morehl—and, it seemed, the selumari as well—Gundakhor was the enemy. Anyone who opposed the vagha thereby became an ally.

Calantha looked at Orric warily, then at the crowd. "No. I have sentenced you. We can fight Gundakhor without you. Guards, take him away."

Carrying his cloak, Orric left in silence. Inwardly he seethed.

The diligence guards escorted him to the highest floor of the building, to the cells. The Supreme Hall had been built by the morehl, who built prison cells far above the ground because separation from the earth was considered punishment. The guards put Orric in a small stone cell with a single tiny window. They removed his shackles and left. No sooner had they closed the door than Orric went to the window and looked out on the road far below. He donned the cloak, then draped it far out the window. Then, breathing deeply, he concentrated.

In moments a raucous cry startled him. Jungle all around—an iron-beaked bird dived at him! He threw himself to the ground, where a thorned vine wrapped around his wrist, trapping him.

The bird circled and plummeted at him again. Twisting aside, he grabbed at a wing with his free hand, wrenched the struggling bird to the ground, and crushed its skull between his legs.

Gasping, with the thorn vine slashing deep into his wrist, Orric concentrated again.

He lay panting on the ground outside the Hall of justice. The cloak had fluttered down after he vanished into the other realm. He staggered to his feet, then ran off, having reached the ground far ahead of the guards who locked him in.

With the dimwitted miner's help, Orric had hidden the last crate of Prosperhome flintlocks near the old imperial tunnel. As he nursed his smoking wrist, he made for that cache now.

Half a watch later, Calantha learned of Orric's escape.

He tried yet again to fool me! she thought.

Disappointed and betrayed, she told the guards, "When you see him, shoot to kill."

"The destruction was total," Count Fohlin said in a dazed voice. "The walls were blasted, Death only knows how, and every piece of furniture shattered. They took or destroyed everything I owned. They poisoned the fungus gardens. It was—I don't have words. My estate is ruined."

Fohlin looked around at the nobles' unsympathetic faces. Whatever the unrest in the city above, these dozen people should feel relaxed here in Cennard's luxurious chambers, lounging at a table laden with food of uncommon savor. Yet the nobles seemed tense. With dread, Fohlin suspected he knew why. He fingered the sphere in his pocket.

Cennard, at least, behaved with his normal humor. Gesturing with his spicemead goblet, the thin priest said, "Come now, Fohlin, you own an entire new estate—and a richer one, I must add. The rioters are a ragtag lot and will soon fall back into obedience. Then you will restore your estate and be doubly rich! Have no worries about refurnishing your chambers. We'll happily donate items of our own. Eh, Krikil?"

The orator smiled thinly. "Indeed, Elder Cennard." As if on signal, Krikil pulled out a kerchief and conspicuously dabbed at his lips.

Fohlin noticed the kerchief's familiar pattern. It came from his own estate crest. The only kerchiefs with the pattern had rested in his bedchamber, until the rioters looted them. Lady Akhien fussed with her hair using a bone comb inlaid with obsidian—the comb Fohlin had used every day for years. And there. Duke Eahrol jingled a leather coin pouch embossed with Fohlin's crest.

Fohlin's heart pounded. He held the sphere ready, out of sight under the table. Anger made him clutch it tightly. These nobles, whom I thought my family, have destroyed my estate?

But he must keep up appearances—for a few moments.

"Why, what—what a delightful joke? I wonder how my little t-trinkets fell into the hands of my dear friends?"

Elder Cennard kept up his light mood. "Fohlin, you must know we are your family. We care for you. If you do well, we are glad. If you go astray, we apply a healthy corrective. And Fohlin, you have gone quite badly astray with this matter of the heir to the throne."

The nobles rose, drew obsidian daggers, and moved hesitantly toward Fohlin.

The traitor has rehearsed them, he thought, *and they have complied, after all my feasts!*

Anger—not panic—flared strong in him and he snatched a weapon of his own which he'd hidden in a sleeve. Fohlin had carried it ever since Dharsi's death at the elder's hand. The attackers looked around in terror, then fled, stampeded, out the chamber's entrance and into the tunnel beyond.

Cennard alone resisted the urge to flee. "You are a much greater coward than I had suspected," the elder said, dropping all pretense. He held up one hand. His eyes rolled back in his head, as they had when he summoned fire from the sky.

Fohlin chose that moment to throw the gnomish talisman. To learn its use, he had paid the last of his gold to a Crafter in Altars. The tiny metallic sphere flashed across the table, struck Cennard in the chest, and clung to his black robes. The elder startled, shook, screamed, shook more violently. Then the talisman did its worst. In an eye blink, the gaunt figure shrank and vanished into the sphere.

Now a sick green, the talisman fell to the floor.

Fohlin seized the tiny ball and, remembering the usual practice with such spirit-prisons, swallowed it. The talisman burned in his stomach, but he did not belch.

He began to breathe again, then to tremble. Thinking of what he had done, what these people had done to him, he fell to his knees, gasping, laid low by grief and despair.

Grief and despair? Such feelings were distinctly un-morehl! In that moment something clicked in his mind. He realized his true parentage. Why he had difficulty in contributing to Deathcraft throughout his life but had occasionally aided in Firecraft.

As if he communed with Death itself and gained supernatural knowledge he understood why he was taller, his features more rounded. *I am half eldarim! A child of morehl and eldarim... but any creature can willingly serve Death if they forsake all other ties.*

In that moment, Fohlin recognized himself as the instrument of Death's will, a necessary check upon an errant people—he was still morehl, after all—and so much more. Only Fohlin could tell that the morehl deserved the doom they planned for others. He intimately knew his peoples' black hearts.

He went to the back of the chamber, recited Cennard's password before the leopard pelt, and watched the shadow slide from it. Entering the Crafter's chamber, he saw a black ring and two scrolls on a table. With great care, he placed the scrolls and the Ring of Stars in a linen bag. He walked out of the room, out of Cennard's chambers, out of the tunnels. After a time he began to run.

In his pounding heart, there rose a sense of unshakable destiny. Fohlin wasn't just a child of the Death god as any other morehl—he was an instrument of that god's will—and *all* would know the wrath of Death.

PART 3
FREEDOM

19

Mountain's concentration had not wavered. Steadily, the sun had slowed in its passage overhead, until he saw it almost as did the tiny things within his crater. Yet now the sky was dark and starry. Remarkable.

New sensations troubled him. No—old sensations, familiar to him. Tiny stings of wrongness, the pinpricks of summoning Craftwork he knew from years ago. The goads of ritual—the Corruptor's work.

Ill at ease, Mountain stirred.

In the Court of Justice, where she had decided the fate of so many others, Calantha sat and pondered her own.

On the dais by her chair stood a small oil lamp. The room was otherwise empty, but filled with a choking odor of lavender. "Look upon her and judge." Her leaden words echoed through the half-dark chamber. "Slayer of morehl. Usurper of the throne. Destroyer of two cities, two races. Guilty of all these crimes and more. Pronounce her fate!"

She laughed hollowly, coughed, and waited for her own judgment. She waited without hope, without need of hope. Death, of course. But what sort of death?

She could dress as a common soldier and stride through the streets, challenging every armed rioter she saw. Her skills with steel were modest—she would eventually fall. No, she might merely be wounded. Then some wretch could find her and arrange for her recovery while she lay helpless.

She might find those goblins from the marsh and learn firsthand what it was to be eaten. A pity she could not remain alert through the meal, to hear their comments about her flavor and texture. What sauce best suited a selumari ruler?

With each new possibility of death, her smile broadened.

A deep voice came from a silhouette in the entryway. "Why does the demarch sentence herself to death, when she knows she deserves a crueler fate?"

She turned. "Count Fohlin? Are my thoughts bits of ash drifting in the breeze, to be caught by any passerby?"

"No, demarch. I regret to report that the dernarch was thinking aloud." Fohlin moved into the chamber, toward the lamplight. His walk was slower and more ponderous than ever.

"What doom, then, would you lay upon me?"

"For the demarch's conquest of my people, none. That was fairly done." As he approached, Calantha saw that his once-fine garments were tattered, muddied. He carried a linen bag. "For the demarch's intent to bring our races together, none. That was nobly attempted. But suppose one takes a dangerous beast and maddens it with injury. What do the ways of Nature tell one to do about this creature?"

"Heal it. Or put it out of its misery."

"Can the demarch heal Karakto?"

"No."

She remained silent. Brooding over how foolish she'd been to think she could undo many generations' worth of evil and breeding enacted upon these people by the wicked Empress.

He stood before her, waiting. The change in him startled her.

Fohlin's features drooped, and by morehl standards he was pallid. "You look unwell," she said with genuine sympathy.

Fohlin swallowed. "I ate something that disagreed with me."

"Perhaps you should change to a simpler diet."

"Yes, demarch. My next dish will be served cold."

"I cannot destroy Karakto, Count Fohlin. I have not the means, nor the right."

Abandoning protocol, he talked with intensity. "You do not need the right, demarch. You have the duty. That is the sentence I would lay upon you: Undo the evil you have done.

"As for the means…" He opened the bag.

In a conference chamber sat Fohlin, Calantha, and her advisor in Craftwork, an old conjurer named Doerinal. Fohlin's gifts lay spread on the tabletop before them.

All but the Ring of Stars. Calantha held it, marveling at its beauty—a ring of the blackest stone, infused with gleaming chips of diamond and other precious gems. She found she could not look at its surface. The eye mistook blackness for unending depth, and gleaming gems for twinkling stars. It seemed a night sky, from some place so distant that the constellations were unfamiliar, captured in the palm of her hand.

Then Counselor Doerinal's words sank in. "What did you say? A dragon?"

"Yes, demarch. This scroll tells how to summon—" The old man's voice seemed to catch in his throat. "How to summon a dragon… it is a—powerful beast. I'm not sure about some of these sigils, but it is certainly a dragon."

She stared, appalled.

Doerinal continued, "The creatures, trapped in whatever realm they go to in their next life, have interbred, making it possible for even a selumari to call a dragon of opposing elements, provided it contains the neutral magic such as what the humans use. I've heard them called hybrid dragons… the creatures must have interbred while in diaspora. I suspect this may be one of that variety."

Fohlin said, "It is the only way, demarch. The Ring of Stars will call a dragon—a manageable one—not one of the Greater dragons such as Hwarrm or the others that leaked as tears from the Mother. Do not fear. This scroll—" he tapped the second parchment "—describes how to destroy the creature after it fulfills its purpose."

Wyrmcraft. Calantha felt a thrill of revulsion, quickly muted by the sana calm. Her thoughts seemed muffled in a wrapping of silk—a shroud. She mused on the idea of a summoning, the most desperate strategy any ruler could devise. "Can it be done?"

Doerinal spoke reluctantly. "I must caution the demarch that dragons, when called from whatever realm they inhabit, are mad, uncontrollable."

"I know that!" she snapped. "I fought with the army that killed Hwarrm on the slopes of this city. Answer the question."

The old Crafter fingered the scroll. "The rite is odd, as Fohlin tells me, this is a fairly new type of wyrmcraft. Odd… but possible. Even with that ring," Doerinal said, "You would need others to draw enough magic to complete this spell. Are you comfortable bringing other spell-casters into the fold for such a task?"

Calantha's face drained of its bood.

"I remind you again that I've never cast such a spell and I'm somewhat uncertain of the writing on this script."

"The mortality faces," Fohlin interjected before Calantha's will could falter. "They link the Crafter with a base of additional power… normally, the flintlocks. They accumulate it like a pool holds water—that 'water' could be drawn on for other pusposes."

Calantha wondered briefly how the count knew of that ring of stone faces, where General Osmaral had died years ago. For all she knew, though, he could have helped build them, long before Emmiria occupied the city. "What of the second scroll?" she asked.

Doerinal picked it up. "This, too, seems workable—if the ring is all Count Fohlin has made it out to be.

The matter of destroying the dragon seemed minor as she stared deep into the abyss of the Ring of Stars and she took Doerinal at his word. "Call for a gathering at the spire—all the morehl, and my personal guards. Remove the mortality faces from the bat cavern and install them at the base of the spire. Then evacuate the selumari, all who are willing to leave."

"Evacuate?"

"Ready the sky ships. Send them north, to the old site of Emmiria. Tell them they will be building a refuge for use if Gundakhor invades. Make sure one ship stands by, close enough to see what befalls us."

"And the morehl?"

Her eyes lost focus, and she spoke flatly. "I should have had them all killed years ago. How odd. Burgard was right, and I wrong. Now our positions are reversed. I must do what he wished then, what he would invade to prevent now—else the poison of Karakto will spread to Gundakhor."

A deathly quiet greeted her words, and she looked up. Doerinal was looking at Fohlin.

"Ah," the demarch said, realizing she'd just condemned his race. "I am sorry you had to hear that, Count Fohlin."

But he showed grim satisfaction. "I am glad of it," he drew her into his confidence and drew back the locks of his hair to show her his ears—more rounded and shorter than his counterparts' even despite his larger and bulkier frame.

Calantha's eyes bulged for a moment when she recognized him for what he was: the product of an eldarim male and an unfaithful mother. His seeming faithfulness to her plan suddenly seemed more rational.

Fohlin bowed and said, "I shall do all I can to help the demarch carry out her sentence."

Under a starlit sky in the plaza of Alliance Square, beneath Karakto's central spire, a crowd gathered—elders and fisherfolk, guards and merchants, many thousands of morehl and a few selumari—summoned by criers, united by curiosity. Whispers flew as thick as a swarm of bats.

Everyone noted the odd stone carvings, huge faces, that workers were setting around the spire's base. The morehl knew of the mortality faces, and they stared with morbid fascination.

Then she appeared on the balcony far above—-the demarch, beloved and hated—joined by Fohlin, Doerinal, and diligence guards. The whispering rose to a loud hiss of anger and praise.

More than she had in ages, Calantha felt assured. The suspicions and uncertainties of years had fallen away, leaving her poised, certain, the image of a demarch in her first year of rule. She looked with detachment at the destroyed Trade Hall and the dark ruins everywhere in the city. She smiled down at the crowd, a doting mother, and raised her hands for attention. The crowd quieted.

Her words, carried by magic means, rang in every ear. "It is no secret that I will not long be demarch of Karakto. Nor does this displease me. I wish my successor the same good fortune and long life I wish upon my city.

"You know about the dwarves of Gundakhor."

She waited, and the crowd did not disappoint her. A hiss of anger resounded in the plaza.

"They come not to kill, but worse, to conquer and enslave. In these last days, you have made known your hatred of the lives you lead. Gundakhor means to trap you in those lives, without hope of change, for the enrichment of its corrupt lords!"

Another hiss came, far louder—pure rage.

"I have dispatched the sky ship navy to meet the dwarven army. But the navy cannot defeat it, merely slow it. We ourselves will defeat it. You will defeat it! Prepare yourselves, cleanse your minds, and our craft will break the spine of the dwarven force. Then you will be free! Free to roll over them like the tide, and bathe in their blood."

The spine-chilling hiss of blood-thirst rose like a wind.

Calantha looked back at Fohlin. He bowed and said, "We have both reached the culmination of our hopes."

She nodded to a guard, who unrolled the summoning scroll and held it for her. Then she donned the ring and felt its coolness against her skin, felt its power resonate in her bones.

She looked out at the thousands who were about to die at her hands, and she smiled.

"Clear your minds and unite your spirits. I shall speak words.

Repeat them back to me in a single voice, the voice of Karakto.

"*Koliaktur.*" It was one of the words of potency spread of old across Esfah.

The crowd whispered the word back. The air spirit turned it into a roar, and the final syllable rumbled through the city.

Calantha mouthed the words and wondered at their meaning. "*Dodaktra Karakto lceyussakor badu.*" They flew to the crowd and then echoed back to her, suffused with power.

Voiced by thousands, the words sounded less like language than like the grinding of stones. The scar on Calantha's neck, the mark Orric had left when trying to save her all those years ago, began to burn.

Below, a light like a torch flame appeared over the crowd. It danced above them, veering as if batted to and fro by every word. It grew large.

Fascinated, she called out, "*Golkiern nahu earrrrn!*"

But those words, repeated by the massed voices, came back to her differently: "*Golkiern na HWARRM!*"

Aghast, she revoked Aihalara at once. She turned to Fohlin.

He shrugged. "I fear I have deceived the demarch. It is no minor dragon we summon. But trust me. Hwarrrm will perform admirably."

"No…" She shook her head. "No! *Hwarrrn is dead!*"

"Say rather, disembodied."

Doerinal was clutching the balcony rail. "Demarch, stop the ceremony! If Hwarrm is recalled, he will seek revenge on Gundakhor and Emmiria alike!"

The crowd, eager for the next words, began calling out.

Frowning, as if recovering from a blow to the skull, she looked down at them. "Devin," she said in a whisper. "You would not know me."

Fohlin moved closer. "Your late husband? Whom we morehl slaughtered? He would cheer you on."

She rounded on him. "Give me the other scroll!"

He handed her the parchment. She unrolled it. It was blank.

In a kind voice he said, "I burned the real one after you looked at it. We can't have you undoing what must be done." He fondly touched the white scar burning on her neck, then gave her a strong push.

She staggered back against the rail—back, and over. She plummeted.

A gust of wind manifested beneath her, a blur of air that bore her and set her upright. She floated above the crowd and saw her guard captain wrestling Fohlin into submission.

Her locket had fallen off. For an instant she felt afraid, started to search for it.

No. No more.

Calantha collected her thoughts. She still might break the rite. Its last line remained unspoken.

The orange light floated up and hung huge before her. In its depths she saw a huge, writhing form she well remembered, and a battle she wished she could forget. Hwarrm fell on Devin, and on the Dawn Blade he held—the sword that banished the spirits of its victims.

Now she realized his sword was the key, a dawn blade of gnomish origin which locked away the souls of its victims must have reacted with the draconic magic. Even a dawn blade could not banish Hwarrm's spirit to whatever pocket where it held its victims. But neither had it sent Hwarrm to the elemental realm where dragons went when dispatched. *Hwarrm could be revived!*

Over long years, well before today's ritual, Calantha herself had opened the way for Hwarrm's return. Calantha had long suspected the faces were the creation of the gremmlobahnd—the gnomes—and if it was their weaponry that had separated the great wyrm's soul from body, surely one of their creations might be capable of reuniting them!

Then the light spoke, shrieked, to the crowd below: *"Iktakyad nahu earrrm!"*

The crowd roared, *"Iktakyad na HWARRM!"*

And the ritual was done.

The light flitted away, toward the seaward rim of the crater, toward the notch Hwarrm had made in his death-agonies.

In terror Calantha cried, "Follow!" The wind carried her after the fleeing light.

The events of the plaza sped by in Mountain's perceptions, and he despaired. The sparks had at least been harmless before. Now he could feel them calling for Hwarrm, calling with the voice of Death—and the leader of the blue sparks was the chief voice among them!

As an elemental—a being of pure spirit and elemental magic, Mountain knew the depravity and power of the Elder Dragons which sprang from the tears of Nature, the Mother Goddess, in a similar fashion as the elementals were made… only the elementals were called to life by the Shara, the "little gods" known as the eldarim who walked the face of Esfah before the colored sparks even existed.

Mountain was made to protect life against the malice of dragons—elementals balanced Esfah against the sorrow of the dragons. He knew that Hwarrm must not be called. The leader had to die to break the rite.

He called up an influence from deep within himself. It surged upward, toward the spire from which the leader spoke.

"We must follow the demarch," said the guard captain as he finished binding Fohlin's limbs.

Doerinal stared after Calantha. "Give me but a moment." He cleared his mind to summon power for a casting.

Below, the crowd began to rush away from the center of the plaza. Doerinal watched, puzzled, as scores of people fell. Then he felt the rumble in the balcony, saw the buildings shaking.

"Earthquake!"

Fohlin laughed.

A pillar of molten rock burst forth from the plaza's center, engulfing a score of morehl. Lava could not immediately burn the race that had risen from it, but in its flow their clothing flamed instantly, and the victims drowned as they would in water.

The shaft of glowing red and yellow rose to match the spire's height. For a moment it stood steaming, filling the air with the stench of brimstone. Then the pillar bent and struck unerringly at the balcony.

In the last moment of his life, the guard captain screamed. In the last moment of his life, Doerinal pondered the pillar reaching for him. Made of red-hot stone, intent on death, it represented all that the selumari loathed. Yet it was eerily beautiful.

In the last moment of his life, Fohlin said calmly, "We must set an example."

They felt a blast of heat, too swift to be felt as pain. Then the lava struck the balcony and poured over them, reducing the selumari to ash and knocking Fohlin back into the railing.

It shattered, and he fell.

Quickly he woke and found himself hanging high above the ground. The broken rail had snagged the sash of his rank at his waist. By reflex he grabbed for the rail. In that instant the sash burned through, and Fohlin fell to his death.

Mountain considered. The chanting had stopped—too late.

The sparks had completed the rite well before his sluggish blow struck home. He had slain some, but the leader had fled toward the earth—wyrm's body. He sensed Hwarrm: the dragon was incomplete—neither living nor dead. Hwarrm was something in between.

He would need another arm. He sent it burrowing upward...

Wind snapped at Calantha's garments and hair. The air spirit carried her swiftly, but the flying glow was swifter still. She saw it reach the volcano rim, where a line of broken rubble marked where Hwarrm's tail had thrashed its last.

The light descended and struck the rubble. The glow traveled through the broken stones, illuminating the gaps between as it leapt from boulder to boulder where bones had been petrified and stone-locked to create a lasting monument to the old war that had ended with Wyrmcraft. It arced up the dead dragon's tailbones, flying over the ridge...

"Higher!" Calantha cried, and the winds lifted her.

On the volcano's seaward slope, the light hurtled down the mound that once was Hwarrm. It traced the length of the shattered body. Stones along its path began to shake, as though stirring within the earth.

Calantha summoned every technique of her Craft to help her gather enough of a connection to Aguarehl. She pleaded with the shadowy copy of herself—envisioned it doing what she needed. *Scatter those stones so no two are touching! Hwarrm must not become complete!*

The light had almost reached the water's edge, where the polished, stone skull of Hwarrm had long ago broken away from its neck and Fallen into the bay.

Waves crashed against the shore. Calantha saw her face in the white-capped froth as her ethereal figure did as requested.

"Yes!" she said aloud. "Please be swift."

The light emerged from the dragon's broken neck and plunged into the waves before them. The water at bay's edge stirred, and something rose from the depths. Black, smooth, rounded, the size of a selumari mansion, it floated to the surface. Hwarrm's skull. Its empty eye sockets glowed orange. It began bobbing toward shore.

Despairing, Calantha shouted, "It's taking too long!" The buffet of air bore her outward, above the fallen form of Hwarrrn. Rocks that had once tumbled away from the body now tumbled toward it, as though years of decay were quickly turning backward. "Strike now, or all is lost!"

The floating skull reached the shore, and sand crawled up to join neck and skull. All along the monsters length, earth and stone flowed to enfold the bones of rock.

Calantha hovered, awaiting the rebirth of Hwarrm, who was among the largest and cruelest of the Elder Dragons. Even so—he seemed to command more dread and power than ever before. He seemed to radiate it!

Finally, his target fell still. Mountain had her. The leading finger of his new arm emerged into the air and began to cool. Still she hovered, unmoving, unaware of him.

Other movement—the stirring of loose soil on his seaward slope. It was wrong. Stillness in the sea at his base, equally wrong. But he could not divert his attention. These sparks moved so fast he could lose his target.

With a motion that was, for him, sudden and savage, Mountain thrust his new arm out into the painful, cool air and struck at the leader.

A stream of lava burst from the mountain slope. Like a lance of light it shot straight at Calantha, too fast for her to escape. She flung a wall of elemental energy to shield herself. Wind struck against the lava, darkening it, hardening it. Mist and fog spread along the lance, cooling it. Even so, a hundred times her weight in super-heated stone struck Calantha in the back and slapped her from the sky.

Falling so fast that her wind gusts could scarcely slow her descent, Calantha smashed into a boulder as it slid across the slope to join Hwarrm's form. She lay broken and bleeding. The agony of seared flesh and broken bone struck, but she knew the worst punishment was coming. She must watch as, for the first time in eighteen years, Hwarrm's head rose from its resting place.

Patches of the marble skull showed forth in the moonlight, gradually obscured as streams of earth leapt from the ground to cover it. The serpentine neck turned to regard the mountain's upper slope. In black sockets, the glow of orange gave way to the gleam of serpent eyes reflecting starlight.

An evening's march south of Karakto, four dwarves of Gundakhor happened on a box in the middle of the road. They gathered round.

It was a large crate, wooden slats visible only at its base. The rest was covered in a black cloth drapery.

Marked on the cloth in chalk were the words, "A present for the saviors of Karakto."

The dwarves eyed it warily. One, shorter than the others and with a curious streak of white matting his beard, scratched his nose as he contemplated the box. "A trap," he announced.

The others nodded.

"Still, we must know. Stand off." He waited until his fellows had withdrawn to a safe distance. Then he pulled the cloth aside and raised the box lid. He studied the contents.

When he lowered it, his eyes were wide. He hastily restored the cloth. "Fall back to the line, all speed. And tell the warlord," he called. "He will want to see this."

Minutes later, Lord Burgard, Jandith, and the advance units of the Gundakhor army reached the prize. Burgard met with the scout. "Well?"

"Flintlocks, sir." He could barely conceal his enthusiasm. The selumari and morehl of Karakto would have a more difficult time defending against the dwarven invaders if the vagha had access to the cursed bullets from the arcane flintlocks which pierced shield and flesh with equal vigor.

"Fresh from the Karakto armory, if I don't miss my guess."

"No treachery boxed with them? Poisons on the stocks, lead blocking the barrels, runes altered?"

"No, sir. I inspected them all."

"Excellent. For your bravery, the first flintlock will he yours. You and you!" Burgard pointed to two bodyguards. "Pitch my tent, then bear this crate within."

"Useless." Jandith dropped the Flintlock into the second, bigger, pile.

"Exhausted, like the rest?" asked Burgard.

"Yes. Of fifty in the crate, only five will function."

Burgard shrugged. "Disappointing, but still worth our time. I shall fetch that scout and one or two others who deserve a reward. When we take Karakto, we shall attune them to the pistols."

He left her. She smiled fondly after him, as any owner would upon a favored pet.

She heard a rustling, like wind tugging at the sides of the tent. She turned. The black cloth that had covered the crate was rising, taking shape? Orric, covered in brambles and bleeding smoky blood from his scalp, stepped forward and clapped a hand over her mouth. "Don't move," he said, as if making a polite suggestion.

Jandith bit his hand. He grimaced and struck her in the stomach, then on the side of her head. She knew no more.

Burgard strode into the tent, with five soldiers behind, and stared down the barrel of the flintlock in Orric's hand.

"Send them away," said Orric.

"Where is Jandith?"

"In the box. Send them away. Or shall I shoot them?" Orric aimed at the brave scout.

Burgard waved his troops hack. "No attempts at rescue," he told them. "I am in no danger."

Orric laughed. When the two were alone, he said, "Turn back your army."

"I think not. We can give Karakto wise, stern rule, better than your mother provided. The city will prosper."

"The vagha will profit, you mean. Your greed has made you hateful, and you would spread it among your kind. Can't you see what has happened to the selumari?"

The warlord shrugged. "What can one expect of the selumari? Beauty and art, yes—but not discipline. We will avoid their fate. *Your fate*." Burgard smiled. "And don't think that slaying me will stop my army. I have many good officers who can lead in my stead. You couldn't kill all of them before they dragged you down."

Cries of alarm came from outside. Then something hit the tent from above, and it collapsed on them.

Burgard was first to crawl out. When he saw what had hit them, he swore violently. Orric wormed his way out, the black cloth over his arm. When he saw what lay atop the collapsed tent, he leapt forward with a cry of anguish.

Calantha. Her fine garments were burned, and bloody scrapes covered her skin. Her left arm twisted at an impossible angle.

Orric touched her brow gently, as if fearing she would collapse into ash. Her eyes opened. "Orric," she said. Her voice was a smoky rasp, like the whispers of the morehl.

"Mother—what—?"

"Shhh. Listen. Hwarrm is not dead. I summoned him."

Burgard's golden skin paled. "Aah!" He seemed to shrink. "You mad-woman! What have you brought upon us?"

"An awful mistake. Here. Ring of Star—use it, call on Mountain. It will kill him. I hope."

While Burgard called for the troops to sound an alarm, Orric shook out his cloak and donned it. "I'll get you to the healing pool."

Calantha coughed and shook her head. "Too late. Unite the morehl, lead them. Help Burgard stop Hwarrm." She held up her right hand, offering the glittering prize within. Orric numbly took it. "Too late," she repeated, and her hand dropped away.

Orric moaned, then touched her throat where once he had scarred her. He stood and, with infinite care, took Calantha in his arms. He winced as broken bones grated. "I must take my mother away."

"She's dead, lad."

"No! There is a pulse."

"Then she will be in a moment. I know how you must feel, but now we must—"

"Lord Burgard, Mother told me how she once entrusted the city to you while she healed me. You honored that trust."

"Orric—"

"Now I give this ring to you. I hope you will act honorably once more." He passed the Ring of Stars to Burgard.

"Orric, hear me! We must think of our city and both our peoples. You can lead the morehl where we cannot. Together we might kill Hwarrm, as the old alliance did before. But believe me, my army cannot defeat him alone!" Burgard looked pleadingly at Orric. "I know of no other way to save the city. For better or worse, fate has chosen you for our ally."

Orric stared him down. He said coolly, "I make my own choices." Holding Calantha in one arm, he swept up his cloak. It settled over them both, and they were gone.

20

The air smelled of roasted meat, and trees scratched at an angry red sky. It would have been a thrilling sunset—but where was the sun?

In this dense forest, the trees bore no leaves. Glistening, covered in something like black leather, they moved ever so slightly, though no breeze blew. The rich soil was dotted with tiny black toadstools.

Orric, carrying Calantha, had finally struggled through to this quiet place.

His rapier was bloody, his flintlock already almost exhausted. He himself was exhausted. He had to haul his mother's body—no, don't think that way—to haul his mother to high ground. There he hoped to survey the land and spot the hill with the healing pool. But to get her there, he needed a sled.

He saw two likely branches twenty paces away. Could he leave her and go get them? Hearing nothing save the clacking of the tree branches, he went to get the sticks. Just as he picked up the first, he turned and saw two huge eel-like creatures slither down from the sky and fasten their bony mouths on Calantha. They labored to lift her off the ground.

"No!" In a frenzy, Orric ran back with the stick in his hand.

He brought it crashing down on the silvery scales of the nearest creature. With a raspy cry it turned to attack. When he saw the eyes, two large circles of obsidian black, he realized with cold horror that he had seen these creatures a decade before—the gentle windsnakes.

He swung again. The creature moaned, fell, and lay writhing.

The second, finding it could not lift Calantha alone, snapped at him with its wide, fanged mouth, cutting his left hand. The vapor of his blood provoked him to greater savagery. With three berserk blows, he drove away the windsnake.

He looked around, gasping. "You won't take her," he said aloud to the world.

Spreading his cloak between the branches, Orric constructed a primitive sled. Selumari soldiers learned to make such sleds in order to move wounded troops off the battlefield.

The morehl had no use for such things. Honor called for death on the battlefield, not off it. Even in this land, he didn't know what he was.

Or where he was.

He remembered Calantha's words: As you are attuned to the elements, so these plants are attuned to the cloak's owner. As you grow, so they grow. That is how the cloak teaches discipline.

Or how it failed, in his case.

She had said that about the garden, a pleasant, neat enclosure like her mind at the time. His own inner world presented struggles, not beauty—striving, not Quietude.

Pulling the sled with care, Orric made his way up a slope that reminded him of the foothills near Karakto. As he climbed, he felt a new kind of unease about the jungle. It was deadly, yet what alarmed him was how it attracted him. The bleak leafless branches, the red sky, the myriad deadly beasts— he found it all queerly familiar, with a twisted beauty. It was his heritage. The morehl, lovers of destruction, were unhappy in the young world.

Put us on a dying world at the end of time, he thought. *Let us brood atop some windswept ruin, and we can be moody or savage to our hearts' content.*

In the distance he saw smoke plumes, and he thought of volcanoes. As a boy, he had once told his mother he wanted a volcano named for him. He recalled a line in one of the sacred plays: "My blood is lava, blood of the mountain."

There were no paths in these woods. Twice, thorn bushes struck out at him. Both struck swiftly, drawing sizzling blood. In time, he reached the summit, a bare dead clearing beneath a red sky. Stones marked with mysterious glyphs covered the ground. Scanning the horizon, Orric saw with surprise that the jungle occupied only this hill. Beyond lay a barren desert of ash, and one distant mountain, its peak capped with green. A narrow, winding river flowed from the mountain peak across the barren land toward the hill where he stood.

For a moment Orric despaired. He was standing on the site of the terraced garden. The healing pool on the gentle hill, the bubbling brook that flowed down into the garden—both had transformed into these awful obstacles. What had happened?

Where had he gone wrong?

He looked down at his wounded mother. He was already tired from dragging the sled. He saw nothing to eat or drink here, either. Could she survive the journey?

A rustling came overhead. He looked up in fear and saw something falling—hailstones! He threw himself across his mother's body as hail fell with bruising impact. The icy stones burned with a green-black flame. The strange trees began wailing in agony. He tried to pick up his mother and shield her body while scrabbling down the ashy slope toward shelter. He couldn't believe how much the stones hurt. More than anything he wanted to be back home, even if it meant facing Hwarrm.

Then that regret gave way to anger. He said aloud, "I shall live by my choices!"

Calantha moaned. *So she was alive!*

With new hope he returned to the sled, and thought about how to return downhill. Down is easy, he thought. That was the secret of Calantha's corruption. At every opportunity she had chosen the path down.

Fighting through the jungle, he reached the base of the hill. There he broke free of the thistles and quickly found the river. Bright blue water flowed in hard-baked banks that were shiny with mica. Orric fashioned a crude raft from branches that lay along the shore, tying them with creepers from the jungle.

While he moved the sled onto the raft, Calantha briefly awoke. "Thirsty," she said weakly.

Orric didn't dare risk giving her water from this river. "Mother, can you summon a water spell?"

No use. She didn't seem to know where she was. She started to sing some selumari children's song—"Little fishes, swim upriver, there you'll find—" She fell unconscious.

Poling the raft upriver, he looked down in the water and saw a school of trout-sized fish skeletons, swimming downriver as though alive. Suddenly, they floated out of the water and swam through the air around him, nipping like deer flies. He let them harry him, unwilling to take a moment away from poling. In time he fought free of their school. Many bends of the river lay ahead. Sighing, he pushed the raft upriver.

A long, long time later, he arrived at the mountain and began pulling the sled up the slope. The forest here was denser than it had been on the small hill. The trees had thorns, and their trailing branches whipped Orric as he passed.

The slope rose more sharply as he made his way up. He found himself puffing and wheezing as he never had in the sulfurous depths of Karakto.

Farther up the slope, patches of thin black wires grew like grass. They tried to ensnare his feet, but with brutal strokes he cut them down and continued on.

In time, Calantha's breathing became labored. Orric had to find the healing pool soon, but they were hardly halfway up the mountain.

The soil grew soft, and he often skidded backward. Once he fell and, while twisting to avoid crushing Calantha, he lost his flintlock. It slid far down the mountain and into a crevasse.

He was so weak now that he was trembling. He needed the pool as much as his mother did.

Something flashed above, a shiny rainbow flash. There it was again—a gigantic moth. Its purple and black wings beat the air in a slow, hypnotic rhythm. *That buzz...*

Moths don't buzz, Orric thought, and then the thought drifted away. *So sleepy. Had to have sleep. As he lay down, all his pain left him. This must be how she feels with sana...*

He jerked awake. Already both he and Calantha were covered with foot-long black caterpillars, weaving silk to cocoon them. He cut and smashed. Their stench was awful. They made little mewing sounds when he crushed them.

The moth flew off, and all was quiet.

Orric pulled himself up and began a determined march. He would get Calantha to the pool. He climbed up, up.

His legs had long since gone dead beneath him, and his flesh numb to the lashing gantlet they passed, when a marvelous smell reached him. The most marvelous smell he could imagine: water.

He neared the peak, climbing now on soft green grass.

Dragging the sled over a mossy boulder, he looked for the pool. A thorn wall of what appeared to be blackberry bushes surrounded it. Looking through, he glimpsed a garden inside, the one he remembered from his childhood. The trees within had green leaves, and as he drew near he believed he could hear birds singing. He could smell flowers in bloom, and water, water!

Pulling the sled, he circled the wall of thorns. After a long while, he found a tiny break in the wall, where a little stream of water trickled out into the ashy soil. The brook, he thought sadly.

He washed his hands in the trickle, then began washing Calantha's wounds. All his toiling fears passed away as he gave himself over to the simple task.

Quickly he realized that her skin had gone cold. Orric felt for her pulse. *Nothing.*

Disbelief, anger, and bitterness rose, one after another. In pure fury, he pounded his fists on her body.

The anger burned itself out, leaving resentment. *All this way, and for nothing,* he thought. *All this struggle so that the best person I ever knew could die in a muddy pool, ten paces from salvation.*

That thought—how odd. The best person he had ever known was corrupt, callous, and deluded by sana. By now, her handiwork had probably destroyed Karakto. Yet he kept thinking of her as she had been, sitting calmly beside him, drinking tea sip by sip. That was the best person he had ever known.

But that person was a phantasm, an illusion of childhood. He knew now that she had never been that pure, mindful person.

Yet she, that ideal Calantha, still survived, in a way. The image of her survived in his mind.

He could try to make himself that person, the one he thought she had been. That new self could become his goal. He tried to picture her standing beside him, guiding him. She would know the way through this wall of thorns. She would walk along the wall, observe it with clear sight—there, for example— and she would discover…

A gap. A narrow crawlspace, just big enough. Right there. He dragged her inside and lay her body gently on the grass. He looked up at the sky—it seemed lighter now—and then he plunged into the pool. He washed away the blood and ash and bones. He sank deep, far deeper than he had years ago. Somehow he understood that he was safe here, that the thousand servants of Death could not enter. He lay quietly in the pool. With each beat of his heart, he saw new things.

He had forgotten this peace, the simple pleasure in the moment. No, not pleasure—presence.

What had Cennard talked about? The awakened will. Reshaping reality by reshaping himself. *That is true magic,* he thought. *And the only moment when I can reshape myself is this moment.*

Quietude—the embrace of the moment, the calm interest in its passing—that was the way to peace.

He wanted never to leave. But he had many choices to live with, and many more to make. He floated to the surface, got out of the pool, and dried off. All around him he sensed spirit creatures, mercurial elementals that drove the wheel of the world. In the heated sky dwelt the fire spirits, and their flickering essences harmonized with his own.

Beside his mother's corpse he saw blackberry bushes. Going to them, he picked and ate a berry. Tartness, then a smooth sweetness that spread across the tongue as each tiny, fleshy fruit burst. Without reflection or judgment he savored the juice, its tang and catch at the throat, its sugary aftertaste. Between one bite and the next, he noted without surprise the appearance beside him of a standing figure—a rippling silhouette that imprinted the air with his mother's outline. At its heart was a curl of mist that glistened as though reflecting a hidden fire.

21

Midnight at Karakto. A few people who stood on the volcano's rim or on the single-masted coral sky ship *Starfish* witnessed the resurrection of Hwarrm.

The dragon raised his head to gaze back at the city he had once almost destroyed. The Elder Dragons fell as tears from the eyes of the Nature goddess—Mother Ghaeial—these were the wisest, most mischievous, and deadliest of dragon race. They could even speak the language of the elder races and of the Shara.

Hwarrm bellowed his triumph. "At last!" he said in a thunderous voice as he shook in place, casting off sheddings of skin that peeled and molted, sloughing off patches of scale and hide to reveal what had grown beneath: thicker scales like dwarven mail but white as snow.

Freee meee, indeed—the spell he'd helped Cennard craft all these years had not only reunited Hwarrm's soul and body, it had also amplified his strength at least two-fold. He was more than free—he was free and nearly limitless, unbound by the constraints of the elements—Hwarrm the White was a product of unbridled power!

"Each day, each moment of these eighteen years my anger has grown! Now I take my revenge!" he reveled in his new form as a dreaded white wyrm, until now, only rumored of and speculated over by arcanists with too much ability and too little magic.

He extended his clawed arms, even as streams of earth still flowed up from the volcano slope to merge with them. His skin regrew under magical impulse and the stone form of the pitiable petrification spells flaked off like sloughed skin.

With a quaking of the earth, Hwarrm stood on shaky, malformed legs, and roared. The mansions and walls of the shoreline district blew apart. As though driven by a hurricane, many stones quarried from Hwarrm's petrified form in years past now flew back through the air and strengthened the dragon, recalled like carrier pigeons.

Hwarrm plucked from his breast the tiny sliver of metal that had split his soul and body so many years ago. The Dawn Blade still shone brightly in the night—until the beast breathed on it, drawing on the power of both earth and fire in his surroundings, and encased the hated weapon in a thick shell of unbreakable stone.

Ccrouching on his four legs, Hwarrm leapt into the air. He writhed like a serpent and splayed fins to catch the currents, much as did the selumari air ships. Unlike the winged drakes who could fly for long times, some wyrms could glide—though only for a short time.

The currents carried him aloft, far out to sea and over an unexplored expanse with depths unplumbed by the selumari. Then he threw the rock encasing the accursed blade with all his might, still farther out to sea, where it struck, sank, and was lost eternally to the depths where it could no longer harm him.

Hwarrm wheeled and flew back toward Karakto. His brilliant white armor reflected yellows and reds from the Daybringer overhead. His revenge, long overdue, awaited.

Mountain was too late. The summoning was complete. The dragon, whose corrupting body had for so long lain against him, rose into the air, painfully tearing away Mountain's skin.

As it escaped its grave, it transmuted, became something greater. Hwarrm's power grew.

The dragon moved so fast that Mountain despaired ever of striking him. Still, he sent more arms burrowing upward. Perhaps in time, the beast would lie down to rest. Then Mountain would have him.

Hwarrm looked down on the darkened city as he glided upon the slipstreams. It looked different through these true eyes, not the tiny, limited senses of his spirit-form. Circling just inside the crater rim, he saw every building, every running creature with beautiful clarity.

The buildings stood firm. The creatures were still flesh, not stone and ash. This had to be corrected.

He dived for a cluster of buildings. They broke like eggshells under him. He heard stone shatter, heard the tiny shrieks of the mortal things buried under a landslide of dressed stone.

Hwarrm inhaled deeply, then expelled a hot breath. It emerged as super-heated dust, washing across all before him. The dust sank into the little blue and red creatures, entombing them in their fragile frames. In an instant, they stood as rock statues.

He sensed movement below. Rivulets of fire were crawling upward, toward him.

Some attack by the pathetic living things? He laughed, blowing more petrifying death across the city. The attack was too slow for Hwarrm. He rose upon his massive haunches and looked for another nest.

Mountain shuddered, knowing that buildings full of the colorful sparks were shaken to pieces by his motion.

Hwarrm flew away, well ahead of Mountain's attack.

Too slow, too slow. The thought brought despair. He moved as fast as he ever had, as fast as he ever could—but not fast enough. He could never strike Hwarrm.

Still, he sent arms to the surface. Perhaps the dragon would tire and fall. Perhaps he would grow careless. Perhaps…

On the northern rim, the stone ridge grew pliable, plastic. It swelled out into a smooth ball of stone, then hardened.

A blow from within shattered the stone bubble. Burgard peered out.

"Good placement, lads. Right on the rim—oh!"

Below, the black silhouette of Hwarrm sat in the midst of what had been the mercy shrine.

His body overflowed the amphitheater. His lashing tail swept through adjacent buildings, shearing them, sending stone and wood flying.

The soldiers with Burgard battered their way out of the bubble and stared in dismay. "We cannot defeat that," the captain said. "We must return, warn the rest to flee—"

"Shut up!" Burgard fingered the Ring of Stars. "We destroyed him once before, while you were still a mewling child."

"With two full armies, yes! How can we gather a force large enough to harm that thing?"

"Risk death now or be certain of it later! Does anyone truly wish to flee?"

They all shook their heads. Some looked with scorn on the talkative captain.

Hard by them, another stony bubble swelled. Moments later, vagha burst out—and Jandith with them. She looked coolly down on Hwarrm and his rampage. "This is no calamity," she told Burgard. "The real city is in the caverns below."

"True." He raised his voice. "Form up! Eyes open for arriving units. When we have enough to make our presence felt, we'll remind Hwarrm what it means to face the might of the vagha!"

The dwarves with him cheered.

To Burgard's ears, the cry was false and hollow. But the Ring of Stars pulsed in his hand, and he again felt its strength and its nature: summoning and direction—Deathcraft and all the elements. He looked to the stars whence the ring had come, and knew how he would command the ring.

Hwarrm waited until he felt the tendrils of fire approaching. Then he rose and crashed through the delicate buildings as if they were lacquered paper.

There before him stood the central spire. The dragon laughed and pushed it over. It shattered near the base, toppled, broke apart as it fell, and smashed half the buildings on Alliance Square.

Tiny screams erupted, as appealing to Hwarrm's ear as trilling birdsong to the selumari. Flame awoke along the collapsed tower's length, burning less hot than his hatred.

Then came a blow, and pain such as Hwarrm had not felt since last he fell! Something plunged down from above, shearing the plated flesh of his shoulder. Hwarrm stumbled and fell in agony. He reared back and poured his ashen breath into the sky, but saw no enemy. What had attacked him?

As pain subsided, he saw a silvery streak high aloft—a shooting star. Then it veered and swiftly grew…

Hwarrm leapt, landing atop the Hall of Justice, shattering in an instant what had taken decades to build. The silvery streak, now flame-orange, smashed into the plaza where he had stood.

Hwarrm smiled through his pain. "At last!" he shouted. "An enemy worth fighting! But where are you, coward, you who lob these stars like a child throwing rocks?" The dragon coiled and launched into the air, climbing high on the heated currents of steam.

A third meteor fell. This time, he felt the source directing it: something on the northern rim. He veered toward it, but the missile seared his skin, cutting through the membranes along his spiny ridgeline; he was too heavy without his patagium to help him snake through the updrafts like a flying squirrel. Helplessly, he banked left and landed hard, sliding through the ruins of Blackshutter.

Impatient, he growled with laughter. "You cannot kill Hwarrm! I am deathless, like the earth itself!" He turned his massive head and took stock of the damage. It was minimal, and he could still glide so long as he kept his core tight. Again he leapt skyward.

When the fourth star fell, he banked right. The fiery stone passed harmlessly—he felt its heat warm his belly before it crashed amid fleeing mortals.

Hwarrm straightened and rose toward the northern rim, toward the tiny figures standing there.

Blackness with gleaming eyes, silhouetted against the city's growing fires—Hwarrm was difficult to spot in the nighttime sky. Still. Burgard managed to bring the sky-stars down with fair aim.

Light glinted off the arcane ring at his fist. *With time, and troops not frightened witless as these are,* he thought greedily, *this will make a mighty weapon!*

Then his last attack missed, and he saw the dragon rushing toward them. "Down and resume!" he cried to the line or troops. "On my signal… now!"

United, the dwarves invoked magic from the earth and imagined a pathway—not so long or complex as the one that had brought them to Karakto. Stone leapt up around them, fusing in huge shells, and drew them into the stony rim. Burgard seized Jandith as his own shell formed and drew them down to safety.

Darkness. Stillness. Then the ground shook as the great beast passed overhead.

"The stones from the sky," Jandith said. "The ring lets you command them?"

"Yes." Burgard uncovered the ring. Its stars shone, the only light in the shell. "Earth from the sky—a mix of elements I have not seen before," he mused. "The gnomes made many of these sorts of items—but whoever tampered with this one to try and improve its power unleashed something new—I suspect it is the only one like it."

"It pulls on all Nature's elements of magic and also Deathcraft?"

"Yes."

He felt her unbuckle the armor at his side. "Not now!" he said.

"Yes, now." Her eyes sparkled with lascivious intent and her voice dripped like honey.

He felt her draw aside the armor against his ribs, and then burning coldness as her knife plunged into his side.

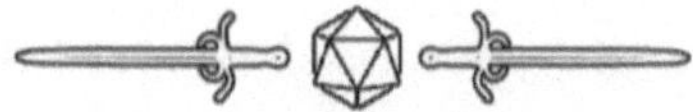

Hwarrm flew past the ridge, out beyond the volcano, and circled the dark skies, waiting.

Moments later, stone eggs popped to the surface all along the ridge. Still he waited.

Then dwarves emerged and looked on the city. They seemed confused.

Silently, Hwarrm glided toward them, his eyes mere slits. Alerted by the wind of his approach, they turned—too late. He poured out his breath, then descended past the line of statues to finish his dread work upon the city.

Jandith's eyes gleamed in the light of the Ring of Stars. "You spoke truly, my love. It does carry with it knowledge of its use."

Agonized, Burgard lay still. If she thought him dead already…

She waved the ring over her head. "Remove," she said. The stone shell dropped away, and the Daybringers glowed in the night sky.

"This is a good stony grave for a good stony dwarf," she said. "I leave you to it. Farewell." And she ran forth into the night.

Burgard wondered what hurt more: the wound of flesh, or that of spirit. She had not taken his life, but something more important: his pride. He would have it back.

He dragged himself to his feet, one hand pressed against his side. Then he saw that not one other dwarf had survived. The elite units of the army of Gundakhor had become dead rock where Hwarrm had spewed his vile breath upon them.

To the west he saw Jandith. She was making for the best path down to the city; Burgard followed.

Just ahead, outside the crater, grew the tall ailanthus where Calantha had persuaded Burgard not to slay the morehl. Jandith laughed at the thought. As she reached the notch in the rim, she turned to make the treacherous climb down into Karakto.

In the lower tunnels she would find allies. They would ride out this dragon-storm and emerge to rule. When they had made their home safe against out siders, they would emerge and call shooting stars down upon the heads of their enemies, realizing the dreams of conquest they'd abandoned nearly twenty years ago.

She heard a sizzling and felt heat from behind—the dragon?

No—Hwarrm was on the far side of the crater, flattening buildings. She turned and saw the tall tree and, beyond it, Orric, descending from the sky on a column of fire! He bore a body in his arms—Calantha, obviously dead.

Orric touched ground. He gently, swiftly, set the body at the tree's root, then looked up. "Jandith! What a pleasure. What is that in your hand?"

"A trifle."

"I want it."

She walked toward him. "Of course. You can make better use of it than I. You can defeat Hwarrm, can you not?" She held the ring before her with one hand, and with the other grasped her knife-hilt behind her back.

"Perhaps." He took the ring, but kept his attention on her.

"Where is Burgard?"

"Slain by the dragon. Burnt to ash. He kept me safe while he perished." She assumed an expression of sadness and waited. In a moment, he would turn to make sad faces at his dead mother, and she would kill him.

"Ah. Then who is this behind you?"

Almost, she laughed. She had not expected such a simple trick from Orric.

"Good—good evening, Orric…"

Hearing the voice, she glanced back. Twenty paces away, Burgard staggered toward them, his gaze fixed on her.

"No!" She brandished her dagger, but thought better of it. Burgard, even weakened, could kill her easily, and Orric was said to be a skilled fighter.

She turned and ran.

Orric's cloak whipped around her legs and threw her to the ground. She stabbed blindly, but her blade caught only silk. Then Orric fell upon her. He twisted her arms behind her back, and she dropped the blade.

He was tying her as Burgard arrived. "Lord Burgard."

"Orric." Burgard sat beside them, ignoring Jandith. "I failed."

"The ring was of no use?"

"It was of every use. With enough strength, I could rain sky-stones on him until he died."

"My late mother spoke of using Mountain."

"I don't know what that means. Gone, is she?" Burgard shook his head. "I fear we are all going tonight." Then he slumped to one side.

Orric pulled bloody cloth from the dwarf's wound. With his newfound awareness, Orric sensed the fire magic bubbling all through the volcano. As he drew on it, his hand glowed red.

Then he touched the wound, and Burgard jumped. Lines of red flame crawled over the vagha's body, then vanished. The wound was not healed, but the dwarf would live.

Burgard sat up. "Firecraft."

"How do you feel?"

"Roasted. And soon we shall all feel stone-hard, unless we find an army to combat that beast." In the distance, Hwarrm reared up again and began a slow, deadly march through another district.

"Look there," said Orric. In the city, a gout of flaming stone burst from the ground and sprayed the ruins Hwarrm had crushed mere moments ago. "See how the streamers of lava emerge? Does the dragon do that?"

"I do not know."

Orric slipped on the black band and extended his perceptions, seeking out the source of the fiery stream. He felt its heat, the magic within it, and traced it down to the volcano's molten heart.

There dwelt a presence, vast beyond reckoning. It was slow but unstoppable: a greater elemental. Its presence shuddered with magic vibrations much like Winter Spear did— only far more powerful.

For a long interval Orric tried to trace its cavernous thoughts, but to no avail. He could not grasp it. He felt very small.

"Mountain," he whispered, wondering.

Burgard looked at him curiously. "What?"

"The volcano itself attacks Hwarrm. Look there, another one." A second fire-stream spattered in Hwarrm's wake, incinerating ruins but leaving the dragon unharmed.

"Remarkable! But it is too slow."

"I see what Mother meant. The mountain itself is our ally—if we can tap its strength. Come with me. We must gather that army you spoke of."

They descended into the crater, a careworn army of mixed races. In the lead walked the demarch's adopted son and the dwarf warlord. Orric and Burgard both held the ring, their hands joined over it. Burgard carried Jandith over his shoulder, ignoring her pleas.

"This cannot succeed," Burgard said. "When the first stone falls upon him, Hwarrm will sense where we are and come for us.

"That is exactly what we want," said Orric. "That is how we defeat him."

Half the city lay in ruins. Hwarrm snarled. That meant half his work lay undone. And when the city above ground was gone, he would batter the warrens beneath and worm his way inside to build a nest to store a horde.

Then it came again, the terrible blow from above. This star seared his left rear flank, throwing the wyrm to the ground. He shrieked, a killing howl that shattered statues across the crater.

He found the source immediately—west this time, in the crater near the center. He rose in a short arc, saw masses of vermin, and descended, readying another cleansing breath—

Orric closed his eyes and gathered to himself the power of Calantha's army. Using the ring, he reached downward. The mind he touched was as large and profound as the sea. He shuddered. Mastering his terror, he sent forth his tiny thought. After long moments, an alien presence crystallized in his mind. He could not interpret its emotion or put its meaning into words, yet—

"I have it," Orric said aloud. He extended phantom hands through the earth until he touched the rising columns of lava.

He guided them, sped them. He had become one with Mountain, leading him as a rider guides a horse.

As Hwarrm descended on a current of smoke, Orric raised a hand, then struck.

A jet of lava erupted from the ground. The glowing stone hit Hwarrm's left flank, shearing through. Hwarrm bellowed as his side blew apart. Hwarrm fell like a stone. His momentum unchecked, he slid through the blocky residences of the poor, hurling walls before him. Crackling and roaring, the great mass of dragon and buildings slammed to a stop, two hundred paces from Calantha's army.

"I feel it," said Burgard. "I understand now."

"Mountain has more than two arms," Orric told him.

Burgard narrowed his eyes and raised a triumphant hand. At Burgard's downstroke, another lance of lava burst from the ground, burning through the beast's tail.

Hwarrm turned toward them. They saw his flanks swell as he took in a breath.

Orric struck again. Lava leapt from the ground and poured across Hwarrm's white head—into his open mouth. The stream disintegrated the beast's lower jaw and ignited whatever anatomy allowed these incredible beasts to spew elemental death. Orric felt his own hand ramming down the dragon's throat.

"Choke on it," Burgard said.

"We must get closer," Orric said. "Mountain wants him, but it needs delicate handling." He took a step forward, but Burgard's grip on the ring brought him up short. Orric scowled.

"Now, Burgard."

"Stay with your city, Orric." Burgard wrenched the ring free.

"I have decided to follow your mother's advice," he said, and hoisted Jandith to his shoulder. "Abandon selfish desire. Desire for wealth, for success! It is liberating."

"We go together," Orric insisted.

Burgard was stern. "Death waits there, Orric. We both know it. I will finish this battle, but you have many more remaining, as you rebuild this city." He blinked in thought. "Send me strength."

Without another word, Burgard raced forward, bounding from toppled building slabs to piles of ruined brick, dancing around flames as they consumed timbers.

Ahead, the ruins of Hwarrm's body rose on two legs. The dragon's head swung aimlessly, confusion in the one surviving eye. Did he seek victims? Answers?

Jandith howled urgently, "Let me go!"

"You said you loved me."

"I do! I do love you."

"Then you'll want to stay with me."

Her voice rose in a wail. Burgard felt crawling tendrils of lava ahead and below. He touched his phantom hands to them. An unlikely alliance—mortal dwarf and ageless volcano!

Hwarrm finally noticed him. His head tilted. He spoke, but the words emerged as an incoherent roar.

"I am Burgard of Gundakhor," the warlord called, "and I have achieved greatness where you have failed. Any dragon can ruin a city. But not any dwarf can slay a dragon!" So saying, he raised his hands.

Lava flows, thicker and brighter than any before, rose from below. They struck Hwarrm from either side, shattering his spine.

At that moment, the ground under the dragon collapsed.

Cracks reached in all directions, with molten stone running along them.

Hwarrm shrieked in death-agony, helpless in the mountain's grip. Then he was half-submerged in the lava, slipping, vanishing—

The ground tilted. Burgard lost his balance and tumbled forward. In his last moments, he fancied he might fall into Hwarrm's eye and wondered if he would hear the thoughts of the dragon. He held on to Jandith almost tenderly, and they tumbled through, vanishing together in the lava's pure heat.

In the last hours of the night, survivors clustered on the western slope and watched the glowing volcano floor cool and darken. Already they were calling the spot Hwarrm's Door.

Orric sat beside an orphaned selumari girl, whom he had rescued from a burning ruin. Her weeping had stopped, and she looked at him now with the clarity and intelligence he remembered from his mother.

"What will you do now?" she asked.

"The army comes from Gundakhor," he said wearily. "Before it arrives, I will declare all morehl free. When it arrives, scouts will see what we did to Hwarrm, and what little is left. I think they will leave."

He took a deep breath. "Then, we rebuild. Perhaps here, perhaps somewhere else. Perhaps the morehl and selumari together, perhaps separately. The spirits that drive us are different."

She nodded. Then, with a wisdom beyond her years, she said, "But different doesn't have to mean war."

He smiled. "Perhaps not." He gestured toward a nearby couple. A selumari man and morehl woman nestled in the attitude of new lovers. "Nature itself is made up of opposing forces—earth and air, fire and water. Before the Corrupter, conflict was the bringer of life to this young world. In conflict, life finds and refines its balance."

Orric's words drifted off in silence as he studied the ruins below, and the ghostlike citizens rising up from them. The city needed tending, the citizens needed tending. Karakto was a garden grown wild, in need of a strong and ceaseless hand. Orric knew it was his duty, his privilege, to tend it—for a time. It was also his duty and privilege, once that time was done, to wander.

The way of Quietude required it of him.

Until you can drink one sip of that tea, you can never drink the tea. Now, at last, he understood.

He was about to express his new resolve to the child beside him when he heard her soft, peaceful snore.

EPILOGUE

"I was living like a hog in a wallow," Yort said as he tended the cooking fire and sharpened the skewers. "I faced no challenges, had no goals. I just wanted security and comfort. But when you get comfortable, you spoil like dead meat. Life is not about comfort. By the way, how are you doing back there?"

"Mmph! Mrrmmummph!" Hornbeam strained at his bindings.

"Good, good… Cubed and grilled, drawn and soaked in brine, frizzled in grease, hmmm…"

The moon lit the midsummer evening, making a sapphire sheet of Hwarrm's Doom Bay. The air, sultry and still, carried only a hint of brimstone from the deserted volcano.

"So, I have had better luck as a wanderer," Yort continued. "I've been trying for years to get home, but I keep getting lost. See what happy opportunities lost-ness brings me, sir? You are saving me from a hungry time."

With the fire burning merrily, Yort looked around. He had seen no other goblins here, not even imps. By now the oldest Wild Thing imps would be, what, thirteen? More than capable of leading their growing number to battle. Likely the males had taken wives of their own and continued the cycle.

This evening, as he had many times before, Yort idly considered finding a new wife and settling down for a week or so. No, it was not the Yort Way.

He had invented the Yort Way' two years ago, after a bad batch of tingleleaf drove him mad for ten days. Waking from weird dreams, he had decided on a new path, a way past his frustrations, and he'd followed that way ever since.

Footsteps approached across the Narcea marsh. Suspicious, Yort ran to Hornbeam, knocked him out with a rock, and hid him among the reeds for safety. The goblin returned to his fire.

Into the fire lit clearing stepped a young morehl man wearing a black cloak. Yort froze. He could hardly tell one red elf from another, but he knew that cloak. *His wife's killer.*

"Good evening to you," said Orric.

"I am meeting a friend near here, a fat dwarf. Have you seen him?"

He does not even remember me, thought Yort. "No." *I can take him by surprise, revenge myself on him!* "Why meet at this deserted place? I only returned here by accident, when I got lost."

"Several years ago we traveled together for a time, south of here. We separated, but agreed to meet back here on this day to exchange news. What place are you looking for?"

"Bent Morass. Have you heard of it?"

"No."

"Pity." Debating various tricks, Yort decided first to lull Orric's suspicions. He gestured for Orric to sit on a nearby stone. "Well, I am as much in the market for news as your fat friend. Why, for instance, does no one live here any more? Did the red and blue elves kill each other?"

"They live on New Emmiria, a volcanic island far out to sea. Ogan the Reef found it for them, though he thought it a nuisance to uproot and make a new home. The selumari and morehl live together still, like standoffish spouses. The selumari live in the old way again, with the Burgardans working for their food as the poor do. Since the morehl higher classes refused to leave Karakto, the virtue of class compliance has quietly been losing favor, and I think the system will wither away."

"What became of the higher classes?"

"See for yourself." Orric gestured to the desolate volcano.

"I thank you, but no." Look-over-there, my-imp's-lost, find-my-treasure… "What of the onetime ally, Gundakhor? Those dwarves lost so many in the war, they must be nursing a grudge."

"What of it? Will they invade an island for no profit?"

"There are no more pistols?"

"The first new edict: 'no more pistols.' At least, not this deadly variety making a name for themselves as Karakto Pistols."

Burning embers in the eyes? No, red elves were mostly fireproof. Yort said, "Still, Death can always plant more morehl in some new volcano. They could devise a way to make them."

Orric wondered if it was possible… *if even one of the mortality faces survived...* he glanced at steaming Karakto. "True. My mother showed me that trying to improve the world is dangerous and, in most cases, unworkable. But we can help one person at a time." He looked straight at Yort. "I am sorry I killed your wife."

Yort froze again. "You knew. You sat here talking with me, knowing—"

"I have thought of that incident many times. For so long, I considered her murder an act of war. But war justifies nothing, certainly not what her murder made of me. What would you have in repayment?"

Yort had no notion, not the faintest idea. For the first time in a long while, he was speechless. He wondered why he had wanted to kill this young man. That was not, he decided, the Yort Way.

Orric said, "I have a talisman that has guided me in mental discipline. If you are struggling with your grief, as I struggled with many emotions, it can serve you well." He pulled the cloak from his shoulders and offered it to Yort. The goblin looked at it, swallowed, and then said, "I thank you. But I need no cloak. Go, and know that I hold no ill will."

Orric nodded. He turned to watch a cloud of moonlit black specks at the lip of the volcano. "The bats have returned to Karakto. They were away so many years… This is fine news."

With a nod to Yort, he walked away into the darkness. Yort stood a while, watching the bats. For one exalted moment he thought of friendship among the First Races, an end to the pointless war.

Then his stomach rumbled, and he saw that the cookfire burned low. "Well, someday, perhaps," he said aloud, going to rouse Hornbeam. "But let us take care of immediate needs, eh, sir? We can help one person at a time, as the man says, and you can be proud that you are helping me."

With a lick of his snout, he set enthusiastically to his work.

THE END.

THE TALE OF CREATION

Canto 1

LISTEN, MY CHILD, and I shall tell you a story — oh! such a story! Listen well as I tell the Tale of Creation, the First Tale, the tale of how our peoples came to be — the tales of our father and mother, and of how the bright shining world of Esfah came to be.

Now, the First One, first of all beings, is Tarvanehl, meaning The All in the ancient tongue — the one whom we sometimes call Father Time. He is everywhere, and he is nowhere. He has no form, no substance, no matter. But he has a mission: to mark the passage of time. He sees all but judges not, interferes not. And listen you well to this: Tarvanehl existed before aught else, and he will endure after all is dust. Think of that when the missiles of the morehl whiz by overhead, deafening you with their sharp retort and blinding you with smoke.

But I digress from the tale, child; let me do so no more…

There is no reckoning, no accounting as to the length of days before Tarvanehl created the Void. This Void was deep, dark, and it had no heart, no soul, no thought. Light and sound did not enter the Void, for neither yet existed. What prompted the First One to create such a strange and morbid thing, we cannot know. But Tarvanehl embraced his strange creation, his thoughts unknown and unknowable, and his touch was bitter cold.

…This cold seeped through the Void, rendering it bleak and desolate beyond measure. We shudder here in our mountains when the winter winds blow, but our cold is as nothing compared to the cold of the Void. Naught but blackfrost, endless in depth, without mercy and without measure, existed in the Void. This cold was an evil, vile thing, and perhaps that is what corrupted the Void so - and not its creator's dispassion.

Canto 2

As time marched on, Tarvanehl touched the Void, now and then leaving behind some fragment of some such substance. What form these shapes took is unknown, but sages whisper that they were spheres of perfect form. The bitter cold held the Void in shackles, however, and it prevented all within — including the spheres — from moving.

These bodies, mostly formless, mindless things, floated through the Void. Despite the frigid chains surrounding them, over the vast, unimaginable stretch of time, there was movement, a tiny flicker of defiance in a barren waste. Such was Tarvanehl's disposition that he had absolute and utter patience, and he let the bodies continue on their minute courses as they would. Then, for reasons all his own, Tarvanehl ignored the Void and no longer embraced it in his cold dispassion. Indeed, some say he abandoned the Void, that time itself stood still. But we know that time can never stand still, my child, not even when Tarvanehl's attention wanders elsewhere. So slowly — oh! so slowly! — the wretched cold within the Void began to give way, much as our winter snows finally melt beneath the warm zephyr of spring.

In this Void, as I have said, Tarvanehl had placed the formless bodies, much like you or I would pick up the pretty shells lining the beaches of the coral elves, placing the bits and pieces on our mantel when we return home. During this endless span of time, Tarvanehl had looked at these… "trinkets" once or twice, most often with dispassion and a curious lack of interest. You may question Tarvanehl's attitude, for he is certainly the father to all in the Void, but would a father look on his children with such disfavor? As I have said, Tarvanehl is The All, the First One. Yes, he paid them little attention, not deigning to see them as gods, though they were the essence of gods, being the handpicked elements of the First One himself. Perhaps they could have become gods with his guidance, but such was not Tarvanehl's way. There was a streak of arrogance in him, bred perhaps during the span of countless millennia. Remember: He was the First One, the One God, The All.

Canto 3

Then, one day, a day of monumental import, Tarvanehl's interest was caught: A god *had* formed in the Void, without his knowledge. In the eons of time, while the Void had been held in the grips of the cold, *he* had formed: Silence, or Selurehl in the ancient tongue.

Selurehl reigned supreme in the Void, for sound did not exist, and Tarvanehl did not interfere, though he watched from afar. For millennia beyond measure, Selurehl filled the Void with savage, silent fury. He spread terror throughout the Void, and none dared oppose his relentless hand — certainly not the beings floating in the Void, who were only now beginning to acquire the glimmer of sentience.

There were, perhaps, a hundred or so such bodies. They were formless, floating lumps of matter — giants composed of gases, dwarfs of dense stone, and others of matter and elements now lost to the winds. Somehow they maintained some semblance of self even as they made their minute passage across the Void. For unimaginable spans of time, they hung in precarious balance, suspended throughout the Void, slowly — oh! so slowly! — making their tortured way across the infinity of space.

Then, my child, in some chance moment, two bodies shifted simultaneously and strayed a hair's breadth closer to each other. Each body abruptly tensed, suddenly aware of a new and unexpected influence: gravity. This strange and mysterious force drew them closer together. They strained against the power, unaware of what would happen should they collide, but instinctively fearing the result. The bodies shifted sideways, hoping to skirt the other, but again the force pulled them together; this time, however, the pull was even greater than before.

Each body's gravity exerted itself on the other... each was drawn ever closer to the other... and each strained away toward the opposite direction. But the force drawing them together was inexorable — and relentless. The titans of stone collided, and the Void erupted in sound and light. The explosive joining of these two bodies reverberated throughout the Void, the ripples trickling off to the farthest ends, but still reaching all.

It was the end of life as all within the Void had known it.

The other bodies could not escape the fate that had claimed their sister and brother. They too were caught up in the deadly force... and one by one each collided with the first two, and all added to the savage sound and fury. A maelstrom of power and light began to swirl throughout the Void, and Selurehl cowered before it. But her hold on her minions was faltering, failing rapidly, and the destruction of herself and her reign drew nigh. Tarvanehl, however, remained impassive as always, perhaps unaware or perhaps merely uncaring of what transpired in the Void he held.

The vortex of sound and color and light expanded as the remaining bodies melded into one huge glowing mass. This mass exploded in size and scope — doubling, tripling, even quadrupling itself in the space of a fraction of a second. Selurehl was dumbfounded. Never before in the long eons of his existence had he encountered anything such as sound or light. His grip upon the Void collapsed, and he vanished, to surface again only in deepest grottoes of the morehl.

The mass increased exponentially; even so, it took some few moments for it to reach the confines of the Void. When it did, Tarvanehl released the Void, and the glowing light exploded into fragments beyond count. Light and sound filled the Void, giving it shape and color, substance and soul. A remnant of the tremendous mass of light remained intact, and we call it Soll or the Sun. Something within the Void flickered and grew; it was the Void itself, at last made sentient, and bound up with the vestiges of Selurehl's wrath and ambition.

Void was a second face upon Selurehl's form, a second nature. The Void was filled with a vision of what it might be. But the millennia of Tarvanehl's patient wait had come to an end. When Tarvanehl touched the Void and bade it sleep, it did as The All Father asked.

The remaining bits of debris and matter scattered about, forming the stars and moons you see in the night sky, my child — as well as the husk of our beloved young world of Esfah, which means the Bright One in the ancient tongue. How many points of light were formed on that day so long ago, none can know — and perhaps not even Tarvanehl, in his immense wisdom, can count the stars.

Canto 4

Now, you might think that is the end of the Tale of Creation, but it is not. For you see, into the Void there entered a spark of life, an animate thing of infinite beauty and grace. She touched upon Esfah and found it to her liking, though barren — oh! so barren! The Void, still so young and new, slumbered on, unaware that the tiny pulse, the flicker of light and color and hope, began to grow.

The spark kept about her task, seeing only that the vastness surrounding her was a vile thing. This nothingness was hateful to her, and she loathed the Void with instinctive hate. One by one Nature — for such was her name, even in the ancient tongue — brought forth the fruits of her womb to help her mold and build the world of Esfah. Nature's firstborn was Earth, or Eldurim in the ancient tongue. He was truly a child of first blood, being the dutiful son and supporting his mother in all her causes. He was a grim being, with his visage of stone, though his heart was true. With his passage into existence the creation of substance, of rock and earth, began. Slowly, oh so slowly, Esfah began to grow and fill.

Into the Void's dreams there crept an image, a vision of life. The Void grew perturbed, its sleep less certain, but still it slumbered on.

Then Nature brought about her second child, Air, or Ailuril in the ancient tongue. She was light of substance and bright of personality, this child of freedom who could not be captured or tamed. Nature could not count on this capricious, whimsical daughter, but Ailuril did gladden her mother's heart, and that counted for much. The child swept across Esfah, pausing to caress the solid fastness of her brother's bones before streaking off into the Void that surrounded them all. Eldurim shook his head at his sister's headstrong ways, but only returned to his work.

The Void's dreams filled with the tempestuous rushing of air as Ailuril's tendrils touched it in her passing. The Void sighed, whether in pain or longing, we cannot know, but still it slept on.

Nature heard the sigh and marveled that the vast nothingness surrounding her might be alive. Her instincts warned her to beware the Void, but she refused to heed any fears. She merely brought forth her third child, Fire, the destructive but cleansing power called Firiel in the ancient tongue. She was a creature of passion and burning desires, with an intensity and purpose that brooked little compromise, and fiercely devoted to her mother. This daughter swept through Esfah, scorching her brother's rocks and stones, melting them and putting her own stamp upon the land. As he had with Ailuril, Eldurim merely shook his head and kept about his work.

The Void rippled in pain at Firiel's touch, and it opened its eyes.

Nature knew her time of fertile creation without interference by another was about to end, and so she hurried the birth of her fourth child: Water, he who is called Aguarehl in the ancient tongue. This son was mercurial in nature, one moment calm and soothing, the next thunderous and violent. He could not be counted on by Nature, who sometimes wondered what her son would have been like if she could have nurtured his creation instead of rushing it. But Aguarehl seemed not to sense his mother's dismay, and he only set about quenching his sister's flames with his own tides, furiously checking fires and volcanic eruptions. Alone of all his brethren, Aguarehl sensed that Esfah was like a vicious sore to the Void, and that the young world's transformation was irritating to the Second God.

Aguarehl tried to halt his siblings' actions, but his efforts were too late; the Void was fully roused and hungry for revenge on she who had awoken it from its slumber, for it knew the true source of its irritation: Nature. The Void fell upon the spark of life and defiled her. Nature cried out for Tarvanehl, and the First One came to her aid. Tarvanehl and Void confronted one another, but then the Void's courage failed and it fled Esfah, hiding away from all prying eyes. During this conflict, none were watching, and in the absence of all entropic forces a life emerged from the primordial mire, the Shara, who saw the faces of the gods and hid for eons, barely understanding their place in the world. They are called the eldarim, which means "from the earth."

Tarvanehl would do no more against his kin, and so he let the Void live, for the sake of Selurehl. He abandoned Nature, not even deigning to comfort the one he had come to protect, but such are the strange and unknowable ways of the First One.

Canto 5

Nature bore a fifth child, a child of the Void/Selurehl and not her own gentle self — and so Death was born. He was an evil creature, with a vile soul and a spiteful heart. The Misbegotten One, as he is sometimes called, spread hatred and despair wherever he went. Eldurim, as ever the dutiful son, tried to embrace this violent sibling into the family, but he was bitterly rebuffed. Firiel stood her ground against Death, neither giving nor taking, her red eyes inscrutable but always upon the youngest child. And Ailuril and Aguarehl? They fled, unable to bear their brother's presence.

This son turned against his mother, and Nature despaired. Death rose up against Nature and moved to strike her, longing only to send his black tendrils into she who had borne him and crush her heart. But Eldurim and Firiel stood by their mother and opposed their brother. Outnumbered, the Misbegotten One spat upon his siblings, then turned and ran.

Nature wept bitterly, her tears of elements falling upon the land; these tears she shed for a child conceived in violence, whom she might have learned to love had he not been so repulsive in spirit. Ailuril and Aguarehl returned to help comfort their mother, taking turns with Eldurim and Firiel to soothe Nature's raw sorrow. So concerned were her children for their mother, and so distraught was Nature, that none noticed the elemental tears form into dragons and wing or crawl away. The dragons hid themselves in the newness of Esfah, marveling shyly at the world and at life. Creeping in the earth and rarely cresting the skies, they were attuned to the Shara: the ancient, powerful creatures that the gods barely took notice of.

Canto 6

Nature tapped the strength deep within her and set aside her grief. The Mother of All turned her attention to the young world of Esfah and her four other children, turning upon them her glad eyes now tinged with the shadow of sorrow. She bade them populate the world, to create guardians for the care of Esfah. Ailuril and Aguarehl were the first to bring forth their children, the Elder Monsters known as the coral giant, the winged gryphon, the sprites, and the intelligent octopus called the tako. These creatures were but the imperfect beginnings of the true guardians of air and water, and before long the selumari — the coral elves — were born. They are the First Race, and many count the selumari as the most beautiful, and the most noble, but in my vaghan heart I know that we are truly the most worthy.

Eldurim and Firiel were next with their creations, experimenting broadly and bringing forth the ugly androsphinx, the reptilian gargoyle, the immense two-headed roc, and the umber hulk. Before long, however, they settled on the design for the vagha — the dwarves, which are attuned to earth and fire. Compact of body and movement and often without grace, we are nevertheless the salt of the earth. We are the Second Race, and we are the pride of Eldurim and Firiel.

Nature was well pleased with her children's work, and for some time Esfah knew only joy and harmony. Ailuril and Aguarehl taught their children, the selumari, the joys of caring for the water and the air. Meanwhile, Eldurim and Firiel taught the vagha how to wield the powers of earth and fire. Even the firstborn creatures, the Elder Monsters, though while not perfect in the eyes of their fathers and mothers, were welcomed in Esfah. Moreover, the selumari and the vagha embraced these siblings with love and joy, and our two races were brothers in spirit if not in body.

Canto 7

Perhaps it was this lack of such care and attention for his own sake that drove Death mad with grief and rage. More likely, the cankerous growth of bile that passed for his heart continued to grow and poison his soul. Whatever the cause, he vowed vengeance on those responsible for his misery, and so he plotted against Nature and her children.

Death violated both Eldurim and Firiel, bringing forth his own children: the trogs and the morehl. Death's races were born fully fashioned. He then corrupted some of these children into the Younger Monsters. From the blood of his goblins, he made the loathsome death naga, the strident harpy, the shambler, and the cannibalistic troll. These fearsome creatures, like the trogs themselves, were wicked creations of death and earth. From the morehl, the lava elves, Death created the nightmarish beholder, the evil drider, the ferocious hellhound, and the fiendish rakshasa — all foul creatures of death and fire.

The children of the elements — the selumari, the vagha, the trogs, and the morehl — fell to fighting for the preservation or the death of Esfah. But you know this part of the tale, my child, for it is the story of your life. And so I will end the Tale of Creation — or at least this Tale of Creation. Others exist, and even the same story I have told may not be the same tale in the homeland of another. But soon I will tell you more, tell you how the Amazons were born, the Firewalkers and, yes, even the dreaded Dead Ones. For now, though, tend to your ways and think long and hard on what you have heard this night.

The world is still young, still malleable, still subject to the forces of Tarvanehl, and Nature, and Death. But we have Eldurim, and Ailuril, and Firiel and Aguarehl to protect and nurture us. They are our fathers and mothers; heed their words of wisdom and all will be well.

All will be well, my child.

THE BEARD AND THE SPEAR

LYANDRA AND ALYANDRA were Amazon twins of great renown. None could best their bow arm in any championship, and the twins won equally, often tying for whatever prize was offered. Likewise, they were the finest charioteers, their reputation for recklessness — and winning at all costs — preceding them. There was often many a wager cast on one or the other of the twins and like as not the bettor went home well satisfied.

They were inseparable, these sisters, always at each other's side as they fought jointly against the trogs, or the morehl, or whoever threatened their homeland. They wandered back and forth between the wars and the competitions that marked the life of Amazon society. And so they spent a carefree existence, and had for the past decade or more, ever since they had become women in the eyes of their sisters.

Then one day they received an invitation to attend a very special competition.

"I think we should go," Alyandra said, looking up from the spidery script traced across the dried mulago leaf.

"All the way to the Ear Seas, though?" Lyandra countered, honing her spear with a Whetstone and then checking the sharpness of the point against one strand of her lustrous dark hair. The sister shook her head.

"No, Aly, it's too far to go. Besides, the selumari are at war with the morehl, aren't they?"

"Yes, but our coral elf brethren wouldn't host the games if they didn't feel it were safe, would they?" Alyandra countered. "Besides, the victor of the preliminaries gets to go up against an Elder Monster."

That should have piqued Lyandra's curiosity, but the sister was wise to Aly's ways. Lyandra only murmured, "Elder Monster? Which one?"

Alyandra smoothed the message. "Hmmm… Ah, here it is. It's shadow. Says here it's the only one of its kind — "

"They say that about all the Elder Monsters, Aly. They're afraid to believe there are more of the terrible creatures. Even if we killed them all, the gods would spawn another," Lyandra interjected.

" — and it's invisible, or at least hard to see," Alyandra continued, ignoring her sister and squinting at the text. "Or at least that's what I think it says." She sighed, staring at her sister. "What do you say, Lyandra?"

When she received no response, Aly added, "There's a purse of a pair of matched grays, Lyandra —— rumored to be the fastest 'round for a thousand leagues. And I'm not sure our team will last another season." Aly's voice turned wheedling.

Lyandra put one last polish to her spear and then stood. "You've a point, sister." Her dark eyes suddenly twinkled. "Besides, I've always wanted to fight a Shadow — haven't you?" With a swift motion that not even Alyandra could follow, the Amazon struck her spear into the soil, straight through the throat of her shadow. Lyandra laughed suddenly, then yanked the spear from the ground. She looked up at the sky of bright cerulean blue and gestured toward the east. "It's a fine day, Aly. If we leave now, we can be there inside a tenday."

Alyandra smiled, well pleased. Of the two sisters, she was the more impetuous, Lyandra the more practical. She seldom went against her sister's direction, however, preferring to get Lyandra to agree with her instead. As always, the two were well complemented. "Then let's be on our way," Aly agreed as the pair headed off into the morning sun.

Ten days of hard travel saw the sisters to the edge of the sea. They paused on the cliffs to look down upon the coral elf city below, marveling at the structures of the selumari. Gilt edged the mother-of-pearl towers and glinted brightly in the setting sun, while the deep green sea likewise glimmered with the sheen of unexpected gold.

It was a magical sight, and the twins were breathless with wonder and anticipation. "Oh, Aly," Lyandra sighed. "I'm glad we came." She gave Alyandra's hand a quick squeeze and flashed her a smile.

The pair wandered down from the hills and headed toward the arena, located on the outskirts of the city. It was a beautiful coliseum, with tall fluted pillars of coral inlaid with lapis lazuli (a gift of the Amazons in centuries past) and broad sweeping steps that also acted as seats for spectators. Now the seats were filling with throngs of people: blue-skinned selumari, golden-skinned vagha, and a few Amazons. There was even the odd trog or two, but not a single morehl was in sight, for the war between the coral and the lava elves was still going on.

Lyandra and Alyandra paid their entry fee, drew their lot number, then sat back with the other contestants to watch the competition. Because of their reputation, the twins didn't need to compete in the preliminary events, which merely tested an individual's skill with the bow or spear against a target.

"There's not a one among them as good as we are," Lyandra spoke critically, pointing out flaws in technique to her sister.

Alyandra nodded. "We'll be in the final rounds then, no doubt, sister. And if luck remains with us, we'll be all alone against the Shadow, gods willing."

The sisters' prediction came true the next day. By midmorning they had bested their opponents in the finals, sending two coral elves and a dwarf to the infirmary in their zeal for victory. The twins were declared the victors of the match, and after a brief recess for the midday meal, the real event of the competition would begin: The Shadow would oppose the Amazons. "Are you scared, Aly?" Lyandra asked as she sat in the gladiators' waiting area, sharpening her spear and her kukri sword.

Alyandra stopped her nervous pacing, then knelt before her sister. "Yes, I am," she said truthfully, fear evident in the large dark eyes so like her twin's. "I don't want to lose you. You are the other half of me, Lyandra, and I couldn't bear — "

Lyandra touched her sister's lips. "Shush, Aly. You, too, are half of me. No matter what, I will always be by your side. Never doubt that. Never."

The gong sounded then, urging the spectators back to their places in the stands. There was time only for a quick embrace before the pair picked up their weapons and returned to the arena. They walked onto the coral sands, the heat of the sun prickling them "a little, but not unpleasantly so. The selumari announcer rattled off their names and conquests again for the audience, then asked the pit master to release the Shadow.

The twins tensed, watching the round granite slab blocking an archway slowly move out of the way. The spectators' voices had dropped to a murmur, and the grating of the rock on the sand could clearly be heard. Alyandra gripped her shield and pair of spears a little tighter; her lips pressed together.

Something slipped forth from the hole in the wall, something there but not there. It moved with furtive speed, darting from one object to another in the sandy arena. But the sun was high overhead, and there were no shadows for the creature to hide in.

The sisters moved forward slowly, stealthily creeping near the puddle of inky blackness that whispered across the coral ground. Lyandra threw her spear first, but she caught only the edge of the Shadow as it streaked away; the spear stuck in the ground where a moment before there had been darkness.

Aly circled around to trap the Elder Monster. She thought she heard something whisper, a tiny trill of pain, but she told herself it was only the wind. The Amazon cornered the Shadow in the crease between the arena's wall and its floor; Aly swore she saw the creature shiver in the narrow shadow there created by the overhead sun.

The young Amazon threw her spear just as the creature hissed and leapt upward. Aly's weapon clanged loudly against the stone wall of the arena, then fell to the ground. Her attention wasn't on the spear, however, but rather on the Shadow.

Strange, nearly solid limbs had formed from its inky depths; these appendages were gripping the wall and slowly dragging the creature's body upward. The shock of seeing a shadow crawl held Alyandra motionless. For a moment, she didn't realize that the sibilant whisper coming from the Shadow was filled with fear.

Lyandra was held in no such thrall, and the twin rushed forward. She swung her kukri sword upward in a wide swinging arc designed to cleave an opponent in two.

Aly shouted suddenly, "No! Don't hurt it!" She flung out her hands in a vain attempt to halt her sister's stroke.

The cry came too late, for Lyandra couldn't stop her momentum, nor even deflect the maneuver. The sword came crashing down upon the substanceless form of the Shadow, and the Elder Monster screamed. Its cry rent the air, the creature's pain tearing at Aly's heart.

The Shadow wrapped around Lyandra's sword, then slithered down the Amazon's arm and fell upon the woman's face. Aly whispered a tortured "No" even as Lyandra's own screams filled the air. The twin collapsed on the ground, dropping her sword and shield. She writhed about in agony, screaming all the time and clawing brutally at her face.

"Kill me!" Lyandra shrieked. "Kill me, Aly, before it kills me!"

The fear in her sister's voice drove Aly forward, and she fell to her knees by Lyandra. Aly straddled her sister's body, preventing Lyandra from rolling about. Lyandra clutched at her face, her fingers streaking through the sooty darkness and emerging red. Alyandra didn't know whose blood Lyandra was drawing, but she prayed it wasn't her sister's.

"No, Aly," Lyandra moaned, her voice ragged and fading fast. "Kill me before it kills me! It'll have my soul if you don't…" The Amazon's voice fell to a whisper, and her hands stilled upon her face.

Alyandra stood up slowly, horror thrumming through her body. For the first time in her life she was crippled by fear, and she could only stumble backward a step or two. She heard the Shadow hiss, a sound at once evil and hurting to Aly's ears, and she wondered if her sister's death sigh was mingled in the sound.

Then Lyandra's hands moved, albeit shakily. "Aly..." the twin whispered, "Aly... kill me, now, before it's too late. Aly, upon my love, kill me..."

With a horrified sob, Alyandra leapt forward, plunging her spear into her sister's belly just beneath the breastplate. Aly threw her weight against the heavy spear, forcing the shaft to dig deeper. Lyandra cried out and doubled over, once, and then was still.

Alyandra pulled out the spear and fell to her knees, her hands held before her in horror. She realized numbly that her eyes would not blink, and she wondered if they ever would again. Then she saw the Shadow's sinister blackness ripple in sudden convulsion. It formed an appendage of half-substance and began probing down Lyandra's body.

"No..." Aly whispered. "No, please..."

But the Shadow didn't heed the woman's terrified words. Instead, the appendage found the wound made by Aly's spear and thrust a portion of itself inside Lyandra's body. The creature shrilled a sound of mingled pain and rage, then bunched up its substanceless form and slithered down Lyandra's still body. Aly watched in horror as the Shadow forced its way into her sister, slowly disappearing from view.

Rage coursed through Alyandra at this violation of Lyandra's body. She stumbled forward and fell to her twin's side. Aly pounded Lyandra's chest and arms, screaming all the while. "Get out!" she screeched. "Get out of my sister!" Tears fell from her eyes, drowning her vision. Aly was aware of only two things: the rhythmic thudding noise of her hands pummeling her sister's body, and the awful desperate ache inside her soul, where half of her had been ripped away.

Then, barely penetrating the rushing noise in Aly's ears, she thought she heard a far-off voice whisper, "Aly, Aly, it's me." But she fought against the insidious noise, for it was not the clear dulcet tone of Lyandra's voice. Only when something caught Aly's hands, holding them still against Lyandra's breastplate, did Aly finally stop. Her breath came in great ragged gulps, and it was many moments before she could calm her thudding heart and open her eyes.

Something lay before her — something had taken the place of her beloved twin's body. It looked back at her with Lyandra's dark eyes, and it had her sister's finely shaped nose and lustrous hair. But it had a body unlike any Alyandra had ever seen before, at least among Amazons, and it had a dark growth upon its face. Aly reached out in fear, certain it was the Shadow come forth again. But her fingers touched only hair.

Aly jerked her hand away, then tentatively reached forward to touch the stranger again. Its eyes looked upon her with such a familiar expression that, for a moment, Aly thought she was looking into the eyes of someone she knew.

"Who?" Alyandra formed the word, though no sound escaped her lips. Her touch lingered on the creature's brow.

"I am Lyander, Aly," the thing said, its voice unexpectedly deep. Then slowly, ever so slowly, it reached up and smoothed Aly's brow in exactly the same gesture.

"I told you I would never leave you, Aly."

And so the first man was born, the first War Chief to lead the young race of humans and their warrior class: the amazons.

The Soldier's Journey

Anonymous Author
With an Introduction by Beloch Malkazahl
vagha Historian

THE EPIC POEM "The Soldier's Journey" was written by an anonymous poet very early in the history of Esfah. Although scholars have conflicting views, the majority attribute the saga to Elius Lawfollow, a selumari poet of considerable renown. Why he never claimed the tale as his own is unclear, though perhaps the dark nature of the work had something to do with his desire for anonymity.

Other scholars speculate that Lawfollow did not use his name because to do so might have been political suicide. Certainly, "The Soldier's Journey" is one of the most famous epic ballads — and not merely because it is so clearly a look at the earliest beginnings of Esfahn history. Indeed, the integral point of contention of "The Solider's Journey" — that there were only three lands corresponding to three races — at the time of its inception was certainly tantamount to heresy in the eyes of our less civilized forefathers.

And that is the whole premise to "The Soldier's Journey," that the epic lay details just three lands: the Abyss, home of the morehl; the Dead Zone, a fanciful term for trogland; and the Bright and Shining Land, clearly a euphemism for the seas and coastlands inhabited by the selumari. There is no mention of a fourth land corresponding to the vagha, which, by all accepted historical accounts, was the Second Race. Certainly at the time this poem was first passed around from campfire to campfire, the dwarven race would have decreed a Death Pact against the author — and certainly Lawfollow would have been very much aware of such a pact. Needless to say, this was one work any author would prefer not to claim as his own.

As a scholar of no small merit — and as a vagha — I find "The Soldier's journey" to be merely an interesting relic of a bygone era. Undeniably, there are passages of historical import (which I have duly annotated throughout the poem) as well as references of truly mythical — and implausible — nature (the Tree of Life, for example). Certainly I am not offended by the omission of my people's race in this epic tale — only, perhaps, slightly mystified. Although I cannot argue with the antiquity of "The Soldier's Journey," I can certainly take exception with its authenticity.

It is my opinion that this saga is merely the words of a talented and fanciful poet — certainly Elius Lawfollow's other ballads feature a notable whimsy — and not a true accounting of a remarkable period in Esfahn history. As such, "The Soldier's Journey" is best enjoyed as a bit of dramatic candy, and not the meat of historical truth.

The reader will likely find the journey of the fictional soldier of interest. The protagonist of the tale starts out in the Abyss, the term used to describe the morehl homeland. He is clearly a morehl himself, though he grows sick at heart in the Abyss. Perhaps there is something defective in his personality, or perhaps he is under the insidious influence of a Seed of Life (one of Lawfollow's several clearly mythical interjections in his tale).

The soldier finds the courage to leave the morehl homeland and journeys onward, into the land known as the Dead Zone, which, according to the tale, surrounds the Abyss. This supposition is problematical, for although historians have long known that distinct boundaries exist between the morehl and the trogs, the races of Esfah have no single homeland — and therefore it is inaccurate to say that one homeland could surround another, since, in fact, there are more likely to be many such homelands. At any rate, the soldier wanders the Dead Zone, tortured by the gray desperation of the land. He knows not what he seeks, and only dimly realizes that he must nurture the Seed of Hope that he still carries. Lawfollow's tale is unclear as to whether the trog homeland affects the soldier to the point that he becomes, in effect, a goblin.

At last the soldier leaves the Dead Zone, journeying into the Bright and Shining Land. Perhaps one thrust of Lawfollow's ballad is that there is an inner connection between the lava and the coral elves, for certainly the soldier identifies with the selumari homeland. Though reluctant at first, he comes to embrace the tenets of the Bright and Shining Land as his own, becoming at last a happy and fruitful being.

Certainly the imagery of Lawfollow's epic poem is obvious: He posits that the soldier — clearly a euphemism for any being — begins life as a miserable, hating morehl who then must endure the gray despair of the trogs before finally developing a soul of lightness and love, a selumari spirit. This is a natural outcome, of course — Lawfollow being a coral elf. As I stated earlier, I am not offended by the exclusion of the vagha in this "evolution of the soul," merely mystified.

I invite the reader to draw his own conclusions.

The Soldier's Journey

Part I: The Abyss

The Abyss
      lies black and careless
      past the wasteland known as the Dead Zone.
The Abyss
      is wrought with rage;
      passions of hate churn there.
      Its walls are of cloven fears
      pegged by spikes of despair.
      In its depths lies the River of No Return;[1]
      the stench of sluggish waters
      couples with terror
      and bears bitter fruit.[2]
The Abyss
      is a land screaming hate and rage
      and all things foul.
      It lashes out with morehlian flames,[3]
      gathering all to its edge.

---

[1] A reference to the ancient River Lethial, rumored to have caused great illness or death in all who drank its waters.

[2] It is speculated that the Tree of Hope (and its subsequent Seed of Hope) mentioned later in this ballad were the result of this union.

[3] Clearly an allusion to volcanic activity, a typical feature of any morehl territory.

The Abyss
>   seeks the soldier's blood,
>   his tears,
>   his warrior's soul.
>   It has the last but thirsts for more,
>   and he hovers on its brink —
>   tempted by the fear of it,
>   fighting morbid lust for it.[4]

The Abyss
>   is wrought with broken souls.[5]
>   It calls him often and draws him nigh —
>   the pain and sorrow and rage it holds
>   can smother his,
>   can make his own pale and faint,
>   can kill him
>   so he needn't feel again. m

The Abyss
>   hungers for the soldier,
>   clutching for its child.[6]

---

[4] The soldier is obviously appalled at the savagery of his morehlian nature, and is fighting against it.

[5] To this day, morehl line the walls surrounding their volcanic cities with the corpses of those killed in battle — including their own dead.

[6] The meaning of this passage is somewhat unclear. Could the author have meant that the soldier was not, in fact, a morehl but rather some being of another race — perhaps a slave — caught in the Abyss, the lava elf community? The last passage seems to deny this postulation, however, confirming again that the soldier is a morehl at birth.

The soldier's heart
    was forged with morehlian blood
    on a day forgotten
    in a life cast off.
    He grew old and bittered
    on a single day, a single instant,[7]
    when the fires of the morehl
    woke him from his slumber.
The soldier's life
    began that day,
    born in the bowels of that dark land,
    near the River of No Return.
    Beside him was a broken bough,[8]
    its end tipped with wilted silver petals
    and a golden nut.
    He kept the Seed,
    its beauty his only talisman against the Dark.[9]

---

[7] Clearly a reference to the ancient belief that each race sprang up, fully formed, in a single day.

[8] Further suggestion that the Tree of Hope was a byproduct of the River Lethial.

[9] Speculation exists as to whether the author intended "the Dark" to be a generic reference to all things evil and dangerous, or whether he instead intended it as a specific reference. If the latter, the question remains: What is "the Dark"? Certainly there is accurate historical information regarding the Elder Monsters, the creatures who were first created when Esfah was young. Possibly this is an oblique reference to the Shadow, an Elder Monster believed destroyed by an Amazon warrior some centuries ago.

The soldier's soul
>fled the Abyss
>by ways unknown or blissfully forgot.
>Long and hard was his tread,
>but stronger still was his fear of surcease.
>Through the mist of pain and rage
>and despair beyond all ken,
>he left the morehlian land behind.

The soldier paused
>upon the perverted ledge,
>gazing back upon his tortured path.
>Blood still flowed between him and morehlian flames,[10]
>and the need to linger grew.
>But he clutched the Seed and turned away,[11]
>and set his foot upon a path
>that led away from the morehlian edge.

The Dead Zone
>drew him nigh,
>drew him to a land
>where all wounds could fester and not heal.[12]

---

[10] Again, confirmation that the soldier began life as a morehl. He clearly feels the tug of his native homeland, via the "morehlian flames" or volcanic activity.

[11] It is interesting to observe the author's use of this literary device to motivate his protagonist. While most of the external trappings of the tale — the settings, for example w are either historically accurate or obvious extrapolations of actual facts, the author persists in referring to the Seed and Tree of Hope as though they actually existed. Yet neither of these can be confirmed in any historically accurate tomes.

[12] A clear reference to the trogs, who often use a spell called reanimate dead This vicious magic was later adapted by the morehl for their own use, who learned it from the trogs.

Part II: The Dead Zone

The Dead Zone
     surrounds the Abyss
     like a poisoned cowl,
     shedding darkness on even that black hole.
The Dead Zone
     is a land devoid of hope,
     of sight and sound,
     of laughter and emotion.
The Dead Zone
     is the color gray —
     a land once fertile with life
     until the yellow-skins came.[13]
     Then the Tree of Hope —
     whose limbs upheld the sky,
     whose roots bled through the land —
     was defiled and destroyed.[14]

---

[13] Clearly a reference to trogs.

[14] The antiquity of the author's work is not in question, and some scholars speculate as to whether his description of the Tree of Hope is, in fact, a truthful one. Certainly there are no historically accurate accounts depicting this tree, and one can only wonder at the author's intent here. Perhaps trogland once was a forest — some references do imply this — but now the goblins' territory is mostly that of a dying swamp. Any trees possessed by the vast fen are dead or decaying remnants of a bygone era. Whatever the case may be, the Tree of Hope certainly does not exist anymore if, indeed, it ever did. Interestingly enough, a small group of revisionist theorists believe that the Tree of Hope is an actuality and not a myth. They are on a search for signs of its existence.

The Dead Zone
    has no heart, no soul.
    To wander there long
    is sure and certain death.
    But it became the soldier's home,
    and he is its gray wanderer,
    its keeper of the last Seed of Hope.[15]
The Dead Zone
    muffles and warps all emotion;
    it hides all sun and eats all life.
The Dead Zone
    is cruel but not without mercy,
    for it allows a life of sorts,
    for those not ready for the Abyss —
    for those who deny the morehlian call.
    It provides a home
    for those too lost to know, too hurt to care.
The Dead Zone
    hides the soldier from prying eyes,
    trapping his soul for its own.

---

[15] Some sages speculate that the Tree of Hope was a giant among trees (as substantiated by the passage on the previous page), that its branches spread through the sky across the lands of all the First Races (excepting, of course, the vagha). This contingency contends that the Tree of Hope dropped its Seed in the Abyss, the land of the morehl, though its trunk existed in the Dead Zone, the land of the trogs. They further postulate that the soldier (the Gray Wanderer to them) journeyed throughout the Dead Zone in search of the mother Tree of Hope 4 ostensibly to find the lifeblood of the Tree to fertilize the Seed he carried!

Raindrops fell the day he entered
    the Dead Zone —
    drops of tears so hot[16]
    he cried in pain.
    What was this new torture
    that welcomed him to this land?
    Where was the expected surcease
    of rage and pain and despair?
Winds howled the first long months (or days or years)
    he was in the Dead Zone —
    winds so loud they drove him mad
    in ways he'd never known,
    in ways he thought impossible.
Gray mist filled the air, his sight, his vision
    of the Dead Zone —
    mocked him with blindness,
    with cataracts of decay.
The soldier's strength
    was sapped anew
    by endless, endless gray;
    the Dead Zone
    did that and more to him.

---

[16] This reference is of particular interest to naturalists. Some such scholars speculate that the heavens once deluged Esfah with a rainfall of volcanic matter, rather than one of water. To uphold this theory, they point to the unusual pockmarks or scars that trace across a number of mountain ranges. Certainly the pocked nature of the rock indigenous to those regions gives every indication of having been subjected to such treatment.

The soldier's spirit
>   was swept aside in the Dead Zone,
>   and only the Seed of Hope
>   kept him whole.
His soldier's pride —
>   his love of words that not even
>   his sojourn in the Abyss could taint —
>   grew dim and dry and dusty,
>   belittled and forgotten
>   by the Dead Zone.
He left for the Bright and Shining Land,
>   shunning the Dead Zone
>   and its hunger for the Seed of Hope,[17]
>   unwilling to share its bounty.[18]

---

[17] Scholars have long debated the intent of this passage. Could the author be referring to the Dead Zone's need for its own Seed of Hope? This would seem to be the most likely explanation. The implication is that trogland itself is aware of the Tree of Hope w perhaps from some ancient memory buried within the land. Some sages argue that this substantiates the existence of the Tree of Hope. However, I believe the author was using this phrase merely as a metaphor to emphasize the nature of trogland. These vast fens are a fetid region, clearly devoid of any natural beauty or bounty.

[18] The psychological struggle evident in the soldier is seldom more poignant than it is in this line. The morehl has clearly found life difficult in the Dead Zone, and he obviously has the means to restore hope (and thus life) to this wretched land. Yet he chooses not to plant the Seed of Hope, preferring to keep it instead. It may be argued that the morehl soldier had become a trog, for goblins are a notoriously selfish race. His travails have clearly not made him into a more noble person, for such a one would have sacrificed his desire for the Seed and planted it for the benefit of the Dead Zone. Indeed, those scholars who believe in the existence of the Tree of Hope must wonder what would have happened to trogland had the soldier planted the Seed.

Part III: The Bright and Shining Land

The Bright and Shining Land
    lies beyond the Dead Zone,
    the gray lands
    surrounding the Abyss.
The Bright and Shining Land
    is a land so bright,
    a wonder so true,
    a joy so rare,
    few can long there dwell.
    Its waters are silver
    its shores white with sand;[19]
    sunlight shines always,
    blinding those who try but fail,
    blinding those who will not dream.
The Bright and Shining Land
    is wondrous beyond ken,
    but a price is asked,
    a price most fear to give,
    for the price is love.

---

[19] Clearly a description of the selumari lands, although some of the coral elves' shorelines have beaches composed of other materials, such as crushed coral — which often produces a remarkable salmon tint — or even obsidian, depending on the proximity to morehl land.

The Bright and Shining Land
    demands a courage,
    a heart and soul,
    from those who would live there
    and eat its glittered fruits.[20]
    Few are they
    who can love so greatly
    they can endure the Bright and Shining Land.
For the Bright and Shining Land
    devours and transforms the soul
    and replaces the husk
    with a thing of beauty,[21]
    a rare and wondrous
    being of love.
The Bright and Shining Land
    is love,
    and it calls the soldier home.[22]

---

[20] Some sages point out that many of the fruits grown in the selumari homelands are inedible by those who aren't native to the region, and that this is the true underlying cause as to why "Few… can endure the Bright and Shining Land." Be that as it may, I happen to know that with a little judicious thought, outsiders can develop an immunity to and even a taste for the fruits of the coral elf islands.

[21] This is a rather graphic depiction of a rite of passage described in ancient selumari tales. Lawfollow, as a coral elf, gives every indication of believing that this metamorphosis is an actual event, though I must demur and contend that he is speaking metaphorically and not literally. The author is referring to a selumari belief that, in the most distant past, at a certain age the coral elves would actually enter a pupal state, metamorphose for an unspecified period, and then emerge fully developed in their next stage of growth. I am often astounded at the things some people will believe.

[22] Clearly, the lava elf has transformed — at least in spirit — into a coral elf.

The soldier journeyed
>to the Bright and Shining Land,
>clutching his Seed of Hope.
>His ragged soul
>matched his blinded heart,
>and he drew them both together,
>prepared to surrender
>should the land but ask.[23]

But the Bright and Shining Land did not;
>instead it wrapped him
>in new clothes of hope and happiness;
>the land nurtured him
>as he had never been before.

How long how short
>the time he spent there,
>he never knew,
>only that his heart mended
>and became whole and hale again.

The soldier wept for boundless joy,
>and on that day he could finally see
>in the Bright and Shining Land;
>he wept again,
>his tears filling his cupped hand.

---

[23] This passage supports the idea that the soldier was, in fact, a selumari slave all along and that he needed only the security of his homeland to restore him to health.

The Seed of Hope
    took root and burst its shell
    of soldier hands;
    it grew sure and tall,[24]
    its blossoms white with dazzle.
The Bright and Shining Land
    loved him,
    loved him enough to let him be.[25]
    The Abyss could beckon,
    the Dead Zone could plead,
    but the Bright and Shining Land
    did neither:
    It let the soldier be.

---

[24] There is much speculation, of course, that a Tree of Hope actually grows in the selumari Islands. The coral elves have declared that no such tree exists, and they have been most cordial in allowing scholars from other races to confirm that statement. To date, a Tree of Hope has not been found. It is likely that such a specimen will remain a footnote of legend, and not the fact "The Soldier's Journey" purports.

[25] The soldier in this epic saga has undoubtedly found, at last, all that he desired: a surcease of sorrow and pain. Some scholars speculate that Elius Lawfollow wrote this poem as a piece of propaganda in an effort to draw members of other races to the selumari homeland —thus winning their wars through attrition. While none can answer that, it is certainly true that the Bright and Shining Land is much more attractive than either the Abyss with its volcanic outbursts or the Dead Zone with its fetid swamps. Still, the author neglected to mention the mountains of the vagha — and in that he has done a disservice to the dwarven race, for the lands of the vagha are the finest in all of Esfah. Naturally, as an impartial scholar, that slight bias has not colored my interpretation of this tale in any way whatsoever.

About the Author

D.J. Heinrich is a pseudonym for an author residing in the wilds of Wisconsin. She is the author of the first two novels of the Penhaligon Trilogy, The Tainted Sword and The Dragons Tomb, as well as the author of "Sight and Sound," a short story in the RAVENLOFT® Tales of Terror anthology. Miss Heinrich enjoys writing science fiction, Gothic romance, and poetry, which she composes in lieu of keeping a private journal. Her current [1995] writing project is an adult science fiction/fantasy novel she began in 1980. "Margaret Mitchell took ten years to write Gone With the Wind," Miss Heinrich quips, "so if time to completion is any indication, when I'm finished it ought to be pretty good." Her passions in life include gardening, Oriental cooking, making barbarian costumes, and a recently acquired teddy bear named "Fuzzy."

HEART OF STONE AND FLAME

Year 496 of the First Age

Iron clanged on iron and echoed down the tunnel and into the chamber. The alarm!

Barakh the dwarf dropped his lava ladle and dashed to the stone bench where the weapons lay. He grabbed a one-handed crossbow, cocked it, and loaded it, before any of the other half-dozen dwarves in the foundry had more than glanced toward the entryway. They stood there, stone-shaping tools in hand, gazing curiously first toward the sound, then at him, as he snatched up a small ax in his off-hand and headed for the door. That's when his father stepped forward and snagged him by the shoulder.

"Hey now, boy, let's not be getting too hasty," the older dwarf said, his golden eyes crinkled and just the hint of a smile hidden among the whiskers on his red-bearded face. "There's no need to be getting your blood all aboil. I know you've been practicing with those things and are eager to prove yourself in battle, but take a good listen to the ringing of that alarm. It's too slow and measured to be signaling an emergency. Why, if there were something calamitous afoot, the sentry'd be banging up such a fierce din, you'd swear the mountain was coming down on us."

He loosed Barakh's shoulder and cast a pensive glance toward the doorway. "This is more likely the presage of some announcement, though I can't imagine what. Why don't you uncock that weapon before you shoot someone accidentally," he said, untying his leather apron and laying it on the weapons table. He gestured with his head toward the back wall, where Barakh had been working. "And then you can go fish your ladle out of the stream. Those things don't hatch from eggs, you know. When you're done, you can follow the rest of us topside."

Barakh almost argued. He almost said, "But what if it is an emergency? What if it's an attack?" But he stopped after the first word, sighed, and dropped his gaze. His father made sense. It was just that Barakh wanted excitement, even if it meant danger—even if it meant an attack on the village.

With that guilty thought, he unloaded and uncocked the crossbow, laying it back on the table, then placing the ax beside it.

The other workers filed out, debating what the alarm might be about. Barakh's father left last, after giving the young dwarf an affectionate pat on the back.

As the chatter wandered away up the tunnel, Barakh took a long pole with a bucket hook and walked back to the lava stream where he had been ladling molten stone into an iron mold for making barrels. Fortunately, the ladle hadn't completely submerged when he dropped it. An inch or so of handle still lay on the shore, though the turgidly flowing rock was slowly dragging it under.

Squinting his eyes against the heat, he hooked the ladle and drew it out, then dropped it into a cooling barrel. Water hissed to steam, and congealing lava on the ladle popped and cracked noisily. Barakh waited while the ladle cooled, imagining what it would be like if the alarm had signaled an emergency, maybe a *dragon attack*...

Barakh pictured himself leading a desperate charge against a rampaging flame drake while the young and aged of Stonehome watched on in fear and in awe. His mind envisioned a storm of dwarven crossbow bolts peppering the monster, most doing little more than scratching its scaly hide. But dashing forward, beneath its very head, its flaming breath searing the air above him, he imagined himself planting a quarrel in the dragon's tender throat just below the jaw. In his mind, the beast reared back in pain, and then Barakh leapt up, ax ready, and hacked deeply into the neck—a fatal blow.

His arms tensed with the imaginary strike.

Barakh pictured the panicked cries of onlookers as the monster thrashed about, threatening to crush him beneath its fiery form. But in his mind's eye, he saw himself rolling to the side, then coming up on one knee and chopping the dragon's neck again, severing its head. Slain, the monster crashed lifelessly to the ground. Then, as the deadly beast reverted to its native element of flame and dissipated, he and his fellow soldiers would turn their attention to the dark elves who had conjured it—the evil morehl—and chase them back into the foul caverns from which they had crawled. Many of the vile morehl would be slain—the rest would learn that Stonehome's defenders were not to be taken lightly.

That night, the clan would feast in his honor. People would repeat the tale of his slaying the dragon over and over, with awe in their voices, while his father and mother watched on, shedding bright tears of pride at his bravery. And his name would be added to the Song of the Ancestors, to be repeated in reverence by future generations of vagha to the end of time. He would become a symbol of courage to his people…

Blinking, Barakh's attention returned to reality. The water was no longer hissing, and the stone had stopped popping. He reached into the cooling barrel and retrieved the ladle, then gave it a solid thump against the floor. The tool's cracked stone coating shattered and fell away, carrying the tool's patina of old rust with it. Freed from its sheath of rock, the iron ladle shone like new.

By the time Barakh got to the meeting hall, most of the clan had already gathered.

Outside the lava tunnels, the sun was westering, sinking below the rim of the canyon the vagha settlement occupied. Long, cool shadows stretched across the faces of the village's low, stone houses, though their roofs and the canyon's eastern wall were still bright with sunlight. A warm breeze swept down off the mountain, carrying a familiar scent of sulfur. It gusted past the mouth of the foundry complex as Barakh exited, and accompanied him to the cluster of buildings below. When he stopped at the meeting hall in the village center, the breeze continued onward, slipping past the gatework that guarded the canyon's mouth and spilling out onto the grasslands beyond.

The young vagha climbed the meeting hall's three outer steps: One for Courage; one for Honor; one for Truth. At his touch, the outer door swung open smoothly, a slab of heavy stone mounted with expert dwarven craft.

Just inside, a pony stood tethered. It munched contentedly from a feed bag, while two beardless young villagers brushed it with great devotion. Nearby, a third worked diligently at cleaning a richly decorated saddle and bridle, while a fourth—the village Eldest's grandson, Barakh realized—stood watch over a heavy battle ax and an ebony crossbow. The young guard nodded curtly, arms folded, as Barakh passed.

In the hall proper, the bulk of Stonehome's population stood around the walls, while their six elders were seated at the council table. Barakh's father was among them. Several of the villagers had conjured a handful of flames and held them high to light the chamber. Each of the elders had conjured a personal flame on the stone table before him, to light his face during the meeting.

A stranger sat at the table as well. The village's ornately embroidered Hosting Cloak rested across the stranger's shoulders, and a golden chalice of wine was placed before him. Obviously, this visitor was someone of great importance, though Barakh didn't recognize him. The young dwarf noted the heavy ruby ring on the visitor's left thumb—the emblem of the High King! For a dazed moment, he wondered if the stranger was the High King himself. But from the attitude of the elders—respectful, but not adoring—Barakh soon realized that this was merely a royal emissary.

"I thank you for your gracious welcome," the stranger was saying. "Stonehome is truly spoken of, in the capital, as a place of great faithfulness to our people's tradition."

"You honor us with your presence," the Eldest replied with a slight bow of his bald, age-freckled head. "Now, will you listen while we have the village Song recited, to recount our history, and our past service to the Crown?"

The emissary seemed on the verge of a smile, but a sudden cough drew his hand to hide his mouth. He took a moment to compose himself, then spread open hands before him on the table.

"Would that I had the time," he said.

A murmur of disapproval passed among the villagers.

The emissary hastened on. "Were the situation less dire, and the Crown's need not so pressing, I would take great pleasure in hearing again the Song of Stonehome. It has been ages since I last heard it sung, and I ache to experience it again and to share the Song of my own native village with you, for neither was I born in the capital.

"But duty calls me to stay just long enough to deliver the High King's message, and then to be away. Before it grows fully dark, I must reach the town of Oxforge, two leagues west, and speak to them as well. I beg you to understand and forgive my haste." He gazed hopefully at the assembled elders.

Barakh's father cleared his throat. "There is nothing to forgive," he said. "We are best honored by those who faithfully serve our king, as you do."

The other elders nodded sagely, and the emissary bowed his head with a smile.

"Please, give us the High King's words," the Eldest said.

The emissary stood and turned, passing his gaze over everyone in the hall. When he spoke, it was loudly, to carry his voice to the whole assembly.

"The High King has pledged our kingdoms aid to the selumari of the Maris Coast, a fortnight's ride north of here. Those coral elves have been hard pressed of late by united forces of goblins and lava elves intent upon driving them into the sea. Should the selumari be defeated, the trogs and morehl would then surely turn their attention south, to these mountains, our own homelands. We all know how the morehl covet this land, and with goblin allies they would doubtless prove a major trouble to us.

"In his wisdom, the High King has decided that it is better to face that threat now, with allies of our own—and on distant soil—than to battle them later, alone, in our very homes.

"He seeks volunteers to come north to Vhandria, the capital, in a week's time, to be outfitted and trained for battle, and to then march to join the selumari at their city of Maris-ta-Sehlim. From there, we will break the back of the trog-morehl alliance, and teach them that the civilized peoples of this world will not stand for their chaos and terror."

The emissary paused to let the crowd consider his message. A moment passed before he asked, "Who among you will come?"

With a roar, every man in the hall thrust a hand into the air, as did many of the women and children. Even the Eldest stood and raised his arm. At his place near the door, Barakh fairly leapt into the air.

The emissary laughed joyously. "Truly, you are a fearsome clan!" he said. "But the High King needs defenders to remain here as well, lest the morehl decide to strike for our heartland before defeating the selumari.

"I am to recruit only two young warriors from your village. With your kind permission, Eldest, I shall take this fellow with the fists like mallets," he took the hand of a youth named Fohviss and raised it above his head. "And as the second," he turned and pointed toward Barakh, "I'll take that bouncing young vagha near the door."

Barakh's heart leapt with pride. Now he would learn to become a true warrior.

Fohviss wasn't much of a talker.

As they labored their way along the rocky trail to Vhandria — back and forth across steep cliffsides, over sharp saddles between peaks lost in cloud, along narrow gorges mist-dampened by spectacular waterfalls, and through the occasional old mine shaft or lava tunnel — Barakh tried time and again to get a conversation started to help pass the hours. But no matter what subject he broached, the other dwarf would effectively end it with one vapid sentence or another.

Barakh's first foray had been, "By the flame, I'm sorely anxious to see Vhandria. Aren't you?"

"Yup," Fohviss drawled, scratching his bearded chin.

Barakh continued. "I've heard that the capital city is so beautiful that once you have seen it, you never want to leave." He looked toward the other dwarf for confirmation.

Fohviss took a deep breath, then nodded, eyes on the trail ahead.

"Have you heard anything in particular about the city?" Barakh asked, hoping to draw the conversation out.

Fohviss merely shrugged.

Frowning, Barakh gave up.

That evening, as the two roasted coneys over a campfire Fohviss had conjured, Barakh tried again. "I've always dreamed of being a warrior," he said. "How about you?"

Fohviss looked thoughtful. He stared into the flames, pursing his lips and working his mouth as if tasting the idea. He stuck his tongue in one cheek and wrinkled his brow. After a bit, he smacked his lips and let out a breath. Then he rocked his head slightly from side to side, as if considering whether to commit himself to an answer. Finally, he turned the rocking into a slight nod, not so much to Barakh as to himself.

Encouraged by the length of Fohviss's thought on this subject, Barakh pressed on. "In part, it's the feel of the weapons, I think." He patted the ax and crossbow lying on his bedroll. "There's something almost elemental in the heft and swing of a good ax, in the way it hisses through the air, the solid thunk of it biting into a shield.

"But a crossbow is even more mystical somehow. The way it butts against your shoulder. The feel of the stone stock against your cheek. The line from eye, to quarrel head, to target. The squeeze of the trigger and the shock of release. The whisper of the quarrel through the air. And the smack of its strike."

Fohviss yawned, pulled his coney from the flames, tested it with a finger, and began to eat.

Barakh spoke a bit louder, to be heard over the sounds of munching. "But what really excites me about being a warrior is the glory of fighting for what's right, of defending the helpless, of protecting our world of Esfah from evil creatures who would despoil it, who think only of themselves, and who take pleasure in the suffering of other beings. Don't you agree?"

"Sure," Fohviss said, licking his fingers. He tossed his roasting stick into the fire and lay down on his blanket. Within moments, he was snoring. "That's all right, I'll take first watch," Barakh said glumly, biting into his own coney.

On the second day's march, Barakh decided to try something outrageous. He was in the lead, and when he reached the crest of a rise, he stopped to let Fohviss catch up.

"You know," he began, "I'm not so sure we really need a High King. I mean, our clan seems to get through life without him most of the time. We only ever hear from him when he needs something from us, like now. So why not just ignore him? The next time one of his emissaries comes by, we should just send the fellow packing."

Fohviss looked troubled. He took a seat on a boulder, beneath the thin shade of a solitary aspen, rested his hands on his knees, and breathed deeply, recovering from the climb.

Barakh leaned back against a rock as big as a mammoth. "Sure. Better yet, when the next emissary comes, first we should flog him for disturbing our peace, and then we send him on his way. No. Even better. We should rob him first, then flog him, then send him packing." He grinned at Fohviss.

"Well," Fohviss said, hesitantly, "I I don't know." He got to his feet and stumbled away with a worried look, eyes averted from his companion. He started down the other side of the slope in something of a rush, quickly putting distance between himself and Barakh.

"Hey! Hey!" Barakh called, hurrying to catch up. "I was only jestingl I swear!"

After that, about the only words the young dwarves shared were "Let's rest a moment," or "Watch your step here," or "See the hawk," or "I'll take first watch; you take second."

Barakh was effectively left alone with his own thoughts as day followed day. At first he resented Fohviss for not being a better companion. Wasn't it everyone's duty to keep relationships smooth with polite conversation?

But slowly, he came to recognize the simple comfort of having someone else present, without feeling the need to keep that person entertained and happy. Traveling by himself would have been lonely, and potentially dangerous. In sharing the travel, and the work, Fohviss lent Barakh a sense of security. Yet at the same time, he left Barakh the mental space to watch the terrain around him, to absorb something of its beauty, its peacefulness, and its life.

Barakh found himself discovering things about the mountain landscape that he had never really noticed before. For one thing, he had never realized just how much water there was to be found among even the higher slopes of the range. It trickled down cliffsides, melting from snows higher up, gathering in a convocation of streams in the bottoms of gorges and canyons. In places, it sprang from cracks in the mountains, chillingly cold from sources deep inside the stone, or sulfurously warm from passing near a volcanic heart.

Nor had he ever really considered just how much vegetation clung to the stony slopes, sprouting hither and yon, wherever a crevice provided a spot for seeds to take root. And with that vegetation came a surprising wealth of living creatures, from insects, to rodents, to birds, to mountain cats. The valley his clan nestled within was so carefully tilled and tooled and patrolled that it took on a very different nature. It was so controlled, so unchangingly dependable, that it begged to be taken for granted.

But this untended explosion of life from such a harsh terrain filled the young dwarf with a tremendous joy, deeper than any he had known before. It was an emotion he now felt sure he would have missed, had he had his way and filled the journey with endless chatter. It bubbled within him, sometimes emerging unconsciously in snatches of song. He found himself humming and singing old vagha hymns about the glory of life, and their words took on new levels of meaning as he realized that this was what their writers had been trying to say. Ironically, it was only in this relative isolation that he came to understand that, and to feel a kinship with those ancestors. It made him consider his native village in a new way as well, as part of the tapestry of life in the mountains over all—an especially fertile part, to be sure, but one hard won by those who had come before, and something to be revered and protected for later generations.

And he came to view this all as a gift—something bequeathed upon him by the Creator of all life, something given to him especially through the strange ministry of Fohviss the Reticent.

As a result, he came to feel a real fondness for Fohviss. And from the gazes Fohviss cast about the landscape, and the smiles he turned upon Barakh thereafter, Barakh was certain that Fohviss felt that bond as well.

Sharing silence, the two grew to be as brothers. It was something of a disappointment to finally reach the capital.

All right, you babies, put your backs into it!"

Blinking sweat from his eyes and growling at the drill master's insult, Barakh slid his shoulders a few inches further down the stone block, planted his boot heels more firmly beneath him, and pushed backward with all his might. At his side, Fohviss strained to do the same. In response, the block slid perhaps six inches along the wall, with a terrible grating sound, then halted. Desperately, Barakh shoved harder, hoping to keep the momentum going. But the stone wouldn't budge.

The drill master let the pair strain a moment more before informing them, "All right, that's done it lads. The block is in place. If you push any more, you'll shove the whole row right off the wall! And then you'd just have to lift them all back into place again."

He leered at the two while they gasped for breath.

"Come on, then," he finally said. "Off the wall with you. Unless you want to be crushed between your block and the next to come. The next team is ready to place theirs."

Limply, Barakh and Fohviss stumbled off the growing wall, astonished that the drill master had let them keep straining even after their block was set, but too exhausted to complain about it. Not that it would do any good. The drill master was as unassailable as a god. In the two weeks that they had been under his tutelage since arriving at the capital, he had dictated when they slept (far too little), when they woke (far too early), when they ate (far too quickly), when they labored (far too long), what work they did (far too hard), what words they spoke (far too loudly), and even—if possible—what they thought. Along the way, he had put them through seemingly endless practices with ax and shield, interspersed with equally endless crossbow training, and even a smattering of battle magic. They had carried their weapons with them wherever they went, ate with their weapons, even slept with them, ever ready to be called upon for a surprise inspection at a moment's notice. And no matter how hard they worked, there was always something more he wanted of them, some nuance of axwork he badgered them to add to their mock battles, or some senseless, back-breaking chore to be done in half the time that was reasonable.

After two weeks of this persecution, Barakh was about to snap. Most of what the recruits were kept busy with seemed to have little, if anything, to do with becoming a warrior. Most of it, like the building of this wall, was more properly the work of draft animals. That weapons training was crammed into the moments between virtual slave labor seemed merely an excuse to keep the recruits here, as far as Barakh was concerned. It made him angry. But it wasn't just Barakh. Even the normally complacent Fohviss had taken to glowering at anyone who crossed his path.

Sheer stubbornness was all that kept the pair going. Barakh was determined to bear up under whatever torture the drill master threw his way. He knew that the "training" couldn't last much longer. Soon, the dwarven contingent being sent to the Maris Coast would have to begin its march if it was to get there in time to be of any use to the selumari, and Barakh meant to be a part of that force. If he had to endure the fiendish cruelty of the drill master to accomplish that, then so be it. Fohviss seemed to be of a like mind.

Wobbly with fatigue, Barakh and Fohviss gathered up their weapons and stood waiting for the drill master's next order. Barakh yearned to sit and rest his lower back. It ached fiercely, but he refused to let the pain show on his face.

While waiting, he reflected that little about this city was as he had envisioned it, though his first glimpse had seemed promising. Cresting a final pass along the trail from Stonehome to Vhandria, he had spotted the spires of the High King's palace before anything else. Shaped by vagha stone magic, the towers were seamless constructions of rosecolored granite, affixed to a glossy white central keep of gold-veined marble.

"I can't wait to see it up close," Fohviss said in a tone of awe.

As they came nearer, the rest of the city became visible, a patchwork of buildings of every hue of stone imaginable, the whole surrounded by a trio of walls of purest black onyx. Between the walls, crops were raised. Outside them, the bulk of the dwarven army billeted in tents of bleached wool.

That was part of the problem. Expecting to tour the city itself, Barakh had been dismayed when, after telling the gate guards their purpose in coming to Vhandria, he and Fohviss had been directed to the tents outside. They had spent their every moment since then training in the billeting area. Barakh got the impression that the Vhandrian citizenry didn't welcome the idea of having soldiers and outlanders tramping through their pristine streets.

Those few Vhandrians who had actually volunteered to join the army merely strengthened that impression. Every one of them was inordinately proud of being a Vhandrian citizen and considered anyone else to be some sort of inferior creature. To hear them tell it, only Vhandrians knew how to live, only Vhandrians were worthy of making legends, only Vhandrians were worth speaking to. Outlanders were little better than cattle in their eyes, marrying young, spawning lots of children, drinking nasty home brew, and spending their every day tending animals and hauling manure. According to the capital dwellers, in Vhandria people ate only the best of viands, drank only the best of wines, attended entertainments that outlanders could only dream of, and maintained vagha learning and tradition virtually single-handedly.

The strange thing was, Barakh was embarrassed at some of the "entertainments" these Vhandrian dwarves talked about. In Stonehome, many of them would have been considered obscene. That his embarrassment branded him as a "hick" only made matters worse. And thatithe Vhandrians almost never left their city walls——those who joined the army would invariably be assigned to home defense within the city itselfmade their claim of superiority all the more infuriating. Barakh was sure that none of the capital city recruits had ever experienced the oneness with nature he had felt on the journey here. He was equally certain that, had he tried to explain it to them, they would have taken it merely as further evidence of his having little more sophistication than a farm animal.

Lost in thought, Barakh almost missed the drill master's next words to him and Fohviss. With one eye on the next pair of trainees levering another block of stone onto the wall, the drill master tossed a comment over his shoulder.

"You've done a good job, men," he said, too quietly for anyone else nearby to hear. "As a matter of fact, I'd say you two are ready to leave our little holiday camp. Why don't you go clean up a bit, get something to eat, then meet me in my office in an hour's time. Bring all your gear. I'll give you your new instructions there."

Barakh and Fohviss stared at him.

The drill master chuckled. "Move along now," he said. "I don't like having to repeat myself."

Gaping at first in disbelief, then whooping and smacking each other on the back, they hastened to obey.

Three days later, Barakh and Fohviss were on their way to Maris-ta-Sehlim as part of a contingent of one hundred dwarven infantry being sent to bolster that city's defenses.

"Only the best men are going, only good soldiers," their drill master had explained. "And don't be mistaken—there is a difference between a soldier and a warrior. A warrior fights by himself; soldiers work as a team. A warrior fights fiercely, but he is a unit of one. Get a hundred warriors together, and you have a mob. Get a hundred soldiers together, and you have an army. Anyone can he a warrior, if he has the stomach for it. But being a soldier takes tenacity—it takes wisdom and self-control. You gentlemen have demonstrated those qualities, and I am proud."

He shook their hands and spoke an old vagha blessing over them. "May the stone guard your days and the flame light your way."

Then he said, "Now get out of my camp, before I put you back to work digging latrine pits."

They didn't have to be told twice.

Before leaving, they spent two days inside the walls of Vhandria, sampling the wonders of the capital. They rented a sleeping room with coinage paid them for their two weeks in training, a novel experience for them both. They ate in streetside cafes, visited museums, walked through elegant parks, and haggled for souvenirs in market squares.

In the end, they decided that Vhandria was just like Stonehome, only bigger. Any variances between the two places were easily ascribed to their sheer difference in size. The people here were still people, with all the hopes, dreams, and petty vices their old neighbors in Stonehome were prone to, if somewhat gruffer in going about their business. With that decided, the young men walked the city with confidence and enjoyed their time within its walls.

On the third morning, they reported to the main gate to join with the other soldiers traveling north. Everyone there was anxious to be off and on their way.

While waiting in line to check in, the soldiers exchanged rumors of what the selumari were like.

"I've heard that they're more fish than human," one dwarf said. "My grandfather says that the coral elves have gills, so that they can breathe underwater."

An officer patrolling the line stopped and scowled from under his ornate helmet. "They cl0n't have gills," he said. "And they aren't part fish, despite the fact that they can breathe underwater at times. It just has to do with their affinity to that element. Just as we vagha can conjure shapes in stone and fire, the selumari work magic with air and water."

"Give me stone and fire any day," the first speaker said, grimacing. "Why, what if one of their watery buildings was to collapse all of a sudden? Everyone inside would be drenched. And then all they'd have is a cold breeze to dry off with." He mock shivered, then burst into laughter, elbowing those dwarves nearest him and gesturing for them to join in on his joke. A chuckle spread through the group.

"Well, aren't you the bright one," the officer said, peering at him thoughtfully. "You know, I've been looking for a cunning lad to tote some of my gear. And you've just volunteered yourself. Come along then, bright boy."

He snagged the "jester" by the arm and turned a stern gaze on the rest of the soldiers. "I am Warlord Marut. I'm in charge of this little expedition," he told them. "You'd all best be keeping in mind that the selumari are our allies, and I'll not be having it said that any of my men were treating them with disrespect or causing offense."

A sober silence fell over the line.

With a nod, the warlord stalked off, with the unfortunate trooper in tow.

Barakh and Fohviss exchanged a glance.

"Let's try to stay on his good side," Barakh suggested.

"Uh huh," Fohviss replied.

The one hundred dwarves set off, on their way to see the coral elf city of Maris-ta-Sehlim.

The bulk of the force consisted of heavy troopers, eighty in all, organized into four companies of twenty each. Barakh and Fohviss, given their familiarity with both ax and crossbow, had been assigned with eight other light troops into a single platoon of sentries whose function it was to scout ahead of the main body. The remaining ten dwarves consisted of Warlord Marut, a master wizard, his six apprentice theurgists, and two mammoth riders, whose beasts each pulled a massive wagon full of foodstuffs and crossbow quarrels.

Barakh rather enjoyed working as a scout. It gave him a freedom that the heavy troopers, marching in unison, did not have. It also gave him a chance to enjoy the landscape as it changed over the next many days from mountain, to foothill, to flatland, to marsh. And as the sky turned gray, and a drizzle set in that lasted from one day to the next with no sign of letting up, and the already marshy ground turned to a virtual soup, he had the liberty to curse the weather for hours at a time without having to worry about a superior officer taking offense. In a black mood, he wended his way through league upon league of tangled wet shrubbery, slipping and tripping in the sticky muck that passed for ground in these parts, and wishing now that he were marching with the main body of infantry, in a path trampled relatively clear by the mammoths.

Late in the afternoon of the third day, Barakh unexpectedly heard someone else cursing fervently, though in a female's voice. Intrigued, he cautiously approached the sound. He found a woman, wearing the bronze body armor of a warrior, wrestling to free her horse-drawn chariot from a sinkhole. She was nearly twice his height, though less broad across the shoulders than he. Could this be a coral elf? He hadn't heard that the selumari sported brown hair, though. According to the stories, their hair was dark green, like the ocean depths, and their skin was pale blue, like an open sky. But this woman's skin was rather golden, though of a far paler shade than Barakh's own——more white, like butter cream.

Barakh decided that the situation bore investigation.

"Ho there," he called, stepping into the open where he could be seen clearly.

The woman spun about to face him, bent in a crouch, coming up with a wicked-looking blade in the process. It was something like a short sword with a slight bend in the middle and Barakh was sure she knew how to use it. Her face was tensed in a battle snarl, but after a moment her expression changed to one of puzzlement.

"You're not a trog," she said, straightening to her full height. "You're far too clean."

Considering the leagues of marsh Barakh had recently waded through, this struck him as funny. He laughed out loud.

"Your skin is like a goblin's," the woman continued, "well, not really pale enough. And your hair it's red rather than dirty black. What are you?"

"My people are the vagha," Barakh replied, with a slight bow. "We dwell among the mountains, not down here in the muck like the goblins.

"But turnabout is fair play, my lady. Who or what are you?"

"My name is Setha. I am human," she said. "My people call themselves Amazons. We dwell upon an expanse of plains far south of here. On occasion we trade with the selumari, and I am part of a band of warriors come north to help them fight the trogs."

The woman's eyes glistened with sudden tears. "Though I fear that I am the last of my band. Most of my sisters were slain by a host of goblins days ago on the coast. We were within sight of a selumari city when the attack came. The goblins had with them many strange, red-skinned elves who carried hand weapons that spat fire and hurled pellets with deadly force. They stood between us and the city, firing into our ranks and jeering at us.

"Our charge caught them by surprise, though. Our chariots thundered down the beach toward them, trailing arcs of sand and spray from the horses' hooves and the spinning wheels. We nearly broke through their mass, but the red elves..."

"The morehl," Barakh interjected.

"The morehl," she tried the word, "they were mad with bloodlustl We slew many, but heedless of their own losses they threw themselves against our chariots, and the goblins followed them blindly.

"In the end, though the sands were drenched with the blood of trogs and morehl only a handful of my sister warriors escaped into these marshlands, pursued by goblins the whole way. We were separated during the rout, and I haven't seen any of the others since.

"My duty now is to return home, to deliver word of this tragedy to my people, and to lead another, larger force back here to avenge my sisters' deaths, to permanently extinguish the madness of the goblins and their red elf allies."

Barakh cast a glance behind him, in the direction of the main body of dwarves.

"I'm part of a contingent come to help the coral elves, as well," he told her. "I suppose I had better take you to talk with our commander. Let's see if together we can get your wagon free."

Setha smiled. "It is called a chariot," she said.

The drizzle died at last, replaced by a light mist.

Shortly before sunset, Barakh and Setha reached the main body of the vagha. The column was setting up camp for the night on a bit of higher, drier ground. Fohviss was already there, waiting for his friend. He raised his eyebrows curiously as the two strode into camp, Setha leading the horse and Barakh pushing the chariot from behind.

Warlord Marut came to meet them, alerted by messenger when they passed the guard perimeter.

"What have you brought me, trooper," he asked Barakh.

"An ally, sir. And a source of information."

The warlord gave Setha a measuring look. "There is water heating in my command tent," he said, "if you would care to wash up before joining us for dinner. I'm afraid we have little more than travel rations, but you are welcome to share in them. Shall I have some of my men attend to your horse?"

"Thank you, sir," Setha said with a gracious nod. "I would be delighted to share in your dinner, and my horse could use tending too."

After a trooper led her away and the mammoth riders had been summoned to groom and feed her horse, the warlord turned his attention back to Barakh and Fohviss.

"You two could stand a good washing as well," he said, wrinkling his nose, then winking. "When you've done with that, come to my fire for dinner." That said, he turned and strode away, bellowing at the mammoth riders to take more care with the Amazon's "war wagon."

The attack came shortly after dinner, just as most of the camp was preparing to bed down for the night. Setha had been describing the location of the selumari city when death began descending on the dwarven camp.

The first signal of trouble was when a sentry stumbled out of the darkness, into the light of one of the outlying fires, clutching both hands to a slit throat. The troopers around that fire raised a cry, but it was cut short by a veritable hail of sling stones from the darkness beyond.

Aroused, the rest of the camp scrambled for their axes and shields. But once armed, they could find no enemy to fight, only more whistling sling stones. Many of the dwarves charged into the night, yelling fierce battle cries. Their cries fell silent quickly, and they did not return from the darkness.

"There is no way to tell how many of the enemy we face," Warlord Marut said, tensely watching the chaos spread. "But one thing is certain: We're perfect targets with all this light. Pass the word to douse the fires." Runners hastened to obey, while troopers began scattering the brands of the fire before the command tent.

"Where is my horse?" Setha demanded.

Buckling on his armor, the warlord spared her a glance. "It should be down near the mammoths," he said, gesturing toward the northern end of the camp. "Barakh and Fohviss can take you there."

Without another word, the Amazon strode in that direction. The warlord favored the two scouts with a curt jerk of his head, signaling them to follow and help her. They had to trot to catch up.

It wasn't easy finding the makeshift corral in the dark camp, with dwarves dashing this way and that, giving challenge every few yards, and with goblin sling stones flying. But the bellowing of enraged mammoths helped lead the way. By the time the trio arrived, however, the beasts had broken free and were trampling through the swamp. The horse was gone, too.

Worse, the goblins were now beginning to move in on the darkened camp, stone axes at the ready.

Fohviss noticed them first. There were dozens slipping through the brush in this area alone. It wouldn't be long before they found the two dwarves and the Amazon.

"What now?" Barakh whispered. "We're cut off from the bulk of the camp. And we're sure to be spotted any minute."

"All we have to do is survive the night," Setha answered. "We can rejoin the rest of the group in the morning's light.

"Assuming anyone survives," she added bitterly, under her breath. "As for being spotted, I still have a trick or two."

Chanting softly, she raised open hands before her and waved them slowly in interlocking spirals, as if spreading dough. In response, the night mists seemed to coalesce near those hands and then spread out, obscuring everything around them in a thickening fog.

"You do water magic," Barakh said, "like the selumari." "My people work with whatever magic is predominant in the land," Setha responded. "Here in the marshes, I can call upon the power of water and earth. Near a great source of flame, I can summon up a bit of fire magic, and under an open sky the power of air is ready for my use."

Barakh filed the information away for future reference. He could hear the goblins drawing nearer.

"Fog or not," he said, "we're soon to be discovered unless we move on."

As quietly as possible, the three fled before the advance of the goblins.

They spent the entire night dodging goblin hordes. At times, they could hear dwarven battle cries and the sounds of fierce fighting in the distance. Twice they came across a scene of great slaughter. In each case, the dwarves had sold their lives dearly, taking two or three times as many goblins with them into eternity, but in the end it made no difference.

On occasion, when Barakh caught a glimpse of Fohviss's face in the darkness, he noted a growing anger there, a bitterness that threatened to sink into his friend's very soul. He only hoped that they would survive long enough to see better days. All of a sudden, the thought of dying in the midst of this hell seemed ludicrous, and he wondered what had ever possessed him to want to be a warrior in the first place.

Near dawn, tragedy struck.

The three were stumbling along, nearly exhausted from the tension of staying constantly alert, keeping constantly on the move. Setha was in the lead, with Barakh flanking to the left, Fohviss to the right. The Amazon paused a moment to catch her breath. She leaned forward, hands on knees, head hanging in weariness.

All at once, a quartet of goblins broke through a wall of brush ahead of her. Before she even had time to draw her blade, three of them were upon her. Their combined weight bore her to the ground. Stunned by the suddenness of it all, Barakh heard her scream with rage. He saw stone axes rise and fall, heard the multiple thuds of their impact. Setha's scream cut short. Barakh's heart seemed to seize up as a wave of shock spread through him. His limbs trembled.

Fohviss was not so hesitant. Already on the verge of snapping under the strain of the night, he launched himself toward the goblins with a purely animal snarl, his dwarven ax drawn far back to the side for a mighty two-handed stroke. When it landed, the blow cut through the right-most goblin at the waist and slammed his corpse into his nearest companion, knocking him to the ground as well.

Abandoning his ax, Fohviss grabbed the third goblin by the throat with one hand, pounding him in the face with his other fist—a fist an emissary of the High King had once likened to a mallet. The goblin clutched at the choking hand, eyes wide with panic, then stunned with pain. Even from aidistance, Barakh could hear the crunch of cartilage and bone breaking.

When the second goblin began crawling out from beneath the corpse of the first, Barakh broke his own paralysis and rushed forward to engage him. The goblin in Fohviss's grip struggled ever more weakly.

But the fourth goblin had hung back in the initial onslaught to draw his sling and load it. As Barakh closed the distance to his own target, the fourth goblin sized up his two dwarven opponents and took aim at Fohviss, who was so caught up with strangling his victim that he didn't even register the danger.

"Nooooo!" Barakh screamed, willing the projectile to miss. Slamming into the second goblin at full tilt, Barakh threw his ax at the slingman, hoping to disrupt his aim. He threw with all his might, trying to rush the weapon through the air, desperate to beat the release of the missile.

He wasn't fast enough. The slingman released his pellet. It hissed through the air, catching Fohviss near the temple with an audible impact. The dwarf's head snapped to the side and his legs buckled. He and the strangled goblin fell together, lifelessly hitting the ground.

A fraction of a second too late, Barakh's ax hit the slingman in the chest. It bit deep; the goblin coughed blood and collapsed, dead.

Barakh and the remaining goblin went down in a tangle. The goblin scratched and bit like a wild animal, but Barakh was beyond the pain. Snatching up a fallen stone-headed ax—one wet with Setha's blood—he put an end to the goblin's struggles.

When dawn came, it found Barakh sitting on the spongy earth between the bodies of his two friends. His right shoulder ached, most likely from a pulled muscle, and his face and arms were covered with bloody scratches. His heart was numb, past caring about what to do next.

But the sun's warmth roused flies and other insects, and Barakh couldn't stand to see them landing on his dead friends. In a fury, he dragged the two bodies to a bit of high ground, away from the goblin corpses. He didn't know what burial ceremonies were used among the Amazons, but he couldn't risk lighting a pyre. So he summoned what earth magic he could, fueled by his rage and grief, and opened a grave for his friends. He laid them in it together, head to head, with their weapons at hand, to watch over each other in death. Then he released the magic and let the earth close over them. He marked the grave with a chunk of stone saved from its bottom.

Barakh stood a long time beside the spot, wrestling with his guilt. Two thoughts chased each other around inside his head. If you hadn't hesitated, said one, if you had acted more instinctively, like Fohviss did, you could have saved him. The other countered, If Fohviss hadn't been so instinctive, so focused on his rage, he wouldn't have needed saving; he would have remained aware of the fourth goblin.

Finally, he grew tired of the debate, and spoke to break the silence.

"I'm sorry, Fohviss," he said.

He let those words sink into the earth.

"I don't know what to do next.

"Maybe I should turn around and go back home. The High King should be told of what happened to his army.

"But you and I both wanted to see the selumari city. It seems a shame to have come so far, just to turn back. And the coral elves are certain to wonder what happened to their allies."

He looked south, toward the mountains. Their peaks were just visible above the passing mists. They seemed to beckon him to return home.

Shouldering his ax, he turned north instead, heading for the coast.

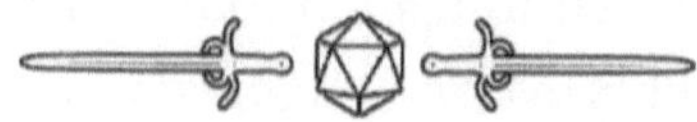

Crossbow cocked, Barakh peered out over the coral city's outer wall, searching for a target among the raiders. All along the wall to either side of him, selumari archers did the same, though they nocked coral-headed arrows to bows of whale bone. Cradling the carved stone stock of his dwarven weapon, with its iron-tipped missile, Barakh felt a surge of homesickness. He was reminded of a conversation he once had with Fohviss, on the trail from Stonehome to Vhandria. But he forced that thought aside with a growl. Battle was not the place for feeling sorry for oneself, no matter how alien the surroundings, no matter how cut off from one's own people.

The cohort of vagha warriors he had traveled with were all dead, but he had come to fulfill their promise to the selumari. Not that he was really much help: one lone dwarf with an ax and a crossbow, and a smattering of stone and flame magic. Even worse, what magic he possessed was dampened here, in more senses than one. In this selumari city, lying as it did on the sea coast, damnable damp salt air interfered with vagha fire magic, and shifting sand was virtually worthless for aiding in spells of stone.

Peering out into the fog, Barakh took aim at a fleeting shadow and fired. With a cry of pain, the shadow dropped. Barakh grinned grimly. From the sound, the victim was one of those thrice-damned morehl. The goblins were foul enough, but there was a madness to the morehl, an evil that threatened to engulf the whole world. Well, now there would be one fewer to plague it. Barakh ducked to cock and reload his crossbow.

Above his head, all along the wall, ghostly flames suddenly sprang to life. The coral elves staggered back, startled and half blind.

"Do not fear!" Barakh shouted. "It's only fairy fire!" He had seen the like before, had even been taught to help conjure it.

The coral elf to his left took heart and, ducking behind a merlon, rubbed his eyes and blinked to clear his vision.

No one else seemed to have heard him. From outside the city, a crackle of lava elf pistols sounded, and blinded selumari fell from the wall, bloodied and broken. The raiders roared a cheer.

Cursing, Barakh drew upon what little fire magic he could. A pale flame flashed across the sky, and a thin cloud of ash began falling over the immediate area, further obscuring attacker and defender alike. It wasn't much, but it might give the selumari enough respite to re-man the wall.

From deep inside the city, a horn sounded a low, mournful note.

"It's the signal to retreat," said the surviving coral elf. "The main gate must have been breached. Our only hope now is to reach the quay and escape aboard ship."

"My people died trying to reach this city, as did an army of Amazons" Barakh said, grimly. "We came to help hold it, and I won't retreat now."

The selumari laid his blue-skinned hand upon the dwarf's golden one.

"Will your death bring your friends back?" he asked.

Barakh ground his teeth. The coral elf's calmness was infuriating. He matched Barakh's glare with a steady gaze.

Barakh sighed. Gathering up his crossbow and quarrels, he drew his ax and gestured toward the stairs.

"After you," he said.

Ten minutes later the pair neared the quay. Three galleys lay at anchor there, their coral hulls floating lightly on the water. Barakh had heard that such ships could even sail through air, given the right magic.

Scores of selumari waited to board ahead of them. Even to the dwarf's eyes, it was obvious that they couldn't all fit.

"Do you see anything wrong with this plan?" Barakh asked his companion. He spat angrily over the edge of the quay, onto the sand.

The coral elf took in the crowded quay and the trio of ships. He gazed down the beach and out across the water. He stood still for a moment, head cocked, as if listening to something the dwarf could not hear, then drew his cutlass. He swung the blade a few times, then rolled his shoulders to loosen the muscles.

"Let's not give up hope yet," he said. "You came to help hold this city, and you may yet get your chance." He walked back to where the pier met city street, and took up a defensive posture, facing the city. Columns of smoke were arising here and there within it, and the wild cries of goblins and lava elves echoed down the streets. The horde was coming.

Barakh stared at the selumari's back for a moment, then hefted his ax and stepped to the elf's side.

The selumari glanced at him and smiled.

"I'm glad to have you here, brother." he said. "Your faithfulness is a testimony to the honor of those who perished along the way."

Barakh nodded, too moved to speak.

From the crowd behind, other selumari joined them, forming a defensive line across the quay's head. All laid a companionable hand momentarily upon the dwarf's shoulder as they did so, as if drawing strength from this alien's dedication to their city's defense. With each touch, Barakh felt a growing bond with these elves, regardless of their strange ways.

He recalled a passage from an ancient vagha hymn, the *Song of the Land.*

> Earth and Air, Fire and Water,
> Intermingled in the land.
> vagha earth and fire master,
> Selumar air, water tend,
> Intermixed, as Nature planned.

As during the trip from Stonehome to Vhandria with Fohviss, the words spoke to his heart in a way they could not have done before. He recognized now that the vagha and selumari were brothers, united in their dedication to the world. It was a concept he felt sure the trogs and morehl, in their worship of death and destruction, could never understand. For a moment, he felt sorry for them.

Then the horde came into view. Down every street they swarmed, converging on the quay, putting torch to anything that would burn, and smashing everything that would not. Their gleeful destruction was chilling to behold.

The invaders spotted the knot of defenders at the quay's head.

With a deafening cry, they charged.

Barakh braced himself, convinced that death lay only moments away and saddened that he would not live to carry his new understanding back to his own people. Still, he was determined to make these death worshipers pay dearly for his life.

Suddenly, from out of the sky, a veritable cloud of tiny winged people descended. Lightning bolts flashed from their ranks, lancing into the mass of trogs and morehl.

A cheer rose among the selumari. "The sprites have come!" Between the selumari and the onrushing attackers, a thick band of frost settled. Swiftly, it grew into a tall, defensive wall. The invaders crashed against it with cries of pain.

Barakh blinked, startled. Obviously, the coral elves had asked for help from more allies than just the vagha and Amazons. And though they were arriving somewhat late, still they had come.

Nor were the sprites the only ones. Now, from the ocean behind, he heard a great splashing of waves, and droplets of chill salt water fell upon him. Turning, he watched a giant man of living coral rise slowly out of the sea. Two others followed. The first giant took one ponderous step over the wall of frost, and the invaders cried in dismay.

Cheering mightily, the coral elf warriors pounded Barakh upon the back.

"Come, let's reclaim our city!" the elf beside him shouted, the elf who had fought at his side on the city wall. He gestured magically, and a gust of wind lifted him upward. He paused to offer Barakh his hand.

I have come this far, Barakh thought, What is there to fear from a little wind? Reaching up, he took a firm grip on the elf's wrist. Together, they rose over the mound of frost, to join the sprites and giants in driving the trogs and morehl from the city.

Barakh stood again beside the grave of Fohviss and Setha.

"I've finished our mission, my friends," he said. "I've been to the selumari city. It's different from the towns of our homeland, Fohviss, but it has a beauty of its own. I plan to return some day. Perhaps with my children. The coral elves have something to teach us, I believe. And we them."

He looked up at his new companions and smiled.

The selumari leader smiled back.

"Lead on," he said.

About the Author

A factory worker turned English major, Lester Smith has been working full time in the gaming hobby for ten years. His published game credits are many, including design of the DRAGON DICE game. His published fiction credits include an Aysle short story in the first Torg fiction anthology, and an ENDLESS QUEST® book, A Wild Ride, for TSR. Les says his career change is a happy one, the result of making an occupation from a preoccupation.

THUNDERFIST AND THE DRAGON

Year 829 of the Second Age

Zephras "Thunderfist" sa'Geril stood on the edge of the mountain road and shaded his eyes against the bright light of Soll. The dwarf twisted his whiskers and watched the battle unfolding in the vale below.

Rannon, the chief spell caster from the vagha city of Balgavarr, stood next to him. He was much younger than Zephras, but had proven himself competent to the vagha warlord. "How are they faring?"

With flinty eyes, Thunderfist stared at the dwarven warriors. "They fight well." He muttered below his breath, "They always attack this same region… for two years now, only this spot." The two leaders had come down to see how the patrol performed and had heard from a scout that a skirmish was likely.

Rannon didn't hear the last part. "Well, they had better be winning," he said sarcastically. "You trained this lot."

Thunderfist bobbed his head. "Fat lot of good it might do em," he sighed. "I've always been a better fighter than a teacher."

Rannon pointed to movement in the trees that hemmed in the battlefield.

"I see em," said Thunderfist. His dwarven patrol battled trog marauders that had come from the Big Wet and crossed the Sareen River. Another goblin platoon was coming up to flank the beleaguered vaghans, unseen.

Thunderfist waved to the small, but elite force that he traveled with. "Come on, boys—let's go join the party before it gets out of hand!"

The crew of thirty warriors whooped and hollered, eager to put down the invaders. Zephras clambered up a mammoth that had a riding standard attached with his banner.

Steering his mount down the trail, the dwarven reinforcements rushed into the fray. Past the far battle line, the sneaky incoming trogs stopped in their tracks rather than engage. They stared, wild-eyed, as Thunderfist and his forces rode in to bolster the dwarven battle group.

The invaders turned and fled, abandoning their comrades to die at the hands of the vaghan defenders. When the remaining trogs recognized Zephras's banner, a red embroidered fist against a yellow background, they too, routed.

As soon as the goblins outpaced their pursuit, the dwarven company mowed down a large number of them with crossbows.

"I so rarely get to have any fun these days," Thunderfist said with a mild pout. He hadn't even a chance to swing his axe.

Rannon shrugged. "Such is the price of fame."

"I think you mean infamy."

"Amongst the goblins, absolutely. They'll never forget how you held the western outpost, almost single-handedly, without even an axe to wield."

Zephras flexed his hands. He remembered it too, but there had been scores of other battles with them, too.

Rannon motioned to the patrol. "Then, you were not much older than they are."

He nodded. It had been his first assignment after training with the military. Only four peers from Zephras's class had survived.

This group they had come to aid had likewise been on their first patrol.

"I had a good teacher," Thunderfist said. His instructor had been his father, Geril, a brilliant community leader and warrior who had passed away two years ago.

Rannon clapped his friend on the back, "And so did these stout soldiers. Come, we've got another group to train when we return." There was an unwritten rule that all male vagha of Balgavarr had to serve at least one tour in service before any female would marry him. Most males trained, and many of the females too, as a matter of civic duty. "I think this crew has a recruit of special interest?"

Thunderfist nodded and turned his mammoth back to the road and thought of his son. "Aye. Ghuren has had his eye on this pretty little lass. Dunno if his heart wants the glory of battle, but it certainly wants to get through training for her." He grinned and then spurred his mount back along the trail.

The lower gates of the Uruzak stronghold opened and belched red-skinned warriors. Lava elves trotted along the western road under their leader's watchful eye.

As his legions swarmed out of the city gate, Merod grimly smiled. He'd been laying careful plans that bartered away the lives of trogs in order to lull the armies of Balgavarr into negligence and routine. At his direction, the goblins always attacked from the same direction and they'd intentionally set the dwarves' expectations very low.

Things had gone badly for the empire ever since the vagha had placed Thunderfist in charge of the border; he took enough care that they'd have to take a long way around to even enter the dwarven lands unseen. Thunderfist's reputation cowed the goblins, who still remembered his legendary stand. Now, however, the Morehl had new allies-allies that knew no fear, allies that crept through the swamps with great stealth and skill. Merod finally saw a path to victory, and their secret allies, new comers to Cyrea, were the key.

The reward for conquest would be great: promotion, wealth, and perhaps, someday, the Obsidian Throne itself. Merod dared to scheme such lofty goals. He had a plan, and too little respect for his Emperor, Saugor, who he thought too young to be worthy of his position. Merod had no fear of the dwarves, or their allies, the Selumari.

As long as the amazons remained in the plains of Seshara, the battle would be his. Once they dared to strike the dwarves, only the humans and their amazon warriors could reach them in time—and these strange invaders from the swamps of

Dereh'Liandor could match the chariots' speed and engage them before they could render aid.

Merod smiled. Soon would come his glorious day, and it would live long in the annals of Esfahan history.

Thunderfist stood with his arms crossed at the front of the room while Baddoch, his lieutenant, instructed the students. In addition to martial combat skills, Balgavarr's military trained its members in tactics. One without the other made an incomplete soldier, and Zephras knew firsthand how important it was to have some skill with both. When he'd made his stand at the tower, all of his superiors had died in the trogs' first attack and he'd never have survived without a well-rounded education.

Baddoch scrawled upon a slate board, *8,000 goblins > 2,000 dwarves*, and then scratched a line through the numbers.

Thunderfist stepped in to explain. "There's more to war than killing the enemy," Zephras told the dwarf trainees. "War isn't about casualties, it's about territory. Controlling a terrain may be the single most important aspect to war. It gives you the advantage, the edge, the power to conquer. Remember that, and your battles will go well. Forget it, and you may as well find a hole and lie down in it."

He hefted his battle axe so that the wickedly sharp blade gleamed in the bright sunshine. "But this, this is also a part of battle. In all war, there are losses, but whether they belong to you or your enemy depends on how well you can think and plan. Strategy is the key to victory."

One of the vagha students raised a hand and spoke. "But if there *was* a mathematical equivalent, how many trogs would equal one dwarf?"

Zephras grinned. "Many factors to consider, Ghuren," he said, flashing a wink to his son. "I dunno that I want to answer that... it gives some vagha too-great a pause for thought when they see the hordes of trogs swarming—that's the kind of pause that sends the weak ones scurrying home and shifting the odds for the worse. You tell me, what do you think the equation is?" He knew his son was smart, had a head for numbers, and would make a fine councilman someday.

Ghuren shrugged. "They out-breed us eight to one... but eight to one only works if dwarves had a child per year. Most vagha have a child every other year, so... it's got to be far better than one to sixteen? Goblins tend to have more litters than dwarven live births in their lifespan."

Baddoch nodded enthusiastically. "We haven't had solid tracking numbers, but let's not forget the low mortality rate of trogs. Many die young because of their nature; they aren't very intelligent and are prone to acting impetuously... but yes, their numbers are typically larger. I'd say that it's nearly double your one to sixteen, at least in seasons without a strong goblin leader who properly bloods his trog warriors."

Thuderfist grinned. "No tracking rates? *I thought we all kept score.*"

"Why? What are you up to, now?"

"Show me yours first," Zephras said.

Baddoch wrote a number on the chalkboard and covered it with his hand. "We'll show at the same time." He offered Zephras the chalk.

The dwarven hero looked at the writing utensil. "I'm gonna need a lot more chalk than this," he teased.

A door clicked at the back of the room. Unmistakable blue skin identified the coral elf soldier who stepped in and recognition lit in Zephras's eyes. The dwarven teachers traded glances; they both knew the visitor.

"That's enough for today," Baddoch dismissed them.

Zephras waved at his son. "Ghuren, stay with us so I can make an introduction."

Aalerd sat facing Baddoch and Zephras, whose son stood behind him. A younger elf sat next to Aalerd, who Zephras vaguely recognized. "You might remember my son, Weldyn?"

Thunderfist nodded slowly as the memory came back to him, and he introduced his own child, Ghuren.

Aalerd placed a bottle of wine before him and removed the cork.

"Ah! Ye remembered," Zephras said, eying the bottle of his favorite blend made by the selumari of Tulgesh. "It's not often we dwarves find much to our liking besides a good ale."

"You spoke so highly of it on your last visit to the port that I thought to bring you some."

After they'd each had a cup, Zephras gave the selumari general a serious look. "The wine is nice, but what *really* brings you to Balgavarr?"

"It's two-fold," the coral elf admitted. "Protective duty, first. Tradesman Riechus is escorting his daughter, Naemyar, through a tour of the Cyrean sights before she travels abroad."

"Riechus, he's the shupping mogul, right?"

Aalerd nodded. "He's showing Naemyar off and letting her see the world in the process. She's got grand ambitions, that one: four different suitors, each a prince of a different selumari kingdom. She's got her pick of them. Naemyar will be a queen, somewhere. First, she's visiting Balgavarr."

Zephras furrowed his brow. "So you're playing at bodyguard? That doesn't sound like your type of mission."

"It's not," Aalerd admitted. "That leads me to my second reason: diplomatic relations. I wanted to tell you about the suspicious movements my scouts have identified."

"Do tell." Thunderfist leaned in.

"I don't have much by the way of concrete evidence to share," Aalerd said, "That's why I wanted to come personally. It's mostly a gut feeling. Subtle shifts. The morehl have kept a pretty regular patrol of their lands' perimeter, but its patterns have shifted lately."

The dwarven warlord tapped his finger to his lips. "If Uruzak was invading Tulgesh they'd have to cross Seshara, and we'd have plenty of warning… so the selumari are insulated. Only south or north are likely invasion routes."

"North of Uruzak lies the Big Wet, the red elves' longtime ally. Some new thing in the south has killed whatever scouts we've sent there, and the humans in Thurisa refuse to go there. It's always been controlled by the lava elves, anyway, but whatever is there is not morehl; besides the lava elves have not historically bothered with it. There's no strategic value there."

"How many troops do you have with you?"

"I brought a decent enough complement under the premise of military exercises while traveling. You're thinking a northern invasion, then?"

The dwarf nodded. "They've wanted our mountains for generations, and if invasion is coming, the morehl will find only death waiting for them at Balgavarr." Zephras stood. "I'll dispatch some scouts immediately."

Aalerd nodded and left the room with his son in tow. "Death has always created chaos," Aalerd spoke once they were out of the room and did not stop. "This alliance of Morehl and Trog will last as long as it is convenient." He paused, then continued sadly, "Unfortunately, so may this alliance of selumari, vagha, and human."

He turned to his son. "Never forget how fragile Death has made things, and strive to stay close to your allies in Nature, Weldyn. Long after you and I are gone, it will be those like your son Matrek who shall lead our people. They must keep the balance."

"Matrek, and those like Naemyar?" Weldyn asked. "She's making certain to build strong alliances abroad."

"Time will tell with her," Aalerd said, as if he had some reason not to trust her.

A hulking bruiser of a trog sauntered into the clearing near where the River Marl emptied into the sloughs of the Big Wet. The Marl was more of an ambitious creek than a river. It stretched from the eastern Kafnysan lowlands to feed the swamps where the goblins dwelt.

Merod and a few of his captains waited for the goblin chief, Gorbak. The lava elf turned to his peers, Cheron, who commanded the morehl cavalry, and Laskar, who led the corps of missile troops who were expert combatants with their flintlocks. "Speak slowly. Gorbak may be a behemoth in a skirmish, he's perhaps the stupidest trog to ever lead the Big Wet."

The massive goblin's stench reached them before he did. Merod ignored the thick odors of mire and decay. "Do you have what was agreed upon?"

Gorbak nodded and pointed to the trees. "Five hundred gobbo soldiers."

Merod could see their silhouettes in the trees at the clearing's edge. He tapped Laskar's shoulder. "Go and count them, to be certain." The elf turned back to Gorbak. "It won't be long now and we shall engage the vagha. With our help, the Big Wet will finally take Balgavarr," he lied, noticing Cheron do his best not to smirk. If the lava elves took the peak adjacent Balgavarr, they'd eventually take the whole mountain range, leaving nothing for the goblins.

"Gorbak gets Balgavarr and lava elves take the standing stones. That is our deal?"

Merod nodded. "You've been sending regular scouts to needle the dwarves in their southeast?"

Gorbak nodded. "Many died, but they were weak gobbos."

Laskar called from the edge. "We had to add a few, but we've got them."

"Excellent," Merod said. "Gorbak, show us the firmest path through Big Wet. Our army musn't be seen or the dwarves will know to expect us, and they will be better prepared."

"Walk anywhere," Gorbak said with a shrug. "Big Wet no care. We don't need roads."

Merod scowled. "Goblins, no. But we *do* need the roads. Moving thousands of troops through mud is not feasible, Gorbak. Guide them on a route through the firmest ground, please."

The big trog scowled and sighed as if he did not understand the request, but he waved them forward and took the lead. Merod's troops had already made it halfway through the swampy terrain, but knew that wetter parts lay ahead.

Laskar led the group of goblins into the clearing while the line of lava elves passed through it and began the journey. If Gorbak's word was good, he'd sent another minor invasion team even now to harass the vaghan border again and draw any eyes away from their movements.

With Gorbak safely away, a patch of muck shifted atop the water of a stagnant pool. A scaley creature emerged who looked much like a cross between a cobra and a man. She hissed, "You have my minions?"

Merod nodded and pointed across the way to the cluster of trogs who waited for orders. "As requested, Sharsyea."

The reptilian sarslayan gave a chirping kind of hoot and forty more of their kind emerged from stagnant pools and stalked through the swamp as they drew nearer the nervous legion of trogs. One of the swamp stalkers carried a stone pot and held it with a special kind of reverence.

Merod knew some sarslayan had taken a foothold in Cyrea after crossing the seas from Dereh'Liandor's Snekdenn Bayou. He didn't particularly care about this new, invasive species. They weren't mountain dwellers, so as soon as they captured Balgavarr, their presence was a moot point... in fact, Merod hoped the sarslayan and trogs would wind up at war so Big Wet would forget about the morehl's eventual betrayal. For now, the saslayan were useful and this shaman who led them had been, so far, easily manipulated.

He grinned. Maybe he could get them to assassinate Emperor Saugor on his behalf... when the time was right. Merod still had to position himself perfectly in order to ascend the Obsidian Throne.

"These goblins will mutate into more creatures like us," Sharsyea flicked her tongue between her fangs.

"I care little about their fate as long as you can deliver on your promise to delay the amazons when they ride to Balgavarr's aid."

"It will be as you say," she responded.

Merod knew of Balgavarr's alliances and expected the humans would arrive shortly after the battle began if it drug out for more than two days. The human city of Thurisa provided the closest support the vagha could receive, and the amazon warriors were renowned for their speed. The sarslayan shaman had promised she could delay their arrival, provided the morehl bolstered their forces... the reptilian species had yet to find a solid foothold in Cyrea, and this would give it to them.

Cheron shot Merod a skeptical look that he ignored. Merod explained, "Once we possess the stones, we can ferret out the exact location of Bagavarr's hidden entrances, and then the morehl will reign supreme in Cyrea."

The sarslayan flicked her tongue with amusement. "You cannot find a simple door? I begin to wonder at your army's skills; we thought the lava elves more intelligent than this."

Merod ground his teeth. "It's not so simple, Sharsyea. The vagha know the importance of keeping their home secret and they are master stone crafters. Every couple of years, they move their entrances... not only resetting the masonry, but their spell casters can mold rock as if it were clay, recasting their entire layout. Thus far, efforts to turn any of their allies to our whims and gain the location have proven less than effective. Whenever we ascertain an entrance's location, it has been moved or sealed up before we ever get a force mobilized."

Sharsyea hissed. "Ahh... you require speed."

"Exactly."

She nodded. "Sarslayan are fast—especially in the water."

"Perfect," Merod said. He unrolled a map and pointed to a spot marked upon the Sareen River. "This is where the amazons will cross when they answer the dwarves' call for aid."

Sharsyea memorized the location, and then she turned and led the way deeper under the cover of hanging moss and bald cypress for privacy. Whatever foul magic she drew upon to mutate these trogs did not matter to Merod, and he didn't care to see it.

Ghuren strolled through the main hall of Balgavarr. The cavernous chamber was a marvel of their stone-crafting skills.

He was on his way to watch the selumari visitors from Tulgesh who were reported to be shopping at the main bazaar and possibly selecting new goods for export. They'd been in town a couple of days now and Ghuren hoped to catch Aalerd and perhaps get an amusing tale or two of his father when he was younger. Afterwards, perhaps he'd drop in on the pretty dwarven mistress he'd been calling on lately.

A barrel-chested dwarf in a scout's uniform blasted through the tunnel that led into the main hall and Ghuren intercepted him. The runner doubled over, panting and half dead from nonstop travel.

"No time," he panted. "Must get a message to Thunderfist!"

All thoughts of recreating left Ghuren. "Zephras is my father. I'll take it straight away. What's your message?"

"Attack… we are besieged." He paused to spit out the phlegm building up in his windpipe and nurse the pain in his side.

"Trogs again? I'm sure that we can…"

"No! Morehl have been spotted in the north. Trogs and morehl both."

Ghuren recognized the seriousness in the messenger's face. He whirled and ran to find his father. Minutes later, he rushed into Zephras's office and found him examining a map with a critical eye.

"Lava elves," he practically shouted.

Zephras raised his bushy brows.

"A runner in the great hall," Ghuren explained in a choppy manner. "He says we are attacked in the north by trogs and the morehl."

Zephras nodded resolutely as he stared at the map. "Uruzak has finally come out for more, eh?" He took a seat at his chair and took up his quill and inkwell. The dwarven warlord scribbled several short messages on tiny rolls.

"Ghuren, take these to the master of ravens. We must get word to our allies."

The younger dwarf looked at the old warrior. "What does it mean, father?"

Thunderfist crooked his jaw as he spoke, but Ghuren couldn't tell if his words were dismayed or excited. "It means war."

A raven descended to the rookery in Thurisa where it had been bred. It alighted on a post and was quickly snatched up by human hands.

Herestia pulled the note from the raven's leg. "It's from Balgavarr," the amazon mumbled as she recognized the sigil on the exterior of the tiny scroll.

She read it quickly and then sprinted for the queen's estate.

Amazon guards, members of the humans' warrior class, let her pass when they recognized her. She was the army's lead charioteer and a close adviser to Queen Alexandria.

Herestia rushed to the queen's side and handed her the note.

The human leader scanned it briefly and then crumpled it up. "The vagha are often suspicious to the point of paranoia," Alexandria said, "but if Thunderfist sees trouble, then the amazons shall go to their aid. I have never known him to call needlessly."

Herestia's face lit with an eagerness for battle that rivaled her hatred for goblins and lava elves. "I can see the faces of the trogs even now. And the morehl must cross through the Seshara, at least in small part, to reach Balgavarr. If they dare attempt to cross our lands, they'll pay dearly for that impertinence. None move on the plains so fast as we, and there will be no escape for them."

Alexandria nodded her head. "You have your orders."

Herestia nodded and departed. She smacked the side of her chariot and cracked her reins, riding out to rally their forces.

Thunderfist arrived on the northern slopes of the Kafnysan range and got to work immediately while Ghuren, Rannon, and Baddoch set up a command post. He dismounted his mammoth and followed the lead vagha scout to the best vantage point and overlook the battlefield.

"We've already had a few skirmishes with 'em, Warlord," the scout reported.

Zephras realized what the morehl had engineered by the layout of the battle below. They'd looped around to come at them from the north, hoping to catch the vagha out of position. Thunderfist asked, "Casualties?"

"The initial patrol who stumbled onto the enemy was fully lost, except the runner who was sent to report their presence. The first wave of defenders fell, a corps of footmen you appointed as early responders. They lost approximately fifty percent of their numbers and yielded the enemy their current position."

The warlord nodded measuredly. He was thankful that the vaghan troops had been so quick to engage an overwhelming force. Had they not, the enemy would be at the top of the mountain by now. Taking the nearby peak was surely their goal;

it could give them a close enough position that they'd finally locate the entrances to Balgavarr before the tunnels could be rerouted by dwarven engineers.

Zephras counted the soldiers spread out across the mountainside. They continued to trickle in from the city of Balgavarr and from regional outposts.

Far below in the foothills, the morehl had gathered for another frontal attack. Zephras turned to the sergeant standing next to him and issued his orders.

"Gather the mammoth and lizard-riders to flank the morehl. Tell them that once the main force is engaged they are to attack from the sides. I'll take a full platoon right into their midst. The marksmen are to hold back and defend our home to the last dwarf."

The terrain below where the enemy mustered was wooded enough that missile salvos would have little effect at this range. They had to make sure that their shots counted. "Tell them they are to fire only if the lava elves break through our line. Only then. If we succeed in driving these cursed red elves back, we'll regroup here for a final assault."

Zephras stared at them for a few long moments as the sergeant relayed his orders. If he was the enemy leader, he'd have ordered a mad charge uphill to try to seize the primary objective before the vagha could get a leg up on them. He spoke to himself wondering, "Why aren't they attacking?"

Gorbak watched as his goblins gyrated and groaned. Some danced, some whipped themselves. Each spell caster had his or her own method of igniting that arcane connection to a deeper source of magic. Each denizen of Esfah possessed it, but for some, the gift was far deeper. Summoning their arcane energies, they came together and surrounded the Big Wet's primary authority on magic, an old goblin mage.

Bryegak shuddered and contorted as he harnessed the corporate pool of energy summoned by his underlings. He could not see and had been born with his head covered in cancerous pustules—but his command of eldritch energies far exceeded any other that Gorbak had known.

Long ago, before the Dragon Crusades, a fiendish black dragon had terrorized this region before a dwarven hero killed him. The vagha called it by name. Gorbak smiled wickedly. He knew that dragon magic, when properly applied, could call specific dragons from the realm their spirit returned to when they were killed on Esfah… and Bryegak had learned the name of this dragon.

Gorbak looked back up the slope and saw the vagha forming ranks. They'd locked into a vanguard to protect the mountain trail that could give the morehl and trogs access to the mountain… and eventually Balgavarr.

The sudden silence that fell over the spell casters unnerved Gorbak. Trog and morehl alike trembled as the mages completed their chant.

A deep black shadow loomed on the horizon, a swirling mass of dark energies moved at the speed of the wind and it moved toward them.

With a mouth of mostly jagged teeth and amorphous growths, Bryegak cackled and called the name of what he summoned. "Morguus Ebraxas."

"Dragon magic," Gorbak mumbled with a certain fearful reverence.

But even as the mighty wyrm began to crawl from the vortex that spawned its creation, the Death mages of Big Wet realized they may have called for more than they themselves could handle. At once the army began to retreat, giving themselves enough distance that the beast would first annihilate the vagha.

Hopefully they could muster enough magic to unsummon the fiend afterwards. "Hopefully," Gorbak told himself.

The great black wyrm thrashed as it emerged from the vortex of magic that opened directly over top of the dwarven vanguard. It screamed with bestial rage as it was summoned, lashing out with its long sinuous tail. Opening a mouth filled with razor-sharp fangs, it spewed liquid putrescence at the vaghan army. A line of unlucky soldiers fell to the ground.

Morguus Ebraxus curled into an arc and only offered the enemy his armored hide as a target. The wyrm was the size of a castle, wingless but with arms corded with thick muscle like a forge worker's and a body that seemed to be half tail, and covered in barbs along the spine.

Zephras raged and spat a string of profanity. "They leave the field to us and the wyrm. If it kills us all, they win. If we manage to destroy the beast, they'll attack as we recover. There's only one way out of this."

"What's that, Warlord?" asked Baddoch whose mount waited on one side of him, Ghuren was on the other.

"We lead the dragon to them."

Before Thunderfist could spur his mammoth into action, a voice called out behind him. "Hold!"

Zephras turned and spotted Aalerd riding down to meet them. A crew of selumari trailed behind him. "I have another idea," the coral elf insisted. "My casters can summon a blue dragon. Dragons are fiercely territorial. The beasts will fight each other and give us the opportunity to engage the enemy."

"Is that wise?" Ghuren protested, he knew his father was not always comfortable using mystic means in combat and he'd heard of the damage dragon magic could cause.

Zephras eyed his son but flashed him a conspiratorial grin. "Son, there are many ways to overcome your enemies, and a wise commander makes use of them all." He smiled grimly. "Still, when it comes down to that crucial moment, give me a sturdy axe in my hand and someone to fight in front of me, and

I will make certain my enemies never forget the name of Zephras Thunderfist." He nodded to Aalerd and authorized the plan. "Make it so."

Another portal split the sky and a blue drake emerged with a raspy shriek. The winged dragon scanned the land greedily, and then locked eyes on the black wyrm.

The wyrm screeched a challenge and the blue drake roared in response. Morguus Ebraxus abandoned the vagha and pursued the intruding dragon, instead.

Both blasted each other with flaming gouts of breath. They clawed at each other and rolled through the trees, snapping old oaks like dried kindling.

The beasts jettisoned any thought of the other creatures assembled against each other and tumbled over a jagged cliff, all fang and tail. The sounds of their battle echoed over the countryside; only one would emerge from the scrap alive—and then it would return to where it was summoned to devour whoever was left.

With the sudden absence of the dragons, the dwarves surged forward. Beards flagged in the wind as they charged into the fray. Blood flew as axes swung, gripped by vagha and trogs. The morehl hung slightly back, letting the goblins take the worst of the dwarves' fury.

Merod howled orders and sent soldiers into positions to try keeping one step ahead of Thunderfist and his troops. He pointed to a weakened position where the goblins' strength was faltering and shouted for troops to shore it up. Most of the trogs seemed over-matched by the well-trained dwarves, except along the front where Gorbak fought and rallied his minions.

Cheron's mount fought through a swarm of enemies as he outflanked them with his giant scorpion. Both the poisoned barb of the creature's tail and Cheron's rapier flashed, and they racked up casualties.

Adjacent to Merod, Laskar loaded and reloaded his carbine and took aim, putting a hot round of ball shot through his vulnerable enemies. Only two of his shots went errant enough to strike a trog who was engaged with the vagha, and on principle, Laskar made sure not to try sniping dwarves engaged with lava elves.

Merod blew a horn, and another wave of goblins emerged from the trees. Little by little they took ground away from the vagha by out positioning them. The dwarves suffered fewer casualties, but were pushed back one cubit at a time.

Laskar chuckled as he sighted his gun on the head of the vaghan warlord leading the troops. "The goblins played their part well, without even knowing they were doing so. The dwarf forces are reduced, if only slightly."

Merod's smile twisted with uncertainty. "I think they'd rather die at the mountaintop than upon its slopes. I'm uncertain if we are pushing them back or if they are tactically withdrawing?"

"They will certainly scatter if their revered leader falls in battle. The vagha will learn to fear our flash-powder." Another few paces and the dwarf would be perfectly exposed. Laskar's enemy would never see Lord Death's hand as it reached for him. "Today you die, Thunderfist."

Laskar squeezed the trigger, but yelped and stiffened as he did so, throwing his aim wide and into the sky. The sharpshooter fell to the dirt, dead. A feathered arrow protruded from his chest where crimson blood and steam leaked.

Merod looked up the slope and spotted the comparatively small team of blue-skinned elves. The morehl wrinkled his nose in rage. "Thunderfist has brought selumari allies to the battle. I guess that explains the blue dragon." He hadn't expected to encounter any coral elves—he'd taken precautions against their involvement, and so they must have already been in Balgavarr.

He scanned the horizon and estimated their size. They were not a large force and Merod assumed their impact would be negligible.

The lava elf spat into the dirt. "I guess we'll be treated to the deaths of both vagah and selumari before this is all done." Merod called a shield bearer to his side, nonetheless, to make sure that he had some protection from the same fate as Laskar. The last thing he wanted was to take an arrow before he had the chance to watch the spark of life extinguished from Zephras Thunderfist's eyes.

Aalerd and his elves loosed arrows over the main battle group and targeted the reserve forces at the rear. Mostly the reserves were made up of morehl who sent the trogs in to do the bulk of the dirty work and soften up the dwarven vanguard.

Tulgesh's evokers joined Aalerd near the stacked stones where they'd taken cover against return fire. One of his magicians glared at the red-skinned enemies. "It is said the morehl fear nothing save their own ambition," the enchanter said, "but we shall make them fear the very skies above them."

Aalerd stared at his enemy. He shared his enchanter's hatred of their racial enemy.

Behind him, the selumari mages began their chants. Winds and fog swept across the battlefield. "Let them see what the magic of the coral elves can unleash!"

Clouds roiled in the skies, and lightning struck among the morehl.

Aalerd frowned. The arcane bolts certainly helped, but the enemy continued to pour into the battlefield.

The magic efforts slowed them, but the hordes continued to advance.

"Where are the amazons?" Aalerd wondered aloud… he'd seen Alexandria's response and expected them at any time. He had really expected them to arrive by now.

Herestia led the caravan as they blitzed across the Seshara plains. At its north-most peak, the Sareen River intersected the Big Wet and the vaghan lands on the far side. There, the Sareen spread broad and shallow; the amazons frequently used it as a crossing.

The amazon charioteer slowed her approach, and the others matched her speed. They made all due haste to aide their allies, but did not want to risk damaging a wheel or axle by carelessly crossing through the shallow rapids.

As soon as the first of the chariots entered the water, snake-like warriors leapt from the reeds. Some tackled horses with scaly bodies capable of matching the ferocity of dragonkin. Others coiled around humans and vehicle alike with elongated serpentine bodies—their pale yellow eyes gave them away, they were more than animals.

Herestia howled, "Attack!" and the humans leapt into the fray with javelin and kukri. They hacked at the creatures and lanced them with spears.

A monstrous fiend rose from the water before Herestia. It towered high with a humanoid body perched atop an anaconda body. Herestia's horse trilled and the pulling shaft broke away from the yoke, tipping her chariot into the drink.

The enemy snapped as the amazon spilled into the water, and the reptile lunged for her. Herestia burst up from the rapids to meet her opponent and slashed with her kukri. Hacking through flesh, she sent the strange creature's body into the rapids and they carried it downriver.

"They bleed like any other!" Herestia screamed, emboldening her army. She'd only heard hushed whispers about these swamp stalkers before and assumed they would put up more of a fight than what she'd got: they were no match for amazon steel.

Amazon warriors shouted their war cries and rushed towards the river.

On the far side of the Sareen, Herestia spotted one of the swamp stalkers watching them with calculating eyes. "Their leader," she spat, wiping wet locks of hair to the side of her face where they stuck like paste. Herestia threw off the chariot's harness from her horse and rode it bareback.

Kukri in hand, she charged across the shallows. Before she arrived, the fiend slipped into the water and disappeared, knowing better than to fight the enraged amazon. Moments later, the majority of the human caravan had finished crossing as well.

Herestia spun a circle on her horse, searching the waters for the cobra-like swamp stalker, but it never revealed itself. Finally, the last remnant of the amazons made it to the dwarven side of the river.

"Casualties?" Herestia asked.

One of her lieutenants did a head count and reported back. "Nearly two hundred lost. Most of them were on foot."

Herestia scowled and scanned the shores. "But where are the bodies?"

Her subordinate searched as well, but they found only a few. Likewise, only a few dead snake-men floated in the current. "Dragged to the depths?"

The amazon commander scowled. "It's waist deep at the most… they took them for some purpose. Whatever that is, they did not intend to kill our sisters and brothers."

They stared at the water a few long minutes more, but the danger had seemed to pass. Wherever their comrades had been taken, the amazons could not follow.

Herestia scowled. The swamp stalkers had taken nearly a tenth of her force, but they had only slowed the caravan momentarily. The casualties were acceptable, but irksome. She blasted a sigh through her nose; Herestia was out of options here and could not linger on the river bank, though she would strongly recommend to Alexandria that they build a bridge after returning victorious to Thurisa.

She gave the signal for them to move out and spurred her horse forward.

The ever-present noise of the dragons' ferocious battle reigned over the skirmish on the mountain slope. Their screeching cacophony suddenly stopped, casting an unnerving pall over the vagha army as they yielded more and more of the slope to the enemy, hoping to wear them down by forcing them to fight uphill. With his archers stationed behind him to provide a picket-line of last-ditch support, Thunderfist hoped that he could soon bring them to bear against the enemy if they gained enough elevation.

Zephras shouted to his commanders and asked where the dragons went. None of his plans would matter if one of the dragons returned before the battle was played out... unless it came up directly on the lava elves' heels.

Ghuren searched and then shrugged. Baddoch did likewise, and Aalerd looked around in vain, unable to spot either of the beasts.

"There!" some nameless scout shouted. The black wyrm stomped away into the distance, furrowing a trail through the trees as he cut a line towards Balgavarr. Morguus Ebraxus had previously met his demise at dwarven hands. The beast clearly held a grudge against the vagha if he abandoned the territory where he was summoned; Morguus Ebraxus's hatred must have run deep indeed to let him fight off the call of dragon magic so that he could return to wreak vengeance against Balgavarr.

Suddenly, the blue drake reared up over the cliffside behind the vanguard and the archers. The dragon was not defeated! It lunged for them.

"Fire!" Zephras commanded, and the archers let loose a mighty barrage, snap-firing with pure instinct.

Unable to dodge at such close range, the drake was hit countless times. Arrows and crossbow quarrels bounced off its thick hide. It collapsed all the same as a single crossbow bolt struck it in the eye and drove deep into its brain.

Lurching forward, it rolled down the slope until its inertia slowed to nothing; the massive body twitched and finally lay still. The blue beast was dead… but Morguus Ebraxus was still released upon the Kafnysan Mountains, and he burned with hatred and the desire to roast helpless dwarves within their homes.

A horn blew just before the first of the amazon cavalry smashed into the morehl's rear flank, catching them mostly unawares. The invaders suddenly found themselves fighting a battle on two fronts.

With the humans now needling their flank, the lava elves regrouped, finally pulling closer to their trog allies. The humans pushed them out and into the open where they could be properly engaged.

Zephras watched as the next wave of amazon chariots thundered past the carcass of the dragon and toward the lines of morehl and trog soldiers. The enemy stood their ground and paid the price as hundreds of spears filled the air and countless numbers of warriors fell. Many trogs turned and fled, dropping weapons as they ran, but many withstood the onslaught, deflecting or dodging the missiles.

"The field is not yet ours," Thunderfist noted to himself. "The final battle lies before us like a dark cloud." He gripped the shaft of his axe so hard it creaked. His heart desired a quick end to this battle so they could pull back as quickly as possible and rescue Balgavarr. He hoped their home's local defenders could hold the wyrm at bay in the meantime.

The amazon chariots withdrew somewhat and the lines of armored human battalions marched forward. Dwarves joined them, two hundred strong and ready to send the armies of Death-worshipers back to their dark Lord.

Zephras turned to find Ghuren mounting a mammoth where their mounts had been tied. He headed towards them and looked back to spot Baddoch marching beside him; his eyes were wide but shone with determination. They knew the battle lines would converge again momentarily. "The fire of Firiel burns brightest in the vagha," he said, "and Eldurim's strength is also ours. If we fall this day, let us take more than our share of the enemy with us."

The Warlord nodded his agreement.

"With you leading, Thunderfist sa'Geril, how can Nature and the gods not triumph this day?" Zephras bellowed laughter, even as the two armies came together a little ways down the slope and the slaughter truly began.

The scorpion-knight dropped from his armored steed and knelt before conqueror Merod. Cheron reported, "The dwarves have taken the highlands. We were unable to outmaneuver them, and the selumari have secured the stones on the summit on behalf of the vagha. What is your command?"

They locked eyes. Both knew the battle had taken a turn for the worse. Merod growled suspiciously; Cheron was a capable soldier—he only asked so that the eventual blame could be firmly assigned if the lava elves returned to Mount Uruzak in defeat... the one who gave the orders would hold all the responsibility.

Merod snarled and gripped his poniard tightly. "If they hold the stones, then we cannot prevent our enemy from using their magic against us. We have no choice but to attack."

Cheron blinked at him. It was a risky maneuver, but if they managed to oust the interlopers, they would hold their target and be able to dig in all the more firmly making it difficult to depose them. *If the peak was held by the spell crafters, it might be possible,* he thought. Casters were not typically adept at combat.

Merod cursed beneath his breath. "The sarslayans have double crossed us… had these amazons not arrived we could have easily wiped them out. And why are the selumari present? They now hold the peak."

He was keenly aware that Cheron stood waiting for confirmation of his orders. "Either these humans are the greatest generation of their warriors or those swamp stalkers are traitors," he mumbled, and then chortled. "Karma is a cruel mistress… perhaps my own ambition for the Obsidian Throne brought this upon me and the goddesses of fate now laugh at me?"

"Orders?" Cheron interrupted his superior's private conversation.

Merod gritted his teeth together. "Circle around the far side of the battle line with your most agile spider and scorpion riders. Kick those selumari off our mountain."

Cheron knew his platoon would take heavy losses. He nodded all the same. "For the glory of Uruzak." Cheron placed a clenched fist over his chest.

"For Uruzak and the Obsidian Throne," Merod returned the salute, but refused to acknowledge the Emperor. *The proper response was, 'For Uruzak and Emperor Saugor.'*

Cheron whirled, and then he was gone.

Rannon closed his eyes and sought the mystic connection he shared with Esfah. He summoned the magic of that connection to his side. When he opened them again, he felt arcane power surge through him in the way his mind interpreted the magic; some spell crafters saw spirits to appease, others saw mathematics to be solved when bridging the connection. For Rannon, the mystic sight was more artisanal. The air in front of him swam with red and gold motes of magic he could form into spells.

He gathered several of the gold sprites into his fist and chanted softly, dedicating them to the earth god, Eldurim. Opening his hand, he revealed a small ball of damp dirt.

Rannon threw it across the battlefield and it flew with unerring accuracy, guided by the power of magic rather than the strength of his arm. He watched with satisfaction as it struck the solid earth and generated a churning caldera of mud, slowing the advance of the Morehl troops.

Morehl cavalry upon spider and scorpion mounts had tried to circumvent the battle line and slip around the vanguard. Their mounts had enough versatility that they could climb the sheer cliff-side where the blue drake had approached them from. They could scale the mountain to its peak, catching the selumari there unawares.

Rannon's magic caught the sneaky lava elves in the muck and mire and slogged them down with the rest where they were vulnerable. His hand swept the air again as he gathered the motes of fire magic and squeezed them, summoning a flash and bang of force from Firiel's domain.

The air around the enemy forces suddenly filled with bright sparkles of blazing lights. They danced around the enemies' heads, effectively blinding them.

"Warlord," Rannon said, turning to Zephras, "the time to attack is now."

"Agreed," Zephras whirled his mount. "And let this battle be over quickly. We've more important things to attend to than these upstart morehl... namely, Morguus Ebraxus. Balgavarr needs us."

Gorbak laughed as the vagha stormed the Trog position. The massive goblin and his platoon of greasy minions were just beyond the affected zone where Rannon's muck shifted the tides of battle.

"Gorbak smite puny mountain dwarves!" he cried. "Trogs kill you all!" The marauder's stone hatchet sent four vaghan footmen to their graves before they could even react. He turned to scream his triumph and wailed as the mighty feet of a mammoth trampled him into the soil.

Ghuren's mount scattered the other goblins. They fled in fear, but didn't regroup with their main battle group as it struggled in the mire. The routed trogs sprinted east in full retreat.

Circling back around to the trog champion who had killed so many of his countrymen, Ghuren found Gorbak climbing to his feet. He swayed, dazed and battered from his near death experience.

Gorbak searched for the weapon he'd lost when the mammoth had stomped him into the dirt. He only found dead trogs that hadn't possess his same fortitude. They lay with parts of their body flattened or burst open from the mammoth's weight.

Snatching one of the dead invader's weapons, Gorbak turned and found Ghuren charging with his axe. Gorbak barely evaded the blow. He took two steps backward each time the vaghan soldier swung, and Gorbak's return strikes fell limply away.

Ghuren easily deflected the goblin leader's efforts. He suspected Gorbak's arm was broken, but the trog refused to relent. Ghuren swung again and pressed him another two steps. Gorbak's foot faltered, and he slid into the milky loam produced by Rannon's magic.

Suddenly dropping a cubit's height, Gorbak's neck was an easy target and Ghuren swung his axe.

Gorbak's head sailed across the battlefield and landed in the middle of a trog crew. The goblins panicked and tried their best to flee, becoming easy prey for the dwarven soldiers.

Ghuren didn't pause to gloat. Instead, he clambered back up the side of his mount and looked for the next target. He spotted a signal fire instead. Balgavarr had called for help. Even at this distance, Ghuren could see the wyrm attacking his city, digging and clawing in an attempt to crack open the mountain and devour what was inside.

Whirling the mammoth around, Ghuren hied it towards the most direct road and rushed away, dashing past his father. "The wyrm is attacking Balgavarr!" he yelled back at him.

Thunderfist watched his son hurry past and growled something unintelligible. "Rannon! You and Baddoch take direct command; Aalerd should be able to help mop this up easily, now. I'll rally whatever troops I think we can spare and follow Ghuren. We can not win this battle only to lose Balgavarr!"

Zephras led a charge up the Balgavarr slope alongside whatever cavalry units remained. They'd even commandeered the horses from their selumari companions; vaghan riders often used ponies and so they directed the larger creatures easily, although they proved wielder than preferred. The horse-mounted dwarves lagged to the back.

The massive wyrm turned and belched a stream of liquid death at them.

Expecting it, the mixed company of riders veered off to one side and evaded the putrid stream. Only the horse riders at the rear failed to get out of its way.

They closed the gap with a shout, watching Morguus Ebraxus's tail whip towards them with the force of an avalanche. It crashed through the cavalry and wiped them out, bowling over mounts and sending the riders flying through the air.

Dwarven warriors skidded across the mountainside with differing degrees of injury. Concerned vagha rushed out from secret openings covered by rockblankets, curtains of threaded stone more finely crafted than any beaded curtain; it functioned as perfect camouflage. The citizens retrieved whatever broken soldiers they could rescue.

"No, no, no…" Zephras cried as he rose to his feet, wincing with pain and knowing those foolish citizens of Balgavarr meant to help, but had just initiated the city's doom. A busted bone protruded through Zephras's lower leg and he worriedly watched as the black dragon noted the location of the entrance and moved for it.

Morguus Ebraxus could not pass through because of his size, but the location provided a weaker point of attack and eventually the dragon would bust it open and gain entry. The wyrm wasted no time, and he smashed whatever dwarves had thought to rescue their kin.

Zephras screamed as he pushed his bone back inside the flesh and picked up his axe. He'd be able to worry about the wound later. "To me! To me!" he yelled, urging whatever vagha remained conscious to charge.

Ghuren lay dazed, but scrambled to his feet along with a handful of other soldiers.

With a roar, Zephras Thunderfist rushed for the monster as best he could on his limping gait and with axe held high. Two dozen others followed him, shooting crossbow bolts as they ran.

This dragon had easily destroyed armies of hundreds in the past. What chance did this small crew of injured and battle weary dwarves have?

Every bolt fired bounced off of the dragon's armored hide. The impotent missiles clattered to the ground as Morguus Ebraxus turned to deal with the pests who dared challenge his might.

The dwarves crashed into the massive reptile and bounced off it with similar effect of the quarrels. Axes blunted, and blades dulled against the dragon's impenetrable scales.

Huge, jagged claws cut down swaths of dwarves and the beast uncoiled its tail. Moguus Ebraxus's body encircled the vagha, cutting off any escape.

Zephras dashed under the behemoth and leapt off a rocky ledge while hurling his axe in a wild arc. The edge of his weapon caught the fiend's belly and split it wide open.

A wave of heat and noxious odors spilled from the growing gash and the attacker screamed as he landed in an awkward stance. Thunderfist nearly collapsed as his broken bone busted through a different part of his leg and hobbled him.

Zephras looked up as the beast reared back to its full height. With its belly slit open, entrails spilled across the mountainside and the dragon shrieked with a failing, croaking sort of groan. The black shadow of Morguus Ebraxas suddenly spread wide as the hideous wyrm's lifeless body rushed towards the ground.

Thunderfist locked eyes with his son, who was lucky enough to be wide of the shadow. There was no time for Zephras to get out of the way, and both vagha knew it. Standing cockeyed on his good leg, Zephras flashed his son a *damned if I do-damned if I don't* kind of grin and a short nod that communicated a wealth of information in so little time.

Ghuren knew that his own voice was howling as he watched, but his mind engaged with his father's nod. He took in everything his father was telling him with it. *I'm proud of you. This is a glorious death. The people of Balgavarr are worthy of great sacrifice. I showed you how to live honorably—this is how one dies honorably.*

With a mighty *whampfh!* The body of Morguus Ebraxas smashed against the mountainside and crushed Zephras Thunderfist beneath his corpse.

Moments later, even Ghuren's voice gave out, and silence reigned atop Balgavarr Reaches.

Days had passed since the fall of Zephras Thunderfist and Balgavarr's army had finally returned from the battlefront after scattering the enemy. They knew the war brewed in long, cold spells. They would be back, eventually, but not for several years. Perhaps even a generation would pass before Balgavarr had to worry about the next significant invasion from the morehl.

Herestia and her legion of amazons had already returned, not waiting to join the victory celebration that was typical of the vagha. She cited some new danger at the Sareen that she needed to bring to Queen Alexandria's attention as soon as possible.

The city elders of Balgavarr had recovered the axe belonging to Thunderfist, Zephras sa'Geril. They presented it to Ghuren during a ceremony meant to honor the hero's sacrifice.

Ghuren thanked each of them in turn and the youngest of the council, a dwarf named Vors, clapped him on the shoulder. "Have you ever considered pursuing public office, son of the Thunderfist?"

He shrugged and mounted his father's weapon in the holster at his belt. "I am not opposed to it," Ghuren stated. "My father was the warrior of our family. I've always been at a loss for my exact path," he admitted. "There's really only one thing I'm certain of in my life's pursuit." He locked eyes on his pretty mistress. She stood at the far side of the room.

Their eyes locked, and her cheeks flushed.

Vors gave him a short bow. "Think about it. Your family name bears great weight and you could do much good if you ever chose to join us at the table."

Ghuren thanked him, and then cleaned his beard, raking out any stray debris and making himself presentable. He walked across the room in pursuit of his love.

Merod returned home at the head of the Uruzak Mountains' army. Sentries at the castle's entrance passed him a note. Merod broke the royal seal and read.

Word of his failure had gone on ahead of them, as expected. Emperor Saugor called him into his presence and demanded an explanation for his failure.

Merod and Cheron were still dirty and weary from the road, but went to the throne room immediately. Sniffing, Merod detected a foul odor lingering in the imperial chamber… a smell like death. He raised an eyebrow; apparently Emperor Saugor was noseblind to it.

Finally, Merod spotted its source. The corpse of a selumari stood propped up near the Obsidian Throne. It startled him momentarily when it moved. *One of the undead has arrived and now appears to act as adviser? This only proves my suspicions. Saugor is too young and foolish to sit upon the throne.*

Saugor caught his servant's line of sight. "That is Leisterbane… a powerful acolyte of Death. He has business in the Shadowlands and is willing to advise us on our future efforts. This war is far from over."

Merod scowled, though he had already assumed as much… but he'd already pledged that it would not be during the current emperor's reign.

"Now, explain your failure," Saugor demanded.

"We were betrayed by the sarslayan. They promised they would stop the amazons from reinforcing our enemies. You can imagine my surprise when a thousand chariots and another thousand human infantry suddenly breached the woods and ripped through our flanks."

Saugor leaned forward upon his royal seat and rested his chin upon steepled fingers. "Hmm. And what have we learned from this failure?"

Merod looked at him wild-eyed.

Saugor explained, "You are an experienced leader—one who I would have assumed could have planned for such contingencies. I hate wasting good resources, and so I am willing to pardon you if we learn something from this failure and use it for future campaigns." He raised a brow, waiting for a response.

Merod nodded and looked at the undead creature beside the emperor. "Perhaps we need better allies. The sarslayan clearly had their own agenda and used us for their own means."

Slow and resolute, Saugor bobbed his head and accepted the answer.

Finally, the icy dread in Merod's gut loosened. He'd felt certain that he would be executed for failing his duty.

The emperor turned and looked at Cheron. "You recall my private orders, soldier?"

He nodded. "My mission is complete."

Merod looked at him quizzically.

"Report," Saugor demanded.

"You asked me to spy on your servant, Imperial Conquerer Merod. He openly spoke of dissension and possible coup," Cheron stated.

Saugor frowned. "Very well," he sighed. "I'd hoped he could be useful in the future, but you have your orders."

Before Merod could even realize that Cheron's whole mission during the campaign was to verify the conqueror's trustworthiness, Cheron pulled a flintlock pistol and put a slug between Merod's eyes.

Sharsyea grinned. The sarslayan shaman ordered her minion to bring out the sacred stone pot. "The waters of Lethial," she hissed reverently, pouring the muddy water into a large cauldron.

Drums began booming from somewhere nearby in the swamp stalkers' home. Nearly two hundred human prisoners sat in a line, bound with damp ropes where they'd been secreted far downriver in the Deepmire where the sarslayans had made their home west of Tulgesh.

The shaman grinned as she emptied the jar's contents; it had originally been a jar of mutating water from the River Lethial, now a dry bed. It had once flowed from Dereh'Liandor's Snekdenn Bayou. Whatever magic was present in the old swamp water remained alive and active so long as it was catalyzed by the blood of the sarslayans' enemies. Now, it was little more than a ceremonial liquid, vastly diluted, but no less potent—it was the magic of ceremony and belief that kept the waters of Lethial filled with Death magic and able to complete the mutation. Sharsyea motioned the first captive closer.

Snake-like men dragged the amazon forward and drowned her in the cauldron. Her screams bubbled, and her body shuddered and eventually went still as she breathed in the mutating waters. Humans made some of the best sarslayan mutates, in Sharsyea's opinion.

The sarslayans released their grip on her, and she lifted herself from the waters. Murky water poured off her head as she looked up with eyes that shone yellow.

Standing aside, the newly converted unit waited and watched as her kin underwent the same drowning and dedication to Death, over and over. Before they were a tenth of the way through, she began to scratch at her flesh as if molting. Her skin sloughed off like badly blistered and peeling sunburnt skin. Her nails fell off as she scratched, revealing talons that had grown in behind them.

With a sickening *schlurking* sound, she peeled off her scalp to reveal the scales beneath.

Sharsyea cackled, and the line progressed, filling their ranks with new members. "These specimens make the transition quite nicely… far better than those nasty trogs. Yes… we shall take a great interest in this city of Thurisa upon Seshara… much interest indeed."

About the Authors

Joseph W. Joiner (1965-2014) was born in Wichita, Kansas. Joe was an avid board-game collector, and loved reading, seeing good movies, and riding his motorcycle through the mountains. His first published book was in the world of Esfah, and he had plans for many more.

Christopher D. Schmitz is author of many Sci-Fi/Fantasy books. He was a child of the 80s basically lived out the plotline to Stranger Things. He lives in rural Minnesota with his family where he drinks unsafe amounts of coffee; the caffeine shakes keeps the cold from killing them. In his off-time he plays haunted bagpipes in places of low repute.

Thunderfist and the Dragon was initially a set of several related passages' worth of flavor text printed inside the Dragon Dice v.3 rules manual. Together, they seemed to tell a part of the prequel to *Chill Wind* that Joiner had mentioned he hoped to write. Schmitz pieced them together during the re-edit for *Chill Wind's* re-release with the game's 25th anniversary and completed the story.

APPENDICES

GLOSSARY
TIMELINE
MAPS
BOOKLIST

GLOSSARY OF TERMS

Abyss - the home of the Void, a realm where silence reigns aside from pockets of terror and chaos where unknown gods reign. This is a similar concept to Greek myths of an underworld.

Ailuril - the secondborn of the Esfahan gods. She is represented by the color blue and has power over the air elements.

Aguarehl - the fourthborn of the Esfahan gods. He is represented by the color green and has power over the water elements.

Amazon - the race of mankind said to have been deposited whole upon Esfah as one of the few races created by Tarvanehl himself. Amazons are the warrior caste of human race.

Areosa - commonly known as the frostwings, a frigid felinoid, winged race with magic resistance.

bloodless - another common name for the undead.

Deadzone – synonym for the Abyss, except from the point of view of the trogs or morehl. Within their respective religions, versions of the afterlife differ wildly and as often as they align in geopolitical goals, neither could imagine spending an eternal afterlife in the company of the other.

Death - the half-brother god who is the child of Nature and Void.

Dragons – these beasts come in two forms: Drake and Wyrm. Drakes have wings, and wyrms do not. Though the dragonkin are a kind of subspecies, they are not the same thing, no matter how similar they are. They used to live hidden across Esfah, but were nearly eradicated in the Dragoncrusades. Dragons have eternal spirits and when they die, they return to the plane where they now dwell. Dragonmagic came in two forms and it summons them from this realm or from nearby (the older form of this magic which has now been forgotten since these mythic beasts have largely gone out from Esfah.)

Drakufreet - the dragonkin come from the same realm as dragons and appear as a type of draconic hybrid race.

eldarim – a human-like race that emerged over eons from Esfah's primordial soup and predated the gods-made races. The eldarim are versatile and have proven the capacity to breed with many of Esfah's races. They are called eldarim, meaning "from the earth."

Eldurim - the firstborn of the Esfahan gods. He is represented by the color gold and has power over the earth elements.

Efflorah - the race of treefolk.

Esfah - the world and one of two planets revolving around Soll.

Empyrea - known commonly as the firewalkers, a war-loving mercenary race.

Faeli - commonly known as scalders or steam dancers. These creatures are fickle and capricious and were once captured and tormented by Death.

Firiel - the thirdborn of the Esfahan gods. She is represented by the color red and has power over the fire elements.

First Age - everything from the beginning of creation to the year 863.

Frehlasuhl - also called the Forsaken or Mudbloods. They are the offspring of selumari and morehl unions. They cannot breed with each other to have children, only with one or the other race, but they are rejected wholesale by both.

Ghaeial - the mother goddess known more commonly as Nature.

Ghwereste - called the "feral folk." These are a hybrid of animal and man created at the dawn of the Second Age.

Gwich'in: "the people of the land" a group of human magicians gathered for study and knowledge (the closest English word might be "coven.")

Leguin - a sister planet to Esfah that also orbits Sol; it can often be seen in the night sky appearing above the horizon like a bright star.

Lich - a powerful undead spellcaster. Lichs often possess necromantic capabilities, though their created undead are maintained by force of will, rather than by other means, such as the Necralluvium.

morehl - commonly called lava elves. They have red skin in addition to their elf-like features and their blood is said to smoke when exposed to air.

Necralluvium - a kind of magical potion with a seeming life of its own. This black filth can kill the living. The dead that are exposed to it become animated.

Rhaudian - the name of the moon. It circulates Esfah twice in a daily cycle.

Sarslayan - commonly known as swamp stalkers. These snake-men emerged in the Second Age as a result of Death using magic to twist the creations of his half-brother Aguarehl. They create more of their kind through magic conversion rather than by reproduction.

Second Age - everything after year 863 of the First Age. This began when Ghaeial walked the face of Esfah and surveyed the damages of the myriad of wars. The 864th year is year 1 of the Second Age.

Selurehl - the name of the second god to emerge after Tarvanehl, usually known as Void.

selumari - commonly called coral elves. They have blue skin in addition to their elf-like features.

Shara – what the eldarim people refer to themselves as when they communicate with each other. It means "little god-in-the-making."

Soll – the sun.

Tarvanehl - the creator god who came first, according to all mythology and story; he is often known as Father Time, or simply The Father.

trog - a synonym for goblin. trogs much prefer to live in boggy areas and tend to pollute the land.

vagha - commonly known as dwarves.

Void - sometimes used interchangeably with the Abyss or, the power or person of Selurehl who is frequently referred to as Void just as his son Malgrimm is more widely regarded as Death. Context determines the meaning.

Warchief - a title of rank among the vagha. Below the king is a Warchief who leads Warlords and Warcommanders under them. It might commonly be understood as a sort of general.

TIMELINE

Included is the general time line of major world events in Esfah. Please note that, during the time before the Mother, Ghaeial, became a goddess and the First Age began, prehistory spanned a scope of time measuring eons, and in that time, verily, only Time existed. Despite the sage's attempts to capture much data and ancient knowledge, they did not begin tracking time and dates until the first passing of the Daybringer. The first three years of history might very well have been hundreds or even a thousand years as the gods (and the earliest race of eldarim) kept time differently.

<u>Prehistory N.D.</u>

Tarvanehl exists and creates within the realm of Void/Abyss and Esfah and Leguin are born; Ghaeial realizes she is a goddess and falls in love with Tarvanehl.

Turambar courts Leguin

Selurehl, third of the brother gods grows angry

Eldurim the firstborn (earth) god-son of Ghaeial and Tarvanehl is born

Ailuril the secondborn (wind) god-daughter of Ghaeial and Tarvanehl is born

Firiel thirdborn (fire) god-daughter of Ghaeial and Tarvanehl is born

Aguarehl fourth born god-son (water) of Ghaeial and Tarvanehl is born

Malgrimm cursed bastard son (Death,) conceived and birthed after Selurehl's violence upon Ghaeial

eldarim are birthed by Esfah and slowly emerge from the mire of her lands and water, evolving over long periods of time. They call themselves the Shara in their own tongue

The First Age

03FA the Daybringer Comet passes Esfah for the First Time, the Sisters of Fate are birthed of Turambar and Leguin, Dragons and the Drakufreet are created during the schism of the god-children

04FA Earliest creations of the gods: "monsters" are formed

15FA selumari are created

16FA vagha are created, trogs are created

17FA morehl are created

19FA The Dawn of War. morehl invaders overthrow the first selumari

22FA Humans arrive on Esfah via Tarvanehl's intervention

28FA Davian Whisperwynd leaves Maris-ta-Sehlim

32FA The proto-empyreans are birthed in the whirlwind

42FA Gundraokh Shatterfist finds the Bands of Turambar and renames the city of Orelod to Gundakhor

96FA Sshkkryyahr the Dread rises to power

103FA Malgrimm attempts to create a new powerful, destructive force within the Shadowlands, but the Areosan's magic resistance helps them maintain mild independence from the Death god and he abandons them to the frost plains

143FA Undead created, Melkior is defeated upon the Raithlan Plains by the gods' chosen Champions

167FA Dilution of the eldarim race and the reduction of the Dragon population via the Dragoncrusades that eliminated nearly all the natural dragons of Esfah; the spells that compelled natural dragons that still remained in the realm became forgotten after this date in favor of those drawing eternal dragons through the interplanar rifts

341FA Existence of the Empyreans is discovered when they aid the elder races in the first major Undead uprising

447FA *Book of the Land, 1st Ed.* is published and immediately begins revisions

520FA morehl city of Karakto falls to the selumari

532FA morehl discover cursed bullets and retake Karakto

544FA Large load of Eldrymetallum discovered on the Karakto slopes

562FA Final version of *The Book of the Land* completed after 23 quintennial installments

836FA The Magestorm Wars erupt with the tectonic cataclysm that opens the Netherwold and nearly splits Dereh'Liandor in two; the Arcana Veil stiffens

842FA Disappearance of the gremmlobahnd and the genocide of the drakufreet

863FA Final battle of the Magestorm Wars ends the first age, the faeli are birthed in the Firequags and captured by the forces of Death and subjected to torments in the pits of the World Wound.

The Second Age

01SA Ghaeial walks the earth and surveys the damage of the elder races

03SA Ghaeial creates the ghwereste

79SA The plagues of the World Wound at its evils continue and the first of the sarslayan emerge from the nearby Snekdenn Bayou

153SA The areosa race emerges from the Shadowlands. They are known mostly as rumors, but their existence is verified to the outside world

209SA Whether the faeli escaped the torments of the World Wound or were released, none know, but they were so twisted by the centuries of abuse that they have become more children of Malgrimm than Ghaeial

233SA Under Ghaeial's wishes, the sylvan efflorah, existing as trees since even before the humans came to Esfah, picked up their roots and first emerged from forest and grove

829SA Zephras "Thunderfist" dies in Cyrea defending Balgavarr from a dragon

967SA Geril sa'Guhren "Dragonsbane" born

1021SA Geril sa'Guhren rules in Balgavarr

1082SA Coryn Sa'Geril is born

1119SA Daybringer Comet makes its pass by Esfah

1122SA Kholkoro Wicebrow writes her commentary *Kholkoro's commentary on Book of the Land*

1127SA The famed "Adventurer King" Hy'Mander sa'Meril is blinded

1139SA Melkior is revived

1142SA Daybringer Comet makes its circuit

Maris Coast
Shen la'Terl
Maris-ta-Sehlim
Vhandria
Brackenhome
The Crethelands
Stonehome
Daurhedge Range
Oxforge
Daur-Bor-Nin
the Darkreach
rnock Range
Mezzoscarp Range
Southern Daurhedge
The Birthla
New E
Lyandrica
0
200
400
Leagues

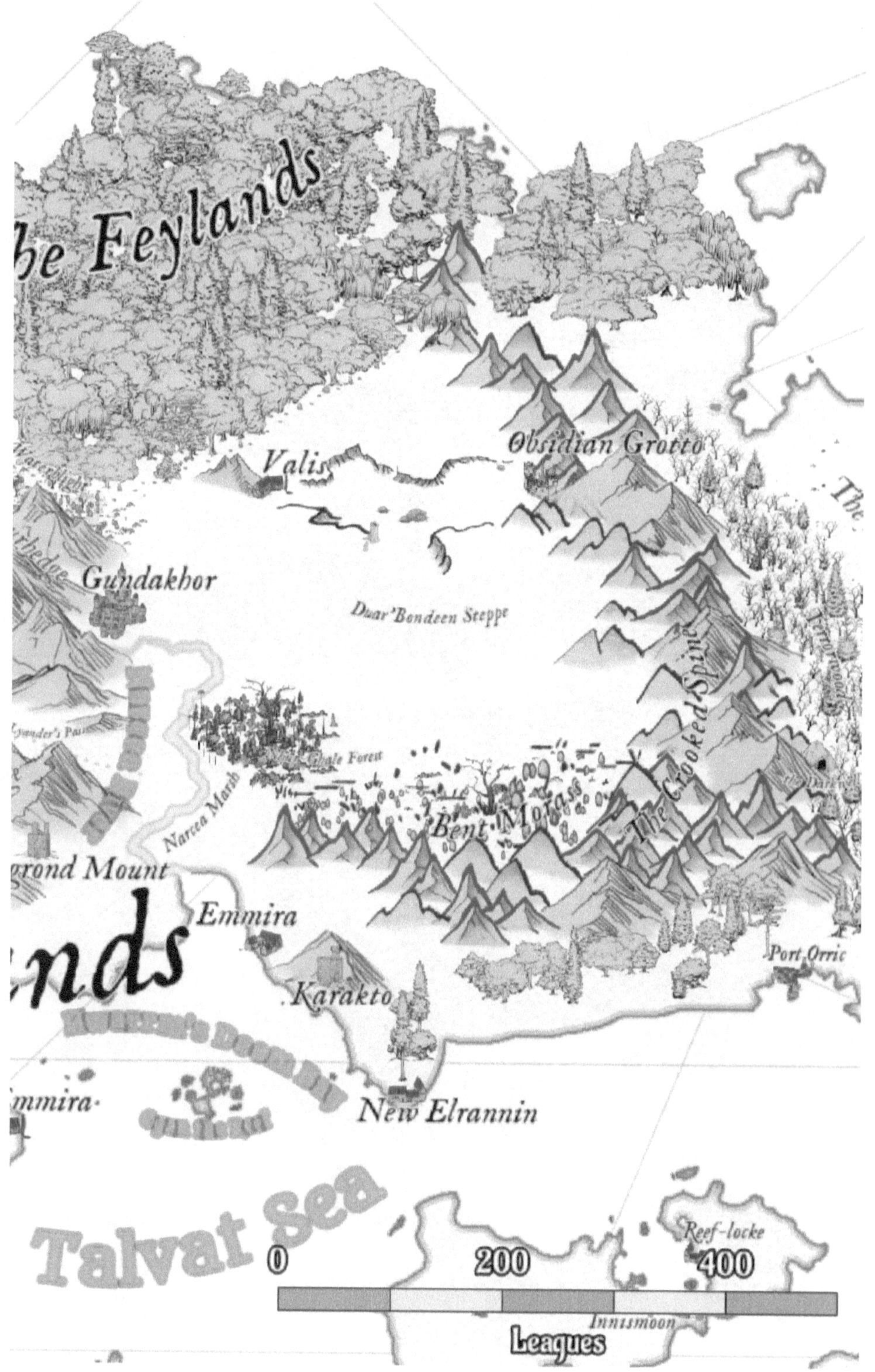
The Feylands
Valis
Obsidian Grotto
Gundakhor
Duar'Bondeen Steppe
The Crooked Spine
Chale Forest
Narcea Marsh
Bent Morass
Lyander's Pass
Emmira
Karakto
Port Orric
New Elrannin
Talvat Sea
Reef-locke
Innismoon
0
200
400
Leagues

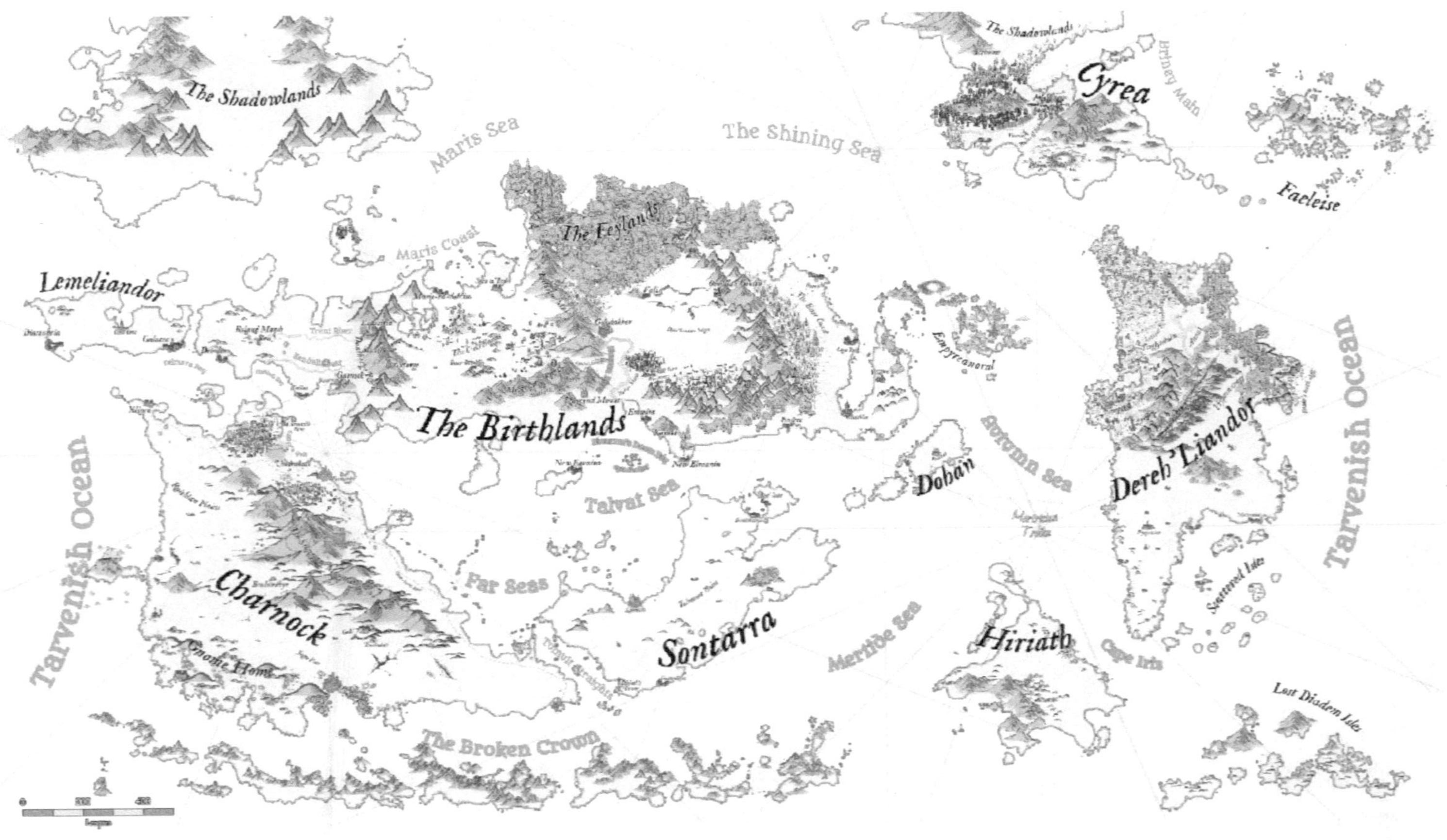
The Shadowlands
Maris Sea
The Shining Sea
Syrea
Brithey Main
Faeleise
The Feylands
Maris Coast
Lemeliandor
Empyreamoral
Dereb'Liandor
The Birthlands
Doban
Aorann Sea
Talvat Sea
Tarvenish Ocean
Tarvenish Ocean
Charnock
Far Seas
Sontarra
Meribde Sea
Hiriath
Cape Iris
Gnome Home
The Broken Crown
Lost Diadem Isles

BOOKS
IN THE DRAGON DICE UNIVERSE
OF ESFAH

Rise and Fall of the Obsidian Grotto
Cast of Fate
Tome of Tarvanehl*
Heart of Stone and Flame*
Ashes of Ailushurai
Rise of the Champions
Drakuwar
Chill Wind
Eye of the Storm
Secrets of the Shadowlands
Army of the Dead**

*These two short books were the first produced by TSR and are included inside the re-released (2020) version of Cast of Fate, which was originally produced in 1996.

**This book was scheduled for release by TSR in the late 1990s but never published. A version of this book was released in 2003 but should not necessarily be considered Esfah canon to the Esfah Sagas unless it is a version rereleased by TreeShaker Books.

Christopher D. Schmitz is author of both Sci-Fi/Fantasy Fiction and Nonfiction books and has been published in both traditional and independent outlets. If you've investigated indie writers of the upper Midwest, you may have heard his name whispered in dark alleys with an equal mix of respect and disdain. He has been featured on television broadcasts, podcasts, and runs a blog for indie authors... but you've still probably never heard of him.

As an avid consumer of comic books, movies, cartoons, and books (especially sci-fi and fantasy) this child of the 80s basically lived out Stranger Things, but shadowy government agencies won't let him say more than that. He lives in rural Minnesota with his family where he drinks unsafe amounts of coffee; the caffeine shakes keeps the cold from killing them. In his off-time he plays haunted bagpipes in places of low repute, but that's a story for another time. He has a special offer for readers on the following page.

You can connect with him via the following links:
http://www.authorchristopherdschmitz.com

Follow him on Twitter:
https://twitter.com/cylonbagpiper
Follow him on Goodreads:
www.goodreads.com/author/show/129258.Christopher_Schmitz
Like/Follow him on Facebook:
https://www.facebook.com/authorchristopherdschmitz
Subscribe to his blog:
https://authorchristopherdschmitz.wordpress.com
Favorite him at Smashwords:
www.smashwords.com/profile/view/authorchristopherdschmitz
His Amazon Author Profile:
amazon.com/author/christopherdschmitz
Follow him at Bookbub:
www.bookbub.com/authors/christopher-d-schmitz

SPECIAL OFFER:

"As a special bonus for you, I'd like to invite you download FIVE ebooks for free as a part of a Starter Library from Christopher D. Schmitz."

To get your free Starter Library, simply visit this link:
https://www.subscribepage.com/p1o9c9
Enter your email address and then collect your books as they are sent to you. It's that simple!

FREE STARTER BOOK LIBRARY

If you like Sci-Fi and Fantasy, you'll love these books, subscribe now to have them delivered right away.

DRAGON DICE

Dragon Dice™ is SFR Inc.'s core product. We are constantly working to create a quality game that everyone can enjoy. Dragon Dice™ was originally created by Lester Smith and produced by TSR© in 1995. After several years, TSR, now owned by Wizards of the Coast, had put Dragon Dice™ on hold to work on other projects. In October of 2000, SFR Inc. purchased the rights to Dragon Dice™ and now will continue to support and create NEW! products for the game.

Dragon Dice™ is strategy game where players create mythical armies using dice to represent each troop. The game combines strategy and skill as well as a little luck. Each person tries to win the game by outmaneuvering the opponent and capture 2 terrains. Of course eliminating your opponent completely is another acceptable way of winning.

Get online today and "Roll your way to victory!"

http://www.sfr-inc.com